A Dream Worth Keeping

Debbie Kaiman Tillinghast

Keep dreaming!

Debbie Kaiman Tillinghast

A Dream Worth Keeping

Copyright © 2020 Debbie Kaiman Tillinghast

Produced and printed
by Stillwater River Publications.

All rights reserved. Written and produced in the
United States of America. This book may not be reproduced
or sold in any form without the expressed, written
permission of the author and publisher.

Visit our website at
www.StillwaterPress.com
for more information.

First Stillwater River Publications Edition

Library of Congress Control Number: 2020922408

Paperback ISBN: 978-1-952521-60-7

1 2 3 4 5 6 7 8 9 10

Written by Debbie Kaiman Tillinghast.

Published by Stillwater River Publications,
Pawtucket, RI, USA.

Publisher's Cataloging-In-Publication Data
(Prepared by The Donohue Group, Inc.)

Names: Tillinghast, Debbie Kaiman, author.

Title: A dream worth keeping / Debbie Kaiman Tillinghast.

Description: First Stillwater River Publications edition. |
Pawtucket, RI, USA : Stillwater River Publications, [2020]

Identifiers: ISBN 9781952521607 (paperback)

Subjects: LCSH: Divorced women--Maryland--Baltimore--
Fiction. | Self-realization in women--United States--Fiction. |
Bakers--Psychology--Fiction. | Friendship--Fiction.

Classification: LCC PS3620.I5155 D74 2020 | DDC 813/.6--
dc23

For my family, with all my love.
You are my reason to dream.

Acknowledgments

Writing is a solitary pursuit, but creating a book requires a community of support. I am deeply grateful to my community of support; without you, this book would have remained scribbled words on a notebook page.

My thanks to Pat Kenny, at Harmony Library, for planting a tiny seed six years ago, and to the Fiction Writers Group—my writing family—Barb, Dawn, Jainne, Jen, and Tracy, for nurturing its growth. Thank you for listening, reading, suggesting, listening again, and for believing in my dream.

Thank you, Rebekah Hamilton, librarian at Hope Library, Kristen Fleischmann Morgan, and Linda Weremay, for your time, insights, and enthusiasm as beta readers.

My profound gratitude to my editor Dawn Alexander, Editor at Evident Ink; your patient guidance made my story better and kept me motivated through all the revisions.

To Bonnie, Carolyn, Elizabeth, Paula, Sandy, and Toni, my heartfelt appreciation for years of friendship and for reading my story and urging me to follow my dream. I couldn't have done this without you.

Sincere thanks to Sobo Café and Vaccaro's for permission to include your names in my book.

My love and appreciation to my son Adam who never stops encouraging me to write.

And thank you, readers, for choosing *A Dream Worth Keeping*. I hope you enjoy it.

"What lies behind us and what lies before us are tiny matters compared to what lies within us."

~Ralph Waldo Emerson

Spring

Chapter 1

The water taxi docked at Fells Point, and Martha tucked her current romance novel into her bag. The fog draped around her shoulders like a cold blanket, forgotten on the grass overnight. It seeped into her bones, reminding her of early spring in New England, and a wave of homesickness washed over her.

She wished that she had listened to her grandmother. Martha had been so sure she had found happily ever after—boy meets girl, dislike turns to love, and they walk hand in hand into the sunset, inseparable, like her parents. But she knew from experience life didn't follow a magical script. *Heroines in romance novels are always gorgeous and have names like Tess or Val. They're never named Martha. The heroes have rippling muscles under their shirts and are named Chad or Blake. I never read a romance novel with a hero named George. No offense, Mr. Clooney.*

The patisserie on the far corner usually tempted her, but today she bypassed it and trudged to the Roasted Bean. A midweek calm surrounded Fells Point, which Martha appreciated. Most shops opened later, and delivery trucks lined Thames Street, instead of hungry diners. On weekends, restaurants offered tables for al fresco dining, and a festive atmosphere saturated the air. Martha didn't feel festive. She entered the coffee shop and waited her turn. The perky barista greeted every customer the same way.

"Would you like to try our new caramel cappuccino latte special?"

"No thanks. Just coffee, cream, no sugar," Martha sat at a tiny table

1

in a quiet corner and retrieved her book, but her mind wandered to the day she realized her attempts to save her marriage had failed.

She touched the spot on her left cheek, healed, but still tender in her mind, then lifted her bag, burdened by the divorce papers. Martha withdrew the cream-colored sheets awaiting her signature and stared at them. She hesitated. Her marriage to Tony had ended, but she hated to admit her dream of happily ever after had ended too.

Martha had requested the divorce, but the reality of it was like a punch in the stomach, catching her off guard. As long as she and Tony stayed married, she hoped their marriage could improve. But the divorce papers arrived four days ago, and her hope disappeared. Martha had wanted to disappear along with it. She'd broken a promise to her grandmother for a marriage that had disintegrated. Guilt and failure battered her insides, and she didn't want to eat, work, or talk to anyone. She had crawled into bed, and stayed there for three days.

Now, as Martha sat in the coffee shop, she couldn't think of a reason to delay any longer. She found a pen and scrawled her signature on the designated lines, then refolded the papers, and replaced them in the envelope bearing her lawyer's name, Ben Simmons.

Might as well get this over with. Martha discarded her half-full coffee cup, squared her shoulders, and stepped out into the spring dampness. Once she'd signed the papers, she didn't want to wait for anything, even the United States Post Office. She'd deliver them herself, then maybe she could move on. She turned left on South Ann Street, past four townhouses painted in vivid colors—blue, yellow, salmon, and lime green. They created a sunny oasis in the midst of all the brick buildings. The doors in contrasting shades of hot pink, purple, green, and magenta added a touch of whimsy and never failed to lift her spirits when she passed them. They reminded her of the seaside cottages of her childhood in Maine, where she had lived with her grandmother, and she tried to absorb their cheerful comfort. Martha wanted to feel Gram's reassuring hug, she wanted to turn back the clock to the beginning, before she had ignored Gram's advice and made the wrong decision about Tony, when her life hadn't fallen apart and she still believed in herself. How

2

different would her life be if she had waited to marry Tony and kept her promise to Gram?

Martha rounded the corner to Aliceanna Street, and walked another block to Ben's office, on the ground floor of a stately brick townhouse. The black shutters on the building lent solemnness to her visit and matched her mood. She handed the sealed envelope to the receptionist Jenna, thanked her, and went back outside.

Quaint little shops lined cobblestoned Thames Street, normally enticing Martha, but today she didn't notice any of them. Head down, she stuck her hands in her jacket pockets and plodded towards the water taxi dock as thoughts of her failed marriage tumbled in her head. The wind had blown away the fog, and maybe if she walked, it would clear her mind as well.

Martha stepped onto the brick walkway that skirted the harbor. She stared at the swaying boats with their fanciful names, Snow Goose, Cricket, and Beach-Plum. The last reminded her of home and the beach plums that grew along the shores. She watched the boats bob at their moorings and thought about the crumbled pieces of her marriage, remembering each one by name. Fun and Friendship stalked out the door first, then Respect departed and took Love with it. She imagined each of them boarding a sailboat and drifting away, leaving her behind. She wondered when she and Tony had stopped spending time together. When had he stopped reaching for her in the night? When had he started blaming all his problems on her? When had loneliness become her constant companion? Martha waved goodbye to her broken marriage and kept walking.

When she passed an athletic wear store, she sensed someone watching her. She spun around and a larger than life image of an Olympic athlete stared at her, with the words, "I WILL," in bold print. The message bored into Martha's brain, and the eyes on the poster challenged her. She took a deep breath and resolved to embrace those two words. *I WILL stop dwelling on the loss. I WILL see the divorce as a gift of freedom.* Martha stared at the image, took a deep breath, and straightened her spine.

The aroma of bacon and eggs collided with Martha's nose and her stomach rumbled, she hadn't had anything but coffee at the Roasted Bean.

She loved eating breakfast in a restaurant surrounded by the homey smells of fresh brewed coffee and warm pastries. Tony had never shared her enjoyment of breakfast. He preferred dinner at the fanciest restaurants, where he could critique the chefs he viewed as his competition. But Tony wasn't here. She had molded herself into the person Tony wanted, and in the process, she had lost her real self. Time to change. *Today, I WILL treat myself to breakfast, and then I WILL do whatever I want to please myself.* Martha strode to the Purple Pear Café and opened the door.

"A table for one, please," Martha seldom ate alone in restaurants, but a thrill of independence shot through her as she followed the hostess.

"What do you recommend today?" She said when the server came to take her order.

"I tried the special omelet, and it's delicious. The chef uses all fresh vegetables and local goat cheese. And the ginger scones are to die for. I sample one whenever the chef makes them, which isn't often."

"Sounds yummy. I'll have one of each and coffee, please." She smiled at the server and returned her menu.

The omelet brimmed with savory sautéed mushrooms, asparagus, and sweet red peppers, and the smooth, tangy goat cheese oozed as she took a bite. She closed her eyes and sighed in appreciation. Light and moist, with chunks of candied ginger, the scone reminded her of the ones she'd made in culinary school, and she longed to recapture the excitement she had felt when she began that adventure.

While she ate, Martha took out her phone and made a list of things she wanted to do, touristy things Tony had said were beneath him. She couldn't remember the last time she'd spent the whole day doing something fun. She and Tony both worked long hours, but whenever she suggested they take a break and spend time together, he replied that she could waste her own time, but he needed to work. Waste of time or not, she needed a day of fun and since the dragon paddle boats topped her list, she'd start there.

Martha left the Purple Pear and retraced her steps past the marina. She heard children's laughter coming from Pierce's Park and went to investigate. The USCGC Taney stood guard from its permanent mooring in the harbor, and three boys chased each other through the bamboo tunnel yelling as one lunged to tag another. Two women stood nearby, they each held a Starbucks cup in one hand, pushing a stroller back and forth with the other. One woman smiled at Martha when she stopped to watch the children.

"Matt, not so fast, you'll scare Myra," the other one called to the boy propelling the merry-go-round. Martha didn't think Myra looked the least bit scared, she sported a wide grin as Matt barely slowed.

Another little girl chased after a soccer ball, complaining as she ran, "Don't kick it so hard, Daddy." Martha thought wistfully that someday she'd watch her own children play in the park while she chatted with other mothers. But right now, she felt out of place without any children in tow. Two boys banged the hanging chimes and they sounded like an amplified version of the wind chimes that hung on Gram's front porch. She forgot her discomfort, picked up one of the metal mallets, and smiling at the boys, added her own bell-like notes to theirs. They grinned and banged even louder.

Then she crossed to the other side of the park to a big metal sculpture, open at both ends like a giant double-horned trumpet. She stood next to a woman with a baby in her arms and watched several children climb up inside one end of the horn and slide down the other side. A small boy ran over and gave the woman a hug. Martha caught his eye, "Looks like fun."

"Yeah, it's awesome," he nodded his head vigorously.

"Does one end make a better slide?"

"No, come on, I'll show you." Martha glanced at the woman who didn't hesitate. "Go ahead, Andy will love the company." He climbed up the tunnel and Martha followed him, hunched over in the small space, as he sat in the middle and slid down the other end.

"Your turn—what's your name?"

"Martha." She followed him down the slippery metal slope. As soon as she reached the bottom he said, "Come on, let's do it again." She raced with him up and down the slide a few more times, until she was out of breath and Andy had to leave, despite his pleas for "just a few more minutes, Mommy."

"I had so much fun Andy, thank you for sharing the slide with me."

"You're welcome." Andy followed his mother from the park then turned, waved, and yelled, "Bye, Martha!"

Martha twirled around, arms outstretched, realizing the oppressive sense of failure and guilt had disappeared, replaced by a lighthearted rush of joy. She inhaled the smell of spring her feet released from the wet grass, and smiled at those who passed by as she left the park and headed to the dock where the colorful purple and green dragon paddle boats waited. Their spiny backs painted gold or red, arching tails, and large eyes made them look more friendly than fierce, and Martha thought, magical. The sunshine had drawn people to the harbor, families with rambunctious children waited in line and she joined them.

George poured coffee from the small pot in his hotel room. He took a sip and opened the pale green curtains covering the wall of windows. The view of the Inner Harbor appeared in his mind, a gray bank swallowed the water and boats below, like the fog that often consumed Cape Cod Bay.

He arrived the previous night and today he planned to explore the area and find a more permanent place to live than a hotel room. He thought about his parents and the old homes his dad resurrected back in Massachusetts, hoping he could find something similar to reclaim here in Baltimore. Although this move took him farther from the Cape, his parents shared his excitement for a new challenge. George ran a hand over a square chin, shadowed by stubble. His mother called it his "stubborn chin" and always claimed he inherited it from his father's side of the family, and she contributed his dark curls and dimples.

George finished his coffee and dressed for a run, hoping to banish the lethargy of a restless night's sleep in an unfamiliar place. He jogged down Light Street to Lawrence and kept going all the way to Fort McHenry, where he looped through the park along the water. George found something mystical about running through heavy fog; the lack of visual distractions made it easier to let his mind explore unexpected paths, and it traveled back six months to early December and the call that had brought him to Baltimore.

"Hey George, it's Nick. Listen, how would you like to come down for the weekend? I know it's last minute, but one of the guys at work gave me two tickets to the Ravens game on Sunday."

"Sounds great, who are they playing?" George hadn't cared about the other team; he hadn't seen Nick in over a year. They had been roommates at Rhode Island School of Design, both majoring in architecture. George had focused on academics and dragged Nick to more than one study group. Nick, on the other hand, always ready for fun, had kept George from taking himself too seriously. Time with his upbeat friend would be a welcome relief from his monotone life and frustrating job.

"Steelers," Nick had said. "Sorry it's not the Pats, but Pittsburgh should give them a good game. Why don't you come Friday and stay here with us? There's something I want to bounce off you."

"What's going on?"

"My company bought several abandoned mills in Baltimore. We want to turn them into high-end condos, but keep the old mill character. We need an architect who specializes in restoration, and I thought of you."

"I don't know Nick, I'm in the middle of a big project right now, I'm months away from finishing." George hadn't expected a job offer. Although he hadn't loved his job, he lacked the motivation to find something new.

"Come on man, you've been burying yourself in your job for five years. You don't even like it."

George had clenched his fist at his side. The comments hit too close to the truth. Nick had pushed him more than once to change jobs. He never missed an opportunity to assert his opinion and point George in a more positive direction, but George viewed it as interference. As much as George respected Nick's professional opinion, he resented it when Nick intruded on his personal life. His initial excitement about seeing his friend faded. He didn't like being told what to do.

"You doing an intervention in my life? Is that why you called?" His voice hardened, although his volume didn't increase.

"No, George, I know you're one of the few people who can do this job. But yes, I do think it's time to get on with your life. Here's a chance to start over with a terrific job. At least take a look and then decide."

George hadn't answered. Nick worked for Jackson and Morrissey, a well-known architectural firm. He'd be a fool to turn down the offer without knowing more about it. Nick remained quiet.

"All right, I'll drive down, because I'm a sucker for free football tickets."

Nick had shown him the mills and shared his vision for the project. When George drove home late Sunday night, ideas for reclaiming the mills swirled in his mind. The position would be far more to his liking than designing modern mini-mansions along the Connecticut shore.

Now George thought about the life he'd left in Connecticut, and the long hours he'd worked to block the painful memories that lived there. He had wallowed in guilt and self-pity for the last five years, since his wife Elaine had died unexpectedly. Nick had been right, it was time to put it behind him, move on and begin again.

By the time he finished his run, the wind had swept away the fog leaving behind feathery wisps. The sun danced off the rippled water in the harbor, and though eager to start house hunting, George didn't want to do anything serious. It had been years since he had taken a whole day to enjoy himself, and today he wanted be a tourist. He'd look for a house tomorrow.

He showered, ate a quick breakfast in his hotel, then headed to the Inner Harbor where he spotted the dragon paddle boats. *What's more touristy than this?* He bought a ticket for a half-hour ride and joined the line of vacationing families.

George found himself behind a woman he guessed was in her late twenties. She gazed across the harbor, oblivious to the noise around her. Wavy, light brown hair, with flecks of gold that glinted in the sunlight, brushed the collar of her jacket. Though the jeans she wore had a one-size-too-big look, they didn't camouflage the trim rounded body beneath. He felt something stir inside him, something he thought had died forever. She tipped her head back to the sun and his eyes traced the graceful line of her jaw where it joined her neck then disappeared into a sea green sweater. He wanted to meet her, *needed* to meet her. And though it was totally out of character, he gave in to his impulse and introduced himself.

8

Chapter 2

Martha held her ticket in her hand and donned the orange lifejacket provided with it. The breeze ruffled her hair and she tipped her face up to the sun, oblivious to the people around her, content to wait for her turn. She felt a tap on her shoulder and jumped.

"Excuse me," a baritone voice said, and she turned to look up into eyes the color of molten chocolate. "I didn't mean to startle you. I wondered if you'd like to share a dragon boat. Might be more fun with two people— unless you're waiting for someone?"

Unlike Tony's smooth good looks, this man's face had a rugged, weathered appeal like the fishermen who frequented Gram's café. When he smiled, dimples creased his cheeks and she felt an unexpected glimmer of heat deep within her. Martha realized she was staring and felt her face flush.

"Oh, okay, it does sound like more fun."

"Great! My name's George," he held out his hand.

"Martha." She smiled and shook his hand. *Why couldn't it be Chad?*

"Martha, what a lovely name, old fashioned, but warm."

She'd never thought of her name that way. It sounded more appealing when he said it. When they reached the front of the line, they handed their tickets to the attendant and Martha took George's offered hand to steady her as she stepped into the boat. Once they were seated, the attendant released the lines and their purple dragon drifted from the dock. They both laughed at their lack of coordination and slow progress. Martha relaxed, relieved George didn't get upset, but found it funny too. Eventually they coordinated their pedaling and easily propelled the boat into the harbor.

"Do you live in Baltimore or are you visiting?" Martha wanted to ask why he was here by himself, but then he might ask the same of her. What would she say, self-therapy for her recent divorce? She'd ask what she didn't mind answering herself.

"I moved here for a new job and I decided to be a tourist for the day. How about you, do you live here?"

"I do, but today I felt like being a tourist too. I've run past the paddle boats so many times and thought they looked like fun, and I decided to give them a try. What other touristy things have you done?"

"This is my first, any suggestions?"

"Fells Point's one of my favorite parts of the city, and the Purple Pear Café has the best omelets." She told him about walking the cobblestoned streets and the charming shops, even her adventures in Pierce's Park, but she didn't tell him about the divorce papers she had signed and delivered that morning, or that she'd hidden in the coffee shop trying to lose herself in a story of happily ever after. Her reason for being in Fells Point didn't matter right now, only this man with the chocolate eyes and dimpled smile mattered, he made her insides feel things they hadn't felt in years, and she wanted to know more about him.

"You mentioned a new job, what do you do?" she asked.

"I'm an architect, I'll be working with a company that reclaims old mills."

"What a great job, it's sad to see the once-imposing brick buildings falling apart. I'm glad you have plans to save them."

"I'm excited to see them come back to life, but I know the first weeks will be hectic. There won't be much time for sightseeing then, but that's okay, I'm looking forward to being busy."

By the time their thirty minutes ended, something had eased inside Martha, as if she had been holding her breath for months and she could finally let it go. At the dock, George took Martha's hand again as she stepped out of the boat, and happiness prickled her fingers. They returned their life jackets and ambled back to the harbor walkway. She looked up at George and thought about their easy conversation. She didn't normally pick up random men, but spending the day alone had lost its appeal. Besides, today was different, she was different, and she followed her impulse before she could change her mind.

"I had fun. Would you like to come with me for a cone of gelato at Vaccaro's, the next stop on my touristy list?" She tilted her head and his smile of pleasure rewarded her impulsiveness.

"I will, under one condition: it's my treat."

"That's not necessary." Martha started walking and George fell into step beside her.

"Please. Besides, I have an ulterior motive."

"Oh?" Martha saw a playful twinkle in George's eyes and her heart did a funny little skip.

"I'm hoping you'll let me join you for the rest of your list. Consider it thanks in advance for being my tour guide for the day."

"Since you put it that way, how can I refuse?" Martha had the urge to twirl, after years of feeling invisible and unimportant in her marriage, George wanted to spend the day doing whatever she had planned. Tony would never have consented to joining her. If she tried to make plans for them, he didn't have time or he'd agree, then cancel or change her plans at the last minute. She didn't need, or even want, a new relationship right now, but she could fantasize for today.

They meandered out of the crowded Inner Harbor to quieter streets and Martha imagined they were a couple exploring the city together. Along the way, she pointed out the Aquarium and the Museum of Industry and told him about the nearby Flag House where Betsy Ross had sewn the first American flag.

"You seem to know all the tourist highlights, have you visited all of them?"

"No, although they sound interesting. Like the paddle boats, I've run past them but never taken the time to stop." She hadn't felt like exploring them alone.

11

"Do you ever run at Fort McHenry Park? I ran there this morning."

"That's a beautiful spot, but most of the time I run through the Inner Harbor to Fells Point or the neighborhoods around Federal Hill. The familiar route clears my mind." But running hadn't freed her mind from the weight of failure.

"I know what you mean, running my normal route helps me think when I'm working on a building design, and relieves the stress of tight deadlines."

"Try running up the steps to Federal Hill Park for stress relief!" Martha enjoyed running by herself. Tony had preferred workouts at the gym, but she could see herself running with George. The thought appealed to her. Maybe she'd invite him running sometime.

They arrived soon after Vaccaro's opened for the day. On warm summer evenings the line for ice cream snaked out the door, but today they were the only customers. The scent of freshly made waffle cones greeted them and they took their time strolling past the display case.

"I never know which flavor to try, they all look yummy."

"Anything with chocolate works for me." George ordered a large cone of double fudge espresso.

Martha continued on, studying each flavor, until she reached the strawberry lime cilantro. As a child, she ate only strawberry ice cream for several summers, and here was a grown-up version. How could she resist? Her first lick exploded in her mouth, the tartness of the lime and fresh taste of cilantro made the strawberry flavor dance and she closed her eyes and sighed with pleasure. When she opened them, George was studying her intently.

"I can tell you *really* like ice cream," he said with amusement. Pink crept up her cheeks and she looked back at her cone.

"You've only known me for an hour, and already you've discovered one of my favorite indulgences."

"One, that must mean there are more. Will you tell me another?"

Martha thought for a moment, and embarrassment warred with delight. George had noticed her ice cream trance but his question sounded interested, not mocking—so delight won.

12

"I smell the flowers." She stole a glance at George as he licked his ice cream cone. Sunlight caught the gold band on his left hand and something squeezed in her heart, how had she missed that? She should probably end their excursion right now and go back to her empty life, she had no intention of becoming involved with a married man. But he wanted to continue their touristy day together and so did she. Well, why not? She could hold on to her fantasy a little longer. She was drawn to him, despite the gold band. Their conversation felt comfortable, although they'd kept it pretty impersonal. Was he living a fantasy too?

They left the shop and George said, "Where to next, tour guide?"

"Well," she continued to lick her ice cream, and tried to think what might appeal to a man who enjoyed bringing life to old buildings. What would be fun for them to do together? After today, they would go their separate ways.

"Do you like trains?"

"Do you know any boy who doesn't? I used to imagine hopping on a freight train and riding it wherever it took me, usually when I got myself into trouble and decided to run away from home."

Martha smiled. "I know the ideal place for an adventurous boy, follow me." She strode down Albemarle Street. They walked up Pratt Street, past commercial buildings and a neighborhood lined with triple-decker row houses. She cast sideways glances at George as they strolled. Not a huge man, George carried himself with an air of confidence and the grace of an athlete. Though she met him just today, she felt safe with him.

❅ ❅ ❅

George wondered where they were going, but it didn't matter. Martha captivated him and he wanted to be with her and share whatever adventures she had planned. He didn't understand this immediate, visceral attraction, he'd never felt anything like it before. He wanted to know all about her, learn all her secret indulgences.

"Have you always lived in Baltimore?" George matched the pace of his longer stride to hers.

13

"No. Oh look, daffodils," she pointed to a tiny, south facing door-yard garden with several clumps of flowers. Martha got down on her hands and knees, and he stopped, surprised by her abrupt action, and watched as she pressed her nose into the bright yellow daffodil trumpet, inhaling as she did. Then she moved to a lone purple flower basking in the sun, breathed deeply and sighed, "Mmmm, heavenly."

"You were serious, weren't you? You actually do smell the flowers."

"Of course, what did you think I meant?"

George laughed and shook his head. Ordinarily he would have felt a little odd standing next to a woman on her hands and knees with her nose in the flowers, but with Martha, it seemed normal.

George knelt beside her and sniffed. "You're right, it is heavenly, what is it?"

"A hyacinth."

George saw her staring at him in amazement. "What?" Did she think everyone should recognize a hyacinth?

"Nothing, it's—not everyone would smell the flowers with me." George saw a brief flicker of pain in her eyes and he wondered if there was a specific someone who wouldn't smell the flowers. They got up and brushed off their knees, but he had the feeling Martha brushed off much more than her knees. He wanted to ask about it, but followed his instincts and kept his question light.

"Are you going to give me any clues about our mystery destination?" He continued walking.

"Soon. Tell me more about your train fascination."

George wondered if she'd purposely changed the subject again or had given him a clue. "I grew up on Cape Cod, and the tracks were about a mile from our house. My friends and I would put pennies on the rail and then come back later to find them flattened and reshaped by the weight of the train. I even took a train ride for my birthday once."

As they approached the corner of Poppleton Street, Martha stopped.

"Okay, close your eyes," she took his hand loosely in hers. Her hand felt warm and George's senses leaped in response as awareness spread through his body. Did she feel something too? Her eyes didn't give him an answer, so he closed his.

"You won't lead me into a lamp post, will you?" He wasn't worried, but he tightened his grip, relieved when she didn't pull away.

"It's not much farther, I'll tell you if we come to a bump or a curb, trust me."

George did trust her, and he relaxed as they walked hand in hand for the last bit of their journey. Martha stopped and let go of his hand, but he wished she hadn't.

"Ta da!"

George opened his eyes, saw the sign that read B&O Railroad Museum, and grinned. "I can't imagine any place I'd like better." She'd chosen a spot that rekindled some of his happiest childhood memories, and his desire to spend more time with her grew.

Martha smiled, "I'm glad you approve." They arrived at the main entrance and he opened the door for her.

"My dad used to take me to the train museum in Chatham," George said. They explored the roundhouse and climbed in the engines. "My favorite was the red caboose, but these steam engines are even more amazing." When they took the twenty-minute train ride, George imagined them leaving on an unchartered adventure together. What places would Martha choose to explore? He didn't care, as long as he could be with her. After the train ride, they walked by the carousel.

"Oh look, it has trains instead of animals," Martha sounded so delighted, George guided her into the ticket line. When the carousel stopped, she said, "I could ride this all day," so he bought two more tickets.

When the second ride ended, they continued their circuit of the roundhouse. George stopped when they came to Thomas the Train chugging along the tracks and through tunnels. He put his hand on Martha's arm and nodded towards a freckle-faced boy who stood watching, enthralled. He looked like George's five-year old nephew, Oliver, also a Thomas devotee, except without the freckles.

"Which one is Thomas?" he asked the boy.

15

"The blue one," the little boy said with a tone of authority, "and the red one is James and Percy is the green one." George acknowledged his expertise and they stood for a few more minutes watching as Thomas repeated his trip again and again.

"I'm not sure which one of you is enjoying this more." Martha whispered, her lips close to George's ear.

"Probably me," George whispered back. He wanted to slip his arm around Martha and keep her close a little longer, but he didn't. Along with her enjoyment of the day, he sensed a hidden detachment and it cautioned him to proceed slowly.

They left the railroad museum and walked towards the harbor. Even though she would declare it unnecessary, George wished he could think of something she would enjoy as much as he had the trains.

"What a fascinating place, and you're a great tour guide!" But she had done more than direct their tour, Martha had twined herself around his heart. He felt bewitched. "How did you know this would be perfect?" *And how can I keep you from leaving?* Neither one of them had shared anything too personal, and yet for the first time since his wife Elaine died, he felt alive again.

"A lucky guess?" Martha shrugged her shoulder. "You restore buildings, the museum restores trains."

"I hate to see the day end," George said softly. "Can I buy you dinner?"

"I should go home." Martha's expression grew distant and sad. George wanted to bring back the delight he'd seen earlier—ice cream, flowers, the carousel.

"How about stopping for a pizza to end our fun tour of Baltimore?"

Martha's face brightened at George's suggestion. "Actually, one of my favorite restaurants, the Corner Pub is nearby. The pizza's terrific and they brew their own beer."

"Corner Pub it is," George felt grateful the shadow that darkened Martha's mood had passed. They bypassed the crowded, noisy lower level of the pub, climbed the stairs to the quieter second floor, and took seats at a

16

high-top table by the window. George looked out over the city. Baltimore looked different, brighter, more inviting than it had before.

"What do you recommend?" George studied the menu, but thought about seeing Martha again. He wanted to ask her out on a real date. He hoped she'd say yes, and he'd see her eyes light up again.

"Cheese and Greens, I always think I'll try something new, but the combination of basil, spinach and garlic is too appealing."

"Sounds good to me."

Chapter 3

Martha didn't need to look at the menu. She took stock of her heart and admitted she'd allowed herself to believe what her mind imagined. She'd become entranced by her fantasy and this man. At some point she would have to walk away. She prepared herself to hear him say, "Thank you for showing me Baltimore, I can't wait to share it with my wife." But she longed for a different ending to the day.

"Tell me what you liked best about the museum," Martha said, while they waited for their pizza.

"It's hard to choose, I loved going inside the engines, and on the train ride I imagined taking off for parts unknown on a great adventure."

"You seemed to enjoy watching Thomas and his small fan." While George watched Thomas, she had watched George. Tony would never have taken the time to notice the little boy, he wouldn't have gone to the museum at all. And George had smelled the hyacinths with her; Tony would have worried that somebody would see him and think him strange. It took only one day with George to confirm how much warmth and caring had been missing in her marriage.

"He reminded me of myself when I was young. I could tell I'd discovered a Thomas expert, and it's always good to have your expertise acknowledged, even if you're five. I bet I can guess your favorite thing," his eyes twinkled. "The carousel?"

"You guessed it." She smiled, but didn't say she liked spending the day with him the best. He'd captured her heart with his kindness and sense of fun, but along with their pizza, the day would soon be gone, which she liked the least.

When it came time to pay the bill, Martha reached for her wallet.

"My treat," George took out his credit card. He leaned towards Martha, arms on the table. "Martha, I can't remember when I've had so much fun, I loved being with you. I don't want this to end, I'd like to see you again, have a real date, would you—"

"What are you talking about?" Martha's jaw dropped open. "You're married!" She had braced herself to hear about his wife, but not for this. The man she'd fantasized about would never cheat on his wife, he wouldn't. When she envisioned them together, she knew it was a fantasy, why didn't he? "I'm sorry if I gave you the wrong idea, but our tourist day is over, I don't date married men."

She grabbed her bag, put some bills on the table and hurried down the stairs. Martha heard George shout, "Wait, Martha," but she kept going, weaving her way through the gathering crowd of diners.

She hurried back to her townhouse in Federal Hill with questions swirling in her mind and anger surging alternately at him and at herself. Why did he ask her to be his tour guide? She saw the ring, why didn't she comment on it? Why didn't he mention his wife? Why didn't she stop their tourist day after the ice cream or ask when his wife would arrive?

She knew half the answers, starting with the sparks she'd felt when their hands touched. They made her feel so alive she had wanted to pretend they were real, pretend she was a different person, for one day. She and George had laughed, done silly things, and she'd had more fun than she'd had in years. He had looked at her like she was the only woman in the world, and he had behaved like a gentleman. She'd thought how lucky a woman would be if George loved her, she'd allowed her mind to follow a path of make-believe, and had imagined he did.

Martha unlocked her door and shuffled into the gloomy emptiness. She shouldn't want to see George, again, but she did. "It's good he's married,"

19

she told herself. Otherwise she would tumble headfirst into the abyss of Happily Ever After—again. She should know by now life didn't work that way. Despite the firm resolution she had made earlier today, her carefree spirit disappeared, and everything wrong in her life came crashing down. All her failures crept out of the walls. She couldn't even get pretending right.

Martha collapsed on herself, slid down with her back to the door, put her head on her knees, and sobbed. Clouds and drizzle outside joined the dusk and hurried darkness along. Exhausted, Martha stood, and without turning on a light, dragged herself into the bedroom, as painful memories crowded around her, nipping at her. Her failed marriage had consumed her one bite at a time. Tony's constant control and belittling words had bruised her soul and numbed her to reality until she believed him and lost herself. *I can't stay in this house. It will suck every ounce of joy from me.*

She dragged her purple suitcase from the walk-in closet and haphazardly threw in a few things, her running shoes, underwear and jeans, a couple of sweaters and basic toiletries. She didn't need a lot, she wouldn't be gone long, she had commitments at the bakery with Sarah, the house would have to be sold, and details resolved. Plus, she had qualified for the Charm City Chocolate Challenge in October, and she'd need months to prepare. If she won, it would prove to Gram that coming to Baltimore had been a good decision, despite her broken promises and disastrous marriage. On an impulse, she'd registered for the Baltimore marathon, also in October. She had challenged herself with two huge events, one week apart, but she wouldn't walk away from either of them. She needed the marathon to prove her own strength and find her true self again.

A well-worn copy of *Travels with Charley*, written by John Steinbeck lay on the table beside her bed where she'd left it the night before. It had belonged to the mother she never knew, and recounted Steinbeck's travels across the country with his friend Charley, a standard poodle.

When she read it, she imagined her mother and the dauntless spirit Martha believed she possessed. She hoped she'd inherited a kernel of that spirit. *Maybe I'll get a dog, and travel the country.* Doesn't the heroine in romance novels always have a dog? A stray appears on her doorstep, becomes her best friend and protector, and knows whether the men she meets are trustworthy or disreputable. She could have used him today.

"Yeah, right, that will never happen," she mumbled. Martha couldn't imagine traveling with a wet dog in the car, and the accompanying obnoxious smell, nor could she imagine an entire cross-country trip without rain.

"I guess I'll have to figure out who is honorable by myself, or I can find a cat with well-developed instincts." Martha continued talking to herself as she clutched the book, then she tucked it into her suitcase and zipped it closed.

She sent a quick text to Sarah, "I have to get away before I implode, no cakes ordered, I'll be in touch." She took a last look around the stark, modern house, devoid of personal items, the way Tony preferred it.

Martha pushed thoughts of George and Tony out of her mind, and carried her suitcase to the car, along with a bottle of water and the last banana from the fruit bowl. On her way out, she grabbed a warm coat and a rain jacket from the hall closet. Thank goodness for the murmur of intuition telling her to keep her own car, even though Tony fussed that they shouldn't have two cars in the city with a one-car garage. She had stubbornly clung to her Honda, and now it would provide her escape.

But where do I go? Heading north would mean the comfort of the familiar, but was that what she wanted? Driving south would mean the challenge of new surroundings. She loved the idea of endless Florida beaches, especially tonight, when a cold April rain had settled in.

"You better make up your mind soon," she told herself. Martha locked the front door, got in the car and pulled onto the Key Highway, leaving her neighborhood behind. She passed Camden Yards and headed towards Route 95. The highway divided, curving right took her north, bearing left would lead her south. She took a deep breath and turned the wheel.

21

Chapter 4

George continued to berate himself as he wandered the nearby streets of Federal Hill, where Martha said she liked to run. He hoped to catch a glimpse of her, but the rows of townhouses remained silent, though his instincts told him she was close by.

Why didn't I tell her? Neither one of them had shared anything too personal, and yet he felt alive again for the first time since Elaine died. He'd tried to stop her and explain, but by the time he scrawled his name on the check and navigated the crowded stairs, Martha had disappeared, and he didn't even have her phone number.

When the drizzle grew to incessant rain, he admitted defeat for the day and returned to his hotel room. His new job would begin on Monday and the weekend stretched before him. Prior to meeting Martha, George couldn't wait to get started on the designs for the old mills. Now his anticipation sat forgotten in the corner of his brain, and thoughts of finding Martha consumed him.

Light faded from the day, and George slouched in one of the comfy green chairs in his hotel suite. He ignored the harbor view and didn't bother to turn on the television. The time with Martha rolled through his mind again and again, like an old movie theatre playing the same show over and over, without interruption. He remembered every detail, and his body relaxed as he reveled in the pleasure of the day, including his excitement when she agreed to extend their adventure through dinner.

Then he reached the last few minutes when she left the pub, distress replacing the joy on her face moments before, and he wished again that he'd told her about Elaine. He could have kept it simple. He thought she would have understood his reticence to share too much too soon; he sensed the same reluctance in her. Every time he remembered that part of the day his gut clenched in anger at himself. He turned his ring around and around. Had he tried to sabotage his own happiness? After several hours of this torment, he decided he had to stop. He wouldn't allow himself to slide back into the dark place that had gripped him five years ago. He had spent an enjoyable day with a woman he would never see again, and it had ended.

George changed into running gear and left the hotel, despite the darkness and a cold rain. His body didn't need another run today, but his mind did. The Inner Harbor and surrounding neighborhoods had ample lighting, so he pushed himself to run hard for over an hour. He swept thoughts of Martha aside and tried to retrieve the forgotten excitement of his new job.

He pictured the first mill he had seen when he came to Baltimore six months ago. A padlocked chain link fence surrounded the property. Unfazed by the newspapers and plastic bags caught in the metal's grip, George had focused on the aged brick and the intriguing lines of the sturdy building.

"Most of the buildings have doors and windows missing, so we fenced them to keep out vandals, but I brought the keys." Nick had tried several of the keys on the ring he held until one fit, and the gate swung open. As George followed Nick up the broken walkway, he looked up and studied the crumbling brick, but saw apartments with skylights and tall vaulted ceilings.

The heavy, off-kilter wooden door, warped by weather and time, creaked on its hinges. They had entered the cavernous mill building, their steps releasing clouds of dust, and he smelled damp wood and disuse mingled with an old campfire scent of burnt timber. When George's eyes adjusted to the dim interior, he saw numerous broken windows and wires swinging from the beams like vines from a tree. Stains and damaged boards scarred the wooden floors and several missing stairs made reaching the second floor impossible. Charred boards rested in a corner beside a pile of dirty blankets, the remains of someone's efforts to escape the cold.

"This is as far as we go without hard hats and steel-toed shoes," Nick surveyed the space. "Too many hidden booby traps. Looks a bit of a disaster at this point, I know."

George scanned the neglected building. The aged bricks seemed to exude stories and warmth, and towering windows would fill the rooms with light and provide breathtaking views of the harbor and city. He hadn't seen disaster; he had seen infinite possibilities.

By the time George finished his run, the exhilaration of a new challenge replaced some of the haunting pain of disappointment, and he felt ready to review the information he had gathered about local real estate. He loathed apartment living; he wanted a house where he could have several projects going at once to occupy his mind when he wasn't working.

He found a handful of older homes in the residential area of Roland Park. They boasted towering trees and large yards, and though structurally sound, needed refurbishing. He bookmarked three of the most promising, he would call the real estate agent tomorrow. By then, fatigue made sleep a possibility. He tuned the TV to a classic movie channel he used to watch with his dad and fell asleep as the Duke won the heart of Maureen O'Hara.

❉ ❉ ❉

When George went out the next morning at daybreak, leaden skies leaked moisture, and most of the Inner Harbor slept. He ran up and down the back streets of Federal Hill where he felt close to Martha. Despite his resolve the night before, George longed to find her. He wanted the chance to explain, to persuade her to see him again, and hopefully rekindle the spark of connection he'd felt yesterday. He saw a few joggers and wanted to stop and ask them if they knew Martha, but he didn't know her last name and George didn't want to seem like a stalker. What would he say?

"I met this woman and her first name is Martha and I wondered if you know where she lives?" Even if they didn't call the police, he didn't think they'd give him any information. George kept running through the steady drizzle. Maybe she would go for an early morning run too; he remembered

24

she mentioned running helped her think. Then he recalled her toned body and well-placed curves, which didn't help him think at all. After repeating his route several times with no luck, he finished his run by jogging up the steps to Federal Hill Park, accepting the solitude of the morning.

George contacted the real estate agent and set up appointments to see the three houses he had researched last night. He parked his car in front of the first one on the list, a wood-framed house with a wraparound front porch that prompted lighthearted childhood memories of Cape Cod. He pictured children playing in the yard and heard their shouts and laughter. The house had clean, simple lines and although now faded and worn, he saw the remnants of a cheerful yellow. He imagined how alive it would look with a fresh coat of sunlit yellow paint to highlight its friendly style.

Several flower beds near the porch needed weeding, but the clumps of daffodils and hyacinths scattered along the front edge of the yard caught his attention. They reminded him of his day with Martha and kneeling beside her in the grass to smell the flowers. He never would have done that by himself, but with Martha it seemed right; in fact, he'd felt comfortable with Martha all day, from the time he touched her shoulder, waiting in the dragon boat line.

He tucked the memory away when a bright red Mazda Miata parked behind him. A woman stepped into the rain and opened an umbrella, but it didn't offer much protection for her black spiky heels. George got out of his car and walked to meet her. *Striking*, dashed across his mind then stopped. He thought of Martha and the immediate pull to meet her—in one day she had managed to claim his heart. This woman inspired nothing except a fleeting observation.

"Hi, I'm Tanya Lavendow, sorry about the weather." She held out her right hand.

"George Henderson, not a problem," he shook her hand. "I think a house shows its true character in the rain."

Tanya led the way up the porch steps and unlocked the front door, revealing a long hallway with a right-angled staircase on the left. "There are three bedrooms and a bath upstairs, living room, dining room and kitchen on the main floor along with . . ." Tanya's voice trailed off as she sped toward the back of the house. George stood for a moment absorbing the details surrounding him. He sensed happy family memories here, and he felt immediately at home. Beneath the dark brown paint, he recognized red oak floors, and a mahogany stair bannister and newel post. He envisioned the finished room, when he completed the painstaking tasks of sanding and restoring the floor and bannister, and saw sunlight reflecting off the polished wood hallway leading to the kitchen in the back of the house. Excitement flared inside him as he remembered the long hours his father worked to restore the house where George had grown up, his father's talent had left a lasting imprint in every room. George wanted a house where he could do the same, and his instincts said he'd found the perfect one.

The click of Tanya's heels returning to the front hall, her automatic spiel on pause, interrupted his reverie.

"The house really needs a lot of work. The kitchen hasn't been updated, nor have the bathrooms. They did enlarge the pantry to make a sunroom that doubles as a breakfast room, but I have other houses I think your wife would like much better."

"I don't have a wife." The sense of emptiness the words trigged surprised George. *It must be the house.* He wanted to reclaim it, but he also wanted someone to share it.

"You don't?" George realized Tanya was eying the ring on his left hand. He put his hand in his pants pocket. Most of the time he forgot he had it on, but he'd have to stop wearing it if he seriously wanted to start over.

"Recently divorced? I know how that is." Tanya fluffed her hair. "Listen, this house isn't what you want, I have another listing that's in much better condition, the renovations are all top-notch. I know the contractor who did the job, plus the neighborhood is quieter, not so many kids. There's a great café on the way, we can grab a bite to eat. Did you have breakfast?"

George had the distinct feeling Tanya didn't want to sell him this house. Maybe the one she described had a larger price tag.

"Do you mind if I see the second floor as long as we're here?" He ignored Tanya's surreptitious glance at herself in the hall mirror and nodded his head in the direction of the stairs.

"Well, I suppose so, but really the bedrooms are dingy, and the bathroom looks like it came out of the fifties."

Perfect. George let Tanya lead the way upstairs.

"The whole house needs to be renovated," Tanya waved her arm around the hallway. George poked his head into each bedroom, they weren't dingy as much as tired, but the large windows in every room offered a promise of future cheerfulness. Someone definitely had a vendetta against hardwood floors, the same dark brown paint coated every one, but like the front hall, he saw them refinished and shining with reflected sunlight.

Tanya was right about one thing, the bathroom duplicated his image of the fifties, complete with gray tile and pink fixtures, but large enough for the claw foot tub he pictured in the restored version.

After the second-floor tour, George asked to see the basement. He needed to check one more thing before he made any decisions. Despite the need for cosmetic renovations, the underpinnings appeared solid. Relief spread through him, he didn't want to deal with crumbling foundations or rotting sills. His instincts had been right.

He investigated the large fenced yard while Tanya waited in the shelter of the covered porch. The rain splashed into a small dip in the backyard and triggered memories of practicing his home plate slides through a similar muddy puddle when he was a boy. Longing tugged him back to the present. He wanted to raise a family here in the yellow house.

"I really wish you'd look at the other house I have in mind," she said, when he joined her.

"What's the difference in price?" George asked, although he had no interest in a fancier house.

"Only about two hundred thousand, but when you figure in the cost of hiring a contractor and doing all the necessary updates on this one, they'll be about even." Two hundred thousand? *That's a lot of updates.* And well beyond the price range they'd discussed.

"What about the other two houses I mentioned this morning. Can I see them?"

"Yes, but again they need work, not move-in condition."

27

George tried to remember if he'd said anything to make Tanya think he wanted a house in "move-in condition," but his mind came up empty. Those houses probably sold at a higher price, he supposed he would push them too if in her position.

The other houses were both large Victorians, charming in their own right, but they lacked the friendliness of the faded yellow house that had captured George's imagination. Tanya droned through all the advantages of each location, but with fewer negative comments than in the first house. Because George expressed less interest, or because they carried a bigger price tag?

"We're not far from the house I think you'd really like," Tanya said when they finished. "Do you have time to go see it?" Since he had nothing urgent to do, he decided to humor Tanya.

"Okay." He might be surprised.

After a short drive, George followed Tanya into the driveway of a brick federal style house in pristine condition. It had clean lines and an impeccably landscaped yard with tidy shrubs, but no flowers. Inside, the house had been gutted and modernized, not restored. Glass, stainless steel, and neutral colors prevailed. George thought it felt sterile and cold, and he couldn't imagine living here.

"Isn't it incredible?" Tanya's voice matched her wide-eyed appreciation. Apparently, this was Tanya's dream home.

"You were right, it is high quality work." *More like high quality sacrilege.* He could feel the original wide curving staircase, now replaced by an angled floating one. Although the exterior maintained its turn of the century appeal, the interior had been ravished into the twenty-first century.

"Perfect, right?"

"Someone obviously put a great deal of thought, and a generous amount of money into it," George looked around the large foyer, "but I don't think it's my style." The yellow house invited him in, this house remained aloof. It reminded him of the condo where he and Elaine had lived. He had suggested changes he thought would make it homier, but Elaine laughed, told him he was a good architect, but he had no talent for decorating. She would have loved this house. While he dreamed of a family and a home they could restore, she dreamed of upscale New York apartments. He realized they had never wanted the same things in life, and he wondered if their marriage would have survived, even if Elaine had.

"Too big? Did your wife get custody of the children?" Tanya's questions jarred him back to the present.

"No." George immediately regretted his sharp tone. "I don't have any children," he said softly.

"I don't either. Frank and I were only married a year before he developed wandering eyes, among other things. Anyway, I'm better off without him. If you don't mind my asking, why are you looking at large houses if you're all alone?" With her last question, Tanya's voice lost its brittle edge, she sounded sincere and he hoped if he answered she would stop trying to sell him the wrong house.

"I hate apartment living, and I know it's hard to believe, but I prefer a house that needs work. I enjoy the process of fixing it as much as the results."

"You mean you plan to do the work yourself?" Tanya's eyebrows arched.

"Crazy, huh?"

"Actually no, it isn't crazy, just an awful lot of work. Not something I would tackle, but when you're finished it'll be a reflection of you, which must be satisfying. So, I'm guessing the first house is your favorite?" George nodded. *Amazing, she gets it.*

"It is, how firm are the sellers on their price?"

"There could be some wiggle room. Make an offer and we'll go from there." Tanya's sales voice had returned.

"Let me think about it, I may have more questions and want to see it again." He waited while Tanya locked the front door, his mind already planning where he would start when the yellow house belonged to him.

"Give me a call when you decide." She smiled as she rested her hand on his arm. "I'm available tomorrow, if you want to see it again, or if you need more information."

"Thanks, I'll let you know." George had the distinct feeling she was available for more than showing him the house. He had no interest in anything else, and he didn't think he'd implied otherwise, but he'd be more careful on future meetings.

He returned to his hotel and resumed his spot in the green chair. He tipped his head back against the cushion and closed his eyes. Tanya's questions about a wife and children opened a door he'd tried to keep secured. Even after all this time, painful memories of Elaine's death shimmered on the edges of his brain. When he stood in the yellow house, the desire to start over and put down roots here in Baltimore surrounded him. He had held on to the agony of Elaine's death long enough, time to let it go and be receptive to love again. He hoped it would be with Martha, but that might never happen. At least now, after meeting her, he could feel again, his mind and body open to new possibilities.

That night, dreams of Elaine haunted him; she told him her death had been his fault, and she continued to yell as the sound of splintering glass and crashing metal bolted George awake in a cold sweat. When his heartbeat and breathing returned to normal, he dozed and dreamed of Martha and the yellow house. The sound of his alarm woke him, but he longed to slip back into sleep and find her again, if only in his dreams.

Chapter 5

Martha pulled into the highway rest stop as the sun peeked through the clouds. She parked beside the picnic table farthest from the food court building to stretch her legs. Coffee and a blueberry muffin sufficed for breakfast, and after a few fortifying sips, she strolled back to her car, dodging puddles on the sidewalk. She removed her rain jacket, spread it on the damp bench, then sat and leaned her back against the table. The rain had stopped, but after driving all night on unfamiliar roads through frequent downpours, her shoulders begged to be rubbed. Martha rolled them a few times, then tipped her head back, closed her eyes, and absorbed the increasing heat of the morning sun.

Something warm and soft nudged her hand. Startled, Martha's eyes popped open and encountered those of a tiger striped cat, that offered a plaintive, "Meow," then climbed onto her lap, as if her sitting position implied an invitation. He blinked his green eyes and started purring and kneading her legs. A missing collar had left a ring of matted fur on his neck, and Martha touched it with the back of one finger. A bubble of tenderness rose inside her. The cat reminded her of Dennis, her favorite of the strays Gram had taken in over the years.

"Well, hello, where did you come from?" She wondered how somebody could leave a cat behind in the middle of a busy highway, yet here he was friendly and seeking affection. She stroked his sleek fur. "Do you have no place to go either? You must belong to somebody."

Martha decided to return to the building in search of a security guard. She placed the cat on the ground, started walking, then glanced back to see if he would follow her, but he sprawled on the pavement, occupied with a bath.

When she told the guard about the cat, he shrugged his shoulders, "Probably got away from his owners, not much we can do." Martha chewed on her lower lip; she didn't want to leave the cat stranded. *Maybe he won't even be there when I get back.* But he had curled on the hood of her car, as if he had already decided she would take care of him. When she scratched behind his ears, he meowed his approval. Martha thought of all the childhood angst she'd shared with various feline companions and knew she wouldn't mind having this one accompany her now.

"I like you too, buddy, but let's stay here a little longer."

When Martha sat down on the bench again, he relinquished his spot on the car, jumped on her lap, and resumed kneading and purring. She offered him a piece of her muffin, which he devoured. Should she bring him with her? From her experience cats and cars didn't get along, but what other choice did she have? She couldn't leave him marooned in the middle of a highway. Martha ate part of the muffin and waited to see if someone would come by searching for a tiger cat with big green eyes and a purr like a rumbling locomotive.

She stroked his silky head and let the sun's heat relax her tired muscles. The cat's gentle purr lulled her to the brink of sleep. Her mind drifted back to what she thought of as *the beginning*, when life's possibilities seemed endless, but she had felt overwhelmed by the enormity of it all. She remembered her relief when someone had reached out and rescued her. As she hovered on the edge of wakefulness, she saw herself walking into the freshman welcome assembly on the first day of culinary school.

Martha had arrived at the small amphitheater, her newly acquired pastry tool kit clutched to her chest. Her heart raced with anticipation and anxiety. I'm here, I'm really here, following my dream. But she didn't know anyone in this city, large compared to her hometown in Maine, and she felt isolated. She nervously scanned the room, until her gaze met that of a petite, slightly round girl with a cap of black, curly hair. The girl sat with a cluster of students, several rows from the front. She smiled, waved at Martha, and called, "Come sit with us."

Martha climbed over a few people in the row. The girl immediately grabbed her hand and pulled her into the seat beside her, "Hi, I'm Delia. You looked a little lost over there, but we're a harmless group. This is Ralph, Amanda, Connor, Tony, and Annie," she waved her hand randomly.

"We're all culinary students but I can tell by your kit you're in baking and pastry. You must have a head for details. I love eating the results, but baking's too precise for me."

The boy sitting behind Delia stretched out his hand, "Hi Cupcake, I'm Tony. Where you from?" Martha felt a fleeting indignation at being called Cupcake by a man who had just met her. She could have told him a pastry chef did a lot more than bake cupcakes, but he had friendly, blue eyes, fringed by the longest lashes she had ever seen. Plus, his slow, sexy smile caused a wave of heat to wash over her.

She heard the other introductions in a fog, her heart pounded, and she lost her ability to speak. From the depths of her numb mind, she realized Tony was talking to her.

"I'm a local boy, I grew up here, so if you need a tour of the city, I'm your man."

A girl with long strawberry blond hair and a lanky frame, offered her hand from behind Delia's head. "Hi, I'm Annie. Don't believe a thing this guy tells you, and be careful what parts of the city he wants to show you."

Martha heard the laughter that had eased the tension inside her, and an insistent nudge from her new friend brought her back to the present. Nothing remained of her muffin, and no one had come to claim the cat.

"Okay buddy, I guess you're coming with me, do you have a name? Since we're traveling together, I think I'll call you Charley." She moved to the car and opened the passenger door. Charley, who sat placidly washing his face, took it as a signal to join her. He jumped onto the seat, circled it three times, tucked his nose under his paw, and went to sleep.

Weird, I never met one cat who liked riding in a car. Evidently, cars didn't bother Charley. Martha worried he might distract her by roaming while she drove, but when she turned the ignition key he continued to nap, his purr reduced to a gentle rumble in his throat. Martha was grateful for the company and a set of listening ears. *At least there's somebody in the world who thinks I'm worth keeping.*

She didn't have a known destination for the GPS, but she gave Charley a pat, pulled back onto the highway and continued south, energized by her dreamy nap, her new friend, or maybe the realization that she had moved on with her life.

✻ ✻ ✻

"Where shall we go Charley, all the way to the Gulf?" Charley picked up his head and blinked his inscrutable eyes. "I know, it's kind of a long drive. Well, what about Nashville? That's not as far, would Nashville be a good place to begin again? Along with all the country singers? What do you think? If Nashville was good enough for Gram's favorites, June Carter and Johnny Cash, it should be good enough for us."

Charley continued to stare at her.

"No comments from you, Charley? Well, for now we'll keep going, but I'm tired of the highway. Let's take some back roads and enjoy the scenery." She pulled off the highway at the next exit and stopped to check the map. Once Martha settled on an acceptable route, she resumed her one-sided conversation.

"For the record, I'm done with men, present company excluded of course, you seem to be an agreeable companion, unlike Tony and George."

"Meow."

Martha patted Charley's head. "Who's Tony? He's my ex-husband. The man I thought I would be married to forever. I remember the day we met, but I should back up, you might as well hear the whole story."

Martha still sought to understand why things went wrong. Maybe if she told Charley the saga, it would make sense to her. "I don't know where

34

your life began, but mine started in a little town in Maine, called Hope Island Harbor.

"My grandmother has a bakery and breakfast café there, and everybody says she's the best baker in Maine. People line up in the morning to get her wild blueberry coffee cake and homemade cinnamon rolls. Her pancakes are light as air.

"She's the one who taught me to bake, and I worked in the bakery all through high school. Gram relied on my help, but I found the weekend early morning hours a challenge, and I overslept more than once, even the day I planned to tell her I wanted to go to culinary school." Martha stopped talking and her mind got lost in memories of that day.

Martha had opened the bakery door as quietly as she could, hoping Gram wouldn't notice her late arrival. Silly, did she think she could pop up from behind the work bench and claim to have been there all along? Those wishful thoughts had disappeared when she saw Gram behind the front counter, placing raspberry muffins in the case. Gram looked up, her eyes went to the accusing hands of the clock. It was 5:30, not Martha's scheduled arrival time of 4 a.m., but Gram didn't say a word. Martha had poured out her excuse.

"I'm sorry Gram, the alarm went off and I thought I was getting up and ready for work, but I must have been dreaming, when I really woke up, I was still in bed." She always felt guilty when she overslept, but that didn't stop her from doing it again.

"The cinnamon rolls just came out of the oven, they're ready to be iced and put in the case."

Martha nodded her head. Gram had mastered the wordless lecture, there would be no further reprimand. The bakery opened in fifteen minutes, she had to hustle to make the icing. How could she ask Gram about culinary school now?

But Gram couldn't stay mad for long, and Martha heard her singing along with Johnny Cash as she rolled pie crust and he "Walked the Line." She promised herself never to be late again, but her future plans buzzed around her and made it hard to concentrate, so she took a chance.

"Gram, I've been thinking, I'll be graduating next year, and I'd like to

35

go to culinary school. Then I could come back and help you, we could expand the café and as business grows, hire someone else too. You could have more time off and you wouldn't have to get up so early."

"Someone has to get up early." Although she saw the hint of Gram's smile, Martha felt her cheeks heat with embarrassment, she hated letting Gram down.

"I know Gram, I messed up—again." Martha finished frosting the last tray of cinnamon rolls and gathered her courage. "I thought we could take a trip together and visit culinary schools, the closest one is in Rhode Island."

"I don't know Martha, you sure you want to sign on for endless hours and early morning wake up calls? There won't be room for excuses in school, or another job."

"I love working here, even the days I hate to drag myself out of bed. I enjoy baking once I'm here. Breathing the smells lifts my mood, and the rolling and cutting, or mixing, all give me space to think."

Another "Meow" came from Charley, as if urging her to continue, and it brought her mind back to the present.

"Sorry Charley, my mind wandered. Gram and I visited culinary school, and when I saw the intricate chocolate creations and spectacular wedding cakes, I knew I wanted to become a pastry chef, but I wanted more than the basics Gram taught me. I wanted to make magical things from chocolate and wedding cakes the bride and groom would remember forever. Gram helped pay for culinary school. In return, I promised I would come back after graduation and work with her for at least a year, but I let her down again, like I did those mornings.

"I met Tony on my first day. He obviously thought highly of himself, and initially I didn't like his superior attitude, but he was so handsome and smart. When he asked me out, I couldn't believe he would be interested in me. We took long walks on the beach and talked about our future dreams. He would be the chef in a five-star restaurant, and I would create renowned chocolate desserts and wedding cakes. In our senior year, he got an offer from Zander's, one of the best restaurants in Baltimore, and he wanted me to go with him.

"I told him I had to go back to Maine and work with Gram, but he wanted to leave Providence right after graduation, he said my talents would be wasted in Maine, and I let him persuade me. I didn't even return to tell Gram that I was moving south instead of coming north to work with her. I told her when she came to graduation, at the same time I told her Tony and I were getting married. She looked me in the eye and said, 'Martha you need to follow your heart, just make sure it's your own heart you're following.' I should have listened to her, Charley." Martha drove in silence for a few minutes, and then continued her monologue.

"And then there's George."

Charley meowed in response.

"I know, I know, it's too soon to even think about meeting someone, but I didn't plan it. Charley, we had such a glorious day together. He enjoyed everything I suggested, he even knelt beside me to smell the flowers, he didn't expect me to change my plans or behavior to suit him. I was disheartened when I saw his wedding ring, and I decided to pretend, for one day, he didn't have one. But I don't understand why he pretended too."

"Meow," Charley blinked his green eyes.

Chapter 6

Martha parked at an overlook and stepped from the car. She stretched and wrapped her arms around herself. Nothing but mountains and a winding, narrow road stretched for miles, despite the awe-inspiring view. *What was I thinking, taking such a desolate route as a side trip?* She stood by the wall guarding the steep drop and felt the wind, bulging with rain, race across the valley. It blew through her soul, leaving her hollow and depleted. A painful lump deep in her chest, her constant companion, gnawed at her. She tried to swallow past it and the emptiness that consumed her. Would she ever feel whole again?

Charley jumped from the car as soon as she opened the door. He explored the nearby bushes and when he finished his investigation, he wound between her legs. Martha gathered him in her arms, nuzzling his velvety neck.

"What am I going to do, Charley?"

Charley meowed, leaped from her arms and back to the front seat.

"I guess you're right, we better get going, I don't want to be on this road in the rain." She returned to the twisty route. Martha clenched the wheel as she drove, unsure of her destination, she felt adrift, and had trouble focusing; Charley's steady purr from the passenger seat anchored her in the moment.

"We're okay, Charley," she crooned, more for her own benefit than Charley's, "I see a sign ahead for the highway, we'll be back to civilization soon."

Martha's cell phone rang, and when she answered she heard the frantic voice of her friend, Delia.

"Martha, where are you? I've been calling and calling. I was ready to contact the police!"

"Delia, I'm so sorry. I should have called you last night, but I was overwhelmed by everything that happened yesterday, and I forgot about our plans. This morning I realized I didn't plug in my cell phone, and I've been disconnected from the world." Martha felt horrible, and selfish.

"I was so worried when you didn't come to yoga last night. We agreed we would go out after class and celebrate your signing the papers—you did sign them, didn't you?"

"Yeah, I did Delia," Martha sighed, "and for a while it really gave me a high. I felt free and—but then so much happened and I met this man, and he seemed nice, and then he was married, and then I felt so down about failing at my marriage, and—"

"Martha, Stop! Don't beat yourself up, it wasn't your fault, and what man?"

"Well, it takes two Delia, I must have done something wrong, somewhere along the way."

"You were young, you chose the wrong guy, but you don't have to live with that for the rest of your life. Come on, meet me, let's go get a drink and—what man?"

"I can't."

"Why not?"

"Because I'm driving, somewhere between Baltimore and Nashville." Martha braced herself for Delia's alarmed response.

"What? What are you doing there? You drove by yourself in the middle of the night?" Delia's mother hen instincts clicked in.

"Well, I was by myself, but I'm not anymore. I have a friend," Martha smiled to herself. "His name is Charley."

"You picked up a hitchhiker?" shrieked Delia, "Martha, what is the matter with you? You can't pick up strange men and give them a ride. Don't you read the news?"

"He's nice Delia, he's really nice, come on, say hi to Charley."

"Hello, Charley." Delia said, in a frosty voice. Charley looked up and blinked his eyes.

"Meow," he replied.

"A cat? Your friend is a cat?" Delia's voice grew louder.

"What? You think I should have picked up a man?" Martha hoped her attempt to lighten the mood would defuse some of Delia's increasing concern.

"You know that's not what I mean, you seem so—oh, I don't know, off kilter, it isn't like you."

"What do you expect, Delia?" Her life was in free fall, and she couldn't find the ripcord. "Yesterday, I signed papers to end my marriage."

"You had to. You couldn't stay after what he did. You know you're better off, now you can get on with your life."

"My head knows it, but right now my heart is having trouble figuring out who gets custody of the memories."

"Oh Martha—"

"Don't worry, I'll figure it out eventually, but I needed some space. I had to get out of the city, I didn't want to think about any of it."

"But why Nashville?"

"I don't know, my car chose south when I got on I-95."

"Well, as long as you've made it that far, you should keep going. Annie has a bed and breakfast in Pensacola, remember? She's told me more than once to come any time. She'll be glad to see you and you can stay there till you get over this weirdness. Take a couple of weeks then come back to Baltimore. I'll call Annie and let her know you're coming."

"No Delia! Let me figure this out, please." *One more reason I needed to leave Baltimore.*

"I'm just trying to help. You seem a little lost." She could hear the concern in Delia's voice.

"I know you want to help, but I'm not a naïve teenager anymore, you don't have to rescue me. I'll let you know what I decide and where I am."

"Okay, stay safe, and don't pick up any real hitchhikers, but tell me—*what man?*" Martha refused to share any details about George, she wished she hadn't said anything. Delia's opinionated advice would steal the little magic that remained from her day, and part of her wanted to hang on to the fantasy a while longer.

"Bye, Delia," Martha disconnected.

"Delia means well, Charley, she's a good friend, but she's as bossy now as she was in culinary school. Sometimes I want to tell her to leave me alone, but of course I don't. She doesn't get it Charley, divorce doesn't only mean the end of pain, it also means the end of a dream."

Martha stopped for gas and replenished her coffee, then found a classic country music station. She listened to the sad stories of Eddie Arnold and Johnny Cash, whose music had permeated the Sunrise Café while Gram baked. She allowed their songs of love lost to soak into her own damaged heart as she drove the last 150 miles to Nashville. A little before noon she turned onto Commerce Street and opened her window to the music surging from bars and restaurants that lined the pavement. Her grumbling tummy reminded her that a blueberry muffin and multiple cups of coffee was all she'd eaten since her pizza with George.

Thoughts of George sliced a different pain through her stomach. She had felt comfortable with him the moment she looked into his chocolate eyes, but it seemed her choice of men remained flawed. She tried to focus on Nashville as she looked for a place to park. Martha saw a car pulling out, so she claimed the spot.

"I'll get us something to eat Charley, and then we'll decide our next move." Martha bought a turkey sandwich to share with Charley. When she returned to the car, he had his front paws resting on the bottom of the window and his tail twitched.

"You don't look too happy." She smoothed his head, "Don't worry, it doesn't feel like the right place to me, either." Martha fed him a bite of turkey. "I guess we should do what Delia suggested after all, let's finish our lunch and then get back on the highway."

Chapter 7

Martha drove through Pensacola to Perdido Key and located Annie's bed and breakfast. Now that she'd reached her destination, the adrenaline that had kept her going evaporated and she felt as if her bones had dissolved. She opened the car door and studied the Plump Pelican. The large Victorian, adorned with gingerbread, was painted the gray of salt-weathered shingles and trimmed in white, with Copenhagen blue shutters. Colorful pots overflowing with pink lantana and purple verbena lined the steps, and a corner porch held a swing and a white, wooden rocker that invited her to sit. The house reminded Martha of being on Cape Cod with Annie. She'd missed her friend. Where Delia pushed, Annie offered, and Martha wished she'd stayed in closer touch.

She should have called Annie, instead of arriving unannounced, but she couldn't, she would have fallen apart as soon as she heard Annie's voice. Besides, Annie would welcome her without question, even if it had been the middle of the night. She climbed the steps and rang the bell. The door flew open and Martha caught a glimpse of delight on Annie's face before she wrapped Martha in her arms.

"Martha, I'm so glad to see you. It's been too long!" Martha tried to respond, but relief and regret paralyzed her throat. She clung to Annie and her pent-up tears spilled down her cheeks, until finally she relaxed in the comforting hug, and Annie's familiar smell of green tea and a fresh summer breeze. She radiated a steady warmth that made Martha grateful for her presence. Annie pushed Martha's bedraggled hair aside and studied her friend's face.

"You must be exhausted."

Martha moved back from Annie's embrace, and sniffed. "You're baking Gram's hermit cookies. Delia called you, didn't she?" She couldn't be annoyed with Delia for giving Annie advance notice, after all, she had done precisely what Delia suggested.

"My guests love those hermits," Annie wouldn't meet Martha's eyes.

"Yeah, right, Annie, no one in Florida has ever heard of a hermit. It's okay, I knew Delia would call you, even though I asked her not to. She can't help herself, she has to meddle."

"She meddles because she cares about you. I confess she called me, and she sounded worried." Martha heard the concern in Annie's voice too. "She said you were headed to Nashville, but she thought you would wind up here eventually. She said you weren't yourself."

"I guess Delia knew I needed to be here, even if I didn't. I went to Nashville, but it didn't feel right. Did she mention Tony and I are finished?" Martha wondered how much Delia had shared, how much she needed to explain.

"Yes, but we can talk about that later, right now I want to meet your traveling companion. I think Delia said his name is Charley?" Martha didn't have the strength to talk about her divorce right now, and she was grateful that Annie didn't ask more questions.

"I hope you don't mind. I think you're going to love him." She descended the steps, feeling safe for the first time since she left Baltimore. Annie had that effect on people, she listened without comment or judgement, and only provided advice when asked.

Martha opened the car door and lifted Charley from the seat. He blinked his eyes and started purring as she returned to the porch.

"Annie, meet Charley."

"Hello Charley, nice to meet you." Annie smiled and scratched him under the chin. Charley leaned into her hand as his purr ratcheted up to full volume. "I don't usually encourage my guests to bring pets, but for you and Charley, I'll make an exception. Come on, let's get you settled. You're in luck, I had a cancellation."

"That doesn't sound lucky for you." Martha didn't want Annie's business to lag so she could have a room.

"It's okay, they've promised to reschedule in a few months. It means you get to have the room I reserve for special guests."

Martha followed Annie up the stairs. It had been several years since she'd seen her friend, and her willowy frame remained fit. A few added pounds had transformed her from lanky to elegant, and she appeared even more graceful than she had in culinary school.

When Annie opened the bedroom door, Martha was sure she had been transported to Cape Cod. The room had a summer beach freshness you only find on the New England seashore. The vaulted ceiling was painted pale blue, a subtle cloud white graced the walls, and a thick carpet the exact color of Cape Cod beach sand covered the floor. The sliding glass doors to the balcony stood open, and the gentle Gulf breeze billowed the sheer curtains into the room. Martha got a glimpse of blue water, less intense than the more familiar waters of Maine, but close enough to carry her back to her childhood. She imagined the smell of the salt breeze at home, peace rippled around her, and Martha sensed every muscle and bone in her body soften.

"Oh Annie, it's perfect." She rested her head on Annie's shoulder, "Are you sure you want me to stay here? You must be able to get a small fortune for this room, you could rebook it."

"There isn't another person in the world I would rather have stay here than you." Annie put her arm around Martha and hugged sideways. "So enjoy it, and we can both appreciate that my bookings are light right now. We'll have some time to catch up. Besides, Danny is on duty at the firehouse, so it's just us girls for tonight. Relax, have a shower, take a nap, whatever you need. I'll be back in a little while and we can talk."

Annie closed the door and Martha stepped out onto the balcony. Two lounge chairs with comfy, blue flowered cushions beckoned, and she longed to snuggle into one of them.

"Shower first," Martha told herself, "too many hours on the road." She emerged from the bathroom bundled in the thick, white robe Annie provided for her guests. Charley was ensconced on the bed, and Martha lay down beside him, intending to rest for a few minutes.

The sunlight had faded when a faint knock woke Martha.

"Martha, you awake?" Annie spoke through the closed door.

"Sort of," Martha sat up, rubbed her eyes and yawned. Sleep tried to tug her back, but she pushed it aside. She wanted to spend time with Annie.

Annie opened the door and the aroma of spicy hermits preceded her into the room. She juggled a large tray laden with a teapot and two cups, as well as a bottle of wine, two glasses, and a plate filled with cheese, crackers, and warm cookies.

"Let's go sit on the balcony," Annie nodded her head toward the open glass doors, "it's ideal at this time of day, and I don't often get to sit and enjoy it. I wasn't sure if you'd prefer tea or wine, so I brought both."

"Tea's fine for now, then wine." Martha sat on the edge of the bed trying to summon enough energy to move, after more than twenty-four hours without sleep, one short nap hadn't done much to revive her. Annie's thoughtfulness and the delicious smells she brought with her persuaded Martha to get up, and they settled into the lounge chairs.

When Martha looked at her friend, she felt like she was back in culinary school. Annie appeared much the same. She had pulled her long strawberry blond hair back from a face generously sprinkled with freckles. Annie had hated her freckles and used to spend money on creams that claimed they would bleach them away, but she must have finally accepted them. Her eyes were the deep blue of Cape Cod Bay, and still filled with kindness.

Martha bit into the moist, chewy hermit, and savored the fragrant spices, mingled with the sweet mix of raisins and molasses.

"Mmmm, these are so good. Maybe even better than Gram's. Tell me the truth Annie, you don't really make these for your guests, do you?"

"You haven't had them for a while, that's what makes them taste extra delicious. I could never improve on your grandmother's rendition. And yes, I do make them for guests, but not usually at this time of year. I bake them in the fall, when I want to trick myself into believing Florida has real autumn weather. Although I make them more for myself, my guests enjoy them too." She continued gently, "You look exhausted Martha, and you've lost weight. Tell me what's going on."

Martha ate the last bite of her hermit and closed her eyes, groggy from her nap. Where did she begin? She hated to admit, even to her friend, that her life had evolved into such a mess. Instead she allowed her half-asleep mind to drift on memories.

"Do you ever long for the Cape, Annie, feel like you're going to shrivel into nothing if you don't get back there, smell the salt air, and see the stretch of ocean that's unlike anywhere else in the world?" Without waiting for a reply, she continued. "The picture over the bed reminded me of visiting you on the Cape." She had noticed it on her way to the shower before collapsing beside Charley, and recognized the steps and faded blue gate leading to the dunes and water below. The painting was hanging in the wide front hall of Annie's parents' home the day she and Tony got married, and she loved the familiar view of Cape Cod Bay, it brought her back to happier days.

"Your folks were so generous, allowing us to use their lawn for the ceremony, we certainly didn't have enough money to pay for a big event." Fatigue swallowed her again and lulled her back to their perfect wedding day, without a cloud or wisp of fog the whole afternoon, and their blissful honeymoon at the nearby beach house. How could that perfect day have led to such a disastrous marriage?

Martha opened her eyes briefly when Annie draped a shell patterned quilt over her, and as she hovered on the edge of sleep, she heard a distant voice say, "You're stronger than you think."

The next time Martha opened her eyes she found Annie standing beside her holding a tray with two steaming bowls of clam chowder. Darkness had tiptoed in while she slept, and the glow of solar dragonfly lights strung across the balcony rim lit the night.

46

"You're spoiling me," Martha took the bowl of chowder from Annie. She realized much of the tension from the last few weeks had disappeared.

"It's what I do best, that's why my guests keep coming back."

"How do you make chowder that tastes like the New England shore here in Florida?" Comfort flowed through her body along with the familiar flavors of home.

"You know whose recipe I use—Gram always made the best chowder."

The two friends sat in companionable silence, enjoying their chowder and the refreshing breeze blowing off the Gulf shore. Lights twinkled in the distance, but stars were clearly visible overhead.

Annie placed her empty bowl on the tray and leaned forward, elbows on her knees. "Martha, when you asked me about missing the Cape, was it because you're missing Maine? It sounds like you want to get on the next plane to Portland and go see Gram." Martha heard concern in Annie's voice, along with more unasked questions. Eventually she would tell Annie the whole story, she didn't have the energy tonight, but she could at least explain why she'd driven to Florida and not Maine.

"I do Annie, but I let her down. I don't want to go back until I can justify not returning to Hope Island Harbor after graduation. She came to Providence that May, expecting me to go home with her, instead I told her I was sorry to break my promise, but Tony and I were going to get married and move to Baltimore. I felt guilty for letting her down, but I was so in love, or thought I was, that I blocked out everything except the next day with Tony."

"What did she say?"

"She asked me why I was in such a rush to get married. I said I knew he was the one. I remember she said, 'Martha, love is a matter of geography. If you were born in Omaha, you'd find somebody in Omaha.'"

"That sounds like Gram," Annie nodded her head.

"When I said I hadn't found anybody in Maine and reminded her Grandpa wasn't from Maine either, she said, 'I knew to my core who I was, Martha, I followed my heart, whose heart are you following?' She could see what I couldn't, Tony had swept me away with his promises, and pushed my dreams aside. Then she said, 'If you're sure this is what you want, I won't try to convince you otherwise.' But I could see the hurt and disappointment on her face, and I've been carrying it with me ever since."

"What did Tony say when you told him about your promise to Gram?"

"He said the job he'd been offered wouldn't wait, and he wanted me to go with him, the same restaurant would hire me as a pastry chef. When we arrived in Baltimore, Tony started working right away, but they weren't interested in hiring me, they already had a pastry chef. He told me he'd find me another job, because I wouldn't find one without his help. I wish I'd gone home with Gram after graduation. Now my marriage has fallen apart, she'll think I'm a failure." Martha feared Annie would think that too.

"Martha, Gram loves you, and she'd be glad to see you anytime. I guarantee she doesn't think you're a failure, because you're not." Annie's voice held compassion, without judgement. "You're an accomplished pastry chef. When we were in school you had more inner drive than any of us. I don't think that's changed. You don't realize how strong you are. Besides, Gram was young once, she'll understand. She's not going to condemn you. What do you want Martha, what do you want to do next?"

"I wish I knew," Martha put her bowl on the tray. "Right now, I'm so at odds I don't know where to put myself."

"You're welcome to stay here as long as you want while you figure things out."

"Thanks, Annie, I might do that, but only if you let me help you here."

"Actually, I could use your assistance."

"Anything. What is it?" She'd feel better about being here if she could repay Annie for taking her in unexpectedly.

"Would you be willing to be the keeper of the Plump Pelican for a few days? Danny and I've been trying for months to get away overnight, not the easiest thing to do when you run a bed and breakfast. Business is flourishing and I'm glad, but it's hard to find any time to ourselves. Between the constant bookings and Danny's schedule at the firehouse, it seems impossible. I've been training an assistant innkeeper, but she broke her ankle in a biking accident and can't work for a couple of months. I'm hoping you'll want to stay until she comes back."

"I'd love to, and I promise not to drive any customers away." She'd planned to leave Baltimore for a week or two, but this felt right. She'd have to let Sarah know she wouldn't be back for a while.

"I'm not worried, you're the best pastry chef I know." Annie laughed, "My one concern is the guests won't be satisfied with my cooking once they've had a taste of yours. But give yourself some time to relax and settle in, forgive me if I'm taking advantage of the situation too soon."

"No, it's not too soon, I'd like to stay for a while, and it'll be good to get my mind off everything, focus on someone—and something—else for a change. I've been living in my own private world of misery for too long. You warned me about Tony, I should have listened."

Martha remembered the day she met Tony and he called her Cupcake. She had been indignant, felt like he was belittling her, and yet he did it with such charm she ignored the red flag and fell in love instead. Where would life have taken her if she had paid attention to that flag?

"Oh Martha, what did I know? Tony had a sharp tongue and a condescending air, but his eyes danced when he saw you. I thought you were the one to turn him around. When you got married at my parents' house, neither one of you stopped smiling the whole day."

"That seems so long ago now," Martha picked at the quilt covering her legs. "Funny, at first I couldn't stand being around him, he acted so superior, but then he pursued me and told me I was talented and beautiful. I thought I'd fallen into a romantic story book, found my happily ever after ending, and life would go along precisely as I planned. How did I mess it up?"

"First, you didn't mess it up, and second, you want a romance novel for your life, but it doesn't work that way. Everyone has problems, and sometimes the solution is to change direction. You needed to make a difficult decision, and you had the courage to do it."

"What about you and Delia? You have perfect marriages, to perfect men."

"You see what you want to see. Sure, Jim's a super guy, but he is far from perfect, and Delia will be the first to tell you that."

"What about Danny? He's a heroic fire fighter and he loves you to pieces."

"True, but he's seldom here to help me. This bed and breakfast was supposed to be a team effort. Now my team is the local plumber, painter, whatever. Danny's either fighting fires or working out so he'll be in shape to fight fires. It's what he has to do. We've made it work, but it isn't perfect Martha, it never will be." Sadness darted across Annie's face, if Martha hadn't chosen that moment to glance at her she would have missed it.

"You must have something special," Martha reached over to touch her friend's arm. "You even survived a long-distance relationship. I remember you couldn't wait to go back to Florida after graduation. I didn't think anyone would get you away from the Cape."

"The day I met Danny I knew he was different." Annie's face softened and she gazed out towards the water. Martha had heard this story before, but she could tell by her wistful smile that Annie enjoyed reliving it, so she listened. "I often wonder what would have happened if I hadn't decided to study at the Florida campus for a year. Or if my dorm mates hadn't persuaded me to go to a bar on a Sunday afternoon when the Patriots were playing the Dolphins. Danny came in with two of his friends and I couldn't stop looking at him. When the half-time whistle blew, he came over to our table and he asked if he could join us until the second half. The rest, as they say, is history."

"Some people are lucky enough to find their soul mate. You and Delia did, I didn't." Maybe she wasn't meant to find love.

"I'll admit sometimes I wonder why it works, Danny and me, but it does, and I can't imagine being with anyone else. I'm sorry things didn't turn out well for you and Tony, but that doesn't mean you should give up." In culinary school, Annie had always found something encouraging to say, and that hadn't changed.

"You could be right." Martha didn't want to think about love tonight, she preferred to turn her thoughts to more practical matters. "For now, I'm looking forward to helping you, starting tomorrow morning. I'll shadow you for a few days and get it all sorted out."

"You need to rest, don't worry about getting up when I do, there'll be time in a week or two. How long can you stay?"

"I'm competing in the Charm City Chocolate Challenge in October, and in a moment of temporary insanity I registered for the Baltimore marathon the week before. I should be back in Baltimore by the beginning of September." She couldn't abandon Baltimore forever, although right now that's what she wanted to do. "I'll need to work on my design for the challenge and train for the marathon here, but I want to learn your routine, what time do you begin tomorrow?"

"If I have guests, I'm up by five. Since no one is checking in until the afternoon, I can sleep late, I won't start until six."

"Okay, six it is. I guess I'd better get some sleep. Thanks for giving me a place to sort myself out." Martha swung her feet from the chaise to the floor. She would put herself back together and move on, without a man.

"I'm glad you're here. Sleep as late as you want." Annie gave her a quick hug and slipped from the room.

Snuggled into bed with Charley curled beside her, a dream carried Martha back to culinary school, when she wanted to make Tony happy and gave him her heart before she knew Tony cared about no one—except Tony.

Martha studied the finished wedding cake. Intricate lace work covered the four tiers, and tiny fondant flowers of trailing jasmine cascaded from a molded sugar arbor on the top. She couldn't wait to tell Tony about her day's accomplishment.

Martha took out her cell phone and found a voicemail from him.

"Hey Babe, let's go to the beach. Pick you up at six, don't be late."

After hours of work and concentration, her arms and shoulders ached with fatigue, and she longed for a refreshing shower. The unusually high spring temperatures made the thought of escaping to the beach appealing, but Tony's plan meant she had only ten minutes to run back to her dorm and change.

"That's my girl, right on time," Tony waited by his car, dark, curly hair damp from the shower. He leaned down to give her a kiss, and Martha inhaled a fragrant mix of aftershave, soap, and Tony—and her remaining fatigue vanished.

An hour later, Tony swung into the parking lot at Narragansett Beach. Martha stepped out into the welcoming ocean breeze. She stretched her arms overhead and breathed in the sweet, salt air.

"Come on, let's walk," Tony squeezed her into a quick hug. They held hands and strolled barefoot along the shore, their toes dancing in and out of the icy water as they moved away from the open beach to the seclusion of a hidden cove. Enveloped in the misty, lavender twilight, their steps slowed and they made frequent stops for lingering kisses, until they stilled, wrapped in each other's arms on the deserted beach.

Tony's hands slid up and down her arms, and his lips drew hers into kisses that melted her bones. He pulled her to the sand, but she pushed against his chest.

"Tony, we can't."

"Shhh, it's almost dark, there's no one on the beach but us, relax." His kisses became more passionate, and his insistent hands slowly caressed her. Somewhere in Martha's brain, warning bells rang.

Don't do this, don't do this. It could ruin everything. Martha wavered, she wanted to listen to the voice in her mind, but Tony's persuasive words whispered seductively in her ear, controlling her body like puppet strings. She couldn't refuse him. The sound of waves sweeping the beach surrounded them, and the last bits of Martha's resolve crumbled around her.

Chapter 8

George ran through the early morning drizzle, nothing like the previous night's monsoon, just a misty coolness as he jogged up and down the streets of Federal Hill. In spite of his determination to put thoughts of Martha aside, he knew his subconscious hoped to see her again, because his feet automatically took him on the now familiar route.

He wrestled with understanding the instant connection he had felt with Martha. Their conversation had flowed naturally, as if they had been friends forever. When she smiled, her entire face glowed and touched off a flame he had never experienced. She had the most extraordinary aquamarine eyes, the color of the water on blue-green summer days at Cape Cod. They sparkled with life, but were darkened with a current of pain, and he wondered why.

George longed to see Martha again, and this time he would tell her about Elaine, and ask her about the shadows that flitted across her face. He wanted to know why they were there, and he wanted to make them go away. He wanted to know everything about her, but she had asked all the questions on their boat ride. Now Martha had disappeared, and he had no idea how to find her.

The few women George had dated since Elaine's death had all telegraphed a hidden agenda, he had felt like they were drawn to his success as much as to him. Sometimes he thought he was on a job interview and had to pass their criteria for an acceptable gene pool or be ousted after the first date.

His day with Martha had been pure fun, and the pain of the last few years had vanished in her company. George found her quirky, but endearing, and their mystery adventure at the train museum made him feel like a kid again.

He thought of the yellow house, the gabled roof and the wraparound porch that cried out for a bench swing, and imagined Martha sitting on it with him while they talked about their days. The possibility that he would never see her again left an aching sadness inside him, but no matter what happened, he wanted to rescue the yellow house. After his run, he returned to his room and called Tanya. She had an opening late in the afternoon and arrived at the yellow house as George got out of his car. She greeted him like an old friend.

"Hi George, so nice to see you again. Have you decided to make an offer? I spoke to the owners last night, and they're excited about your interest." Tanya didn't mince words when it came to making a sale, but he had his own methods.

"Slow down Tanya, I need to review a few things before I decide one way or another."

"Of course, at least you can see the roof doesn't leak, even with all the rain we've had." She unlocked the door and opened it for George. "Take all the time you need. This is my last appointment for today."

George already planned to make an offer. He'd learned over the years to trust his first instincts, and his gut told him he needed to buy this house. He had an amount in mind, but he wanted to see it again, and take notes on the renovations he contemplated, so he knew how much room he had to negotiate. He also wondered how motivated the seller was. He spent time in each room and made casual conversation as he went.

"How long has the house been on the market?"

"Since the fall," Tanya followed him through the house. "The elderly couple who owns it have been spending winters in Florida. They lived here from April to October, but last September, Mr. Taylor had a stroke and he's confined to a wheelchair. They decided they couldn't keep traveling back and forth. This time, when they went to Florida they stayed permanently. They put the house on the market before they left."

"Has there been much interest?" George wrote in a small brown leather notebook while he listened.

"Quite a bit at first, but it fades when people see how much work needs to be done to update everything. Most buyers anticipate contractor's bills that equal the price of the house, so they make an offer to offset that, but the Taylors have been unwilling to accept such low bids. One potential buyer wanted to gut it, modernize it, and flip it. The owners want to sell it to someone who won't destroy the original charm, someone who will stay and raise a family here. They refuse to settle without meeting the buyer first."

"Interesting," George smiled to himself. He wasn't worried about the labor cost, he would provide the labor, it relaxed him. He intended to leave the structure the same and return the interior to its original beauty. He wanted to make sure he hadn't missed any hidden problems and estimate the material cost, which from his experience usually exceeded expectations. When he finished his notes and mental calculations, he gave Tanya his offer.

"If you're sure, I'll call the Taylors right now." George nodded, now that he'd made a decision, he wanted things to move forward.

"As I said before, they'll want to meet you before signing any papers."

"Not a problem, let me know where and when." George wasn't worried, he felt confident the Taylors would approve of the renovations he'd planned. It would remain a family home, but with its original warmth and character restored.

"Okay, give me a minute." Tanya took out her phone as she retreated to the next room and made the call. After the first vibrant, "Hi, Mrs. Taylor, this is Tanya Lavendow," Tanya's voice became muffled, so he went outside and waited on the front porch, imagining the swing he would build and hang there. Tanya worked out the details and came out of the house smiling.

"Mrs. Taylor has a trip booked to check on the house in three weeks, can you wait until then?"

"Sure, I need to focus on work right now anyway." Although disappointed in the delay, the first few weeks of the job would be demanding, and the yellow house would have been a distraction. By the time he met with the Taylors, he would be comfortable in his job and ready to enjoy his restoration project.

"Fabulous," Tanya checked her watch, "it's getting late, how about stopping for a drink and a bite to eat?" She quickly added, "to celebrate."

George ran his hand over his head. He didn't want Tanya to think he desired more than a business connection, but he felt like celebrating. He'd made an offer on a house and its restoration required work that he loved. It confirmed his readiness to move on and begin again.

"Why not? I've no doubt the Taylors will approve the sale."

"There's a great Irish pub not far from here, they have live music on Sunday nights, why don't we go there?"

"Sounds good, I could use a beer." He liked Irish music and it beat an empty hotel room for celebrating.

George and Tanya entered the pub as the band played a lively rendition of "Galway Girl." They found a corner booth, where they could talk over the volume of the music, and ordered burgers and beer.

Tanya launched into her life story and somewhere between her city childhood and her broken marriage, George tuned out. He should find Tanya appealing—tall, slender, long-legged, she could easily have stepped off the pages of a fashion magazine. In fact, she reminded him of Elaine, they both had the same sense of impeccable style, but like Elaine, her edges were hard, and that wasn't what he wanted. Then George thought of Martha smelling the daffodils, and he smiled, apparently at an inopportune time in Tanya's monologue.

"It really wasn't funny." Tanya frowned at him. George had no idea what she meant and tried to cover his distracted mistake.

"Oh no, I'm sure it wasn't," he said. "I'm sorry, the music makes it difficult to hear clearly."

"It is noisy," Tanya leaned closer to George. "We could continue our conversation someplace quieter?"

"Thanks Tanya, but it's been a long week and I start my new job tomorrow. I think I'm ready to call it a day. Let me know when the Taylors want to meet." He signaled their server for the check. He should have known celebrating by himself would have been a better choice. Tanya wanted more than a real estate client and he wasn't interested.

"You don't have to do that, I invited you out," but she made no effort to take the check. George felt guilty for ignoring Tanya while he retreated to his own world, and picking up the check helped assuage his conscience.

"My pleasure." George escorted Tanya to her car.

"Call me if you have any more questions." Tanya touched his arm gently. He nodded and returned to his own car.

Chapter 9

*M*artha woke to the smell of brewing coffee. She opened her eyes feeling a bit disoriented, then located the clock on the bedside table. Nine o'clock registered. "Oh shoot!" She threw back the covers and ran to the bathroom to splash water on her face.

"Charley," she called, "why didn't you tell me it was so late?" She returned to the room and realized Charley wasn't on the bed.

I wonder how he got out without waking me? She slipped her feet into comfy, white, terry cloth slippers and headed for the bedroom door, then glanced down, remembered she wasn't at home, and grabbed her robe from the foot of the bed. Martha followed her nose to the kitchen, where she found Annie removing trays of lemon blueberry muffins from the oven. Sun slanted through the patio doors and glistened off the sugar-capped muffins covering the large work island in the middle of the room.

Charley sat on the floor, in a patch of sunlight, peacefully washing his face. He paused long enough to look at Martha and blink, then continued with his morning ablutions.

"Smells like I overslept," Martha leaned down to scratch Charley under the chin. "I wanted to help, and I'm sure I set the alarm. I don't know what happened."

"After driving all night from Baltimore without sleeping, I would have done the same thing. You're exhausted. Anyway, no guests this morning, so there isn't a lot to do. I'll freeze these muffins for busier days, and you can relax. Grab some coffee, and I'll make you breakfast. Anything special you'd like to do today?"

"As enticing as breakfast sounds, I think I'll have coffee and a yogurt for now, and if you're sure there's nothing I can do to help, I'll try to run the cobwebs out of my brain. Any suggestions for a good route?" Martha poured her coffee.

"You could do a loop down River Road and back by Perdido Key Drive. It's probably three miles. If you want a longer run, Johnson's Beach Road and back is about five miles round trip, and you can see the water on both sides of the road as you run."

"Sounds perfect, I love running near the water. It soothes my mind and distracts me from the first mile, which I hate." Martha leaned against the counter, eating strawberry yogurt.

"One more question. Do you know anyplace I could work on my chocolate challenge entry? I've got to transform my thoughts into actual designs. If I'm going to stay for a while, I need to practice and have a plan in place when I go back to Baltimore."

"I've a friend who owns a chocolate shop in Pensacola. She makes the most amazing truffles, almost as good as yours. Last time I saw her she had more orders than she could fill and was putting in long hours. She said she wanted to hire more help but couldn't find the time to interview anyone. I bet she'd let you use her equipment in exchange for work in her shop."

"That would be great, if she's open to the idea." She didn't want to impose her experiments on Annie's kitchen, and it would be much easier to work in a space customized for chocolate creation.

"I'll call her as soon as I finish here."

"Thanks, Annie, I'll be back in an hour or two, depends on what my legs decide."

59

Martha put her foot in her running shoe and felt something crinkle in the toe. She shook it upside down and a folded paper fell into her hand. It charted her daily marathon training schedule. She thought she'd left it behind in Baltimore. Reassured, she took it as a sign that she should train in Florida.

Shaken by the divorce, Martha had ignored her training the past few weeks. She had a long way to go if she wanted to be in shape for the October marathon. Martha laced her sneakers, consulted the schedule, and traced her finger to her last entry on the chart. It required she log eight miles today. That might be pushing it since she hadn't increased her mileage for several weeks, but she'd give it a try. These cool mornings wouldn't last, so she'd best take advantage of them.

The clear, soft air stroked her face, and strands of her hair fluttered in the breeze. She did some easy stretches and took a few deep breaths before she jogged along the route that Annie suggested. She never ran with music; she found the sound confining and preferred to give her brain space to ruminate. As always, the first mile dragged, until she found her rhythm. Then magically, her body powered forward, like a car changing gears as it reaches cruising speed. She heard the consistent beat in her head, and her breathing became steady and even. Without realizing, she picked up her pace as her mind drifted back to the beginning days with Tony, and the moment when she knew she couldn't stay married any longer.

What went wrong? After they were married, the initial closeness she had felt deteriorated. She kept thinking if she tried harder, if she accommodated all his wishes, things would be all right. And she had tried for years, then finally, he went too far. When he crossed over the line, his giant step had brought her world crashing down, and she had known she couldn't stay. The day played back in her mind.

Martha sat at the counter drinking a cup of tea and opening the mail. She froze as she read a notice from the bank, informing them their checking account was overdrawn, and they should contact the bank as soon as possible. That can't be right. She balanced their account to the penny every month, and she had checked it a few weeks ago. She hadn't withdrawn any money, and Tony hadn't mentioned that he had either.

"The bank must have made a mistake," she muttered to herself. *But she thought about how edgy Tony had been. He barely spoke to her, and when he did, he sounded surly. Her tea sat untouched and grew cold as she paced from room to room, running her hands repeatedly through her hair. The bank had closed a while ago, and Tony wouldn't be home for another couple of hours. She needed to move, and automatically slipped into her running shoes, then grabbed a water bottle and went out the door.*

Darkness had already claimed the late February day, but Martha hardly noticed. Fueled by frustration and anxiety, she sprinted towards the steps leading to Federal Hill Park. Even when her breathing became labored, she pushed herself to increase the pace. At the top of the stairs, when her lungs screamed, she paused, then found her normal rhythm, and ran until her mind calmed. She walked the last few blocks home, the clenching in her gut had diminished, but not her concern about the notice. She took a shower and cooked dinner while she waited for Tony.

The front door slammed, and Tony's heavy steps resounded as he came into the kitchen. "I need a drink," he took a bottle of scotch from an overhead cabinet.

Martha seldom confronted Tony, but this had upset her so much, she felt compelled to question him. "We got a notice from the bank," she held the paper in her outstretched hand. "They said we've overdrawn our checking account."

"Not now, Martha." Tony looked over his shoulder.

"But it's a mistake, right? Everything was fine a couple of weeks ago when I balanced the account."

"I said I don't want to talk about it." He poured himself a generous drink.

"You mean it isn't a mistake, we really are overdrawn?" Shock and betrayal slammed into her; Tony had endangered their hard-earned financial stability and hadn't bothered to tell her. Why did he need the money? The last threads of connection she felt to him threatened to break.

"For God's sake, Martha, give it a rest!" Tony downed his drink in one gulp.

"I need to know what's going on, how can we be overdrawn?" Martha's voice grew louder. "I deposited my last paycheck a week ago."

They stood in the kitchen, face to face. Tony trembled with anger. If she kept pushing him, she would regret it, he wouldn't speak to her for weeks. But she couldn't stop the words from pouring out.

"Why did you take out so much money? You never said anything."

Tony stood in front of her, rocking from one foot to another, pacing side to side but going nowhere. His arms hung at his sides, his fists clenching and unclenching. The rocking from foot to foot quickened, as did the clenching and unclenching. Martha tensed.

He's going to hit me. Martha froze in place. Her subconscious registered the blow a fraction of a second before it came, and she retreated enough to prevent the full force of Tony's slap from knocking her off her feet.

Stunned, she put her hand to her cheek, and saw the shock she felt reflected on Tony's face. He reached his arms towards her, "I'm sorry Babe, I'm so sorry." She cringed from his touch, and backed away.

"Get out! Now!"

He stared at her for a moment, then left without another word. The door latched behind him and Martha sank to the floor, shaking. She wrapped her arms around her body, trying to hold herself together. She didn't know what to do next. She couldn't tell anyone, too humiliated to admit that Tony had hit her.

Martha felt the slap again, and though tears threatened, she ran harder and harder until depleted so that she didn't have the strength to cry. She walked the last few blocks to the bed and breakfast trying to collect herself before she saw Annie.

"Martha, I talked to Darcy—" Annie called from the kitchen.

"Great, I can't wait to hear about it, I need a quick shower first, then you can tell me the details." She let the steaming water sluice away the last of her distress. By the time she sought Annie in her office, Martha had regained her composure, and wore her usual cheerful smile.

"Thanks for calling Darcy, what did she say?"

"She liked the idea, but she wants to meet you before she commits to anything. She said you could come in anytime today."

"I'd like to meet her too. I'll drive to Pensacola now."

Chapter 10

When George arrived at his office at eight Monday morning, Nick greeted him with a handshake and a smiling rendition of the company's slogan.

"Welcome to Sloan and Company, 'Where everything old is new again.' How was your first weekend in Baltimore?"

"Eventful, I put an offer on a house." George braced for his friend's response.

"You're kidding! You just got here, how did you have time to look at houses, never mind buy one? Where is it?"

"Roland Park, in an older neighborhood."

"That's great, I'm glad you've found something you like. But why so fast? You're not usually this impulsive."

"I can't keep living in a hotel room, and I hate apartments, I want a house. When I saw it, I knew I had found the right one. Here," he took his phone from his pocket and showed Nick a picture. "Besides—"

"Nice lines, but it looks like work. Besides what?"

"Nothing, but—you were right, time for me to move on." Despite his initial response, George was grateful Nick had pushed him to leave his stagnant life. "Wait till you see it, hardwood floors and hand-crafted woodwork, all buried under brown paint." George paced around the office. "The house needs me to bring it back to life, and I can't wait to start sanding, but right now I'm ready to get to work here."

Now that George had found a permanent place to live, he could focus on his job. It would be at least a month before he could move into the house, possibly more by the time he met with the Taylors, the inspections were done, and they scheduled a closing date. He could live in the hotel for another month, and if he got stir crazy in the small space, he would spend a weekend with Nick and Mandy. Nick assured him he had a standing offer.

"Okay, you can tell me more about the house later, let's grab a coffee and I'll bring you up to speed."

Nick reiterated a more detailed version of the long-term goals of reclaiming the mills, and creating elegant living spaces within the sturdy buildings. They left the office to survey the first project. When they arrived at the site, both donned hard hats before entering the deteriorating building.

"This one will be the poster child, so to speak." Nick opened the heavy door. "Although every mill will have unique features, we'll tweak this basic pattern on future designs."

They crossed stained wooden floors and George took in the dirty bricks and broken windows. In spite of some crumbling walls, the supporting beams looked solid. George's eyes saw the repairs required for safety, but his mind saw light-filled apartments with vaulted ceilings, enormous windows and massive beams sanded and refinished.

The specific layout of the rooms would be determined as the project progressed, but George wanted to include open space and natural wood, with nothing hiding the warmth and color of the refurbished brick. He visualized the building entrance with a living wall of plants maintained by a built-in watering system.

Boutique shops would occupy the first floor, along with garden apartments, each incorporating a small green oasis protected by a wrought iron fence. Upper floor balconies would overlook the harbor, and a clock tower in the middle of the complex, surrounded by colorful gardens and brick walkways, would serve as a focal point.

George and Nick returned to the office, where George transformed pictures in his mind into actual drawings of the finished building. He preferred to do the external rendering by hand, sketching in the building details as well as his landscape ideas. The computer would create three-dimensional designs of the interior, after he rebuilt the mill visually first.

George hoped his father would be more accepting of this job. He had hated it when George started designing mini-mansions along the coast. They blocked the view and intruded into what his father considered the natural order of things. He told George he had sold his soul to the Devil and asked him why he'd abandoned his dreams of reclaiming, instead of continually building. The two men had always been close, bound by their love of restoration, but as George watched his mansion designs take shape, he sensed a wall growing between his father and himself. He missed their connection.

His father specialized in restoring and preserving the old Cape Cod homes, many of which had been built by sea captains in the 1800s. George had learned carpentry skills from him, along with an appreciation for retaining the essence of each home. George wanted his father to be proud of him, but he felt as if he'd disappointed him. This job would merge his love of creating with his compulsion to preserve the past, and he hoped his father would approve.

❊ ❊ ❊

Martha drove into Pensacola and turned right on West Garden Street. She found Darcy's chocolate shop tucked away around the corner on East Intendencia. A long, narrow, shotgun house had been converted to The Dancing Dolphin, and flowerpots filled with a riot of colorful *Portulaca oleracea*, impervious to Florida's heat, lined the short walkway.

She parked and got out, smoothed nonexistent wrinkles from her jeans, then surveyed the tidy building. The front window, sheltered by a wide, roofed porch, featured a pod of dolphins leaping from curling chocolate waves. As she opened the door a tiny bell tinkled cheerfully and reminded Martha of her grandmother's bakery. She inhaled the chocolate aroma and felt her whole body loosen.

No one stood behind the counter.

"I'll be right with you, feel free to look around," a friendly voice called from the back.

Martha recognized the surprising hint of a Boston accent, softened by the smooth roll of the South.

"Take your time." Martha slowly turned, surveying all the display cases before moving closer and inspecting each one individually. The first held truffles, both dark and milk chocolate, in exotic flavors like mojito magic and elderberry wine. The next housed chocolates molded in unique shapes representing the Florida seashore. Tiny pelicans perched on chocolate posts, detailed cranes stood on one leg, and individual dolphins jumped from their own chocolate sea. In a glass case all its own, a string of white chocolate, truffle-filled pearls spilled over the rim of a molded chocolate oyster shell. The store vibrated with a sense of anticipation, as the chocolates sat waiting to be tucked inside scallop shell boxes.

Her excitement grew, this would be the perfect place to create her chocolate design.

Martha noticed a footed glass plate with miniature chocolate truffles, each sitting in its own doll-sized fluted paper case. A small cardboard tent sat in front, with neatly lettered words, "Please try one." Martha placed the tiny confection in her mouth and held it on her tongue, letting the warmth melt the chocolate. She closed her eyes and concentrated as the layers of complex flavors peeled away in her mouth. She noted each one as it appeared, the initial intense, dark chocolate, followed by the sweet, rich ganache, tinged with the raspberry flavor of Chambord. When it formed a puddle on her tongue, she swallowed, and as it trickled down her throat, the lingering bitter taste accented every other flavor. Martha sighed in appreciation.

Intent on enjoying the truffle, she didn't realize she was no longer alone.

"How can I help you?"

Martha's eyes flew open. "I got lost in appreciation. These truffles are exquisite and your chocolate work is superb. Are you Darcy?"

"Thank you, and yes, I'm Darcy." Several inches shorter than Martha, she had spiked black hair and eyes the same green as Charley's. Behind their mischievous gleam resided a hard edge of determination.

"I'm Martha, Annie's friend," she extended her hand.

"I'm so glad to meet you," Darcy's smile warmed by several degrees. She balanced a tray of chocolates on her hip with one hand as she reached over the counter to shake Martha's hand with the other. Her nails were short, unpolished and filed to the rounded shape of her fingertips, much like Martha's own. Although she had several piercings in both ears, Darcy wore no jewelry, but a line of tiny blue-gray leaping dolphins adorned each arm. They started above her wrist and disappeared under the short sleeve of her white T-shirt.

"Annie told me you've been selected to compete in the Charm City Chocolate Challenge." Darcy filled the case from the tray of dark truffles she carried. Her hands flitted from tray to case reminding Martha of a tiny wren. "That's quite an honor. Don't you have to qualify to even be considered?"

Martha felt pleased but a bit embarrassed by the praise. She still had trouble believing her entry had been accepted. "Yes, and I thought I'd be in Baltimore to plan and practice my final design, but things didn't work out that way."

"Annie said you're going through a rough patch." Darcy sounded sympathetic, but she didn't stop working. She set the empty tray aside and started lining boxes with blue tissue paper, until they were neatly stacked, ready to be filled with chocolates.

"You could say that, but I'm determined not to give up my spot in the challenge, and I have so much work to do between now and then. I understand you might be looking for help. I'd be glad to trade work for use of your space and equipment to perfect my design."

Darcy remained silent as she finished lining boxes, and Martha waited, hoping Darcy agreed to let her work here. After tasting the truffle, she couldn't imagine going anywhere else. Darcy finished her task.

"Come on, I'll show you the kitchen," she pushed though the swinging doors. "It isn't spacious, but it's efficient." Darcy continued her explanation, she moved with a dancer's grace and a resolute manner, and Martha followed her rapidly retreating back.

Darcy never stopped working, and poured molten chocolate onto a marble slab as she spoke. "I prefer to temper the chocolate by turning it on the marble. It takes a little longer, but I have more control over the cooling temperature, to keep it smooth and glossy." Martha nodded her agreement but didn't interrupt. The equipment she saw would be suitable for her needs, and the kitchen offered ample space for two of them to work at the same time if necessary.

"The enrober is new." Darcy looked down at her chocolate streaked apron and laughed.

"I swear I enrobe myself every time I do that job." She continued her verbal tour of the kitchen while she moved the warm chocolate with a spatula, scraping and turning in a steady rhythm. "Annie's right," Darcy looked at Martha. "I need help. I'm thrilled with the success of my shop, but I can't keep up this pace indefinitely."

Did Martha miss something? Did Darcy agree to her suggested arrangement? For a moment she wondered if she had spoken out loud, or if Darcy had read her mind.

"Based on how she raved about your talents, I'd be a fool not to take advantage of your offer. When can you start?" Unlike Annie's soothing, restful presence, Darcy emitted constant energy, and Martha felt like she had been invited on a great adventure with a kindred spirit.

"Tomorrow?" She beamed with anticipation.

"Great!" Darcy scraped the cooled chocolate from the marble. "I open at eleven, so you can come at ten."

"Okay, see you tomorrow." Martha waltzed back to her car, where she shouted, "Yes!" to the world.

Chapter 11

George left for work in high gear because he had an appointment with Mrs. Taylor that evening. He hoped they could work out the details of the sale; he was impatient to move out of his hotel room and into the yellow house. As he entered his office, his cell phone rang, and he recognized Tanya's number.

"Hi Tanya, everything set for the meeting tonight?"

"Hi George, no, I'm sorry to say, we have to reschedule. That's why I'm calling. Mrs. Taylor's daughter went into labor four weeks early and she has to fly to Chicago to take care of her two-year-old granddaughter. She apologized, and said she'll be back as soon as she can and hoped you'd understand."

"Of course, please tell her I hope her daughter and the baby are okay." George's good spirits collapsed. How long would he be stuck living in a hotel room? His plan to finalize the purchase of the yellow house today evaporated, and the weekend loomed before him. Five o'clock came and went but he kept working, hoping to take his mind off his disappointment.

Nick poked his head in George's office door at six o'clock. "You going to spend the weekend here? Come on man, it's Friday, time to relax."

George pushed his chair back from the drafting table and stood, stretching his arms overhead. "I was trying to resolve a structural issue, and I guess I lost track of time." He tossed a pencil on his desk. "You and Mandy have plans for the evening?"

"Mandy's friend Lucy is in town, we hoped you'd join us for dinner."

"I don't know, Nick, it's been a long week, and you know I hate blind dates." He frowned at Nick.

"I know, but Mandy's known Lucy since they were kids, she's part of the family. I think you'll like her. Besides, Bethany and Jonathan have been asking to see you. Come on, it'll be fun."

"All right, what time? I miss the kids."

An hour later George knocked on Nick's door, showered, shaved, and not at all sure dinner was a good idea. He wished he could think of a reason not to join his friends. The few blind dates he had been on always ended in disaster—awkward evenings when he and his date had nothing in common, and he didn't expect any more from this one.

However, his best friend knew him well. If Nick thought George would have a good time tonight, George would try to be positive, even though he'd much prefer to go back home, don his workout gear, and run in the warm Baltimore night.

Nick opened the door as he dried his hands on a dish towel.

"I was afraid you weren't going to show."

"I did consider it." George grinned sheepishly.

Jonathan came barreling across the room yelling, "Uncka George, Uncka George!" He wrapped his arms around George's legs and hugged him. George bent, hoisted Jonathan above his head and twirled him around, eliciting delighted giggles. A carbon copy of Nick, he had the same straight dirty blond hair, hazel eyes, and mischievous smile. Mandy came in holding Bethany's hand, the baby toddled toward him, and George scooped her into a hug. He loved spending time with Jonathan and Bethany, even if it meant he had to endure a blind date.

"Hi George," Mandy said. "Lucy will be down in a couple of minutes. The kids are hoping you'll read them one book before we go."

"Sure, what's it going to be tonight, guys?" George walked to the living room, holding Bethany, and sat on the couch. Jonathan climbed up beside George and handed him one of their favorites, *When Dinosaurs Say Good Night*. George drew him into the curve of his arm and snuggled him close.

"Make the funny voices," Jonathan said.

George complied with Jonathan's request as he read the story, and when he finished the last page, he closed the book, then glanced up when he heard clapping. The unexpected audience didn't bother him, he enjoyed entertaining the children with dinosaur sounds. A pretty woman with a riot of curly blond hair and glasses stood in the doorway, and George responded to her infectious smile and easy manner. Perhaps the evening wouldn't be a disaster after all.

"No wonder Jonathan was jumping out of his skin waiting for Uncle George to arrive," she extended her hand and stepped forward. "Hi, I'm Lucy Stevenson."

George struggled to stand as Bethany twined around him monkey style, and Jonathan clung to his arm. "Hi. George Henderson." He disentangled his hand so he could take Lucy's outstretched one. "It's nice to meet you."

Mandy walked in with the babysitter. "I think it's time for these two monkeys to head for bed," Mandy said. "Give Uncle George hugs and Andrea will read you one more story when you're all tucked in."

Nick drove and the four arrived at Woodhaven Grill a few minutes before their reservation.

"Have you been here before, George?" Lucy asked.

"No," George shook his head and studied the huge brick building. "Whoever did the restoration work knew what they were doing. They kept the original detail, and the outdoor seating area looks like it's always been here."

"It used to be a flour mill. The whole complex has been repurposed from its industrial days." Nick opened the door to the restaurant. The hostess showed them to their table in front of a huge arched window. High vaulted ceilings and brick walls were little changed from its factory days, but a nearby fireplace created a cozy atmosphere, and a stack of wood behind the bar fired the brick oven and grill.

"This is one of our favorite places," Mandy said, after they were seated. "The chef uses local foods and the menu changes often, but it's always amazing."

"What brings you to Baltimore?" George asked Lucy after their server took their order. "Just a visit or did you have another reason?"

"I've been working as a traveling nurse, but I'm sick of darting around the country and I'm searching for a home base."

"I'm trying to persuade her to stay in Baltimore, Johns Hopkins Medical Center is here, so it's the perfect spot." Mandy buttered one of the warm rolls.

"I'm trained in Pediatric Cardiology."

George felt an immediate connection to Lucy. His sister had been born with a valve defect and had required open heart surgery as an infant.

"What about you?" Lucy took a sip of her wine. "Nick tells me you started a new job recently."

"I've always loved reclaiming old buildings, like this one, and Nick offered me a position redesigning vacant mills. He convinced me it would be my dream job." Without including painful details that led to his move, he added, "So far, he's right. I love the job and I'm enjoying Baltimore."

"What's happening with the house?" Nick asked George after the server brought their dinner specials of grilled rockfish, garlic roasted new potatoes, and sautéed asparagus.

"I had an appointment to meet with the owner tonight, but she had a family emergency and had to cancel." George took a bite of his fish.

"So, you decided to work late."

"You know me well." George grinned at his friend.

"George wants to buy a house and you want to find a job," Mandy looked at Lucy, "hopefully you'll both have something to celebrate soon."

"You want a house and not an apartment or a condo?" Lucy sounded surprised.

"Restoring houses is my hobby, and I found a perfect one. Structurally sound, but needs a little care and imagination to make it vital again."

"Where is it?" Lucy asked with interest.

"Roland Park, in an older section." George continued eating, but the yellow house occupied his thoughts. "The house drew me to the area, and I'm hoping to move out of my hotel room soon."

They ended dinner with strawberry rhubarb tarts for dessert. When they returned to Nick and Mandy's house, the couple said goodnight to George, and excused themselves to check on the children. Lucy accompanied him to the door.

"Thanks for a nice evening." George smiled ruefully, "I admit I was dreading it, but I enjoyed myself."

"Me too, on both counts," Lucy nodded her agreement. "I love Mandy, I've known her forever, but she figures my time for settling down is long past. She's made it her mission to matchmake until I do."

"I think Nick's on the same page." George opened the door. "How long will you be in town?"

"I'm not sure. I'm staying with Mandy and Nick for now, but I don't want to remain there indefinitely. I'll spend a couple more weeks job searching, and if I find something that interests me, I'll look for a more permanent place to live."

"Good luck with your search." George turned to leave, then changed his mind.

He expected to end the evening with a sigh of relief, but he had fun tonight. "While you're here, would you like to have dinner again sometime?"

"I'd like that," she said.

George leaned over and gave Lucy a chaste kiss on her cheek, but as he walked back to the car, he thought about Martha.

�✖✖

George looked at the two tickets for the Red Sox Orioles game tomorrow. He'd intended to take Nick as a thank you for recommending him for the mill job, but Nick already had plans with Mandy and the children. His dad wouldn't be able to get here on such short notice. He could go to the game alone. Instead, he picked up his phone and scrolled to Lucy's number. He didn't even know if she liked baseball, but he hit Call anyway.

"Hey Lucy, I've got an extra ticket to the Orioles game tomorrow, I wondered if you'd be interested in going?"

She immediately responded. "I'd love to. My dad used to take me to the Orioles games, and I haven't been to one in years."

George drove to Nick's house filled with anticipation. He hadn't been to a baseball game for a long time, and Lucy had been excited to go.

"Hey, I can see the competition is on," he said, when she opened the door wearing a bright orange Orioles T-shirt and an Orioles cap over her curly hair.

"I should have known we'd be rooting for opposing teams," she said and laughed. George sported a Red Sox hat and T-shirt.

"Where are we going to sit? We'll be thrown out by both sides." Lucy locked the door.

"That's okay," George said, "I think Baltimore's used to having Sox fans in their territory, but we have to promise not to boo the other team."

"Agreed, but I can't promise to cheer for them either." As they walked to his car, she said, "How about a little wager, to spice up the evening? The winning team has to buy pizza and beer for the losing team."

"Sounds good to me," George opened the passenger door. "I can spring for pizza and beer."

"Don't be too sure, the Orioles have been hot the last few games."

When they entered Camden Yards, George inhaled the familiar stadium smell of popcorn and roasted peanuts and his excitement ratcheted up another notch. He grinned at Lucy and saw delight in her eyes when she smiled back. *It's going to be a fun night.* They found their seats behind the first base line, and he wanted a hot dog right away, like when his father took him to a game. He waved at a nearby vendor and bought one for each them.

"You said your dad used to take you to games." They munched on hot dogs and waited for the seven o'clock game to begin. "Did you see the Orioles play often growing up?"

"I did. My dad loved baseball, and he took me to my first game for my tenth birthday."

"Did you enjoy it?"

"At first this was my favorite part," Lucy held up her hot dog. "But baseball became our thing, a way to have fun and spend time together, and

74

eventually I caught his love for the game."

"Any other baseball fans in your family?"

"My mom died when I was nine and I'm an only child, so it was just the two of us."

"That must have been hard." George thought about how close he'd been to both parents and his sister growing up.

"At first, but my dad was always there for me." Lucy paused and looked across the field. "He even coached my softball team. Did your dad take you to see the Sox play?"

"Occasionally, maybe once a season, but most of our baseball watching took place on Sunday afternoons in front of the TV. He did grill hot dogs for us to eat while we watched."

The game began and their conversation stopped. Lucy focused on the field and whistled and cheered for every Baltimore run. He enjoyed the game even more than he expected because of her enthusiasm.

The score teetered back and forth, and although Boston won, the game went into extra innings and didn't end until almost midnight. They both stifled yawns.

"Looks like I'm buying. Do you want your pizza and beer now, or would you prefer to wait for another night?" He hoped to wait for an evening when they could spend more time together, but he let her decide.

"Another night, I think." Lucy covered another yawn. "I had a busy week of job interviews, and I might doze off in the middle of my pizza."

"I feel the same way." When they got back to Nick's, he walked her to the door.

"Thanks for inviting me George, I had a wonderful time."

"I had fun too, let me know when you want to collect on our bet." He gave her a quick hug and smiled as he walked back to his car.

Summer

Chapter 12

Martha's days fell into a comfortable rhythm. She set the alarm for five, went for a run, and returned in time to help Annie serve breakfast. Then she drove to the Dancing Dolphin to work with Darcy. After the shop closed, she focused on designs for the chocolate challenge.

She had only been at The Plump Pelican for six weeks, but it felt like longer. She enjoyed the routine and the guests raved about the scones, cinnamon rolls, and other pastries she baked for breakfast.

Annie came into the kitchen one morning as Martha loaded the dishwasher. "I sent the Millers on their way." She reached for the coffee pot. "No guests until the weekend, and then only two rooms reserved. Do you think you're ready to be an innkeeper for a few days?"

"Absolutely!" She appreciated all of Annie's support and wanted to give her a break to have more time alone with Danny. Plus, it would give her a chance to confirm her desire to own a bed and breakfast someday. "Are you sure you're ready to leave your 'baby' with me?"

"I was ready the day after you arrived, but I wanted you to feel rested and relaxed before I took advantage of your help."

Took advantage? She'd been the one taking advantage of Annie. With her friend's trust, Martha was another step closer to believing in herself. "I'm happy to do it, where are you and Danny going, and when do you want to leave?"

"We thought we'd go to Seaside today, when Danny's shift ends. It's not far, a nice leisurely drive, and we'd be back Sunday night."

"Anything special there?"

"It's a quirky little town, and we like eating at the food trucks, several of them are always lined along Main Street, and the food is amazing. Danny's favorite one makes twenty varieties of grilled cheese. The beach is endless, perfect for long walks and romantic, sunset dinners."

"Sounds enchanting, you and Danny deserve some time to yourselves."

"We do need to get away, we never have time to talk." Annie's voice grew wistful and Martha wondered if something was troubling her, but Annie always sidestepped her questions, and Martha didn't want to pry. "No guests tonight, and only three tomorrow," Annie's voice grew stronger. "The Reillys are coming for a week to celebrate their fiftieth anniversary, so they'll have the room you had the first night."

After her second night at the Pelican, Martha had insisted on moving to a less luxurious room. She'd chosen the smallest of the third-floor rooms and loved its sunny day atmosphere. The walls were painted a smooth, buttery yellow and the molding, doors, and bedspread were bright white. Martha imagined she was strolling through a field of daisies whenever she opened the door.

"There's also a single man, Jake Whitfield, who happens to sound VERY sexy, by the way." Annie smiled, mischief in her eyes as she added the last bit of information.

"I'm not interested." Since her day with George had ended so abruptly, Martha had resolved to concentrate on work. "And how do you know he's single?" Not interested didn't mean not curious.

"He said he's on an extended sailing trip, and his boat required some repairs. Since he made a reservation for one, I assumed he was single. Anyway, he'll be here for three nights, but I told him if he needed to stay longer, he could."

"I'll let Darcy know. It shouldn't be a problem, since she doesn't have any special orders this week."

"Thanks Martha, I really appreciate your doing this, I know it disrupts your schedule."

"Don't be ridiculous, after all you've done for me? Besides, I'm looking forward to being the innkeeper, I want to see how it feels."

Martha stayed late at the Dancing Dolphin, knowing she would work fewer hours over the weekend. She returned home after dark, grateful for the lights Annie had left on. She locked the door behind her, slipped off her shoes and padded to the kitchen. Charley had been sleeping on a flowered chair cushion, but he stretched and jumped down to greet her, winding through her legs and purring.

She found a note from Annie on the table, but she scooped Charley into her arms, and nuzzled his neck before she started reading.

Hey Martha,

Thanks for taking care of the Pelican for a few days. Danny and I left on schedule this afternoon. You'll find grilled chicken and veggies in the fridge. I figured you'd work late and be too tired to cook when you got home. Have fun, relax, call my cell if you have any questions. See you Sunday night.

Love, Annie

Martha smiled, typical Annie, taking care of her, even when she wasn't there. She could feel herself healing cell by cell with Annie's kindness and support.

Martha set Charley on the floor where he meowed his protest, then rolled her head from side to side, trying to stretch her neck and shoulders. They felt like someone had tightened them with a winch. Darcy had received a last-minute order, and Martha helped her finish it. Then she'd had a brainstorm about her chocolate sculpture and worked a few hours on the design before driving home.

She thought about dinner, and mentally tasted the fresh basil, oregano, and garlic Annie would have used to season the chicken and veggies. She weighed food against a hot shower. The shower won, but first she put her supper in the oven to warm. After her shower, Martha wrapped herself in the white terry robe Annie had insisted she keep, and came downstairs. The house felt different tonight, empty and cold, instead of welcoming and cozy. It sensed she and Charley were here alone and creaked its discomfort.

Martha took her supper to the small table by the window. She often had breakfast standing at the island counter, but her whole body felt drained by the hours she had worked today, and she welcomed the comfort of the cushioned chair. Charley sat on the floor beside her and meowed.

"Oh okay, come on," Charley didn't need any other invitation. The words were barely spoken before he hopped into her lap, circled to find the most comfortable spot, then closed his eyes and purred while she ate.

"We're on our own Charley. I'm glad you're here." She stroked his furry head. Loneliness joined them and Martha longed to talk with Gram. They usually spoke every week or two, but Martha had avoided calling the last few weeks. Gram would sense something wrong, and she didn't want to tell her about the divorce and her feelings of failure and humiliation. She remembered when she was alone in Gram's house, how it seemed to be holding its breath, waiting for Gram to come home, as if it knew Martha wasn't in charge. Gram changed the whole atmosphere and the house sighed in relief when she came back, as did Martha. She picked up her cell phone and found Gram's number.

When a sleepy voice answered, "Hello?" she kicked herself for forgetting the time difference. Her grandmother had probably been in bed.

"Hi Gram,"

"Martha, is that you?"

"Yes, I'm sorry if I woke you, I forgot about the time." Despite her guilt, Martha relaxed at the sound of her grandmother's voice.

"It's okay, I was dozing in my chair. Is everything all right?"

"Yes, I wanted to call and say hi."

"I'm glad you did, how are you, dear?"

"I'm fine Gram, but I miss you." A lump formed in her throat as she spoke and the pain and guilt of abandoning her grandmother ached deep inside her. She tried to keep her voice normal and halt the threatening tears.

"I miss you too. How are things in Baltimore?"

"Actually, I'm not in Baltimore, I'm in Florida, near Pensacola."

"What are you doing there?"

"Remember my friend Annie, from culinary school? She has a bed and breakfast here in Perdido Key and she needed some extra help, so I came down for a few weeks."

"Is Tony there, too?"

"No, he couldn't get away. I'm planning to come home to see you, Gram." Martha couldn't bring herself to talk about the divorce. Gram would be so disappointed in her, and the longer she waited the harder it got. She'd already hurt Gram, but she wanted to explain everything in person, not over the phone.

"Oh wonderful, I hope you come soon. Next week, maybe?"

"No, probably not 'til fall."

"Oh, that long?" Weariness flooded Gram's voice. "Well, whenever you can, I'll be glad to see you. You know, you always have a home here." Although the words were Gram's, the defeat Martha heard in them wasn't normal.

"Are you sure you're okay Gram? You don't sound like yourself."

"I'm fine dear, just tired, I had a busy day. When I got home, Beal stopped by, she pops in now and then. She teaches music at the high school now, you know? What a voice that girl has."

"Yes, she used to sing when we ran. I'm glad she stays in touch." They both said goodnight and I love you before ending the call.

"As soon as the chocolate challenge is over, we're going back to Maine, Charley." She rubbed his fur, waiting for his rumbling purr to soothe her, but the ache of missing Gram persisted, why did she wait so long?

⚸ ⚸ ⚸

Martha wanted to make sure everything was ready for the guests before she left for work. She looked into the room where the Reillys would stay. When Martha slept in this room, its seaside air had created a wave of peace that washed over her, but today it filled her with a surge of homesickness. She missed Maine, and she missed Gram.

Annie had readied the last room on the second-floor hall for Jake. Every room had its own lighthouse knocker on the door, and the name of a town on the Cape. This one said, "Wellfleet." She opened the door and peeked in. The pale green walls, ivory woodwork, and cushiony gray carpet reminded Martha of the dune grass that grew on Cape Cod. Like the Reilly's room, she found it spotless. Reassured all was guest worthy, Martha left for the Dancing Dolphin.

✵ ✵ ✵

"Hello, anybody here?" Martha was in the kitchen of the Plump Pelican when she heard the deep male voice.

"Yes, I'm in the kitchen, I'll be right there." She finished pouring the batter for wild blueberry cake into the pan and slid the cake into the oven. Martha came through the swinging door to the front hall as she wiped her hand on a towel.

The owner of the voice had broad shoulders and slim hips, with a thatch of pale blonde hair skimming his forehead. He blocked the sun streaming in the front door, and consumed the surrounding space as he stood with his tan muscular legs spread slightly, and his hands resting on his hips. She had to tip her head back to meet his eyes. *Wow.* Martha visualized him in the prow of a Viking ship, sailing into battle.

"Hi, I'm Martha. You must be Jake." She recovered her poise and offered her hand in greeting. "You're booked for three nights, correct?"

"Yes, for now, but I asked Annie if I could stay longer if necessary, and I gathered it wouldn't be a problem. My boat's being repaired, and it should be ready in a few days." Sailboat living explained why his thick, shaggy hair was bleached almost white, but his eyes caught her attention. They were pale blue, and though his smile spread seductively across his face, it didn't reach his eyes, which remained cool, unreadable.

Martha felt a shiver run down her spine, but she shook it off and chatted as she completed the registration process. She wished Annie were returning today.

"It isn't too busy this weekend. Annie's normally here, but she and Danny are away and I'm filling in for now."

Before she could say more, Charley ambled in from the kitchen. Jake bent down to pet him, but Charley looked at Jake, arched his back and hissed as his tail grew enormous.

"Charley! Be nice to our guest," she turned shocked eyes to Jake. "I'm sorry, he doesn't normally behave like this."

"It's okay," Jake smiled briefly. "Your cat must smell my dog. He usually sails with me, but he's recuperating after trying to corral a skunk at our last port."

"Oh dear, is he all right?"

"He will be, but he's not the most welcome traveling companion right now. It's not the first time, either. For some reason Oscar thinks it's his job to pursue every skunk that comes within five miles of him. Unfortunately, he managed to get a little too close this time, and he's suffering the consequences. You'd think one dose of skunk spray would cure him of his hobby, but it hasn't." Jake shook his head and smiled again.

Martha felt herself relax a little, anyone who kept a skunk-chasing dog named Oscar must be pretty easygoing. His story reminded her of Gram's favorite movie, "The Odd Couple." Jake looked meticulous, in his pressed khaki shorts, white polo shirt, and boat shoes, like Felix, while his rogue dog Oscar got himself in trouble chasing skunks. She chuckled to herself, shooed Charley back into the kitchen, then gave Jake a copy of his receipt.

"I'll show you your room. It has a private bath and a small balcony overlooking the canal." She led the way upstairs and tried to sound welcoming, even though Charley's behavior still unsettled her.

"There are several local restaurants you might enjoy for dinner. I have menus in the kitchen if you'd like to see them."

"I passed a place called Perdido Shores on the way here. The sign said fresh seafood, so I thought I'd give it a try."

"Good choice, it isn't fancy, but the fish is fresh and simply prepared."

"Can I convince you to join me?" The casual words stepped into her space with their intimate tone and Martha stiffened, uncomfortable with the request.

"Thanks, I appreciate the invitation, but other guests will be arriving this evening, and I need to make sure everything is ready. Here we are," she opened the door for Jake. "If you have any questions about the room, or anything else, please let me know. What time would you like breakfast in the morning?"

"Is eight, okay? I usually run first."

"That's fine. I run early myself, then come back and serve breakfast."

"Do you have a favorite route? I'll come with you."

His words crowded her, and Martha withdrew to the hall. Why did she tell him she ran too?

"Oh, I'm up at the crack of dawn, I need to get back and prepare breakfast. I have a local street map though. I'll give you a copy and suggest a few possible routes." She had no desire to spend time alone with Jake. He made her uneasy, but she couldn't say why.

Martha removed the blueberry cake from the oven while Charley wound between her legs, purring.

"Don't try to butter me up, Charley Boy, I'm still annoyed with you. You're not allowed to hiss at guests. You better be nice to the Reillys, or I'll have to lock you in a room by yourself."

Charley meowed his apology, then curled himself into a ball on the cushioned rocker in the corner.

❋ ❋ ❋

Martha heard the doorbell and went to greet her newest guests.

"Welcome to the Plump Pelican, Mr. and Mrs. Reilly."

Martha filled out the necessary paperwork and led the way upstairs.

"You're in the room reserved for special guests," she opened the door and stepped back. "I gather this trip is a celebration for you."

"Yes, Frank and I were married fifty years ago on Sunday. What a gorgeous bouquet." Mrs. Reilly stood gazing at the lace-cap hydrangeas and yellow roses Annie had arranged. "Hydrangeas are one of my favorites,"

"Annie's away, but she wanted to wish you a happy anniversary, so she left the flowers for you."

"How thoughtful." Mrs. Reilly lightly touched a blue blossom.

"Let me show you the balcony. It's a charming place to sit in the evening."

"I feel like I'm back on the New England shore." Mrs. Reilly was clearly thrilled with their accommodations.

"I felt exactly the same way the first time I saw it. Are you from New England?"

"Yes, we're both from Rhode Island, but Frank was stationed at the Navy base in Pensacola during Vietnam. We had planned to be married the following year in Newport but then he received orders to ship out."

"I asked Catherine if she'd be willing to get married before I left, I couldn't believe it when she said yes." Love shimmered in Frank's eyes, and he smiled at his wife. Martha wondered if a man would ever look at her with so much affection or love her the way Frank loved Catherine.

"I flew to Pensacola, and one of Frank's buddies and his girlfriend stood up for us." Catherine's eyes sparkled as she told the story. "We came back to see our friends, Bill and Lois Jennings, and celebrate with them."

"How wonderful you can all celebrate together." The Reillys had found the happily ever after Martha longed for. "I hope you'll be comfortable here. Let me know if you need anything else. I have warm blueberry cake if you would like a piece, and there's always iced tea available."

Martha met Jake on the stairs as she returned to the kitchen. "Are you all set, is there anything else you need?"

"Yes, for you to join me for dinner, any chance you changed your mind?" Jake stepped closer to Martha as he spoke.

"Thank you, but not tonight, maybe another time." Jake kept pushing with his invitation, and she wanted to push back, but she didn't want to be rude to one of Annie's guests.

"I'll hold you to that," he said smiling.

Martha hurried down the stairs without responding.

Chapter 13

The alarm rang at 5:00 a.m., and at 5:15 a.m., Martha headed out the door for her run. The cool gulf breeze that lulled her to sleep the previous night had been swallowed by a wave of humidity. The sultry air was so thick she felt like she needed to push it aside to run, and the smell of trailing jasmine, usually delightful, suffocated her today. Although she began with a slow jog, a moist sheen soon covered her skin and she found it difficult to breathe. The soft air in Florida made Martha miss the crisp, clear days of Maine, where she welcomed a sudden warming after the hard days of winter. Florida days lacked contrast, one dissolved into another, each hotter than the preceding one, until Martha felt like she would melt away in a puddle of sweat. Fortunately, her training schedule required a short five miles, but she hadn't planned on running in a steam bath.

How will I train for the marathon if it's like this every day? Martha watched the road flow under her feet and focused on breathing steadily and picking up her pace. She approached a curve and tried to imagine the cool salty air that fueled her summer runs in Maine. The sound of screeching brakes startled her and she jerked her head up. A red pickup careened around the bend, barreling directly at her. Martha lunged off the road into tall grass and fell. She slammed her head on something hard when she landed. Stunned, she lay stationary until the dizziness subsided. *Breathe, just breathe.* She pressed her hand to her head and gasped in pain. She shifted her weight.

Still in one piece.

"Are you all right?"

Martha opened her eyes. Jake leaned over her.

Where did he come from? She forced herself to sit up.

"I think so." Something wet ran down her cheek, she touched it and took her hand away. *Blood.*

Jake pulled a clean bandana from his pocket and offered it to her. "Here, use this and apply some pressure. I don't think it's too bad, cuts on your head always bleed more than you think they should." She took the bandana and pressed gently but it still hurt.

"Ow!" She winced.

"I saw somebody on the ground, but at first I didn't realize it was you. What happened?"

"A truck came flying around the corner and skidded on the gravel. I thought he was going to hit me, so I dove off the pavement. He saw me at the same time and managed to swerve back onto the road." Embarrassed by being found in a heap on the ground, she said, "I usually have a good sense of balance, but I must have caught my foot on something."

"Do you think anything's broken?" Jake stretched his hand toward her ankle. Before he could touch her, she pushed his hand away. She could determine on her own if she had any other injuries.

"I'm fine, really, I'm fine. I fell and bumped my head, that's all."

"I'm going to get my car so you don't have to walk back."

"If you're going back to the Pelican, I'll come with you. I'm sure I can walk." Martha started to push herself from the ground. Jake placed his hand on her shoulder.

"No, don't try to get up yet, my car is right beyond the curve. I'll be back in a minute." He was gone before she could ask him why his car was parked so close to where she was running. She managed to stand unassisted, but her ankle hurt more than she expected, and she sat down again. Although relieved she didn't have to walk, Jake's immediate arrival seemed strange. She wondered if he had been heading out to check on his boat, or wanted to follow a running route she suggested, or had he hoped to run with her?

Jake returned from moving his car and helped her to stand. When she tried to walk, pain shot through her ankle and she sucked in her breath.

"I think you should go to the emergency room." Jake put a steadying hand on her elbow.

"I'll be fine, just take me back to the Pelican so I can get breakfast ready." She refused to let Annie down the first time she filled in as innkeeper. She could stand on one leg to cook if she had to. She gritted her teeth against the pain and made it back to Jake's car.

"You need to stay off that foot." He started the car. "Don't worry about breakfast." Martha didn't want to talk about her foot and she wished Jake would stop telling her what she should do. It was bad enough she had to trust him to drive her home, plus she wondered how he had arrived so conveniently when she fell.

"What a fortunate coincidence you were nearby," Martha aimed for a casual tone. "I thought you planned to run this morning."

"I looked at the map you gave me, and this seemed like a pretty good route, but I wanted to go check on my boat too. I left the car here so I could drive to the marina when I finished my run. I arrived right after you fell, good timing I guess."

Martha thought about her route, if he started running before her, she would have seen his car. Maybe he came later and didn't run as far, that made sense. They drove the rest of way in silence, and when they reached the bed and breakfast, Jake helped her inside.

"Go clean up and lie down. I'll take care of breakfast. Trust me, I'm a pretty good cook. I'll get some ice for your ankle." Jake gave her a gentle nudge towards the stairs and Martha brushed his hand away.

In her head she yelled, "Stop telling me what to do," but to him she said, "Thanks, but I can handle it. Besides, you need to go check on your boat. I'll be down in fifteen minutes." Martha clenched her teeth as she tackled the challenge of climbing two flights of stairs. She resorted to sitting and going up backwards, one stair at a time. At least Jake had gone to the kitchen and couldn't see her. With any luck she'd be back down before he had a chance to start cooking. She didn't want a guest taking over Annie's kitchen without her permission.

Exhausted from the effort, she turned the shower to hot and let the water run over her bruises and sore muscles as she washed the blood from her hair. She stepped from the shower and automatically put her full weight on the sore ankle, then gasped and grabbed the side of the tub.

When the flash of pain subsided, she hobbled back to her bedroom to get dressed. Martha found the pain bearable if she descended the stairs one at a time, half hopping on her good foot. She said a silent thank you for all her yoga classes, especially tree position, it made balancing on one foot much easier.

As she slowly worked her way down the stairs, Martha thought about breakfast plans. Last night she had set a table for three in the sunroom, her favorite spot in the house. The glass-topped, white wicker table and blue chintz-covered chair cushions appeared cheerful in the morning light. She added a bouquet of daisies and violet-blue cranesbill, because they made her think of summer days at home. Annie served breakfast in the dining room for large groups, but the Reillys would enjoy the coziness of the smaller space, as well as the view of the gardens and canal behind the house.

Martha limped into the kitchen and found Jake standing at the stove stirring a pan of scrambled eggs. She could feel irritation rising inside her; she didn't need another controlling man in her life. Annie trusted Martha to serve guests gourmet breakfasts as good as those she made. Martha had no intention of relinquishing her responsibility to Jake.

"Jake, you didn't need to do this, and although the eggs look delicious, I'm serving something else for breakfast today. Go check on your boat, I'll finish here."

"I've already cleared it with the Reillys. They're fine with scrambled eggs and they're enjoying coffee in the dining room."

Martha warred with herself, she didn't want to be rude to a guest, but though she told Jake she could make breakfast, he ignored her. Frustration won, she had to say something.

"Jake, this is my responsibility and I can handle it. I'm not serving scrambled eggs. The crepe batter is already prepared for strawberry crepes, and I set up the sunroom for breakfast last night. I'll take over from here." She moved abruptly towards the refrigerator, and much to her chagrin, her right ankle buckled under her. Martha yelped and would have landed on the floor if Jake hadn't moved quickly and caught her. Annoyed with her inability to continue, she admitted defeat and allowed Jake to support her.

"Martha, please sit down and I'll get some ice and ibuprofen for your ankle. It may not be what you planned, but eggs will be fine, and I thawed some muffins I found in the freezer. You can serve crepes in the sunroom tomorrow, or I'll serve them if your ankle isn't better."

"You're right," Martha nodded. She hoped she hadn't offended him, but he sounded concerned, not upset. "I'm sorry, this ankle hurts more than I expected, and I do appreciate your help." She shuffled to the living room, collapsed on the couch, and stretched out her leg on the cushions. Hopefully, her ankle would feel better tomorrow. She refused to ask Annie to cut her mini vacation even shorter. She thanked Jake when he came in with ice.

"Would you like some coffee?"

"Don't worry about me, serve the Reillys their breakfast." She knew her tone was curt, why was she being churlish, not at all the way Annie would expect her to treat guests? Jake hadn't signed on to be a cook, and yet he stepped in and helped without any complaint. She should be grateful.

Martha sighed and found a pillow for her head. She leaned back and closed her eyes; she'd apologize again later for her behavior. Jake's manner reminded her so much of Tony and the way he had treated her, always assuming he had a better idea, and that she should adapt to his plans.

She remembered one particular weekend when they had been in school. They had a rare Sunday to spend together and she had packed a gourmet picnic for them to take to Jamestown Island, one of Martha's favorite spots. The lighthouse, jagged rocks, and crashing surf all reminded her of the Maine coast. At the last minute, Tony changed their plans to dinner with his parents. If she didn't agree, he wouldn't speak to her for days.

Jake chatted with the Reillys, and Martha heard the hum of their conversation. He obviously didn't mind cooking in an unfamiliar kitchen or meeting new people. She didn't like being stuck on the couch when she should have been the one serving breakfast, but she tried to relax and be thankful Jake could fill in. The smell of coffee mingled with sweet, spicy muffins, drifted over her. Jake must have found the pumpkin chai muffins, and she was glad she'd placed them in the front of the freezer. Since he hadn't come to ask any questions, she assumed the Reillys were content. She had planned to serve the muffins tomorrow morning but admitted to herself it wasn't a big deal to swap the menus for the weekend. Annie and Dan would be back tomorrow night, so she had one more breakfast to serve.

The background noise of clinking glasses and silverware, and the gentle mumble of conversation lulled her to sleep. Her run in the heat and the stress of falling had worn her out more than she realized. Jake's voice startled her awake.

"Hey sleepy head, you ready for breakfast?" He placed a tray on the coffee table beside her. She normally had fruit and yogurt for breakfast, but after her earlier behavior she couldn't refuse the eggs and muffin he brought her. She sat up and scrubbed her hands over her face.

"I didn't think I'd fall asleep. Thank you for making breakfast for the Reillys and me, don't worry about cleaning up, I'll take care of it."

"All done," Jake flashed a self-satisfied smile. "I'm going to check on my boat, unless you need me to stay here."

"No, please, you've done enough. The Reillys won't need anything for the rest of the day." She took the plate of eggs from the tray. "I'm sorry about my behavior earlier. I'm not usually so ungrateful." Her apology helped ease the guilt that kept nudging her, so she could let it go.

"Pain can make you short-tempered, besides, I'm glad to help. I'll be back in time to make you dinner, and you can tell me your plans for tomorrow morning. There's no way you'll be ready to walk on that ankle, I'll handle breakfast again." Martha saw no need to explain that pain hadn't caused her aggravation, and she didn't want him to continue to wait on her. Hopefully, after a day of rest her ankle would improve. If not, she'd think about seeing a doctor on Monday.

"I appreciate your concern, but I'll spend the day reading and heat something from the freezer for dinner. I won't be running in the morning, but after a day of rest I'll be fine to cook breakfast tomorrow. Go enjoy your day."

"I'll check on you later anyway," Jake waved and left. Martha resolved to take care of herself, Jake's assumption that she needed him to do everything caused mental fists to clench inside her. She didn't resent his assistance so much as the way he dictated it. She couldn't help thinking about how different George's manner had been and she wondered what he would have done. She imagined him offering to help, then respecting her decision and helping to prepare the breakfast she had planned.

Martha called Darcy and told her she wouldn't be in until tomorrow, and gave her an abbreviated version of her accident while Darcy made sympathetic noises. Martha hated to renege on her commitments again, but at least Darcy didn't have any big orders for today. Then she spent the rest of the morning enjoying the luxury of reading a favorite romance novel. She lost herself in the story of two people clearly in love, even though neither one would admit it. They argued with each other constantly. Martha knew right away they were meant for each other, and she could feel the heat between them searing the pages. She sighed and closed the book on Tulia and Dominic and their happily ever after world.

Who wouldn't be blissful on a sunny Greek island with nothing to do every day but roam the pristine beach, swim in the indigo bay, and have mind-blowing sex every night? Martha let her mind drift back to meeting Tony in culinary school, and the happily ever after she longed for. She had been consumed by Tony's passionate desire for her, but she'd been oblivious to his equally passionate need for control.

Chapter 14

*M*artha discovered she was adept at hopping, as long as she took her time. In fact, she relished the challenge of getting to the kitchen for a glass of iced tea and a sandwich for lunch. She sat at the kitchen table sketching ideas for the chocolate challenge while she ate, lost in thought, when she heard the front door open. She groaned inwardly, expecting Jake to walk through the door, but Catherine Reilly poked her head in and relief replaced her annoyance.

"Hello dear, we came back for a little rest and then we'll be gone for the rest of the day. We're meeting friends for dinner. How's your ankle?"

"Feeling better, thank you." Martha found the older woman's obvious concern touching, and she'd do anything she could to make their stay perfect. "Would you like a glass of iced tea and some fudge brownies?"

"Oh, I probably shouldn't, but they sound marvelous. Would you mind if I took them to our room? We can sit on the balcony and enjoy them."

"Sure, I'll fix a tray for you," Martha hopped over to the counter. She arranged a plate of brownies, poured two glasses of iced tea, and added cloth napkins decorated with plump pelicans.

"I'd offer to bring it to your room, but I'm not sure I can navigate the stairs and carry iced tea." Martha hated to ask a guest for help. If her ankle didn't improve by tomorrow, she'd have to figure out another solution.

"I can take it, don't worry." Mrs. Reilly lifted the tray and inhaled.

"These smell divine, I can't wait to try one. We'll see you in the morning. I hope your ankle feels better, dear."

"Thanks, enjoy your evening, and let me know if you need anything else." Martha returned to her design sketches and worked for another hour on the plans. She had so many ideas buzzing in her head, she couldn't settle on one. She studied her sketches waiting for something to speak to her and tried to decide which ones to transform into samples. After putting her dishes in the dishwasher, she hopped back to the couch, and returned to her book.

By late afternoon, boredom set in and she returned to the kitchen to make ginger scones and more pumpkin chai muffins to replenish the supply in the freezer. She stood on one foot, resting her bent knee on a chair, and worked until her rumbling stomach reminded her of dinner. She warmed a piece of seafood quiche, a breakfast favorite of the guests, but she preferred to have the rich tart, filled with shrimp, crabmeat, and Jarlsberg cheese for dinner. She sat at the small table, placing her injured ankle on another chair. Charley jumped up and curled himself next to her foot.

When the front door opened, "It must be Jake," flitted through her mind, and she resigned herself to more of his directives. He came into the kitchen carrying a large pizza box.

"I knew you wouldn't feel like cooking, so I bought a pizza for us." He appeared pleased with himself, and his tone implied she should be too.

"I appreciate your thoughtfulness, but I warmed some quiche." She indicated the plate in front of her.

"Forget the quiche, have some pizza," he opened the box. "I got it with everything, that's the best way." He took a plate from the cupboard and looked over at Martha. "One piece or two?"

"Thank you, but I don't want to waste the quiche. You enjoy it." She kept her voice calm even as her irritation at his assumption grew. She reminded herself it wouldn't be polite to throw pizza at a guest.

"Oh, come on, have a piece." Jake put the plate on the table and served himself as well, then sat at the counter. Martha kept eating her quiche. She preferred her pizza smothered with veggies. Tony always ordered it with meat, until she finally persuaded him to request half with vegetables.

"How's the work on your boat progressing?" She hoped there would be no delays to cause him to stay longer than planned.

"They'll finish today or tomorrow, I'm hoping to take her out for a sail on Monday, you should come along."

"Thank you, but I have to go back to work at the chocolate shop on Monday. Do you plan to continue your trip as soon as your boat's ready, or will you need to extend your reservation?"

"I'll be able to move back aboard, but I'm going to take several day sails and test the repairs. Sure you don't want some of this pizza?" He took a bite of his and pushed the other plate toward her.

"I'm good thank you, I'm not very hungry." Martha rose from the chair. "I think I'll say goodnight. Do you need anything else?"

"No, but let me get breakfast in the morning, you can sleep late."

"I couldn't sleep late even if I wanted to. I'll be fine." She tried to channel the voice Gram had used when she meant, 'Don't argue with me, I'm not changing my mind.' "Enjoy your morning run."

❋ ❋ ❋

After serving breakfast Sunday morning, Martha sat in the kitchen and savored a second cup of coffee before loading the dishwasher. She had mastered the art of cooking while standing on one foot, but it required more frequent rests. She'd set up a buffet on the counter and asked the guests to help themselves. Not ideal, but it worked.

Charley was purring on her lap while she planned her day, when her phone rang.

"Hi Martha, it's Annie, how are you doing at the Pelican?"

"Great!" Martha looked down at her foot resting on the chair and Charley sitting in her lap. "Aren't we Charley? We're doing just fine." *Under the circumstances.*

"Dan managed to swap shifts with someone at the firehouse. We could stay one more day and come back Monday morning, if you don't mind." Martha heard Annie's joy as well as her pleading unspoken words: "We're having such a wonderful weekend, please say you'll be okay for another night."

"Of course, Annie, enjoy yourself."

"Are you sure everything's okay? You sound a little worn out."

"Everything's fine, Charley and I are relaxing." Although she'd been looking forward to Annie's return, her ankle had improved since yesterday, she could manage one more breakfast, and no way would she ask her friend to cut short her minivacation.

"But what about the chocolate shop?" Annie sounded concerned.

"Don't worry, I'll make breakfast for everyone, then go to the shop."

"What about Jake, is he as sexy as he sounded on the phone?" Martha recognized her friend's teasing tone, and tried to match it so Annie wouldn't fret.

"I hadn't really noticed, besides, I told you it doesn't matter." Some women might find Jake sexy, but his controlling manner negated any sex appeal in Martha's mind.

"I'll take that as a yes. See you tomorrow, and thanks, I owe you."

"You don't owe me anything, I'm glad I can help YOU."

The remainder of the day passed uneventfully. Despite her sore ankle, Martha baked cinnamon rolls, raspberry muffins, and lemon curd scones to stock the freezer. Since the Reillys mentioned plans to spend the day sightseeing with friends, she didn't expect them back until late. Jake waved to her as he headed out to work on his boat. When he returned around five to check on her, he tried to entice her to join him for dinner. But she refused, and he left for the evening. Exhausted after a day hobbling on her ankle, Martha went to bed early, without seeing her guests.

The next morning, Martha rose at first light and limped to the kitchen. She could put partial weight on her ankle now, as long as she did it carefully. She drank her coffee on the back deck, and watched the sun make its morning debut. The steamy air hung in ribbons around her, and she was glad she didn't feel compelled to run today. She managed to walk, but her ankle wasn't ready for running steps.

When she finished her coffee, she started making blueberry stuffed french toast. Gram always made it with tiny wild Maine blueberries, but Martha settled for the juicy, organic ones she found at the farmers' market. She remembered making it with Gram while they talked about school or whatever else Martha had on her mind. Real maple syrup sweetened the cream cheese filling for the bread and made it easier to spread, one of the tricks Gram taught her as they worked. She poured a custard of eggs, milk, and cream over the bread, then set it aside so the liquid would be absorbed before it baked. Martha sighed; she missed those days of baking together.

Jake came in dressed for his run. "Good morning Martha, how's the ankle? Want me to take over?"

"No, I'm fine, thank you, go enjoy your run. Breakfast will be ready when you get back." She walked to the oven and slid the casserole in to prove she didn't need his help.

After Jake left, Martha cut fresh cantaloupe, pineapple, mango, and strawberries. In cut-glass bowls, the fruit looked like colorful jewels, and she set one at each place, then filled a small, white enamel pitcher with maple syrup. She had set the table the night before and arranged roses and deep blue delphinium in a large white enamel pitcher, like the one she remembered from Gram's kitchen. The roses' delicate fragrance wafted through the room and their cherry red petals contrasted with the blue check tablecloth. She found it satisfying to make breakfast beautiful as well as delicious.

When Mrs. Reilly came into the kitchen, thick slices of bacon sizzled in the cast iron skillet and sent out an enticing aroma. "Something smells scrumptious," she came to stand beside Martha. "How's your ankle, dear? Do you need any help?"

"No, it's much better, but thank you for offering. I set the table in the sunroom, coffee's already there." She appreciated Mrs. Reilly's caring inquiry, unlike Jake's question which made her hackles rise.

Martha heard Jake come back from his run and nodded to herself with satisfaction. She'd managed to get everything ready without his help. As she carried the platters of French toast and bacon to the table, he walked through the kitchen door.

"How was your run?" She smiled briefly at him. Whatever negative feelings she had about Jake, he was still a guest.

"Great, I'm starving and breakfast smells good." He gave her a slow smile, which Martha chose to ignore.

"It's all on the table, help yourself." She checked to see if her three guests needed anything, then started tidying the kitchen. Her ankle had kept her home for the weekend, and she wanted to get to the chocolate shop. The Reillys thanked her for breakfast then left for the day. Jake poked his head around the door as she finished wiping the counters.

"I called the marina and I can live on my boat again; they finished the major repairs. Looks like your ankle's better, so I'll be on my way as soon as I settle my bill."

"My ankle is fine, thanks, and I'm sure you're excited to move back to your boat." Martha did a happy dance in her mind. Jake would be on his way and she wouldn't have to dodge his invitations anymore. At least he hadn't assumed he should stay until Annie returned. "I'll print your bill for you before I go to the chocolate shop." She hung her apron on a peg and gave the kitchen a last check as she spoke.

Jake followed her to the front desk and waited for his bill. "I'm planning to stay in the area for a week or two, make sure everything's okay, I'd love it if you'd come for a sail before I leave." His tone surprised Martha—friendly instead of commanding—then he continued, "Let me know what works for you." *If I say yes, which I won't.* She intended to return to her normal routine and forget about Jake.

"I'm going to have a busy week," Martha processed Jake's credit card. "Thank you again for your help when I hurt my ankle, and I hope your boat is all ready to sail." She followed Jake from The Plump Pelican, relieved to see him leave, and hurried to her own car, energized by the thought of returning to her chocolate designs.

�֍ ✖ ✖

When Martha sagged through the front door of the Pelican after nine o'clock, she found Annie in the kitchen preparing for breakfast the next morning. The Reillys would stay through the week, and two other couples had requested a late evening arrival time.

"Hi Annie, how was your trip?"

100

"Amazing," Annie said happily. She had dinner waiting and after encouraging Martha to sit down, she proceeded to quiz her for information. "Why didn't you tell me you hurt your ankle? We wouldn't have stayed the extra day."

"Did you see Jake?" Maybe he forgot something and came back. She hadn't planned to mention her fall.

"No, the Reillys. They both extolled your qualities as a trouper and told me you served them breakfast Sunday and Monday, hobbling on one foot. They also reported Jake pitched in and helped. How's your foot? Tell me exactly what happened, and why you didn't call me."

Martha sighed. "First of all, it wasn't a big deal."

"Mrs. Reilly claimed a truck ran you off the road!" Annie cut a large serving of vegetable lasagna and paused with it suspended over Martha's plate.

"I went for a morning run, as I was going around a curve, a truck swerved towards me." Martha downplayed her accident and briefly told Annie the story of catching her foot and twisting her ankle.

"Jake pitched in, he was there right after it happened, I'm not sure why or how." He'd explained his timely arrival, but it seemed like too much of a coincidence to Martha, maybe she should accept it.

"Good that he was," Annie said with relief.

"Mmmm maybe, anyway, he brought me back here, and insisted he would get breakfast." She took a bite of her lasagna. "This is yummy, thanks for saving it for me. Turns out Jake's a pretty good cook, he made delicious scrambled eggs, and found the muffins I put in the freezer so the Reillys were content. Jake pumped me full of ibuprofen and I fell asleep, and when I woke up, he'd cleaned the kitchen, and the Reillys had left for the day. By the next morning I could serve breakfast. If it'd been a real problem, I'd have asked Jake for more help. I had trouble keeping him out of the kitchen." Martha took another bite, ready to change the subject.

"I still wish you'd called me. We'd have come home."

"Did you enjoy your extra day?" Martha leaned across the counter and placed her hand on Annie's, she didn't want her friend to feel guilty about not coming home.

"Yes," Annie smiled, and her eyes sparkled with hope, in a way Martha hadn't seen since she arrived. Martha guessed it had been a special weekend for her friend, which made it worth every minute she worked with the discomfort of her sore ankle.

"I'm glad you had a good time. I'll be back to normal and running again soon."

"I think we should invite Jake over for dinner, unless he's sailed away," Annie placed the remaining lasagna in a container.

"He told me he's going to stick around for a while, to make sure the repairs don't have issues," Martha took a final bite of her lasagna. "He'll go for local sails until everything checks out." Annie wouldn't be satisfied unless she showed her gratitude to Jake, so Martha didn't argue, though she had no desire to see Jake again and thought a phone call would suffice.

"Good, I'll call him and invite him for dinner. What night will you get home early?"

"I'm not sure I will get home early." Nor did she want to have dinner with Jake. She appreciated his help, but something about him nagged at her.

"You don't have to do anything except show up. I'll plan it and make dinner, and we'll serve it out on the patio. How about Saturday, say seven-thirty?"

"I looked at the schedule, you've got a busy week coming up Annie, you don't need to cook another dinner. Even if you do make the best veggie lasagna I've ever tasted." Annie planned to serve an anniversary dinner for the Reillys. Their family and friends had flown in for the occasion and there would be twelve people for dinner Friday night. By Saturday, Martha knew Annie would be ready for a break.

"If you insist on inviting Jake, why don't we at least go to a restaurant?" Martha could endure one more evening with Jake if it made Annie happy. "How about the Gulf Breeze?" Annie checked the calendar and reluctantly agreed.

Saturday night, Martha arrived at the Gulfside restaurant where Annie, Dan, and Jake were already seated on the patio. Her aqua sundress matched the color of the water and made her feel cooler in spite of the lingering heat. She promised herself to keep an open mind about Jake and enjoy the evening. He had helped when he could have complained about the service, and his last invitation to sail had sounded sincere, maybe she misjudged him.

"Sorry I'm late, I had to work longer than I'd planned."

"I just got here myself," Jake rose and held her chair when she approached. "I took the boat out for a shake-down sail." Martha breathed in Jake's expensive cologne. He wore khaki shorts and boat shoes with a pale blue dress shirt that made his icy blue eyes even more riveting. The rolled-back sleeves revealed tan, muscular arms, and with his sun-bleached hair he looked like he had stepped off the cover of *Yachting Magazine*. She couldn't deny his arresting good looks, but she'd fallen for those before and she wouldn't make the same mistake again.

Their server came to take their drink requests and returned with wine for everyone. Annie lifted her glass for a toast.

"Here's to guests who help in an emergency." Martha remained silent when they all laughed, and Annie thanked Jake for the second time since Martha had arrived. Jake stressed that Martha couldn't have managed by herself and he was willing to help. She bit back the comment she wanted to make, "I would have coped fine on my own," then took a sip of her wine and said, "Let's order."

"I think I'll have the seafood special." Martha read the description, "Locally caught Grouper, baked in wine, butter and fresh dill."

A chorus of "Sounds good," followed. Jake kept the mood light as he regaled them with tales of Oscar's escapades and skunk encounters. Martha laughed, but despite Jake's entertaining stories, she felt on edge. Dan asked him about his sailing plans, and Jake said he'd be on his way after a couple more minor adjustments. Once dinner ended, she wouldn't have any reason to see Jake again, Martha thought with relief.

"I'm hoping to leave next Sunday. Why don't you all join me Saturday night for a bon voyage picnic on board?" Although Jake included Annie and Dan in his invitation, he looked directly at Martha.

No! She looked down her plate, how could she get out of this? Dan was on duty, and Annie declined due to the number of incoming guests. Martha opened her mouth to say she needed to help Annie, but before she could get the words out, Annie responded for her.

"Martha would love to join you, wouldn't you Martha? You've been missing Maine, and even though it isn't New England, I'm sure it would be delightful to have dinner on the water."

"I don't know," Martha said, frantically searching for a plausible excuse. "I've got a busy day Saturday, and I want to be there to help you with the weekend guests." She wanted to kick Annie under the table.

"Don't be silly," Annie said, "you covered for me so Dan and I could have a weekend away, now it's your turn for some relaxation."

"Why don't you come to the marina around seven?" Jake spoke before Martha could protest further. "I'll have everything ready, and we can eat on the boat, maybe go for an evening sail."

Chapter 15

"Annie, I'm not sure this is a good idea." Martha stood in the kitchen drumming her fingers on the counter as Annie spread the thick batter for macadamia fudge squares in the waiting jelly roll pan.

"Why not? You haven't stopped working since you got here. You're either training for the marathon, designing your chocolate entry, or helping me. You need some time for yourself."

"Those things are relaxing—well, maybe not running in the Florida heat—but my mind goes to another place when I work on my chocolate designs." She sat on a nearby stool. "I love trying different ideas, and working with you at The Plump Pelican has made me rethink my future. Maybe someday I'll open a bed and breakfast."

"You could use a little fun in your life, a little male companionship."

"I know, but I'm not sure it should be Jake." Annie found Jake charming, maybe Martha should trust her judgement, still— "Charley was decidedly unimpressed with him."

"Charley's a cat. He's unimpressed with everybody, it's beneath him," Annie slid the pan in the oven.

"He sure seems to like Danny."

"Because Danny's always slipping him pieces of his tuna fish sandwich. Charley knows how to endear himself to someone who'll give him treats. If Jake had smelled of tuna fish and offered treats, Charley's response would have been different."

"Mmmm, maybe." Unconvinced, Martha thought about her encounters with Jake. *How can someone so intrusive and irritating also be so charming and entertaining? I bet Charley would like George.* The last unexpected thought was followed by, *Where did that come from?* Martha realized Annie was speaking to her.

"Hurry up, go get dressed." Annie made shooing motions with her hands.

"What do you mean? I am dressed." Martha looked down at her cut-off jeans and T-shirt with "Chocolate Is a Food Group," written on it. "What's wrong with what I'm wearing? It's just a picnic supper on a sailboat."

"Yes, but I saw a picture of Jake's boat and I don't think it's what you're expecting."

"I don't really care." She didn't feel the need to impress Jake, he did that all by himself. Martha swiped her finger around the empty bowl and tasted the batter, "Yum."

"Come on Martha, make an effort."

"Oh, all right." Martha flounced upstairs. She'd bought a couple of summery outfits on a rare afternoon of retail therapy after Darcy insisted on paying her for her expertise, and she chose her favorite. Annie wanted her to have a special night out, she might as well dress for the part. She returned a few minutes later wearing white linen capris and an aquamarine silk top that accented her turquoise eyes, and softly hugged her slender body. She had exchanged her sneakers for gold and white strappy sandals, and tucked her wavy, golden brown hair behind her ears to reveal dangling, gold dolphins. The sun had given her cheeks a natural blush, so her make-up was limited to a touch of mascara and peach lip gloss. Annie looked up from loading the dishwasher.

"Wow, I'm impressed." She gave Martha a hug. "Relax, have fun."

"I'll eat dinner and then I'm on my way home." Martha wished she could think of a reason to stay at the Pelican, she'd prefer dinner with Annie. "I promised I'd do breakfast for you tomorrow."

"Don't worry about breakfast, I can cover it if you want to extend your evening."

Martha rolled her eyes and went out the door. That wouldn't happen. Jake didn't inspire romantic dreams.

She made a left into the parking lot of the exclusive marina and was surprised to find most of the slips empty. "That's odd," she thought, did she get the directions wrong? Martha shielded her eyes against the sun as she searched for a boat that fit Jake's description, dark blue hull with a teak deck, and named "My Escape." When she couldn't find it, she looked toward the nearby building. He must have been watching for her, because she saw him wave as he stepped from the office door with a smile on his face.

"I had to move my boat to one of the other slips, because they're getting ready to paint this dock tomorrow. It's a short walk on the beach. Here, take my hand, those shoes aren't designed for walking in sand." Martha glanced at her sandals. "You're right." She slipped out of them and dangled one shoe in each hand, so she didn't have to hold his. When they came to the pier where his boat was tied, there were no others nearby.

"Why is yours the only boat here?" Martha slipped her sandals back on and looked around, an uneasy current ran through her. Should she claim a sudden headache?

"The boats get scattered when they paint the main section of the pier. They tried to do it earlier in the spring, but it rained so much they weren't able to." Martha thought about how many times her runs had been delayed by rain and accepted his explanation.

They walked onto the pier where his sailboat was docked. *Wow.* Annie had been right, not what she expected. A table in the stern of his forty-foot Beneteau was set for two with gold rimmed, dark blue china and silver flatware. The boat rocked gently, and the white damask tablecloth fluttered in the evening breeze. A silver bucket held ice and a bottle of champagne. If Jake's goal had been to impress her, he had succeeded. If he hoped for a romantic interlude, he'd be disappointed.

Martha hesitated, then stepped on board in one graceful motion. She kept her feet steady, and refrained from kicking the dock with her trailing foot.

"This isn't the picnic supper I expected!" She admired the elegant setting and Jake stepped on board.

"I wanted to treat you the way you deserve, Martha. You don't realize how special you are, but I've come to recognize it over the past couple weeks we've spent together."

Spent together? Where did he get that idea? "We haven't seen each other that many times Jake—a few days at The Plump Pelican and dinner with Annie and Dan. I appreciate all your efforts, and I'll enjoy dinner, but you didn't need to go to all this trouble." The edgy current ran through her again, a little stronger this time.

Jake poured them each a glass of champagne, accompanied by assorted cheeses, water crackers, fresh figs, and grapes. He had sailed most of the eastern seaboard, and she found him to be a fascinating storyteller. He served a lightly dressed lobster salad nestled in bib lettuce, and tiny brioche rolls, with sweet butter in the shape of a scallop shell, with a second glass of champagne.

By then, the prickly current had disappeared. Annie had been right, she needed a break from constant work, and what could be better than dinner and conversation with an attentive and handsome man? Martha tasted the salad.

"I don't usually order lobster in Florida, being a Maine girl, but this is delicious."

"The chef at the yacht club owed me a favor, and he special ordered the lobster. Tell me, how did a Maine girl wind up in Pensacola?"

"I went to culinary school in Rhode Island then moved to Baltimore where I started a wedding cake business. I came here to help Annie." She had no intention of sharing personal details with Jake, so she asked about his next destination instead. Content to talk about himself, he told her about his plans for sailing to the Caribbean. They lingered over chocolate truffles and watched the sun set. The champagne, barely rocking boat, and glowing water connected to the sky by a ribbon of vibrant pink, carried Martha away to an imaginary romantic island. Jake's face morphed into George's and she melted inside.

Jake's words brought her back from her reverie. "I want you to come with me." She glanced at him and found his eyes riveted on her. Martha realized she shouldn't have had a third glass of champagne. Her head felt a little muzzy. She knew the instant Jake realized it too. "Be careful," kept flashing in her brain.

"Let's go for a sail, the Gulf is quiet and seductive this time of night," he took her hand. The warning current sizzled through her again. She looked at his pale blue eyes and saw a predator, ready to pounce. Her head instantly cleared, but she kept her smile casual. *Leave now!*

"I appreciate the offer Jake, but I'm on breakfast duty tomorrow and I need to get back. Dinner was lovely." Her eyes darted around the boat, searching for an escape. Jake sat between her and the dock, how could she get past him?

"We won't be gone long," Jake's smile didn't reach his eyes.

"Perhaps another time," Martha rose. Jake trapped her hand in his much larger one. The warning current streaked to fear, and the champagne and lobster roiled in her stomach.

"Let's go for a sail Martha, don't I deserve a little more of your time after spending a fortune on dinner and champagne?" The calm words belied the message in his eyes, "You're not leaving yet." He gripped her hand and Martha stood paralyzed as he released the stern line, tied so he could free it from the boat.

She saw no way past him, and the stern gradually drifted away from the pier. She had seconds to flee. Her mind flashed back to childhood days in Maine, when she jumped an expanse of frigid water to prevent the wind from crashing her small rowboat into the dock. Could she do it now?

Jake let her hand go and moved forward to release the bow line, Martha saw her only chance. In one swift motion, she slipped out of her sandals and stepped on the gunwale, without any thought except landing on the pier. As the bow line fell, she leaped across the four-foot expanse, falling hard on her hands and knees when she landed. She heard Jake swear and took off running, ignoring the complaints of her recently injured ankle as she crossed the soft sand towards the parking lot.

Her heart pounded in her ears, and she didn't slow down until she reached her car. Desperate to get far away from Jake, she dropped her keys.

"No!"

Martha glanced quickly back towards the boat as she swept them up, then got her car unlocked and slid behind the wheel. She repeatedly checked her rearview mirror as she drove, even though it was unlikely that Jake would follow her back to the Pelican where she wouldn't be alone. Martha careened around corners, exceeding the speed limit, but she didn't care, and she didn't relax her grip on the steering wheel until she screeched into the driveway of The Plump Pelican and slammed on the brakes. She wouldn't feel safe until she made it inside.

Martha shut the front door of the house and leaned against it, eyes closed, her chest heaving, and waited for her heart to slow. Annie came from the kitchen.

"You're back early, how—Martha, what's wrong? You all right?"

Martha took a ragged breath to regain her composure, *I'm safe.* She opened her eyes and looked at Annie. "I'm okay," she paused, "but I won't be seeing Jake again."

"Come sit down, tell me what happened." Annie put her arm around Martha's shoulders. "Start at the beginning. Do you want a glass of wine, a cup of tea?"

Martha shook her head no as she ran her fingers through her hair. She took another deep breath and told Annie everything that happened, from the moment she first arrived until her return to the Pelican.

"Oh Martha, I'm sorry I encouraged you to go out with him. We need to call the police," Annie picked up her phone.

"He didn't do anything to report to the police."

Annie put her phone back on the counter. "Well, I'm at least going to wake Danny, he'll go down there and have a few words with Jake."

"No! I don't want Danny to get into trouble. I don't think Jake will be interested in me after my reaction. I bet he'll leave in the morning."

Chapter 16

The next morning, Martha poured herself a cup of coffee and sat on the kitchen floor beside Charley. He purred as she stroked his head, then he angled it for his favorite ear scratch.

"That's it, Charley, I'm done with men. I don't want them in my life, I'm capable of surviving on my own."

"Who are you talking to?" Annie entered the kitchen.

"I'm venting to Charley, he's such a good listener, he never gives me any unwanted advice." She realized her words might offend Annie and wished she could take them back.

"Jake's just one man, they aren't all bad."

Charley climbed onto Martha's lap and she continued to stroke his head, relieved that Annie didn't sound hurt, but sympathetic.

"Tony was the first, then George, and now Jake, three strikes and you're out, and I'm done."

"Wait a minute, wait a minute, who's George? And you never did tell me what happened with Tony." Annie poured coffee for herself and sat on the floor.

"It's such a long story, Annie, and I need a glass of wine to tell it. Can we talk tonight? Right now, I desperately need a run to preserve my sanity." Martha finished her coffee and gave Charley a final scratch.

"Go for your run, I've got to get ready for the guests anyway. You can tell me all about it tonight."

When Martha went out the front door, she tripped over something on the top step. She looked down—her sandals. A shiver went down her back and her stomach clenched, but she crept upstairs to leave the shoes in her room. She didn't want Annie to worry.

※ ※ ※

Late that afternoon, Martha sat at the work bench, her head resting in her hands. Sketches and tiny models of carrousels lay strewn around her. All her designs looked flat and uninspiring, the carrousel reminded her of her day with George and the painful way it had ended. She kept telling herself to forget about George—he was married. Then she thought about his warm smile and chocolate eyes, and how much fun she'd had with him, how natural it felt. She knew it had been a fantasy, not reality, but she couldn't let the memory go.

"Everything okay, Martha?" Darcy walked into the kitchen. Startled, Martha looked up and brushed away the tears that ran down her cheeks.

"Did you decide on the carousel?" Darcy sat down on a stool beside Martha. "Are you having trouble with the design? I know how frustrating that can be."

"I can't decide on anything." Martha ran her hands through her hair. She let Darcy assume her tears resulted from frustration over her design, she didn't want to explain about George. "Nothing seems to speak to me. I thought the carousel would work—"

"But it doesn't?"

"No, not at the moment." Martha picked up a sketch then tossed it aside. How could she create a design that sparked joy when it triggered this ache inside her?

"Remind me of the requirements," Darcy studied the discarded sketch, "the design has to be something from Baltimore, right?"

"Yes."

"Forget about that for a minute. When you think of Maine, what matters to you there? What feeds your soul?"

112

"Easy," Martha said and smiled, "the ocean and lighthouses. Gram used to say, 'You can't live in a fishing village and not be connected to the lighthouses.' I think I've been to every one along the Maine coast." A picture flashed in Martha's brain and she grasped her friend's arm.

"Darcy, you're a genius. The lighthouse in Baltimore's Inner Harbor isn't like any in Maine, but it served the same purpose. I'll put it back in the ocean, where it belongs."

�֍ �֍ ✖

That evening, Martha sat in the white wicker chair on the back porch overlooking the canal, eyes closed and feet resting on the railing. The setting sun bathed the water in a rosy glow. She had put in a long day in the chocolate shop, and her shoulders and arms ached from the hours of painstaking work.

"Martha?" Annie said after she stepped onto the deck. Martha dropped her feet from the railing and smiled at Annie.

"Hey Annie, sorry, I didn't hear you come out."

"Were you sleeping or just far away?"

"Far away," Martha sighed.

"How about a glass of wine and some cheese and crackers?" Annie sat on the chair next to Martha and put the tray she carried on the small white, wooden table between them.

"Ahh, you're a life saver, what a day." Martha sampled a piece of cheese.

"Did Darcy keep you busy?"

"She has a big wedding this weekend and I made all the chocolate boxes for her to fill, then I wanted to try a few new ideas for the chocolate challenge. I'm going to recreate the round lighthouse in Baltimore's Inner Harbor. I don't even remember eating lunch."

"Sounds perfect, you love lighthouses." Annie poured them each a glass of wine. "Is that where you were when I came out?"

"No, I was thinking about my marriage and wondering what happened to me. I went to culinary school with all these plans and dreams and then I allowed myself to be talked out of them. When I met Tony, I was so dazzled I lost myself. I let him take over my life and I convinced myself that his dreams were my dreams. I remembered all the romance novels where two people annoy each other at first, but eventually realize they belong together." She'd been so naïve back then and it had taken her a long time to face reality. She took a sip of wine.

"They say love is blind, but true love isn't blind, it sees the good and the bad and loves the whole person. Lust is blind, I think Tony and I were in lust." She took a sip of her wine. "He never cared about my plans, he wanted me to mold to his life. I can be angry at him, but it was my fault too. I gave in to him and broke my promise to Gram. If I'd been more insistent, told him going back to Maine was non-negotiable, things would have been different."

"Maybe, but maybe not," Annie spoke thoughtfully, and Martha could see her weighing her answer. "Marriage isn't all hearts and flowers and happily ever after, you know. It's arguing and disagreeing and getting so mad sometimes you can hardly speak. But yes, ultimately it is caring enough to work through all those differences and wanting the best for your partner, as well as yourself." Annie set her glass on the table and took a slice of cheese.

"And it isn't hitting her," Martha whispered to herself, then shrank inside.

Annie froze, shock registering on her face. "What did you say? Tony hit you?"

"Yes, and something snapped inside me when he did. I told him to get out." She didn't mean to tell Annie, but talking about it might help her move past her embarrassment, besides, her friend deserved to know what happened, even if she thought less of Martha.

"I'm sorry Martha, I knew when Delia called that something was wrong, but she refused to tell me any details." She touched Martha's hand. "It must have been awful for you."

"I was humiliated, I didn't want to admit to anyone what happened, not even Delia. I kept avoiding her until she showed up at my door one night and wouldn't leave until I told her what had happened." Martha studied the iridescent water. "Things hadn't been good for a long time. Tony hated following someone else's orders. He had his eye on a restaurant for sale, but he needed more money. Whenever I asked him about it, he'd say he was still figuring it out. He invested with a friend in what he thought was a sure thing, only it wasn't. Then he entered the Top New Maryland Chef competition, convinced he'd win the fifty thousand dollar prize. When he lost, he was furious and blamed the judges for his failure. He already drank heavily, but it got worse and he tried to find his money solution at the casino.

"We received a letter from the bank saying we were overdrawn, and I asked him how that was possible. He didn't want to talk about it, and I needed an answer. When I refused to let it go, he exploded and slapped me. I found out later he'd taken the money from the checking account to pay his gambling debts, convinced he'd win it back before I missed it." Humiliation flooded her again. How could she have been so foolish? She should have known Tony's anger stemmed from more than his competition loss and questioned him sooner. Annie laid a comforting hand on Martha's arm, but she didn't speak.

"Delia assured me it wasn't my fault," Martha continued, "and when she asked me what I was going to do, I said, 'File for divorce.' I didn't know until that moment it was what I wanted. Then, when I received the divorce papers, I questioned my decision all over again. I thought I should be able to fix it. But our marriage was broken beyond repair, I think it was broken from the beginning." Martha sat lost in thought, and the truth of those words sank in, their marriage had been built on illusion, not reality.

The darkness triggered the solar twinkle lights, and she watched them come to life.

"Delia told me you met someone," Annie said.

"Yes, the day I signed the divorce papers." She felt again the thrill of looking up into those dark eyes for the first time, her decision to share a dragon boat had resulted in a magical day.

"What's his name?"

"George."

"And?" Annie drew out the word.

"And nothing, we spent a day being tourists together."

"Sounds like fun, what'd you do?"

"Rode the paddle boats, had ice cream, toured the train museum, and went out for pizza. We walked, and talked, and laughed." Martha swallowed past the lump in her throat. George had seemed perfect until—until he wasn't.

"Martha, what's going on? There must be more to it than that. When you described your day with him your eyes sparkled like a Christmas tree. What makes him so special?"

"I had more fun than I've had in years, actually since I married Tony, and I felt like I'd known him forever. He didn't mind my strange quirks either."

"You mean like sighing over ice cream and smelling flowers?" Annie said, and Martha laughed. "Is he drop dead gorgeous? Did he sweep you off your feet and take you to bed for fabulous sex?" Martha could tell by her teasing tone that Annie didn't believe that happened.

"No, and no! But when he smiles, his whole face changes, he has dimples on both cheeks and his eyes make you wish he would take you to bed for fabulous sex, but we didn't get that far. We didn't even get to a second date." Martha still tried to convince herself that's what she wanted.

"Why not? I thought you believed in love at first sight."

"In romance novels, not in my life, even though at first I thought he might be someone special," Martha paused. She denied believing in love at first sight, but didn't she still hope for it?

"But—"

"But he's married, I saw his wedding ring when we stopped for ice cream. I decided to pretend for one day that we were together. Then, after we had pizza, he asked to see me again, he didn't say anything about a wife. The man I spent the day with wouldn't have done that, and I left."

"Oh Martha," Annie said sympathetically, "maybe he's recently divorced too, and he didn't want to talk about it."

"Thanks for your optimism, but even I don't think that's true." She needed to accept that her dream George didn't exist. "I know it seems like I believe my life will follow the pattern of the stories I read, but that's not going to happen. I'll never see him again. I met him once, he's married, and that's the end of it. I'm not thinking about him anymore..." But she did think about him, every day.

"I'm sorry things didn't end the way you expected," Annie gave Martha's hand a sympathetic squeeze, "but there are lots of loving men in the world, someday you'll meet the right one and you won't have to pretend."

Not likely. For now, she'd pursue her dreams alone. Martha pushed thoughts of George into a mental closet and shut the door.

Chapter 17

A few weeks after the baseball game, George's phone rang. He glanced at the screen and smiled when he saw Lucy's name. "Hey, Orioles Lady, are you ready to collect on your pizza?"

"Sure am. I got a job offer today, and I thought it would be fun to celebrate with you buying me pizza and beer." George could hear the excitement in her voice, and he looked forward to celebrating with her.

"Congratulations! You can tell me about it over pizza." George kept working as he talked, it had been a hectic day and the thought of a lighthearted evening with Lucy appealed to him.

When he arrived to pick her up, George gave her a quick hug. She wore jeans and a silky pink top, and the faint smell of citrus floated around her. Although happy to see her, his body didn't instinctively respond as it had to Martha.

"Where we headed?" he said as they walked back to his car.

"There's a great pizza place called Corner Pub right near the harbor that I haven't been to for a while." George stopped walking. He didn't want to think about Martha right now, but she captured his mind. As much as he wanted to find her, he didn't have a lot of hope, being at Corner Pub would poke the open wound of missing her. What would he do if their paths crossed tonight? He hoped to see her again, but alone, when he had time to talk with her.

"Is something wrong?" Lucy said.

"No, nothing, Corner Pub it is." *Tell her*. He didn't want to talk about Martha and he'd told Lucy to choose the restaurant, so it would be rude to suggest another place. He opened the car door for her but remained quiet.

"I get the impression you're not thrilled with my choice," Lucy said, her voice no longer excited.

"No really, it's okay." Although he would have preferred a different restaurant, he'd rather not explain why. His thoughts of Martha threatened to intrude on Lucy's celebration. He started the car and pulled into the street.

"Are you sure?" Lucy rested her hand on his. Her gentle touch reminded him to get over himself and enjoy the evening.

"I'm sure. They've got great pizza and beer." George briefly turned and smiled at her and the frown on Lucy's face relaxed and so did George.

"Tell me about your job," George said after they found a table at the pub.

"It's in the Johns Hopkins pediatric cardiology unit," Lucy said. "I guess my experience in hospitals around the country paid off. I'm excited about the job, and now I won't have to bounce from place to place every six months. I found the ideal apartment on Butchers Hill. You've got to come see it when I get settled." George absorbed Lucy's contagious enthusiasm and tucked thoughts of Martha to the recesses of his mind. They chatted while they ate, then Lucy took the last bite of her pizza and set her plate aside.

"Yummy, just like I remember," she said. "How's your new job going?"

"Challenging, I'm glad Nick persuaded me to come and see the mills, but right now I can't wait to move into my new house. I heard from the realtor today, and I'm meeting with the owner next week."

"Does the house need a lot of work?" George appreciated her interest and didn't need any encouragement to talk about the house.

"I want to update the kitchen and bathroom, but mostly it will be sanding and refinishing. I can feel the family memories there, so I know I made the right choice. I can't wait until it's officially mine, but while I'm waiting for the sale to go through, I decided to train for the Baltimore marathon. I asked Nick if he wanted to run with me, and he said, 'Run twenty-six miles all at once, are you nuts? That's twenty-six days of running as far as I'm concerned.'"

Lucy laughed. "Nick and I are on the same page. But I'll come cheer you on."

"Thanks, it always helps to have friends supporting you, especially when you feel like you can't take another step."

George caught Lucy studying him, a thoughtful expression on her face. He felt like she could read his mind. Did she sense another woman lurking in his heart? He liked Lucy and wanted to focus on her, so he changed the direction of their conversation.

"Do you need any help moving?"

"Thanks for offering, but it's only my clothes and a few personal items. I move so often I've rented furnished apartments until now. Of course, I'll be living in an empty space until I go furniture shopping." Their server brought the check and after George paid, he took Lucy home.

"Thanks for a fun evening, George. I got to celebrate my new job precisely the way I wanted, and you can consider your gambling debt paid," Lucy's eyes twinkled with humor as she spoke, and George laughed.

"Glad to hear it, I had fun too. I'll call you when I get things sorted on the house." He hugged her and said, "Good luck with your new job and let me know if you decide you need some help moving."

❋ ❋ ❋

George knocked on the door of the yellow house and excitement thrummed in his chest. Once he bought the house, he could finally move out of his hotel room. He couldn't think of any reason the Taylors wouldn't sell it to him, but life didn't always need a reason for the unexpected. A woman with short, white hair and the deepest blue eyes he'd ever seen opened the door.

"You must be George," she smiled in welcome. "I'm Edith. I made some iced tea, would you like some?" Warmth filled her voice, and the tension George hadn't realized he felt melted away.

120

He followed her to the kitchen and his nose told him she had made more than iced tea. The kitchen table held a plate of chocolate chip cookies, and Tanya sat holding a half-eaten one in her hand.

"Hi George, wait till you taste these, they're delicious."

"It may sound silly, but I wanted to bake once more in my old kitchen before I packed everything away." Edith looked around as she spoke, a faraway look in her eyes, then sat at the table with Tanya.

"Doesn't sound silly at all," George pulled out a chair. "Tanya told me you raised your family here. This house must hold lots of cherished memories."

"It does." She poured a glass of iced tea for George. "We bought it soon after we were married and part of me hates to leave, but my husband isn't well, and the house is too big and the winters too cold for us to stay. Tell me George, why do you want to buy our house?"

"The first time I saw the house, I felt like I'd come home." He explained his immediate reaction, hoping Edith would think he'd be the ideal buyer. "It reminds me of houses in New England, where I grew up. I can tell it needs some attention, but I love restoring old homes. My dad's a carpenter and he taught me to look beyond the wear or disrepair and see the natural beauty."

"What are your plans for it?" Edith said, with concern. "Tanya tells me you're an architect, do you want to gut it and start again?" George remembered Tanya mentioning some buyers intended to do that, and he understood her hesitation.

"No, absolutely not. The house is designed for a family, the rooms are cozy and warm, which I won't change. I'll keep its character in mind with everything I do. The structure is sound, but it does need fresh paint, and I want to update the bathrooms and kitchen."

"What about the floors, will you leave them as they are?" George saw a glimmer of challenge, was this her test of his sincerity? Had the Taylors painted all the floors brown, or did she think the same thing he did about them? He didn't want to offend her, but he had to be honest.

"I'd strip all the floors and restore the natural wood, the bannister too."

"Oh good, anyone who cares about the house would want to refinish the floors, they were painted when we bought it, and we always planned to refinish them. When our children were young, we were too busy and too broke to do anything to them. Over the years, they became a part of our home's personality, and we decided to leave them alone. If you're willing to put that much effort in, you must plan to stay. Are you married?"

George hoped his lack of a wife wouldn't disqualify him as a buyer, but he didn't want to get into his life story, so he said, "My wife died."

"Oh, I'm sorry," she sounded as if she regretted asking the question.

"George will take good care of your house. He'll restore it and make it his own." Tanya's comment eased the uncomfortable moment.

"But do you think you'll stay, live here, be part of the neighborhood? Or do you want to fix it and flip it?" George sensed her need for reassurance. So many of her family memories lived here, he understood why she wouldn't relinquish it without asking every question she thought necessary to make sure it would be well-loved.

"I recently began a new job in Baltimore, I don't plan on going anywhere, and I want to make this my home." He also hoped he wouldn't be living here alone, but didn't say it, he had the feeling Edith wouldn't hesitate to ask for more details.

"I think our home will be safe with you, George," she smiled and offered her hand for him to shake.

George barely contained an internal *Yes!* But he shook her hand and said, "Terrific, I can't tell you how thrilled I am!"

"I hope you'll be as happy raising your family here as John and I were," Edith turned to Tanya. "Do you have any papers for us to sign, Tanya?"

When they finished, she walked with him to the front porch. "This is your home now George, take good care." He saw tears in her eyes and leaned down to hug her. Even though happiness engulfed him, he could feel Edith's sorrow over leaving her longtime home and his throat thickened. He wanted to comfort her.

"I will Edith, thank you for trusting me, I promise you won't be sorry." He returned to his car, looked back at the house and considered his good fortune. He had a challenging job, the yellow house belonged to him, and someday—maybe he'd have a family too.

✖ ✖ ✖

George moved into the yellow house and began the restoration work. A call from Lucy interrupted a relaxing Friday night of sanding.

"Hi George, I'm sorry to call at the last minute, but I've had a terrible week, would you be willing to meet me for dinner?" She sounded so forlorn he couldn't refuse, and his evening plans faded away.

"One of my newborn patients needs surgery tomorrow." She waited until they'd arrived at the restaurant and ordered burgers. "I can usually keep my perspective, but the parents tried so long to have this baby, and now—my heart aches for them." George reached across the table and rested his hand on hers. He thought about how much he wanted children and tried to imagine how painful and frightening it would be to see your child face major surgery right after birth.

"I don't know how you do what you do, it must be so sad."

"It is sad sometimes, but more often it's rewarding, and being able to help is an incredible gift." George's mind flashed back to Elaine and their fights over having children. They hadn't discussed it before they were married, and he'd assumed she wanted children someday as much as he did. After many arguments about her returning to work, it became clear Elaine didn't want children at all.

"You okay, George?" Lucy said, her concern now focused on him. "I'm sorry I brought my dismal conversation to dinner."

"No apologies needed," George squeezed her hand. "I let my mind wander where it shouldn't go."

"I asked you to rescue me from my troubling thoughts, now it's your turn. What's bothering you?" Lucy needed comfort for her heartache, not a sob story about his past issues.

When he hesitated, she said, "Please, it will take my mind off this family." He might as well tell her. Mandy probably had said something already.

"My wife Elaine and I fought about having children. Although our arguments began with a difference of opinion over how to raise them, she didn't want a family and I did. We had a huge fight right before she left for work one morning. On the way home, her car went off the road and she died in the crash."

Even after all this time those memories tore him apart. He swiped his hand over his face then took a drink of his beer, in an attempt to regain his composure.

"Oh, how awful, I'm so sorry." George heard such compassion in her voice, he felt as if she had touched him.

"I didn't mean to dump my baggage on you." He felt guilty for even mentioning Elaine. "You have enough to worry about tonight."

"I think we both need cheering up," Lucy grabbed his hand, "let's go to Vaccaro's, it's my favorite place for ice cream."

"Sounds good to me." George smiled at Lucy. When they entered the familiar shop, thoughts of Martha and their day together surged through him again. He worked hard to keep those thoughts closeted in his mind, but sometimes they swept over him in a whoosh of melancholy. However, he kept the mood light for the remainder of the evening for Lucy's sake.

The yellow house felt unusually empty that night, and George missed its friendly warmth. Loneliness wrapped around him, strangling him and the hope he had when he bought it. He closed his eyes and tried to picture Lucy in the house, he felt the ease they enjoyed, but the picture he saw had Martha serving dinner with him, entertaining Lucy and her faceless husband. As much as he enjoyed Lucy's company, she would never ignite the fire inside him that Martha did.

George decided to call Lucy the next morning, she deserved to know how he felt, even if he didn't mention Martha. He punched in her phone number, intending to invite her for coffee, and tension coursed through him while he waited for her to answer. He didn't know what to say.

"Hey George, I thought you'd be hard at work on your house."

"I'm taking a break, want to meet me for coffee? There's something I need to tell you."

"I know George," Lucy said, "we don't have to meet."

"What do you mean?"

"I know what you're going to say."

"You do? How do you know?" Had he said something to imply he didn't want to be romantically involved?

"You're one of the nicest guys I've ever met, I enjoy the time we spend together, and I will always want you for my friend. I'd be happy if we were next door neighbors and our kids grew up together." Lucy paused as if searching for the right words. "But we won't be walking hand in hand into a sunset. I get it, and it's okay, I feel the same way. I keep waiting for you to tell me there's someone else, because I know in my bones there is."

Wow! George slumped into a nearby chair. Relief flooded him, Lucy didn't want more than friendship either, but her words caught him off guard and left him speechless. He finally found his voice.

"Thanks for understanding, and I'm glad we can stay friends." He didn't try to explain about Martha, he struggled to comprehend his own feelings.

Chapter 18

Martha woke to the sound of rain pounding on the porch roof and tried to hang on to the dream that swirled in her mind. She closed her eyes, searched back in her brain and found her chocolate design like a three-dimensional picture, it shimmered for a few seconds, and then disappeared. She switched on a light, and sketched madly from memory, aware that it would be an engineering feat, as well as the most challenging chocolate work she had ever done. Daylight seeped through the curtains, and she looked down at what she'd drawn, amazed at the detail she'd captured.

The rain streamed from the gutters, so she decided to change the order of her day and packed her running clothes before heading downstairs. No guests were at the bed and breakfast this morning, but Annie was already up making coffee.

"I thought you were going to sleep in this morning." Martha came into the kitchen.

"I was, but the rain was so loud it woke me. I figured I could get caught up on paperwork. You're not planning to run in this monsoon, are you?"

"No, but it's supposed to be over later today. If you don't need me, I thought I'd go to the chocolate shop now. When it clears, I can run in Pensacola. I need a change of scenery."

"No problem, everything's ready for the guests checking in later. I'm going to keep at the paperwork, it's my least favorite part of this job. Want some breakfast before you go?"

"Don't worry about me, I'll grab coffee and take a yogurt with me." Martha donned a rain jacket and ran through the downpour. Her usual half-hour drive stretched to over an hour as she crawled along flooded roads, worried her car would stall whenever she drove through a lake-sized puddle.

She filled orders for Darcy until after lunch, when incredibly, the sun appeared, and the puddles shrank. When she finished, Martha changed into her running clothes. The meticulous work Darcy's order required left no room for Martha's mind to wander. She needed to revive both her energy and her creative juices before working on her own chocolate project. Although she loved the design she'd created, transforming it into chocolate would take untold hours of work, and she had to be ready in two months. She needed a plan.

She ran along Garden Street to Spring Street, running through the old residential area of North Hill, a route she had recently discovered. Every one of the sprawling old houses had a porch with a swing swaying in the breeze, like the one at Gram's house. They seemed so welcoming and reminded her of the hours she'd spent there with Gram. Although she enjoyed her runs along the water in Perdido Key, this route offered more variety, as well as more hills. The marathon course in Baltimore wouldn't be flat. As she ran, her mind drifted to her difficult first days in Baltimore. Tony had landed a sous chef position and told her he'd find a job for her too, but she wanted to find one herself.

She had left the house in the morning determined not to come home until she found a job. After visiting several bakeries without success, her spirits fell. She'd been counting on her portfolio to open doors that weren't budging. Then she discovered a tiny café called Sweet Selections. The small white tables circled by blue and yellow chairs were cheerful and inviting, and pictures of local farmers who supplied many of the ingredients lined the walls. The coffee beans were from Baltimore Joe, a local roaster, and the combination of brewing coffee and baking pastry smelled like home. She had closed her eyes and imagined she was in Gram's café on a cold Maine morning.

When she opened them, she saw a friendly face studying her from behind the counter.

"I wondered if you were okay, but then I saw you smile, and decided if you fainted it would be from pleasure."

"It smells like my grandmother's bakery in Maine," Martha was unfazed by the observation of her aroma trance, "and I was imagining myself there on a winter morning."

"Those sound like happy memories. What can I get you so you can taste your memories too?"

"I need coffee, but your cinnamon rolls look amazing. I don't think I can resist. My grandmother also makes them, and I used to help her."

"Excellent choice, would you like it warm?" The woman scooped a roll onto a waiting plate.

"Yes please. Have you been here long?" Martha looked around while she waited. "It seems quiet."

"We've been open a year next month. After a rush for coffee and pastry in the morning, there's usually a lull before lunchtime, when we serve soups and sandwiches. I come in early to bake and help cover the counter when it's busy, then work on special order cakes in the afternoon."

"Wow, that's a busy schedule. I'm Martha Coutu," she reached her hand over the counter.

"Sarah Evans, nice to meet you." She shook Martha's outstretched hand.

"I'm a recent culinary school graduate and new to Baltimore. Would you be interested in hiring a pastry chef for wedding cakes?" Martha waited, hoping her instincts were right.

"I'm guessing you have pictures of your work with you," Sarah indicated the portfolio under Martha's arm. Martha nodded her head yes.

"Well, let's take a look."

When Martha walked out the door of Sweet Selections, she had a job. Before long, her reputation had spread, not only were her wedding cakes one of a kind, but she had begun to offer chocolate creations as well, bringing added business to the bakery and more orders than she could fill. When she received the divorce papers, she'd left Sarah in the lurch, like she'd left Gram.

Martha ran up one street and down the next, her feet slapping and splashing on the wet sidewalks. Guilt ran with her, and she couldn't hide from the pattern of behavior it painted in her mind. She had to find a way to redeem herself to Gram and to Sarah. She ran around the park on Russet, and then south on Barcelona. By the time she returned to the chocolate shop, she'd made temporary peace with herself, and she'd developed a strategy to begin the design work she'd sketched that morning. The remainder of the day vanished while she immersed herself in translating her lighthouse dream to chocolate reality.

The next morning Martha came downstairs ready to run before the heat set in. She saw a light glowing beneath the door to Annie's office. When she heard sobs, she paused. Should she intrude? She remembered the flash of sadness she'd seen on Annie's face when she first arrived. She'd seen a faraway look in her friend's eyes on more than one occasion, but Martha had been too engrossed in her own problems to ask Annie about hers. She'd ask now. Martha knocked softly, and without waiting for a response, she opened the door.

"Annie, you okay?"

Annie started and rubbed her hands over her face. "Just feeling sorry for myself, but I'll be fine." Martha closed the door and came over, sinking down in front of her friend.

"What's wrong?"

"I was convinced I was pregnant, but I'm not." Annie looked down and clutched the tissue in her hands. Annie's despair twisted inside Martha, but she didn't speak, sensing Annie had more to say.

"We've been trying for two years to have a baby, we're both so busy and stressed, but I thought some time away would solve the problem. When you watched over the Pelican for us, we had a romantic, stress-free weekend. I was sure this time I wouldn't be disappointed. I didn't realize I'd done such a good job convincing myself, until I discovered this morning that nothing has changed."

129

"Annie, I'm so sorry, I had no idea you were struggling with this." Martha remembered Delia's excitement when she first thought she was pregnant and imagined how upset she would have been if it hadn't happened after all. Annie would be a devoted mother and Martha felt disappointed for her, but she couldn't do anything to make this better, so she settled for giving Annie a hug.

"If you want to get away again, let me know. I'll take care of the Pelican for you."

"Thanks Martha, I'll keep that in mind, but we're crazy busy for the next few weeks."

"The offer stands no matter how busy it is, but for now, I'll go make some coffee. Do you want anything?"

"No thanks, I'll be out in a few minutes."

Martha went to make coffee and decided to warm a muffin for Annie. She saw a long white envelope addressed to her on the kitchen counter. Martha made coffee then opened the letter and sighed. It confirmed what she already knew, she had to return to Baltimore soon.

When Annie joined her, Martha handed her a cup of coffee and said, "I have to face the fact that I need to make plans to return to Baltimore in a couple of weeks."

"So soon?" She should have told Annie before, but then she couldn't continue to live in her world of denial.

"Part of the divorce agreement was that the house would be sold, and Tony and I would share the profits. Except it turns out there's a second mortgage, so there won't be any profits. I don't know how he managed without telling me. The house didn't go on the market until the divorce became final in July. It gave us both time to find another place to live, except I came here instead. She tossed the letter on the counter and gazed out the glass doors.

"When I decided to stay, I told my lawyer to let me know when it sold, and I'd come back and sort everything out. He called soon after the house went on the market and told me he'd found a buyer, pending the sale of their house, but he didn't think it would go through before autumn. Turns out things moved faster than he expected, and this letter verifies what he told me when he called again a couple weeks ago. They want to close at the end of the month."

"Why didn't you say anything?" Annie sounded as distressed as Martha anticipated.

"I guess I didn't want to believe I'd have to return to Baltimore soon. When I left, I thought I'd take a week or two, sort myself out, then go back, find a new place to live and get the house ready to be sold. But when I got here, I realized how much I needed time and space to heal. I'm grateful you gave me that luxury." She'd lived in a safe bubble for the past few months. But if she wanted to achieve her dreams, she needed to go back and face reality, prove to herself she could be independent.

"I don't want you to leave," Annie walked over and placed her arm around Martha's shoulders. "I've enjoyed your company as much as your help."

"I've loved being here Annie, but I have to go back. I have to pack all my things, find another place to live and somewhere to prepare for the chocolate challenge, and I need to continue to train for the marathon." Martha draped her arm around Annie—she hated the thought of leaving her friend.

"What will you do? Where will you live?"

"I don't know." Martha paced around the kitchen and ran her hands through her hair. "But I know I have to go back and finish what I started."

"Why don't you go to Baltimore for the marathon and the chocolate challenge, then come live in Pensacola? You and Darcy can be partners, and you and I can be partners. Hasn't it worked out well? I'd love to get away more often, and you're a born innkeeper."

"Oh Annie, there's a part of me that's saying 'Yes, yes, do it, it's been perfect here.'" She and Annie had reconnected, and she'd miss seeing her every day. "Well, close to perfect," she remembered the distressing encounter with Jake. "But I've realized something during these summer months. I know that as much as I've loved being here with you, Perdido Key will never be home. I need to go to Maine, I need to see Gram, and I want to stay there for a while. I miss the rocky coast and the cold salt air, even the snow."

Annie shook her head, "You know you're weird, just plain weird?"

Martha laughed; her friend's comment released the clutching tension in her body. "I know, who in her right mind would choose a Maine winter over a Florida one? It's more than that, Annie. I need to see Gram and tell her the whole story, instead of skirting the truth. I told her I came to Pensacola because you needed help at the bed and breakfast. It's true, you did need help, but that's not why I came. I came because I needed help."

Chapter 19

Later that day, Martha returned to the chocolate shop. She had to let Darcy know about leaving soon, and she wanted to ask for her help at the chocolate challenge. The first thought left a lead sinker of regret in her stomach and the second released twitchy butterflies. How could she persuade Darcy to leave the Dolphin for a week? She found her in the back, removing dark chocolate surfboards from their molds.

"Hey Darcy."

"Hey, Martha, I thought you weren't coming in until this afternoon, but as long as you're here, would you help me with these? I got a rush order for a surfing-themed bridal shower, and I need to have a hundred favors ready by tonight."

"Sure." Martha washed her hands and grabbed a clean apron and gloves, then joined Darcy at the work table. This wasn't the best time to talk, but her nerves couldn't stand waiting any longer. She wanted Darcy to have time to make the chocolate challenge work. Martha chewed on her lip and placed a surfboard on the waiting tray.

Her words tumbled out in a rush. "I have to go back to Baltimore."

"But not till after Labor Day, right?" Darcy continued to focus on her meticulous task.

"No, in a couple of weeks."

"But you'll be back, right? I have that huge wedding in late September, I don't know how I'll do it without you." She stopped working and looked at Martha.

"I never intended to stay permanently." Martha hated to let Darcy down, and guilt smothered her excitement about asking for Darcy's help at the chocolate challenge. "I told you that in the beginning."

"I know, I know, but we work well together, you've added so much to the shop, and you hadn't mentioned returning to Baltimore. I guess it was wishful thinking that you'd decide to stay." She sounded resigned, and although Martha felt flattered that Darcy relied on her, it also made it harder to leave. She and Darcy worked in an easy rhythm, which she'd miss, but even before the house sold, she had planned to leave by Labor Day.

"I didn't think our house would sell so quickly, but now we have an impatient buyer and things have gone on fast forward. I have things to resolve in Baltimore." She would have liked to tell Darcy that she'd come back as soon as she moved her things out of the house, but she also had a commitment to Sarah that had been niggling at her.

"Why can't you go to Baltimore and sort things out, then come back here?"

Martha chuckled, in spite of her distress. "Have you been talking to Annie? She suggested I do the same thing."

"No," Darcy shook her head, "we both appreciate all you do, and having you here has been a treat. You're incredibly talented, Martha, neither one of us wants to lose you."

"I'm sorry Darcy, but it makes more sense for me to stay in Baltimore. I'll be less stressed if I focus on my chocolate design there, rather than going back and forth to Pensacola. I need to run some of the hills on the marathon course, otherwise I'll never be able to finish, plus I have fall wedding cakes ordered."

"I know you're right, but boy am I going to miss you." She resumed moving surfboards from their molds.

"I'll miss you too, but I have a proposal for you. I know it's a lot to ask, but—" Martha paused and took a deep breath "—would you consider working with me on the chocolate challenge? We're allowed one helper to work with us. I can't think of anybody I'd rather have there than you. You're the most talented chocolatier I know."

"Wow!" A surprised smile lit Darcy's face. "That's quite an honor, but I don't know, how long would I have to be gone?"

"We can do most of the planning over the phone or on the computer. It would help if you could come at least a few days, or a week, before, so we can work out the final details and decide who's going to do what."

"The end of October's the beginning of the busy season. Whew." Martha could almost see the idea tumbling in Darcy's mind. "I'd love to say yes on the spot, but—"

"But maybe?" Martha said.

"All right, maybe, let me think about it, and see if I can figure out a way to keep the chocolate shop open and get away."

"When was the last time you took a break from the Dolphin since you opened?" She didn't want to pressure Darcy, but she couldn't imagine working with anyone else, and Darcy wouldn't buckle under the stress of competition.

"Never," Darcy said.

"Well, consider this a vacation, albeit a working one. It'll be fun, and a challenge."

Chapter 20

George turned off the table saw and took a drink of his coffee, now cold and flecked with sawdust. He heard a knock through the lingering hum in his ears and wondered who it could be, since he hadn't met any of his neighbors yet. When he opened the front door, a petite woman with short, curly, black hair was descending the porch steps.

"Can I help you?"

"Hi." At the sound of his voice she spun around. "I didn't think you heard my knock, I tried the doorbell first, but decided it didn't penetrate the background buzzing."

"Actually, the doorbell doesn't work, and I didn't hear your knock until I killed the saw. Sorry it took me so long."

She came back up the stairs and offered one hand while balancing a towel covered plate in the other. "I'm Delia Walsh, we're neighbors. I made you these cookies to welcome you to the neighborhood." She held out the plate. He thought of his mom, she liked to greet new neighbors with home-made cookies or bread.

"George Henderson, and thank you. Smells delicious, chocolate chip?"

"Sort of, they're my kids' favorite, even though I don't tell them about the oatmeal, raisins, and whole wheat flour I sneak in. They think chocolate chip cookies are supposed to be like this." George removed a cookie from beneath the towel.

"Works for me," he took a large bite. "Wow! Your kids are right, I think these are my new favorite too."

"We live in that monstrous purple Victorian next door, with bikes spilling off the porch and five hundred children playing on the swing set most afternoons."

George laughed. "I've seen the kids, but I didn't realize there were five hundred."

"Well, maybe not, but it seems that way sometimes, even when it's only my four. The neighborhood kids have decided it's the best game in town, so they all like to congregate in our yard."

"If you're feeding them these cookies, I know why." He took another bite.

"I wondered who had bought this house," Delia looked around the porch. "It's been lonely since the Taylors moved to Florida, it needed someone to make it happy again. I've seen your car at night, so I assume you live here and aren't a hired contractor."

"I'm both. I live here and I'm my own contractor." George had forgotten what it was like to live in a neighborhood where everyone knew what was happening in everyone else's life. It didn't bother him, the town where he grew up had been that way too, and he found it a welcome change from the more impersonal nature of condo and apartment living.

"Would you like to come in? As long as you don't mind sawdust, things are kind of a mess."

"Thanks, another time, Maura and Colin are napping in their car seats, I left the car running and I need to pick up Patrick and Deirdre." Delia walked to the stairs, then stopped.

"I almost forgot the main reason I came by. I wanted to invite you to our annual block party. Actually, it's the whole neighborhood, our yards all run together because no one has put up a big fence. Anyway, the party is two weeks from Saturday, unless it rains. We usually start around four. People leave when their children are ready for bed, and those who don't have any are welcome to stay as long as they want. The kids run around, the grown-ups play cornhole or volleyball, depending on who's there. Do you have kids?

Mine hope you do, even though we haven't seen any."

"Sorry, no kids." Did he want to go to a family backyard party by himself? It might be fun, and it would be an easy way to meet everyone in the neighborhood.

"Wife?" Delia said and George chuckled. Somehow she managed to make the question sound interested, not nosy.

"No wife either," he thought sadly of his missed opportunity with Martha, but he continued to smile. "I hope that doesn't make me an outcast in the neighborhood."

"Not at all, we're a mixed bunch of transplants here, some married some not. Agnes and Everett Townsend are the only originals. They raised their family here, but now their children have all grown and moved away. You'll see them out walking hand in hand, which gives the rest of us hope. They've been married for sixty years." Delia bubbled with friendliness and George liked her immediately.

"I better get going," Delia descended the steps and when she reached the car she waved. "I hope you can come to the party."

Chapter 21

Martha left Pensacola in a curl of smoky dawn that evolved into blazing orange as she drove into the day. Her emotions simmered in a stew of confusion. She would miss Annie and Darcy terribly, and although she wanted to complete the marathon and the chocolate challenge, part of her dreaded going back to Baltimore. Then she thought of returning to Maine to see Gram, and her heart smiled.

"I can't wait to get back to Maine, Charley. I'll help Gram in the bakery like I promised. Maybe she'll want to expand the café, and we can serve lunch as well as coffee and pastries." Charley lifted his head and blinked his eyes, then without further comment he returned to his purring nap.

Martha's thoughts drifted from Maine to Baltimore, she would have to pack all her things and find another place to live. Whatever wouldn't fit in a small apartment, she'd sell or put in storage. As she neared Baltimore, she thought of the chocolate challenge, and her stomach tightened. She clenched the steering wheel, and her heart pounded in her chest. Her return made the competition real. If she felt this nervous now, what would she do when the actual day arrived?

Martha aimed her mind down a different path. The house she and Tony had bought together would soon belong to someone else. She expected to feel a sense of loss, but the relief surprised her. Anger and loneliness had ousted the happy memories, and she realized she would be glad to move on.

She'd failed at marriage and that hurt. It seemed she wasn't cut out to share her life with anyone. "Chin up, Buttercup," Gram used to say, get over it and keep going. *Just as well George is married.* That avenue was closed, even if part of her wished it weren't.

Martha arrived at her house in Federal Hill and sat in the car, surveying the area. She rolled down the windows and breathed in the familiar August scent of heat and humidity; it felt like Pensacola, but without the Gulf breeze and without Annie's comforting presence, which she missed already. She stepped from the car and studied the tiny white townhouse squeezed between two larger brick ones. She had always thought of it as the filling in the sandwich, which was the best part, but this sandwich had gone moldy with neglect and she would be happy to cast it out of her life. Martha unlocked the front door and deposited Charley on the floor.

"Here you go Charley, you can stretch your legs and go exploring. This will be home for at least a few days, until I can get us packed and ready to move. I wish I knew where." Normally Charley explored his surroundings extensively, trotting from room to room, tail held high, sniffing as he went. Clearly the Baltimore house did not pass muster with him; he slunk from room to room, hissing as he went, tail dragging on the floor. He stopped outside the door of the extra bedroom Tony had claimed as his office. He wouldn't go in, but stood there with his tail now plumed to twice its normal size, and twitching a warning.

"Don't worry, Charley, he isn't here. I should've had you with me in culinary school, my life would have been different." Martha brought her few possessions in from the car, then wandered through the vacant rooms. Tony's personal things were gone, along with his desk and the TV. He must have come back after she left. The blinds were all closed, and the house felt cold and hollow despite the heat outside. Martha shivered, gathered Charley into her arms, and settled on the couch. She took her phone from her pocket and punched in Delia's number.

The phone kept ringing, Martha opened her mouth to leave a message, and Delia's breathless voice said, "Hello."

"Hey Delia, I'm back from Florida."

"Martha, I'm so glad to hear your voice, hold on while I sort the kids and groceries." Martha heard scuffling noises in the background and then the sound of the TV. "When can you come and visit?" Delia said. "There's a new man in the neighborhood I want you to meet. He's perfect for you."

"I've been back less than an hour. Once I get some sleep, I have to find an apartment, get the house ready for the closing, and arrange a place to work on my chocolate design." Martha scratched Charley's head. "Forgive me if I don't come see you right away, I wanted to say, hi and let you know I'm here."

"All right, I'm sorry, I do get carried away sometimes, but I miss you." Delia sounded as if someone popped her balloon, and Martha regretted her abrupt words.

"I miss you too," she yawned and rubbed her hand over her face, fatigue from her long drive tucked around her. "Do you want to meet for dinner, the two of us, so we can catch up?" She loved being with Delia's four children, but quiet conversation never happened.

"Sounds great, I'm ready for a girls' night out. And you can come to our block party in two weeks, I invited my neighbor."

"I'll call you when I get the house sorted, but I don't have any interest in meeting a man right now." Martha stretched out on the couch and closed her eyes.

"Oh, all right," Delia gave an exaggerated sigh.

"Kiss the kids and Jimmy for me, I'll call when I can." Martha ended the call and smiled to herself.

The next morning Martha went to see Sarah, afraid she would be upset after Martha's abrupt departure the previous spring. She was pleasantly surprised when Sarah greeted her with a hug and an invitation to resume her work at the bakery. Martha asked if she could practice her design for the chocolate challenge there too.

"Of course. We'll be famous when you win."

"Thanks for the vote of confidence. I hope I live up to your expectations." Martha had explained to Sarah that Darcy would be helping her at the challenge, and arriving a week before so they could finalize the details.

"Win or not, I'm glad you're back. I missed you, and so did our customers."

"I'm sorry Sarah, I had no intention of staying in Florida for that long, but I couldn't face coming back any sooner."

"I knew you were struggling with the divorce, and the day you brought me that cake to taste, you were a wreck. I wasn't surprised you needed some time away."

Martha thought back to the day she'd crawled out of bed three days after receiving the divorce papers, and remembered the appointment she had with a future bride. She'd baked a sample layer of parsnip chai pound cake, because the bride wanted flavors that would remind her of autumn in New England. Martha knew in her head the experimental recipe would be delectable, but her stomach had felt as if fire ants crawled inside and she couldn't think about taking a bite. She'd cut a generous slice of the warm, fragrant cake, grabbed a container of ginger cream cheese frosting, yanked a hat down over her hair, and run to the bakery.

"Try this for me," Martha had thrust the cake towards Sarah without preempt. She couldn't stand still while she waited, her insides burned.

"Are you all right?" Sarah had placed the cake and frosting on the counter.

Martha shook her head no, "Sarah try it, please." She fidgeted from one foot to another. Sarah had tasted the cake first, then added a dollop of the cream cheese icing and spread it around with her fork, she sampled a bite with both. She'd closed her eyes and sighed.

"Martha, this is genius, and I will buy the recipe from you." She hadn't been back to Sweet Selections since, but now she resolved to honor her commitment.

Fall

Chapter 22

The morning of the block party, George started sanding right after breakfast. He wanted to finish the hardwood floor in the living room. He intended to skip the party, which had been delayed several weeks by rain, and work through the evening. Late in the afternoon, the sounds of laughter and children's delighted squeals drifted in the open windows and tugged at him. He'd finished sanding and decided the polyurethane could wait for another day. He wanted to meet more of his neighbors. After a hot shower, he found his favorite myrtle wood salad bowl tucked away in a box in the back room. He gave it a quick wash and dumped in the pre-packaged ingredients he had bought at Wegman's the night before. Grabbing a bottle of wine, he crossed to Delia's yard through a break in the low picket fence.

George followed the noise to the backyard where Delia ran back and forth between the house and the picnic table, keeping up a steady stream of conversation as she did.

"George, I'm so glad you decided to come," Delia set a bowl of fruit on the table. "You didn't have to bring any food."

"It's not exactly gourmet fare, but my kitchen's not ready for that yet. I figured every cookout can use an extra salad and a bottle of wine, though they can't begin to compete with your chocolate chip cookies."

Delia smiled with pleasure. "Come meet my husband, he's the grill

145

master." A tall, lanky man stood beside a large round grill and settled an electric starter in a bed of charcoal. "Jimmy, this is our neighbor, George." The two men shook hands. "I'm going to introduce him to everyone."

She took George's arm and led him away. "We'll start with our resident grandparents Agnes and Everett, and don't be put off by their imposing stance. Agnes always delivers a hot meal to any family with a new baby, and Everett's teasing has cured more than one case of the afternoon crankys."

George chatted with the older couple, and he and Everett compared the prospects for the Ravens and the Patriots reaching the Super Bowl. Jimmy came over to join them, "Let's get a volleyball game going. Everett, will you keep score?" They soon had two teams with adults and kids on both sides and played until Jimmy declared the grill ready to cook.

Later, the party grew quiet when the families with children disappeared, and George and a few others guests remained. Those that lingered helped with the cleanup, despite Delia's assurance that they didn't need to.

George had found his neighbors so friendly, for a while he forgot he was alone. Although not everyone was married, all the other singles had partners, and loneliness curled inside him despite the warm welcome he'd received. He made a last trip to the recycling bin in the garage, then looked across the yard to his house. He had left the porch light on and it shed a warm glow over the front door. He imagined what it would be like if he had someone special in his life, and they went home together. Longing consumed him, as it often did whenever his thoughts wandered to Martha.

Delia came over beside him. "I hoped to convince a friend of mine to come tonight, but she got tied up with work, and couldn't make it. I think you two would be great together."

"Thanks Delia, but I'm not interested in meeting anyone else." He didn't want another blind date, no matter how great she might be.

"Ohh, so you do have someone waiting in the wings. I figured you must be working hard to finish that house for someone special." Delia sounded pleased with herself for reaching this conclusion. "What's her name?"

George stood with his hands in his pockets, one toe scuffing at the random blades of grass growing through the driveway. Did he really want to have this conversation? Would Delia think he was crazy?

"I only know her first name."

"Okay, this is way too intriguing not to hear the whole story. Come inside and I'll make some coffee." George didn't pour out his heart to strangers, but for some reason he wanted to tell Delia about Martha. Maybe if he gave voice to the story, he would see how ridiculous his dream was and stop thinking about her.

"No coffee for me," George followed Delia into the kitchen.

"How about a beer or some wine?"

"Beer would be good, thanks." Delia took two beers from the refrigerator, gave one to George and sat at the kitchen table. Jimmy came into the kitchen and put his arm around Delia's shoulders. "Hey Babe, George, I'm going to go check on the kids. You all set?"

"I'm good," Delia looped her arm around him, "George is going to tell me about a mystery woman."

Jimmy grinned at George before he left the kitchen, "Watch out, Delia's in matchmaking mode, be prepared."

"Okay, begin at the beginning," Delia poured her beer into a glass. "How long have you known this nameless woman?"

"I met her by chance last April. We were both in line to ride the dragon paddle boats and we struck up a conversation. One thing led to another and we spent the day together."

"Was it love at first sight?" Delia leaned forward and clasped her hands under her chin, clearly intrigued by George's story.

"I don't know about that, but it was the best day I've ever had."

"So, what happened, why don't you know her name?"

"I screwed up dating 101. I had my wedding ring on, and I didn't explain that my wife had died. I didn't tell her anything about it. We exchanged first names and had fun being tourists together. At the end of the day, I told her I'd like to see her again, but she had seen my ring and said one day was fine, but she didn't date married men. Then she ran off and I didn't get to tell her why I wore the ring or ask her for her phone number."

"Didn't you follow her?" Delia frowned, as if she couldn't believe he let her walk away.

"I tried, but I got hung up leaving the restaurant. For the next week I explored the streets in the area on my runs but I never saw her again."

"What's her first name?"

"Martha," George said, and Delia sprayed the table, and him, with her last sip of beer.

Chapter 23

*M*artha stood in the shadow of Camden Yards and waited with the gathering crowd of runners. She couldn't eat more than a bowl of oatmeal for breakfast, and even that was threatening to rebel, as her stomach clenched with nerves.

What was I thinking, signing up for this marathon? She rocked from foot to foot, breathing the crisp morning air, and hoped her daily five-mile runs, with sporadic ten- or twelve- mile jogs, would see her through the twenty-six point two miles ahead.

Martha had registered for the marathon on a cool, sunny Baltimore spring day. She thought she would have time for miles of training before the summer's heat and then resume her long runs in the cooler fall days. She hadn't intended to head south. Florida summer days were not conducive to marathon training. She detested running in the heat. She had managed a couple of fifteen mile runs after returning to Baltimore, would they be enough? She refused to think about it, her legs had to keep going because she was determined to finish this race.

The gun sounded and a surge of adrenaline shot through her as the sea of athletes pressed against her. Martha jogged in place near the back of the pack, not wanting to be carried away in the seething mass of faster runners. The swarm of bodies thinned, and Martha watched the forward movement trickle back to her. She fought to cling to her own rhythm, which pulsated in her brain. It felt like trying to corral a runaway train, everyone around her seemed intent on a fast start that wasn't her style.

The clear, freshly washed October air reminded her of autumn days in Maine. Gradually, as her legs joined the race, she glided into the familiar beat that always accompanied her. It freed her mind to travel on a personal journey of its own, back to her first days of running.

Martha's best friend Beal had begged her to run with her when she trained for the cross-country team. Martha had never run before. She told Beal she didn't have time to study, work in the bakery, and run too, but Beal assured her it would help make the studying go faster. Baking fed her soul, but she had to pay attention so she didn't add salt in place of sugar. Martha discovered that running cleared her brain when she felt overwhelmed, it freed her mind to fly wherever it chose to go, or sometimes nowhere at all.

They had been inseparable in high school, and Beal claimed Gram as her surrogate grandmother. She hadn't been in touch with Beal since they went to college, but her grandmother mentioned her often. Martha suddenly longed to see her friend, and thought maybe they could run together again when she returned to Hope Island Harbor.

The complaints of her body brought her mind back to the race. Near the twenty-mile marker, Martha saw the finish line at the top of the next rise and the vision spurred her on, but it kept moving ahead of her, and she never could reach it. She crested a steep hill, bent over gasping for breath. Could the desire in her brain overcome the exhaustion in her legs? They possessed a stubborn will of their own and ceased running. Though every particle in her body hurt, she desperately wanted to keep moving.

Her brain yelled, "Run, damn you, run!" but like two petulant two-year olds, her legs shouted, "NO! We're done, we're not moving!" She sensed her legs seizing up, like Colin, Delia's young son did, stiffening his whole body when he didn't want to be put in his car seat. How would she move from this spot? Somewhere in the recesses of her brain, she heard footsteps thwacking in a steady rhythm from behind her.

"Don't stop now, you're almost done," a disembodied voice said. "Picture the finish line, you can do it. Drink some water."

Debbie Kaiman Tillinghast

Hands resting on her knees, chest heaving, Martha gasped, "I don't have any left."

"Here, drink some, and then eat this." Two hands reached towards her, one held a water bottle and the other a packet of energy gel.

"It's diluted Gatorade. It'll help." She guzzled a long drink from the water bottle then collapsed again, hands resting on her knees. She shook her head, refusing the snack, but the opened gel packet reappeared in her hand.

"You've hit the wall. You need to rehydrate and replenish your glucose supply." Still in a fog, she squeezed the gel into her mouth and swallowed.

"Jog easy, just easy," he took her hand. "We're going to finish this together."

"No, you keep going, you're obviously doing fine, I'm done. I'll slow you down."

"You're not done, and I'm going to stay with you until you finish." Martha hadn't looked at her rescuer, but as the haze cleared and recognition penetrated her brain, she knew that voice. She found the energy to turn her head and looked into a familiar pair of chocolate eyes. When they connected with hers, she saw the same shock she felt.

"George?" she croaked.

"Martha?" he said. "I was so focused on reviving you that I didn't recognize you. I didn't know you were running this marathon."

"Me either, at least not for sure, until last night when I picked up my race packet."

Martha wanted to ask George about his wife, or tell him she didn't date married men, but exhaustion prevented her from thinking clearly. Numb with fatigue, she gave in to his insistence to keep moving.

Gradually the nourishment kicked in and she felt like she might finish the race. She'd been ready to give up, but tenacity overcame her acceptance of one more failure. Martha had no idea how much time passed, but she heard cheers and applause from the sidelines. A mirage couldn't make that much noise, and George shouted, "I can see the finish line!" Martha heard triumph in his voice.

151

"Go!" She yelled above the spectators' shouts, "At least cross that at your own pace." George looked doubtful, but Martha gave him a gentle shove, "I'm fine, don't worry, I won't stop now."

George nodded and his powerful legs propelled him forward. Martha followed, as she focused on moving her legs and repeating, "I can do it, I can do it." Applause, whistles and shouts sounded from the crowd. Finally, she heard her name announced, and realized she'd done it. Success at last, no matter what her time, she'd finished! Euphoria kept her upright until George, waiting near the finish line, enveloped her in a hug, and lifted her, feet swinging like a rag doll.

"You did it, you finished!"

Martha nodded and gasped for breath. When George released her, she would have crumpled to the pavement if he hadn't put his arm around her again.

"You need to walk, let's get more water, and something to eat, and there are massage stations." Though hardly able to move, reality sank in and Martha's mind shouted for joy. She followed George to tables laden with fresh cut oranges, whole bananas, juice, water, pizza, and assorted sandwiches. She grabbed a banana and a bottle of water.

"Did you see your time when you crossed the finish line?"

"No, I was concentrating on getting across it without collapsing."

"Three hours and twenty-five minutes, that means you averaged under eight-minute miles—impressive!"

"Really? No wonder I struggled, that's my pace for five miles, I never expected to keep it up for the whole course. Wow, I can't believe it!" Martha beamed, ecstatic that she'd not only finished but run faster than she imagined possible.

George guided her toward the high tables, where the runners could have their tired muscles kneaded and stretched.

"Can we go somewhere and talk after?" George kept his hand on her elbow. "Coffee, lunch, dinner, your choice."

"I appreciate your help, I wouldn't have made it otherwise, but I'm exhausted. I want to go home and sleep for a week." Part of her wanted to

152

agree, her depleted body responded to his nearness, but she didn't date married men.

"How about tomorrow, after you've had a chance to recover. I want to explain Martha. I'm not married, and I'd like to see you again." He held up his ringless left hand.

What? Not married? Had she heard correctly? The words ricocheted off her brain, but she couldn't absorb them. "I don't know, maybe—I need some time, I can't even think right now." Martha shook her head and moved to take her turn for a massage, perhaps it would help her mind as well as her body function again.

Chapter 24

*M*artha left the runners only area and joined spectators waiting in front of Camden Yards. A Bluegrass band played in one corner, and scattered food trucks scented the air with garlic and onions. She spotted Delia supervising her four children. Colin, Patrick, and Deirdre sat at a picnic table munching hot dogs and drinking lemonade, while Maura slept peacefully in her stroller, oblivious to the shouting and music.

"Delia, I didn't expect to see you here. I'd give you a hug, but I'm pretty gross."

"I don't care," Delia, grabbed Martha in a tight embrace. "The kids wanted to come cheer you on and so did I. It took a while to get through the crowds, but we saw you cross the finish line, then they claimed starvation, so here we are. You looked fantastic running in, how do you feel?"

"You mean other than the fact that every part of me hurts except my eyelashes? I feel great!"

Delia laughed. "Why don't you come home with us? I'll feed you dinner and then bring you home, or you can spend the night, and I'll bring you back in the morning. I'm sure you don't feel like cooking. Besides, I've been itching to talk to you. I didn't want to bug you because I knew you barely had time to breathe, between the marathon and the chocolate challenge, but I think my neighbor knows you. He's the one I wanted you to meet, his wife died. I'm telling you Martha, he's a keeper."

Martha thought about dinner with Delia and her family for about one second. It would be delicious, and chaotic, but she didn't have the energy to talk about a new man, she wanted to sleep.

"Thanks Delia, but I don't even feel like eating. I want to go home, take a hot shower and sleep for the rest of the day, or maybe a week." Delia lifted a now wakeful and cranky Maura from the stroller.

"Delia?" a male voice said, "I thought I recognized Colin sitting at the table, but I wasn't expecting to see you." Delia looked up and Martha followed her gaze. George came toward them with a towel draped around his neck and a bottle of Gatorade in his hand.

Martha felt her stomach clench. *Delia knows George?* Their recent conversation zipped through her mind. *"There's a man I want you to meet."* She tried to sink into herself and disappear, but Delia reached out a free hand and grabbed her arm before she could fade into the shadows.

"This is my friend Martha, the one I mentioned at the party last week."

George nodded and said, "Ahh." Martha perceived a depth of hidden meaning in that one syllable. "Hey Martha, you feeling better?"

"Yes, you were right, the massage helped." Martha gave up thoughts of disappearing.

"George you must be exhausted, why don't you come over for dinner? Martha's coming too, aren't you, Martha?" Martha ignored Delia's innocent look and glared at her, then glanced at George.

He gave her an understanding smile, "Thanks, Delia, but I'm meeting friends." As if on cue, Martha heard someone yell, "George," and turned toward the sound.

A man carrying a child who was a tiny replica of himself, a woman with a toddler in her arms, and another blond woman approached with wide smiles.

"Hey, guys," George said, "thanks for coming."

The man slapped George on the back, "You looked great out there."

"Thanks. Meet my neighbor Delia and her friend Martha. This is Nick, his wife Mandy, and their friend Lucy." George tickled the little boy. "And the two imps are Jonathan and Bethany."

155

"Hi, nice to meet you," Martha's eyes included all the new arrivals.

"Congratulations on running the marathon," Lucy looked directly at Martha. "We saw you cross the finish line."

"I never would have made it without George's help. I was about to collapse and give up, but he shared his water and energy gel."

"You looked great, George," Lucy gave George a hug. "I don't know how you can run that far, once around the block is enough for me." Martha studied Lucy surreptitiously. She seemed too excited not to be more than Nick and Mandy's friend, but George hadn't said, "My girlfriend." She wondered how good a friend Lucy was. She told herself it didn't matter, she didn't have time for a man in her life anyway. But it did matter.

Martha took advantage of the distraction caused by new arrivals to make her escape. "If you'll all excuse me, I'm going to go home and sleep for a week. I'll call you, Delia. Nice to meet you," she said to no one in particular. "Thanks again for your help, George."

"I'm glad we had a chance to run together. Remember to rehydrate for the rest of the day." George offered his hand and after she shook it, a tiny folded paper remained in her palm. She closed her fist around it. Martha plodded back to her car, grateful she didn't have far to go, her legs felt like cooked spaghetti.

She flopped into the driver's seat, tipped her head back and closed her eyes. She'd told George she didn't want to see him, but she had to admit that wasn't true. Besides, Delia liked him. She opened the hand that held the small paper, unfolded it, and read the phone number and below it, written in neat block letters:

GEORGE HENDERSON
CALL ME ANYTIME

Martha stumbled through the front door of her apartment. Charley came from the bedroom, stretched, yawned, and meowed a greeting.

"Hi Charley, did you have a good nap? Catch any phantom mice?" Martha leaned down, gave him a scratch, and headed to the bedroom. She intended to go straight to the shower, but the bed looked so inviting she fell across it, face down, arms and legs splayed. Charley sprang onto the bed, then climbed on Martha's back and started kneading his paws. Martha fell instantly asleep, dreaming the masseuse had come home with her, as Charley curled into a ball and went to sleep too.

When she woke a few hours later, every muscle in her body had stiffened. She stretched and groaned when they reminded her she needed a hot shower and a session on her yoga mat. Her hand still held the folded paper and she dropped it on her nightstand. She'd think about it later.

Thoughts of George and his kindness during the marathon followed her into the shower. She would never have finished without him. She remembered his muscled legs taking off to the finish line, his request to explain, Delia's words, "His wife died. He's a keeper," and the blond woman hugging him which gave her an unexpected jolt of jealousy. Martha wrapped herself in her white terry robe and came back to the bedroom rubbing a towel over her wet hair.

"What do you think, Charley, should I call him?" She unfolded the paper again, *"Call me anytime."* Charley had no comment, he sat on the bed purring and blinked his eyes. He left this decision to her.

Martha dressed in her comfy blue sweatpants and Maine sweatshirt. Too tired to cook, she definitely needed food. She picked up the paper, then put it down and went to the front hall where she'd dropped her bag. She rummaged until she found her phone and brought up the number for her favorite vegetarian take out, The Green Grocer. They delivered, so she could do yoga while she waited. She scrolled through the menu, but her usual favorites had no appeal.

She thought of the pizza at the Corner Pub and her stomach rumbled. Before she could think any more, she retrieved the paper and punched George's number into her cell phone. Maybe if they went back to Corner Pub, they could rewrite their last encounter. The call went directly to voicemail, and she disconnected, without leaving a message. Disappointment drove hunger from her mind. George had said he had plans with his friends, but she had still hoped to reach him.

Chapter 25

*M*artha slumped on her bed and dragged Charley onto her lap. "Looks like you'll be my dinner companion tonight." She scratched under Charley's chin, "I have a busy day tomorrow, so it's probably good he didn't answer," she said, but she wished he had. The phone rang and she jumped up, spilling Charley on the floor.

"Hello?" Nerves and anticipation collided, making her voice squeak.

"Martha? This is George Henderson. Sorry I didn't hear the phone. I hoped the missed call would be you." George sounded pleased, which gave her courage to follow through on her impulse.

"I was thinking about getting a pizza at Corner Pub, and I wondered if you'd like to join me." She held her breath.

"I'd love to." She could hear the smile in his voice and breathed again, then gave him her address. After all, Delia approved of him.

Half an hour later, Martha met George at the door; he wore jeans, a navy French rib sweater, and sneakers. The wind had tousled his dark hair, and he smelled deliciously of fresh air, woods, and ocean breezes. Today's exhaustion and tomorrow's busy schedule slithered away, replaced by memories of meeting George the first time.

"Hi George," she held Charley in her arms. Unexpected delight spread through her along with a few first-date jitters. Would she feel the same connection she had that April day?

"Hi Martha, who's this?" George scratched Charley, who twisted his head and stretched his neck, encouraging George to find the perfect spot. Martha put Charley down, left them to get acquainted and went to get her jacket. She trusted Charley's instincts. He had immediately disliked Jake. When she came back, George held Charley in his arms and the cat purred contentedly.

"Charley, it looks like you found a new friend. You don't by any chance have a tuna fish sandwich in your pocket, do you?"

George chuckled. "No, but I grew up with cats, he must have sensed that."

"Mmmm," but she believed Charley sensed something else, and any lingering doubts about her decision to call George faded away.

"Want to walk?" George waited for Martha to lock her door. "It's not far and it'll help loosen any muscles that are tight."

"Any?" Martha snickered. "They're all tight."

"How do you know Delia?" George ambled towards the pub.

"We went to culinary school together. I grew up in a small town in Maine and the size of the school overwhelmed me. Delia took me under her wing." She looked up at George and when his dark eyes met hers, the magic of that April day came flooding back.

"What led you to buy a house in Roland Park?" Delia lived in a family neighborhood; did he have children he hadn't mentioned?

"I enjoy restoring older homes, and it needed some TLC." Martha noticed George's wistful tone and wondered if he had other reasons he didn't want to share. Before she could ask why he wanted a house and not a condo, they arrived at the restaurant.

Once they found a table and placed their order, George said, "Have you ever run a marathon before?"

"No, I've been running since I was in high school, but never a marathon. I'm not sure what possessed me, but I know I wouldn't have finished without your help. How about you? I'm guessing you've run a marathon or two."

"You're right, I played soccer in college, then after graduation I needed a sport that didn't require a team. Running and biking took the place

159

of grueling soccer practices and marathons provided the excitement of competition, especially when I wanted to prove something to myself."

Martha squirmed under his questioning gaze. Did he suspect she had something to prove too? She chose to hear his story before sharing more of her own.

Their food arrived and Martha said, "Oh good, I'm starving." She devoted her attention to her pizza. After devouring half of it, she plunged into the question hovering between the lines of their conversation.

"Delia told me your wife died, but you wore a wedding ring the last time I saw you. Did it happen recently?"

George took a deep breath and blew it out through pursed lips. He might not want to talk about this now, but she needed an explanation. "My wife died five years ago. I hadn't been able to take the ring off."

"I'm sorry. You must have loved her very much." But he had taken it off, why now?

"I did love her, but that's not why I wore the ring." Martha studied George as he spoke and heard the strain in his voice. He ran his hands over his face and Martha waited. "When we got married, I thought we both wished for the same things. But her career consumed her, nothing else mattered to her. I wanted to start a family, and she didn't. We bickered all the time. One morning we had a terrible argument. When she left for work, I was still angry." George flipped his fork over and over. Martha thought about her last fight with Tony, had George's ended in a similar manner? No way could she keep seeing him if it had.

"She called to say she'd be late, and I fell asleep on the couch, determined to wait for her so I could apologize. I woke when I heard someone banging on the door and blinking red lights streamed in the window, I knew she wasn't coming home."

Martha gasped and her hand flew to cover her mouth. How horrible for him.

"What happened?" She asked softly.

"It was raining hard that night, and her car hydroplaned on a curve. It landed upside down at the bottom of a hill, against a tree. She didn't have a seatbelt on and died instantly." Martha recognized the guilt beneath the sadness in George's voice. The hard edge of her own guilt surfaced and her throat constricted.

"How awful, you never had a chance to tell her you were sorry." Martha stretched her arm across the table and rested her hand on his. "I can only imagine how you must have felt." A surge of gratitude merged with the pain she felt for George, knowing she'd see Gram in another week. George must hate revisiting that night, and she regretted pushing him for an explanation.

"I've eaten my limit of pizza," Martha tried for a cheerful tone, "why don't we head home?"

"I'm sorry," George said when they left the restaurant. "I didn't mean to ruin your appetite, but I wanted you to understand why I wore a wedding ring that day. I've been punishing myself for the past five years."

"I asked you to tell me, and I can see it's hard for you to talk about, but it was an accident, and it wasn't your fault." She imagined how she would feel if she didn't get a chance to apologize to Gram.

"It felt like my fault. I didn't think I deserved to care for anyone until I met you, but I still wrestle with giving myself permission to live again. I forgot I was wearing my ring. I don't blame you for running out on me. I tried for weeks to find you. Your neighbors must have wondered if I was a stalker. I ran up and down the streets near the restaurant, peering in the face of every woman that resembled you."

Martha laughed at George's attempt to lighten the mood.

By the time they returned to her apartment, Martha had faded from the rigors of the day. She needed time to process everything he'd told her. When George asked if he could see her again, part of her wanted to agree. She relished his company as much as she had the first day, and now she understood about his wife. But she had so much work to do for the chocolate challenge. She needed to focus all her energy on that. Besides, Darcy would arrive the next day, so they could work out the final details, and she'd meant it when she told Delia she didn't want a man in her life right now.

Martha explained briefly about the challenge and said she couldn't even think about a social life until that was behind her. And then the blonde woman she'd seen at the marathon popped into her head, but that question would have to wait.

"Thank you for explaining about your wife, and don't worry, I enjoyed the pizza and the evening." She held out her hand, but George leaned down and brushed his lips lightly over her cheek.

"You're welcome, I enjoyed it too. Get some rest."

Chapter 26

*M*artha groaned when her alarm went off at six the next morning. She had fallen into bed the night before as soon as George left her at her door, and slept so soundly the blankets remained undisturbed. Charley meowed his displeasure when she moved him to get out of bed.

"I know Charley, I feel the same way, but Darcy will be arriving soon and I have to meet her plane. Shower first, then coffee," she mumbled as she shuffled towards the bathroom, yawning as she went. Hopefully the shower would both revive her and relax stiff muscles from the marathon.

By the time Martha left for the airport, caffeine from three cups of coffee coursed through her bloodstream and she felt more like herself. She parked in the airport's passenger pick-up zone where Darcy waited by the curb, and rushed from the car to hug her.

"I'm so glad you're here," she put Darcy's bag in the trunk. "How was your flight?"

Darcy settled into the passenger seat. "Uneventful, but I'm desperate for coffee and breakfast."

"You're in luck, we're going to the best bakery in Baltimore." When they arrived, Martha led the way into Sweet Selections, where a line of customers waited at the counter. Sarah came over to greet them.

"There's a pot of coffee in the back for you," she motioned them through to the kitchen. A plate of buttery apricot almond scones, filled with sweet dried apricots and coated with sugared, sliced almonds, sat on the table beside the coffee pot. Martha offered one to Darcy, who took a bite and said, "Mmmm."

Martha and Darcy spent the next week practicing the difficult pieces and devising their schedule for the chocolate challenge. Like choreographing a dance, there could be no wasted motions, and no confusion about who would do what, as timing would be critical. They arrived at the bakery every morning as soon as it opened and worked past closing every night. Then they returned to Martha's apartment and collapsed with exhaustion.

Saturday morning, Martha checked supplies off her list as Darcy packed them into the appropriate box. Martha didn't want to be late for their designated arrival time at the convention center. She finished scrutinizing the last page of necessary equipment, and when her cell phone rang, she glanced at it, not intending to answer. But she saw Gram's number, smiled, and set her list aside. Gram probably wanted to wish her good luck at the chocolate challenge.

"Hi Gram," she waited for Gram's cheery voice.

"It's Beal, Martha, Beal Drumlin." The light beat of anticipation transformed to a thud of dread, why did Beal have Gram's phone?

"I'm with your grandmother, she's in the hospital. You need to come home."

"What? What do you mean? Gram's fine." Panic seized Martha and she clutched the throat of her shirt.

"She's been fighting cancer, and now she's developed pneumonia."

"Why didn't she tell me?" Martha closed her eyes and remembered the last conversation she'd had with Gram, and how tired she'd sounded. Why hadn't she pressed her grandmother to tell her what was wrong? She'd called Gram because she needed to hear her voice, never thinking that Gram needed her. Guilt washed over her.

"She didn't want you to worry,"

"Oh Beal, I'll book a flight home."

"I think you should come today, Martha."

"Is it that bad?"

"She's in intensive care. The doctor said she's stable, but even if she recovers from the pneumonia, I don't think she has much time left."

Suffocating pain clamped her throat shut, and she couldn't speak. She'd thought of Gram as invincible, counting on her to always be there. She gripped the phone, and wished she could turn back the clock, she'd failed again to tell Gram how much she cared about her. Martha drew a ragged breath, "I'll check on flights and call you back as soon as I figure it out."

"Let me know when your plane gets in, and I'll meet you at the airport."

"Okay. And Beal, thank you." Martha disconnected and stood motionless, staring into space, tears streaming down her cheeks.

"What's wrong, Martha?" Darcy abandoned her packing and walked over to Martha. "Who was on the phone?"

"My friend Beal, from Hope Island Harbor. She called to tell me Gram's in the hospital. She has cancer and has developed pneumonia. I don't know what to do." The challenge started soon and if she left, she'd relinquish her chance at winning, along with the fifty thousand dollar prize. But if she didn't, she might not see Gram alive again, an unthinkable alternative. Martha stood glued to the same spot with the phone held limply in her hand. "I've got to get back."

Darcy wrapped her arm around Martha's shoulders and drew her close. "From what you've told me about her, I think Gram would want you to do this." Darcy was right, Gram had been so excited for Martha and told her she looked forward to hearing about her win when she came back to Maine, but right now, fifty thousand dollars didn't matter.

"I told Gram I'd be back after the chocolate challenge, but I'll worry about her the whole time. I've got to catch the next flight."

"Let's see what's available. Portland, right?" Darcy took her own phone from her pocket and searched for flights.

"The next one leaves in fifteen minutes, and you'll never make that. There isn't another flight to Portland until six tonight. You can finish here and still make that one." If skipping the chocolate challenge meant getting to see Gram sooner, Martha would have left in a heartbeat, but it didn't. Despite her desperation to get back to Maine, she couldn't make the next flight, and driving or the train would take too long. She'd get through this event and then go to Gram.

"Go ahead and book the flight," she rested her head in her hands and tried to collect her thoughts. All her plans scrambled in her brain, and her body remained paralyzed.

"Come on, Martha," Darcy encouraged, "we'll make it, everything's ready to go."

Martha nodded and forced herself to concentrate.

"Let's get the car loaded." She had to keep moving. "The challenge starts in half an hour; we'll have to hurry to get to the convention center and set up before the deadline." Beal's call had drained away her excitement and replaced it with gnawing worry, and she moved as if in a trance.

Martha had gone through this so many times in her mind, but when they arrived at the chocolate challenge, she felt like her stomach had been flayed raw, and her heart pounded so hard in her chest she could barely breathe. Her hands trembled as she opened boxes, and sweat ran in rivulets down her back, in spite of the cool temperature in the staging area. Part of her longed to turn and flee, she wanted to be transported to Maine, but she had to focus on the challenge facing her here. They unpacked everything in their assigned area and waited for instructions.

She looked over at Darcy, who appeared at ease. She smiled at Martha, "Relax, you've got this. You've practiced it so many times, they could turn off the lights and you'd be okay." Martha closed her eyes and the finished chocolate scene shimmered in her mind. She visualized every detail down to the chocolate ropes that tied the carved chocolate rowboat. Martha took a deep calming breath and opened her eyes.

"You're right, we'll be okay, but I wish I knew how Gram was doing."

The emcee introduced the contestants and judges, and reviewed the rules. Martha heard him say they had four hours to complete their chocolate creations, and she mentally performed her first task. She knew what she needed to do and moved quickly when the starting bell sounded. Martha blocked out everything except her contribution to the detailed design, and she trusted Darcy to do the same. In the background, she heard other teams yelling instructions or arguing when something went wrong, but Martha worked quietly. She and Darcy moved like synchronized swimmers, floating smoothly around each other without colliding.

Martha had decided to recreate the Seven Foot Knoll Light, now in Baltimore's Inner Harbor, at its original site at the mouth of the Patapsco River. The scene depicted a daring rescue performed in 1933. The rocky shoal and base for the chocolate sea were already in place, but they had to construct the lighthouse, carve heaving swells into the water, then add the foundering tugboat, and the rescue craft that had gone out into the storm. It was a dramatic scene, a tribute to lighthouse keepers, emphasizing their importance when poor visibility and the rough waters made rocks and shoals even more treacherous.

Martha poured the tempered chocolate into the double-sided, cylindrical mold that would become the lighthouse, she hoped it would harden in time to successfully remove the hinged metal pieces. Then she carved all the interior parts to recreate the lighthouse keeper's living space. She shaped a small skiff, but it made her think of home, which triggered her worry about Gram, and she lost her focus. Minutes ticked by while she sat motionless, staring at the chocolate in front of her, but seeing Gram lying in the hospital instead, and wondering how she'd survive if Gram didn't recover.

"Martha," Darcy hissed. Martha flinched at the unexpected sharpness in Darcy's voice. She looked down at the chocolate melting in her hands, surprised to find it there. She nodded and her hands moved again, but she'd disrupted their exacting time plan. Now she'd have to rush, which didn't bode well for the finished product. She set the softened chocolate aside and picked up the piece that would become the tugboat. Her fingers flew, and soon the ship emerged as if the design had been stamped on the chocolate. She heard a paper rustle and looked up into the eyes of three judges who watched her and made notes on their clipboards. Her confidence disappeared. How long had they been standing there? Had they seen her blank out?

Her eyes followed them when they moved to study Darcy as she piped the tempered chocolate into lattice for the legs, it needed to be strong enough to support the lighthouse, while giving the impression of an open iron grill. She would complete several duplicate layers and sandwich them together, so they wouldn't take too long to harden.

Martha returned to putting the finishing touches on the chocolate tugboat. Darcy would create the raging sea, carving waves into the chocolate base, and frosting them with white chocolate, tinted with shades of deep blues and greens. After Darcy capped the cresting waves with white, Martha placed the finished tugboat in the swells. The sea looked as ominous as Martha had imagined, and she said a silent, "Thank you," for Darcy's expert and unflappable assistance.

The judges returned, and Martha held her breath when she removed the mold from the lighthouse walls, her hands trembled, but she couldn't make a mistake now. A sigh of relief escaped when her plan worked. The outside walls had been molded in two sections, then stacked one on top of the other. A large chocolate disc formed the floor between. She carefully carved windows into the chocolate walls, then painted the outside of the lighthouse with melted white chocolate tinted red. She worried that the finished lighthouse would be too heavy to rest on the chocolate legs. Although it had worked when they practiced, that didn't mean something wouldn't break at the last minute.

Time was running out. Once the pieces were assembled, Darcy placed a tiny battery-operated LED bulb inside the cupola to flash its warning across the water. Martha held her breath as they balanced the finished lighthouse on the legs, then she painted melted chocolate on the connections to secure them in place.

"Thirty seconds, chefs."

Panic rose in her throat. They still needed to move the finished sculpture to the judges' table. Would they be able to lift it and keep it in perfect balance? It was the longest ten feet Martha had ever walked. Their arms strained under the weight, and their unequal heights made it difficult to keep the lighthouse level. They hadn't practiced this last step, but if they didn't get it to the judges' table before the final bell sounded, they'd be disqualified. They inched their way forward, attempting to keep the lighthouse steady.

Any movement could send the whole design crashing to the floor.

The bell rang as Martha rescued her fingers from under the edge, and Darcy retrieved hers as the announcer said, "Hands up please, step back from your designs."

❈ ❈ ❈

Martha bent over at the waist and let out a whoosh of relief. Then she and Darcy hugged, but worry flooded Martha and smothered her joy.

The judges circulated among the contestants. Martha looked at the clock, if they didn't get to her soon, she'd miss her flight. She shifted from one foot to another and her heart raced with second hand on the clock. *Come on, come on.* By the time they finished their scrutiny of Martha's entry, her cushion of time had vanished.

"I've got to go Darcy."

"Can't you wait for the judges' decision? What if you win?"

"I have to go back to my apartment and pack a few things, then call for a ride to the airport. I hate to leave you, but do you mind finishing here?" She couldn't miss that flight, she had to see Gram, tell her how much she regretted breaking her promise and staying away so long.

"No, of course I don't mind." Darcy hugged Martha close. "I hope your grandmother is okay, and I'll let you know what the judges decide."

"Call me if we win," she said, and was already walking away.

Martha ran down the concourse, reaching her gate as they announced the last call for her flight. She collapsed into her seat and tried to slow her breathing to normal. Beal would meet her in Portland, but for now there was nothing she could do but pray.

Martha spotted Beal as soon as she entered the airport lobby. She looked the same as she had in high school, red hair haloing her shoulders, long shapely legs encased in skinny jeans, curves hidden beneath a bulky wool sweater, and arms folded against the world. Then she noticed the tears spilling down Beal's cheeks, was she too late?

Chapter 27

The smells of antiseptic and disease filled the hospital room where Martha stood surrounded by the sounds of beeping monitors and Gram's raspy breathing. She looked so fragile, Martha had always thought of her as feisty and strong, but now her spare frame barely made a rise in the blanket. The doctors said that they had done all they could, but the cancer had left Gram weak and vulnerable to the pneumonia's assault. She took Gram's frail hand, leaned over, placing her own cheek against Gram's papery one, and tried to force words past the lump in her throat.

"I'm here Gram, I'm sorry it took so long, I came on the first available flight. I completed the Charm City Chocolate Challenge, though. My friend Darcy helped, she thought you'd want me to do it, and I hope she was right." She wiped her own tears from her grandmother's face, then dragged a chair close, so she could sit and hold Gram's hand. The machines kept beeping in the background, their lights glowing eerily in the darkened room. Martha closed her eyes and pictured her grandmother sitting across the table from her, not here, lying in a hospital bed, holding on to life by a tenuous thread.

When her parents died, Gram and Grandpa had stepped in and raised her. Gram's well-cushioned lap had been a steady source of comfort when Martha was hurt or sick. Now Martha started talking, not sure if Gram could hear her or not, but she needed to explain her absence the past eight years.

"As usual, you were right, Gram. I didn't follow my own dreams when I married Tony, I followed his. I thought they were the same, but his were the only ones that mattered to him. It's my own fault, I got carried away by his attention and the attraction between us. I convinced myself that I'd found the romantic hero of my dreams.

"At first Tony said he needed me, and I believed him," Martha paused and swiped at her tears. "He told me we were a team, and my talents would be wasted in Maine. I believed in his fantasy too, but in reality, he needed to be in control of everything, including me."

Martha kept talking, although her grandmother remained silent, her eyes closed. She told Gram the parts of her life she'd withheld over the years, Tony's constant anger and fault finding, and that they never made love. She knew she had talent, but as her success grew, so did Tony's frustration, and she'd allowed his words to fuel her self-doubts. "You'll never make it without me, you need me."

"I wish I'd come back that summer to help you, and if not then, at least later for a visit. But I was ashamed to admit my marriage was such a mess. I thought if I tried hard enough, I could fix it." Martha resolved to tell her grandmother everything, including the moment when Tony hit her, and she realized she couldn't stay any longer. "I was humiliated, my marriage had failed, and so had I." Martha took an unsteady breath.

"I didn't want to come home until I did something to make you proud of me. That's why I waited until after the chocolate challenge. I guess we didn't win, because I haven't heard from Darcy." Martha told Gram about trying out for the chocolate challenge and signing up for the marathon in a frenzied need to prove herself. She told her about meeting George and the magical day they spent together. And she told her about fleeing Baltimore, leaving Sarah in the lurch and the real reason she landed on Perdido Key.

"Annie has recreated Cape Cod in Florida, and when I stayed at her bed and breakfast, The Plump Pelican, I realized how much I wanted to see you, how much I missed Hope Island Harbor. I did help her, but that's not why I went. I went there to help myself, and to heal." She told her about finding Darcy and her incredible Dancing Dolphin chocolate shop, and she even told her about the dreadful date with Jake.

"I knew when I left Perdido Key that I'd come back to Maine, but I had to stay in Baltimore long enough to compete in the marathon and complete the chocolate challenge. My days of running out on my commitments are over." She lingered over her marathon story, and told her grandmother about seeing George, and his help when she thought she couldn't run another step. "He wanted to see me again and at first I refused, because I thought he was married, but it turns out his wife died. He told me the whole story, and like our first meeting, I wanted to talk with him forever." Martha leaned closer, holding Gram's hand in both of hers. "I'm sorry I stayed away so long Gram, will you forgive me?"

Martha felt a gentle squeeze on her hand, then all the blips and beeps changed to a steady hum and the lines went flat. The sound of running feet filled the room and the doctor pushed Martha aside. She started to shake; fear wrung her stomach into a knot. *No, not yet!* She stretched her arm towards Gram, if she touched her, Gram would be okay, but she couldn't. The doctor bent over her grandmother, and when he straightened, his eyes were sympathetic, "I'm sorry."

Chapter 28

R ain drummed on the roof when Martha rose after a sleepless night at the hospital and a few restless hours in Gram's bed. She'd collapsed there when she returned to Gram's house, seeking comfort from the lingering smell of her grandmother. The hours of incessant tears had left her throat dry and raw. She brewed a pot of tea then sat at the kitchen table, hands wrapped around a blue mug with Sunrise Café emblazoned over a lighthouse silhouette.

Memories of the hours spent here with Gram whirled in her mind, and the room remained unchanged from her childhood like a time capsule. Sun and countless washings had bleached the blue and white gingham tablecloth and curtains, and the sheen on the white bead-board cabinets had long ago been scrubbed away, but they still radiated light, even on dreary days like today. A black cast iron woodstove hugged the inside wall, despite the addition of a modern range. She suspected that on recent chilly mornings, the aroma of fresh bread, baked in that stove, had filled the kitchen. Gram always swore nothing baked bread like a cast iron cook-stove. She also preferred it for savory, bubbling soups.

A curved, white enamel pitcher held the season's last beach roses. Martha touched the few remaining pink petals that clung to the faded stem.

Gram must have picked them. Tears streamed down her cheeks and mirrored the rain sheeting from the porch. How could Gram be gone? Wasn't it yesterday when she showed Martha how to make roll-m-ups? She could still hear Gram's patient instruction.

"Pull a chair over Martha, and you can help me make the Roll-m-ups from the leftover pie dough." Martha remembered the feeling of the dough in her sticky fingers, she'd wanted to squeeze it through them. But Gram's words had stopped her.

"Remember we have to be gentle with the dough. Don't make it when you're angry, or the pie will be tough. You have to be happy, it'll make your hands gentle."

In culinary school Martha had a reputation for creating the most tender and flaky pie crust, even better than the instructors. *Did I ever tell you, Gram?*

The cuckoo clock in the corner ticked rhythmically as the pendulum swung back and forth, the only sound, except for the beating of her heart. Though Martha wanted to feel Gram here, right now, she hurt too much. She felt bruised and beaten by her own absence. She never got the chance to sit in this kitchen and laugh with Gram again, to tell her how much she loved her, and how grateful she was.

All during her illness, Gram waited, without asking, for Martha to return, but Martha had been too busy trying to prove herself, to fix her failed marriage and sort out her life. Too busy to realize none of that mattered to Gram. She'd loved Martha no matter what, and would have welcomed her home. Now it was too late, and grief knotted in her stomach making her ill. She didn't think she could take another breath, she didn't want to.

"I'm so sorry Gram," she whispered.

Why didn't I come back?

The wind rattled the windows in response, and Martha needed to move—she didn't care about the rain. Before she left, she started a fire in the woodstove, something she hadn't done for years, but part of her brain remembered how to get it going. She took tiny pieces of kindling from the wooden box beside the stove and adjusted the damper to garner the most heat

174

without releasing billows of smoke along with it. Once she heard the fire crackling, she added a couple of larger logs, donned Gram's yellow rain slicker and rubber boots, and then went out the front door, her head bent into the rain.

Martha followed the path to the shore road that bordered the narrow stretch of the bay touching Hope Island and the summer colony of grayed frame houses. The rocky island offered little shelter from storms, and the winters were hard. With no electricity, it remained much the same as when Gram used to deliver freshly baked pastry there every morning. In fact, she'd met Grandpa there. Martha remembered the faraway look in Gram's eyes when she told the story.

"Ezra and his family stayed in one of those summer cottages on Hope Island to escape the Boston heat. I worked in the Sunrise Bakery, and part of my job was rowing out to Hope Island every morning with fresh doughnuts and muffins. He sampled the warm pastry I sold on the dock, and often came to the mainland. He bought coffee at the bakery, claimed he got bored on the island, and I made sure I waited on him. Ezra captured my heart, but in September he went back to Boston and college, and I stayed in Hope Island Harbor. I didn't expect to see him again.

"Your grandfather came back the next summer, and although his family lived on the island, he stayed in a boarding house in town. He asked me to the movies and summer dances, but the winter had hardened my heart, and I didn't want to be an annual summer fling. I pretended I didn't care, but he saw through me. He stopped asking me on dates, but came to the bakery for friendly visits. Despite my resolve, he charmed me all over again."

Every summer Gram had vowed not to let him into her heart. Then he enlisted to fight in the war, asked Gram to write to him, and hoped she'd be here waiting when he got back. After the war, he proposed. She told him she couldn't leave Hope Island Harbor, her soul belonged here, and she had to stay.

"That's okay, I'll stay too," he'd said. He'd moved here, learned to be a stone mason and a carpenter, and built the house where Martha had grown up. She'd loved her grandfather and she remembered him as strong and tender-hearted. Gram had remained true to herself and still found enduring love. Martha hoped someday she would too.

Her grandfather died when she was ten, and Gram had supported her through that grief, but who would see her through this? Pain radiated from her heart and tore through every nerve in her body, until it shook with wrenching sobs, but the sound got lost in the pounding surf and the howl of the Northeast wind. The temperature had been steadily dropping, and soon tears and salt spray froze on her face. Although she no longer knew if the shuddering in her body came from within or without, she knew the time had come to return to Gram's house.

Martha heard a sharp crack and her anxious gaze flew to the hill above her. The ancient oak tree, that had stood for over a hundred years, quivered in the gale and a huge limb hung to the ground. The storm had intensified, and a sense of urgency gripped her, trees didn't survive forever either. Martha scrambled to keep her footing on the narrow rocky path. The wind at her back pushed her along, as if the storm wanted to warn her to hurry and get home to safety.

She clambered up the porch steps as the wind chimes swung violently, and she struggled to turn the doorknob with her icy fingers. At least she didn't have to worry about fumbling with a lock, nobody locked their doors in Hope Island Harbor. She opened the front door and stopped, *I'm sure I left a light on.* The storm had knocked out the power, leaving the house bleak even in mid-morning, but the kitchen remained warm and cozy, thanks to the cast iron stove.

Martha filled the teakettle with water and placed it on the woodstove, then spooned loose tea leaves into her grandmother's cobalt blue china teapot. While she waited for the water to boil, she wiggled her fingers over the stove to thaw. There were things she had to do today, but her brain couldn't focus on what they were. She'd grieved when her marriage ended, but that was the sting of a scraped knee compared to now, when she felt as if her heart had been cut out.

The sound of the cuckoo clock startled her. She had an appointment with the funeral director at one, enough time to drink her tea and take a hot shower before she had to leave. Then she remembered what happened in Gram's house when the power went out. Since a well supplied the water, no power meant no pump, which meant no water for a shower. She managed to fill the tea kettle with water left in the pipes, but that would disappear the second she started the shower.

Martha sighed as she poured the boiling water into the teapot. She left the tea steeping and took the kettle upstairs where she tipped the remaining water into the sink. It would be cool enough to wash her face by the time she drank her tea. Hopefully the power would be back by afternoon.

The rest of the day passed in a blur, with Martha lost in a fog of exhaustion and grief. She met with the funeral director, the florist, the minister at the Baptist church, and Jeanette, the manager at the bakery. News had traveled ahead of Martha in the small town of Hope Island Harbor, and Jeanette told her the women at the church had arranged for light refreshments after the service. Thankful she didn't need to do anything, she allowed the town's love for Gram to envelop her.

When she arrived home, Martha stood looking at the white clapboard house. She tried to imagine it without Gram, but it was like imagining a school with no children, or a football stadium with no players, it was a building, with all the life drained from it. At least the power had come on, and the lights she'd turned on that morning glowed from the kitchen windows.

Martha filled the kettle again. When she opened the cupboard for tea, the childhood scents of molasses cookies and gingerbread floated around her, and she closed her eyes and breathed in Gram. Her stomach refused to consider anything solid, but the local honey she added to every cup of tea gave her a few calories.

While she waited for the kettle to boil, she looked at the shelf above the sink, and studied the photograph that had been there as long as she could remember. A woman resembling a younger version of Gram stood holding a baby in her arms, her expression vacant and lost, not new baby joyful. She never realized how much pain the camera captured until today. Martha touched the silver frame. Had her mother been happy when Martha was born? She hoped so. Judging by the age of the baby in her arms, this picture must have been taken after her mother learned that her husband, Martha's father, would never come home.

Dinnertime came and went, and sorrow ballooned into every corner of her body, leaving only enough room for sips of tea. How would she survive the next few days? Then she remembered her conversation with Darcy when she had called to tell her about Gram.

"I'm sorry Martha, I know how much you loved Gram." Darcy's sympathy touched Martha like a hug. "I'll cancel my flight to Pensacola, and I'll drive your car to Maine with Charley. The Dolphin will be okay for a few more days." Martha had called Delia and Annie too. For once Delia didn't tell her what she should do, but asked, "What can I do?" But there was nothing anyone could do, Gram was gone, and Martha had to figure things out for herself. She knew how hard it would be for Delia to get away and leave four children behind, so she told her not to worry about coming. But when Delia ignored her words and said, "I'll fly out tomorrow," Martha sagged in relief.

She placed her teacup in the sink. Bolstered by the prospect of company, Martha nestled into the squishy, faded, blue couch to wait for Darcy. She pulled the colorful granny afghan over her and fell asleep. A car door slammed and Martha woke with a start. Disoriented, it took her a moment to remember where she was, and who was knocking on her door in the middle of the night. She wrapped the afghan around her shoulders and shuffled to the front hall. When she opened the door, Charley sprang from Darcy's arms to the floor with a loud meow. Darcy greeted her with a wordless hug as Charley wound through Martha's legs, his purr volume turned to high.

"I'm so glad to see you, how was the drive?" Martha scooped Charley into her arms, and rubbed her cheek against his smooth fur, the tension in her body eased. Charley purred his squeaky, ecstatic purr and pushed his head against her chin, he'd missed her too.

"Come into the kitchen and I'll make you a snack." Martha sliced cheese and a local Cortland apple and put them on one of Gram's lighthouse plates. She ran her finger along the edge, and a lump formed in her throat, they had been Gram's favorite. She slid the plate towards Darcy, then put the kettle on to heat for tea.

"You're not eating, are you?"

Martha saw worry in Darcy's eyes.

"I drink lots of tea," Martha poured water into two mugs, "but I can't seem to get food past the knots in my stomach."

"You have to eat, Martha, what would Gram make for you?"

Martha closed her eyes and imagined Gram beside her, a hand smoothed Martha's hair as she set a plate in front of her. "Cinnamon toast, and a cup of sweetened tea, her cure for everything, from an upset stomach to a failed test or a broken heart." Charley finished his explorations and jumped onto Martha's lap.

Darcy rummaged around the kitchen until she found the essentials, and soon placed two pieces of warm cinnamon toast, each cut in four triangles, in front of Martha.

"How'd you know about the triangles?" Martha looked up.

Darcy shrugged and smiled, "I think triangles taste better." Martha found herself able to eat for the first time in two days. She didn't know whether it was Darcy's arrival or Charley's quiet purr as he sat in her lap, but the knots in her stomach had begun to loosen. As she munched her toast, Martha sensed Darcy's gaze and looked up.

"What is it?"

"I'm sorry," Darcy said, "but we didn't win the chocolate challenge. We got second place."

"I guessed that when you didn't call. The chocolate challenge seemed so important last summer—I wanted to prove to Gram that I wasn't a failure. I'm disappointed we didn't win, but right now, it doesn't matter. Gram is gone, and nothing I do will bring her back."

Martha finished her tea. "You must be exhausted, I'll show you the guest room, we can unpack the car in the morning." Then she crawled into

Gram's bed and fell asleep with Charley's familiar warmth curled against her.

✖ ✖ ✖

Annie and Delia flew in the next afternoon, and Darcy offered to drive to Portland and meet their flight. Martha went through the motions of making decisions, but the thought of driving overwhelmed her.

"Why don't you stay here and take a nap before they get here?" Darcy was ready to leave for the airport. Martha shook her head and tears consumed her again.

"I can't sleep, and I don't want to be alone. I know I have to write something to read at the funeral, but not yet."

Darcy hugged her. "Let's go then, you can navigate and I won't need the GPS."

Martha slept most of the ride home and was surprised when Annie nudged her shoulder. "We're here." By then, the rain that had threatened all day hung in a misty curtain. The women of the Baptist church had tucked casseroles and kettles of soup and chowder into the refrigerator while they were gone. A fresh apple pie sat in the middle of the kitchen table and the fragrance of cinnamon greeted them. Martha discovered a bottle of wine in the refrigerator and retrieved glasses from the cupboard. She set the table and Darcy heated the chowder and ladled it into bowls.

The friends gathered in the kitchen and Annie and Delia reminisced about the care packages Gram had sent to school that Martha always shared. Martha heard their conversation in the distance, but her mind wandered to early days of learning to bake with Gram. She remembered pictures of herself standing on the stool next to Gram in the bakery, her round tummy protruding under the tiny white apron Gram had fashioned for Martha to match her own. As she sat thinking of Gram, sadness engulfed her.

Martha shot up from her chair, "I'm glad you're all here, but I need to walk." She grabbed a jacket from the peg near the door. "Make yourselves comfortable. I'll be back soon." She rushed out into the starless night. The rain had subsided to a light mist, but it painted her face with cold when she moved from the shelter of the porch.

She followed the uneven path to the shore despite the darkness and fog, her feet instinctively recognized every curve and protruding root along the way. The waves, energized by the storm, roiled a white froth across the rocks, and the high tide left a narrow strip of shore.

She settled on a flat rock, and listened to the pounding around her, and felt as if the angry waves, hardened by grief, pulverized her body and soul. She wound her arms around the pieces of herself, and unseeing, rocked back and forth, keening into the wind.

An arm slid across her back, and with eyes closed, Martha leaned into the comfort of the shoulder beside her and sobbed. The woodsmoke and lavender scent of Gram's house clung to Annie's sweater, she didn't say a word, but held Martha tightly against her. Gradually the tide of grief receded, and when Martha lifted her head and opened her eyes, she was alone. Annie must have slipped away, knowing she couldn't talk right now. She sat a little longer, and the wind blew an uneasy peace through her, then she retraced her steps to the house. When Martha came into the kitchen, Annie, Delia and Darcy sat at the table. They'd finished the wine and moved on to hot tea, and Delia held a knife poised over the apple pie.

"There you are," Delia faced her. Martha managed a weak smile and looked at Annie.

"Thanks for coming down to the shore Annie, it helped." Annie looked puzzled, "I haven't left the house, too cold out there for me."

Martha turned to Delia. "Wasn't me."

Darcy shook her head. "Me neither."

Martha smelled the blend of woodsmoke and lavender again, and felt the softness of Gram's favorite, well-worn sweater, and she knew whose shoulder had consoled her.

Chapter 29

The next morning while her friends slept, Martha tiptoed from the quiet house and trudged along the shore. A gray flannel fog obliterated the world, and cars drove by in the distance like silent specters, disconnected twin halos traveling along the road. Only the nearby waves remained unmuffled and continued to pound the shore. The beach had no beginning and no end, no destination beyond the next few steps. Martha walked into nothingness, the cloud around her beaded on her hair and impeded her breath. She'd hoped to find her grandmother again, but all she found was sight gone to gray, and the eternal wash of the sea.

❈ ❈ ❈

Martha sat in the front row of the Baptist church flanked by Annie and Delia on one side, and Beal and Darcy on the other. She closed her eyes and let the words of the familiar old hymns, "Abide With Me," and "How Great Thou Art," seep into her soul, then carried the peace they inspired to the front of the church to give the eulogy.

"My grandmother loved Hope Island Harbor, she often said she'd been planted here, and it had grown into her body and soul, the nutrients of love and friendship it provided seeped into every pore and made her who she was. Many of you called her Jessie, I called her Gram." Martha's voice broke, and she couldn't swallow past the thickness in her throat. She drew a wobbly breath and wiped away the tears blurring the page before her. "Gram was as constant as the tides, as tenacious as the rocky coast, and as warm as the summer sun. She loved to bake, and to garden, she loved my grandfather and she loved me." Martha struggled to continue as guilt compounded her sorrow, but she tried to channel Gram's resilience and her voice grew stronger.

"She sang in the church choir and she lived her faith. She refused to open the bakery on Sundays, except in an emergency, no matter how much business she lost. Many of you remember the ice storm in 1998 when Gram kept the bakery open around the clock, providing hot coffee and muffins for the repair crews.

"Since she grew up here, some of you knew her for all, or most of her life. Those of you who are new to the town, that is, you weren't born here," Martha managed a shaky smile, "knew her as the welcoming face at the Sunrise Café. Her hermits soothed the pain of many a skinned knee, and her apple pie signaled autumn as surely as her strawberry rhubarb did spring."

Regret wound her heart in a strangling thread. She'd missed so much by staying away.

"If you're a lobsterman or a fisherman, she filled your thermos with coffee and provided the muffins and cinnamon rolls to start your day. She opened the bakery on the coldest winter mornings, even in the midst of a blizzard, and she always made fresh, hot coffee to fill your mugs.

"I learned to cook beside her and she instilled a love of baking in me, as well as the importance of precision. Generous with her praise, she had a subtle way of pointing out my mistakes." She looked up and saw several people smile and nod, they knew this side of Gram too. "The first time I made molasses cookies on my own, she told me they were yummy, then she picked two from the batch and put them on a separate plate, one tiny and over-baked, the other much larger and underdone in the middle. She didn't say anything except, 'Those are delicious Martha, keep practicing.'" Martha cherished the memory, she'd carried it to culinary school where the criticism had been much harsher.

"Friendship mattered to Gram, and she frequently took homemade soup and a fresh pie to anyone ill or grieving. Helping others was as much a part of her life as breathing.

"Gram supported me from the day I was born, and she raised me when my parents weren't there. She encouraged me every day and helped me fulfill my dream of attending culinary school. She loved me unconditionally, and I love her more than any other person I know." *I'm sorry Gram, please forgive me.*

Martha sat down, hands clutched in her lap. Annie placed her hand over Martha's trembling ones and kept it there, even when the trembling stopped. Beal's clear voice filled the church and ended the service with "Amazing Grace."

Chapter 30

Although Annie, Delia, and Darcy all offered to stay longer, Martha sent them on their way. They had lives to resume, and she had decisions to make that were hers alone. Beal volunteered to help in any way she could, even if Martha just needed someone to listen. Beal understood Martha's pain the best, because she felt it too.

Henry Berg, Gram's lawyer, asked her to stop by his office. He told her unofficially that Gram had left her the house and bakery, along with the decision about what to do with them. As Martha rose to leave, the lawyer stopped her and held out a letter.

"Your grandmother asked me to give you this."

Did Gram want to tell her more about the bakery? She took the letter home, made a cup of tea, and settled in the comfy chair beside the woodstove. She pictured Gram sitting at the kitchen table, writing. When she removed the letter from the envelope, she ran her fingers over Gram's tiny, meticulous script, and heard Gram's voice as she read the first two words. Tears rose from her throat and shuddered through her, and she closed her eyes and waited for them to subside.

Dear Martha,

If you're reading this it means that I am no longer here to give you a hug and try to guide you with the wisdom I accumulated through the years, but I fear my wisdom failed me. I think I made a mistake years ago.

Your mother loved your father so much she couldn't bear to be apart from him for even a day. She went everywhere with him until she found out she was pregnant with you. She was so excited, but she refused to travel anymore. Your dad loved her and was thrilled about the pregnancy, but he also loved to travel and write.

He tried to settle in Hope Island Harbor, but he couldn't adjust to small town life, and his restlessness drove us all crazy. He left to cover one more story in the Middle East and promised after that he'd stop traveling if your mom agreed to move from Maine to Washington, D.C. but the helicopter transporting him crashed.

I told you all this when you were growing up. What I didn't tell you is the truth about when your dad was killed. I know you assumed your mother had died too, because I said she became ill and was no longer here to take care of you. I let you believe it. In fact, she became severely depressed, almost catatonic. She sat in a chair staring out the window, and wouldn't hold you, or even feed you. Then one morning she was gone, but she left a letter asking me to take care of you, and to tell you she had died. She thought you'd be better off without her. I had no idea where she went, but I hoped she'd heal and change her mind.

But the healing never happened, at least not enough for her to return and take care of you. The summer stretched into fall, and the fall into winter, and still she didn't come back. After a year or so, money orders arrived sporadically, always with the words, "For Martha," but I could never trace them.

She asked me to keep her secret for the rest of my life, but I find I cannot die without telling you the truth. I don't know when the time will come that you read this, but when you do, I have one request. I hope you will forgive me, but even more importantly, please forgive your mother. She loves you, but her heart died with your father.

Feelings exploded inside Martha—anger, hurt, devastation, and ultimately betrayal. She read the letter so many times the words imprinted on her brain. Her mother might be alive? Where was she now? Gram had told her about her parents when she was old enough to start asking questions, but it seemed her grandmother had omitted crucial details.

186

She knew her mom had been an artist and her dad a writer. As newlyweds, they drove across the country and her dad wrote articles about spectacular scenery and their daring adventures. Whitewater rafting in Colorado, hot air ballooning in Arizona—these fueled his writing, and he became famous as a freelance journalist. While he wrote, she painted. His stories had shifted focus, concentrating on natural disasters and political unrest. His job had demanded he travel all over the world, and her mother had accompanied him.

She stormed back to Henry Berg's office, her anger erupting. "Why didn't you tell me my mother was alive? What else are you hiding from me?"

"I'm sorry Martha, your grandmother wanted to explain in her own way. She told me your mother sent money, and I helped her manage it. She shared what she wrote in the letter, but I don't know any more than that." Her grandmother had used the money to help pay for her culinary school, and generous graduation and wedding presents. "At some point, after you graduated, the money stopped."

Martha went through the motions of living. She walked the shore again and again, immersing herself in the damp, salty air, and hoping to find her grandmother's presence. She lived on toast and tea, and refused to answer her phone.

The words in the letter tumbled over and over in her mind, and she kept asking herself, "What next?" She could go back to Baltimore and continue her wedding cake business in the bakery with Sarah, and see George again. She could return to Pensacola and work with Annie and Darcy, or she could stay here in Hope Island Harbor and keep The Sunrise Café open. She heard Gram's words in her head, "Sometimes you have to step forward in faith in order to know if you've chosen the right direction." Which step forward should she take?

Martha shoved her hands into her jacket pockets as she followed her favorite path along the shore. The Northeast wind that blew across the bay felt like it was delivered directly from Labrador, and it coated telephone wires and individual twig fingers, turning them into crunchy clear popsicles. The weather seemed to know when the calendar page turned to November. Overnight, a raw dampness loomed from the bay, skulked into the corners of the house, and found its way beneath the heaviest wool sweater to chill her bones. The promise of snow hung heavy in the air, and the sun retreated for days at a time.

Her friends didn't understand how she could find more pleasure in this wind than she did in the tropical breezes that blew across the Gulf. They had none of the bite of this north wind, and they lacked the briny seaweed smell that meant home to her. In Florida she had no reason to relish a bowl of hot homemade chowder, or sit beside a blazing fire—she wanted to escape the oppressive heat in the chill of air conditioning.

Normally, Martha loved the barren weeks of November, but this year her heart felt as leaden as the skies overhead. Gram's letter had confused her, and she couldn't make a decision about the bakery.

Chapter 31

Martha wandered through the house pondering Gram's letter and her conversation with Mr. Berg. She pictured Gram, her eyes focused in the distance, and tried to remember Gram's exact words when she had asked about her parents. "Your mommy loves you, but after your daddy died, she got sick. Grandpa and I took care of you when she no longer could." Martha felt like she was trying to solve a jigsaw puzzle with a few critical pieces missing, lost in the years that had passed. Gram never said her mother had died, she said she was no longer here, and Martha had filled in the missing parts for herself.

Because of her father's death, she interpreted Gram's explanation to mean her mother had died too. She had been too young to have any memory of them, so Gram and Grandpa were the parents she remembered. When she saw pictures of her mother and father, she would make up stories in her mind to fit the images she wanted to see. Through the years, she found them in every romance novel she read, and imagined their undying love.

The lingering scent of Gram's favorite lavender sachet tugged at Martha whenever she walked by the doorway of her bedroom. Gram's rocking chair nestled in a sunny alcove and Charley slept on its flowered cushion. The radiator next to him sang and whistled and kept the room toasty. She walked over, snuggled Charley in her arms and set him on her lap, then rocked him as her grandmother used to rock her when she was sick or had a bad dream. His purr never missed a beat, and her tension evaporated.

Grief came unbidden and found her. It stole into the room like the fog that prowled across the bay, changing a warm sunny day to one of gloomy damp. One minute she stroked Charley's silky fur, lulled by his sonorous purr, and in the next moment, the pain of loss seized her, and wrung wrenching sobs from her throat. For an instant, she felt the excruciating pain and hopelessness that had devoured her mother, leaving an empty husk incapable of caring for a child.

Why do some people heal and go on and others crumble? She thought back to her grandfather's death, she had sometimes awakened at night to her grandmother's muffled sobs. Silent tears had escaped down Gram's cheeks, but soon she had returned to the bakery and her normal routine. Martha scrubbed the tears from her face and decided to follow her grandmother.

"I'm going to the bakery, Charley. I think it's time I decide what happens next. What do you think?" There was no response, he'd already gone back to sleep. Martha sat for a few more minutes, enjoying the comfort of her grandmother's room and Charley's purr, then she eased him back on the cushion and went to get her jacket.

❈ ❈ ❈

Martha stood outside the Sunrise Café and visualized it as she remembered, sparkling white paint trimmed with blue around the windows, and a cornflower blue door. She blinked and saw the peeling white paint and trim dulled by salt and sun. She guessed as her grandmother's health declined, the building's upkeep did too.

When she stepped inside, the familiar smell of coffee and freshly baked apple pie enveloped her. The fisherman had come and gone, they were there when the café opened, but a steady flow of customers stopped by for coffee, pastry, and the latest gossip. Martha looked around, surprised to see pictures of herself lining the walls. She had been too preoccupied to notice them when she came in before the funeral. A framed copy of the article that had appeared in *Baltimore Style* magazine, naming her as one of the best new pastry chefs in the city, hung above the cash register. She remembered telling

190

Gram about it, but she hadn't sent her the picture. Gram had found it on her own. Martha slipped into the coat of Gram's pride and gathered it around her. Gram never saw her as a failure, and yet, Martha had spent so much time worrying about proving herself to Gram. *What a waste.*

Jeanette set a tray of hot apple pies on the counter and came over to hug Martha.

"Hi Martha, I've been hoping you'd come in. Can I get you some coffee?"

"No thanks, but can we sit and talk?"

Before Jeanette could answer, Bertha DeLoy scurried over. Like Gram, she had lived in town her whole life, she and Gram had been friends for years.

"Hello, Martha dear, I'm so sorry about your grandmother, she was a faithful friend. I don't think a day went by when I didn't see her, either here or at church. If the weather was bad, we chatted on the phone. She'll be sorely missed by the whole town. I don't know what the bakery will do without her. You are going to keep it open, aren't you? She always hoped you'd be back one day."

"Thank you, Mrs. DeLoy. I'm trying to sort everything out. I have commitments in Baltimore too." But as she spoke, it wasn't Baltimore that tugged at her.

Jeanette took a white paper bag from the countertop and handed it to Mrs. DeLoy. "Here are your hermits, fresh out of the oven, so they're still warm."

"Oh, thank you dear, it's my turn to bring refreshments for our book club this afternoon, and everyone adores Jessie's hermits. I'm glad you're back Martha, your grandmother would have been happy too." The words cut through Martha, and regret for hurting Gram festered inside her.

Martha and Jeanette moved to the privacy of the bakery kitchen. "Thank you for keeping Sunrise Café open when Gram was in the hospital." Martha wished she'd come back last summer, when Gram sounded so tired. "It meant long hours for you, acting as manager as well as trying to do the extra baking." She could see the lines of fatigue etched in Jeanette's face.

"Jessie kept baking right up until she contracted pneumonia," Jeanette's eyes filled. "She worked so hard, I couldn't let her down, besides the bakery matters to me too." Martha remembered when Jeanette worked in the bakery as a teenager, first she waited on customers, then Gram taught her to bake. Jeanette grew up in Hope Island Harbor, and though ten years older than Martha, she considered Jeanette a good friend.

Martha had been mulling over her options, selling the bakery being one of them, but somewhere in the middle of the conversation with Mrs. DeLoy, she realized she wanted to stay. Sarah would be disappointed, but she would understand, as long as Martha followed through on any cakes currently ordered. Wedding cakes were in high demand at the holidays, but the Sunrise Café would also be busy. She didn't know how she'd make it work, but she would, even if it meant flying back and forth to Baltimore for a while.

❋ ❋ ❋

At daybreak, Martha tightened the laces on her running shoes and jogged down the shore road. Her body required a last run in the bracing sea air before she drove to Baltimore; it did more to energize her and bolster her mood than any amount of coffee.

She thought about leaving Charley behind, but he would be miserable and so would she. Besides, he loved car travel and would offer his feline opinions on the plans she had for the bakery. Jeanette had offered the cat carrier she used for her calico Gwendolyn, but Charley would be offended by the suggestion that he needed a carrier. Jeanette pulled into the driveway as Martha ran breathless up the hill from the shore. Martha recognized the white bakery box and the sweet spicy aroma of cinnamon rolls wafting from it whenever her friend moved.

"You smell like a cinnamon roll," she peeked in the box. "Thanks for fortifying me for the trip."

Jeanette laughed. "You're welcome." She followed Martha into the house.

Charley must have sensed the pending trip, because he sat inside the front door instead of his preferred spot on a cushioned chair by the wood stove. After a quick shower, Martha packed snacks and water. She would refill her coffee mug at the first rest stop, and indulge in one of the café's cinnamon rolls.

"Okay Charley, you ready to travel?" Martha opened the passenger door and Charley bounded in. He sat, paws tucked in and tail wrapped around his hind legs, then looked up and meowed his impatience to get moving.

"Travel safely and let me know your plans." Jeanette came to stand beside the car. "The bakery will be waiting when you get back."

Martha hugged Jeanette and assured her she would return as soon as she finished her commitments in Baltimore. She placed her travel mug in the holder, gave Charley a pat as he curled on the passenger seat, and waved to Jeanette. She looked forward to the long drive, it would give her time to think about the bakery as well as saying goodbye to Baltimore—and to George.

Ideas for the bakery tumbled in Martha's head as she drove. Once on the highway, she gave voice to her musings.

"You know Charley, I told Gram we should become a farm-to-table restaurant, and keep the menu seasonal. But in reality, Gram did that long before it became fashionable. No wonder she nodded her head without commenting, she already used local ingredients, and didn't need a fancy culinary school student to tell her how."

All Gram's pies and pastries were seasonal; she didn't make strawberry rhubarb pie in January, she made it in June when the two fruits emerged together. She knew intuitively their tart sweet tastes of spring would make luscious companions. She featured blueberry pie in August, and apple pies lined the shelves from September right through winter, along with pumpkin and squash. When days grew warm and nights stayed cold, the sap started to run, and locals and tourists flocked to Hope Island Harbor for her maple chiffon pie, seldom found anywhere except the Sunrise Café.

Martha wanted to enlarge the café, open a chocolate shop, and someday a bed and breakfast. Her mind meandered around town as she thought of the best location for the chocolate shop, and she deliberated on appropriate names.

"What do you think, Charley? Lighthouse Chocolates? The Chocolate Seagull? How about Laughing Gull Chocolates?"

"Meow," he replied.

"I like that one too, and someday Laughing Gull Chocolates will be famous." There were so many possibilities, and she wanted to make them all a reality. She would make a list, starting with her obligations in Baltimore.

Thoughts of what she would leave behind in Baltimore led her to thoughts of George. It had been exciting to see him again, but it would lead to heartache. He had a new job in Baltimore, and she intended to return to Maine. This time no man would stand in the way of her dreams—she had made a promise to Gram and she was finally going to keep it.

Twelve hours later she drove through the Fort McHenry Tunnel.

Martha pulled up to her apartment. "We're here Charley, and we got lucky, there's a parking spot right by 601." She tipped her head back, sighed in fatigue and thought how different this return felt from the one a few months ago. Then the tasks ahead—emptying the house, finding a new place to live, finalizing her chocolate design, and getting in condition for the marathon, had overwhelmed her.

Fortunately, everything had fallen into place. Sarah had welcomed her back to the bakery, happy to give her space to practice for the chocolate challenge. She also had introduced Martha to a friend who needed to sublet her apartment. The lease ran until January first, and it gave her time to decide if she wanted something more permanent.

Thoughts of returning to Hope Island Harbor and seeing Gram had charged her with a current of excitement as well as anxiety. She had hoped the latter would ease when she completed, and possibly won, the chocolate challenge.

Now Martha carried the heavy pain of loss that would haunt her for a long time, but she also looked forward to starting over in the place she loved, and fulfilling the dream she had abandoned when she married Tony. She couldn't help thinking Gram would be looking over her shoulder, cheering her on and subtly helping her right her mistakes.

Charley climbed into her lap and meowed his impatience. "Okay, okay I know, you've had enough of the car, I feel the same way." Martha grabbed her overnight bag. When she unlocked the apartment, Charley scooted in ahead of her.

"Let me know if you find anything amiss, Charley." Martha chuckled as he stalked through the rooms, tail held high, master of his domain, assured nothing had changed since he left.

She turned on a light and plucked the mail off the floor. She dropped it all on the table, and took her suitcase to the bedroom, flicking on light switches as she went. Her eyes fell on the crumpled piece of paper on the nightstand with George's number. Whether it was fatigue or the burden of grief she didn't know, but she longed to be held, and without thinking she picked up her phone and brought up his number.

Did she want him to answer or not? But on the first ring, she heard his resonant voice.

"Martha?"

"Yes—" Before she could explain her call, he continued as if he had been expecting it.

"I'm so sorry about your grandmother, Delia told me it was sudden. Are you still in Maine?"

"No, I drove back to Baltimore today, I just got in."

"You must be exhausted—and hungry, have you had anything to eat?"

"Lots of coffee and a few snacks along the way." She collapsed on the bed. "I wanted to get back as soon as possible."

"You need some real food, let me take you out to dinner, or would you like me to pick something up and bring it to you?"

She sighed. "Take out sounds lovely, I'm so tired I don't want to move."

"What would you like? Chinese, Italian, or some homemade soup?"

"Mmmm, a bowl of hot soup would be perfect."

"Soup it is, I'll be there in half an hour."

While she waited, Martha showered and changed into her favorite light blue sweatpants and a navy sweatshirt with the Pemaquid Lighthouse beaming across the front. She ran a comb through her damp hair and was pulling it into a loose ponytail when she heard the doorbell. Martha opened the door and immediately burst into tears.

"I'm sorry, it hits me at unexpected times." She gave in to the wash of grief, and hoped George would understand.

His arms encircled her and drew her close, he rested his head on hers as she sobbed into his chest. His tender, comforting touch traveled deep into Martha's soul. She remembered sitting on the rocks in Hope Island Harbor wondering how she would survive this loss, and in that instant, she realized George would be there to help, even if he lived here and she returned to Maine.

When Martha's tears subsided, she took bowls from the cabinet and George ladled chicken soup into them. "This is delicious, as good as Gram's. Where did you get it?"

"My freezer, I'm glad you approve, high compliments indeed coming from you."

"You made it? I'm impressed." Charley chose that moment to join them and jumped uninvited into George's lap.

"Charley, not everyone is willing to share dinner with you," Martha looked apologetically at George. "Charley thinks when anyone sits at the table it's an invitation for him to eat. I guess I spoil him." George laughed, and eased Martha's concern. Charley's presumptuous behavior hadn't annoyed him.

"No problem," he smoothed Charley's head. "My sister and I tried to feed our cats unwanted vegetables. It worked best if they were in our laps."

"My grandmother always had a cat." Grief and guilt threatened to drown Martha, should she tell George about Gram? Maybe it would help. She took a few minutes to absorb comfort from the soup and George's presence. "Gram owned a bakery in Hope Island Harbor, and I promised her I'd go back after culinary school to help. I dreamed of making it a patisserie and chocolate shop. Instead, I married Tony and moved here. I broke my promise to her for a marriage that failed." Martha looked up from her soup, worried at what he would think, but she saw compassion in his eyes. Encouraged, she continued.

196

"Gram left everything to me. She told me to use it to follow my dream, which means I could sell it and open my own shop in Baltimore." She stirred her soup, as if she could find the answer there.

"Sounds like Gram wanted you to decide what you want, and not stay in Maine because you think that's what she wanted." George scratched Charley's chin.

"You're right, but I also know she hoped my Hope Island Harbor dream would be fulfilled someday. I love Maine, and when I stood in the Sunrise Café yesterday, I thought I had made the decision, but now that I'm here, staying in Baltimore has its own appeal." Martha felt George's gaze like a caress, which intensified the confusion in her heart.

"You've got a lot to think about, but you look exhausted," George rose and put the bowls in the sink. "I'm going to head out, is there anything else I can do for you?"

"No, but thank you, soup was exactly what I needed tonight."

"Will you be in Baltimore for a while?" He shrugged into his jacket and walked to the front door. "Would you like to have dinner again, in a restaurant next time?" He smiled and Martha felt a warm rush despite her fatigue.

"I'll be here until I get things sorted at Sweet Selections, then I'll be back and forth through Christmas. Holidays are busy in both places, and I have several wedding cakes ordered for Thanksgiving and Christmas weddings here. Meanwhile, I need to decide what I'm going to do." Her mind seesawed. In Maine, the decision to follow her original dream appeared clear, but now she was unsure again. "Yes, I'd love to have dinner." Perhaps more time with George would reveal which dream she should follow.

"Get some sleep," he leaned down and kissed her tenderly on the cheek, "I'll call you tomorrow, to see what night works with your schedule." He opened the door, then brushed her lips with his, "Good night."

Martha shut the door behind him, she closed her eyes and felt the brief touch of his lips on hers, along with her racing heart. *Do I really want to move back to Hope Island Harbor?*

❈ ❈ ❈

George drove home feeling as confused as Martha had looked. When he held her close as she wept in his arms, he never wanted to let her go, he longed to keep her safe with him. He wanted to tell her more about the house he'd bought and restored with dreams of raising a family there. He hadn't told her about the yearning inside him every time he thought about her either, but he'd have to wait for the conversation he wanted to have. Martha hadn't shared the details of her divorce, but when she spoke about it, George heard her self-recrimination, she thought she'd failed along with her marriage.

Though too exhausted to realize it herself, she'd already decided to move back to Maine. He could see the determination to follow her dream in her eyes, she'd changed direction for a man once, she wouldn't do it again. As Martha painted her dreams for her grandmother's bakery, his dream to share his life with her faded, and he wondered if she would ever live in the yellow house. He refused to give up; he'd relish any time he spent with her, and try to figure out a way to share his feelings—staying hopeful that they might have a future together.

Chapter 32

The next morning, after a quick cup of coffee, Martha drove to Sweet Selections. Sarah bustled behind the counter, filling orders for the breakfast rush. She finished serving a customer then dashed over to give Martha a silent hug. Martha appreciated Sarah's sensitivity; she would have crumbled under words of sympathy.

"Grab a coffee and I'll be there in a few minutes." Martha nodded, helped herself to coffee and took it into the kitchen to wait. The sweet, spicy fragrance of cinnamon rolls and apple crumb cake enveloped her like a soothing hug.

Sarah brought her own coffee into the kitchen and put a plate holding two cinnamon rolls on the table. "I'm so sorry about your grandmother, how are you doing?" She sat down and squeezed Martha's hand.

"This morning I'm okay, sometimes I'm a mess. I have to decide what comes next, Gram left me the bakery and the house in Hope Island Harbor."

"Isn't that what you've been dreaming about? Having your own patisserie and chocolate shop? Now you can. What's to decide?" Puzzlement creased Sarah's face.

"I could move back to Maine and expand the bakery, or I could sell everything and open my own patisserie here."

"Could you? Could you sell everything? You were so excited about going back to see Gram and finally spending time with her. You didn't even want to find a permanent place to live. I know your grandmother's gone, but isn't your dream for her bakery worth keeping?"

"I saw George last night." Martha twisted her coffee cup back and forth, if she shared her confusion with Sarah, perhaps it would clarify her conflicting dreams.

"He held me when I fell apart. It seemed—right, to be with him, like the first day we met, he even brought me homemade soup."

"You gave up your dreams once for Tony, do you want to do it again for George?" Sarah's words gave voice to the question plaguing Martha.

"I don't know, I think one thing when I'm surrounded by work and another when I'm with him, but right now I have four wedding cake orders for Thanksgiving and four more for Christmas. Even if I don't take any new orders, I'll have to scramble to get those cakes made and be in Hope Island Harbor to help with the holiday rush."

"I think you've made your decision," Sarah said, "if you weren't going back to Maine, helping them with the holiday rush wouldn't matter."

❊ ❊ ❊

Martha sat at the kitchen table in Sweet Selections and planned her baking and travel schedule. Her phone rang, and when she saw George's name, she floated up from her chair.

"Hi George, you have perfect timing, I'll soon be elbow deep in cake batter." Martha donned an apron as she spoke.

"Sounds like fun, I won't keep you long, I wanted to ask you when we could have dinner."

A flush of pleasure crept over her, and the prospect of seeing George sent plans for Gram's bakery into hiding. "I'm going to be baking nonstop for the next few days, how about Friday night?"

"That's good, I'm finishing a project at work, sounds like we'll both be ready for a break by then. Six-thirty?"

"Perfect."

Martha set her phone down and smiled. The kitchen gleamed like it wore a fresh coat of paint, and the lingering fatigue from the past week vanished. She hummed as she started weighing sugar for the lemon almond pound cakes.

Martha fell into the rhythm of measuring ingredients, but her mind addressed a different issue, as her hands followed the recipe on their own. She considered Sarah's words, and wondered if she'd been right. *Have I already made the decision?*

❈ ❈ ❈

Martha baked continuously, arriving home late every night. By Friday, weariness engulfed her, but she didn't have time for a nap. George would arrive in less than an hour. Excitement rushed through her, erasing her need for sleep. She gave Charley a quick snuggle, then headed for the shower.

"What shall I wear, Charley? George hasn't exactly seen me at my best, so I want to improve on sweatpants and jeans." She rummaged through her closet to find something festive as well as warm. Though nothing like Maine, a cold snap had hit Baltimore, ushered in by a freezing drizzle.

Martha settled on her favorite cream tunic sweater and black leggings that hugged all her curves. She piled her hair into a loose bun on top of her head, and looped a light woolen scarf, swirled with the flaming colors of autumn in New England, around her neck. Her earrings, topaz teardrops suspended from fine gold chains, caught the golden highlights of her hair. Anticipation swirled around her along with a spritz of her favorite Chanel perfume, and she declared herself ready.

Charley trailed her into the kitchen, where she filled his food and water dishes and gave him a scratch under the chin.

"Okay Charley, enjoy your evening, I won't be late." The doorbell rang and Martha hurried to answer it, her heart skipped along with her.

"Hey Martha." George held out a bouquet of yellow roses. "I saw these and thought of you."

"They're beautiful George, thank you." She buried her nose in them and inhaled. George continued to touch her heart with his thoughtfulness.

"Mmmm, they smell delicious. I'll put them in some water before we go."

"I made reservations at The Blue Hydrangea, I hope that's okay," George followed her into the kitchen.

"It's one of my favorites, small and cozy, and the menu's always changing." She arranged the flowers in a tall, footed vase.

"I'm glad you approve, I remembered you love Fells Point." He helped her with her coat and opened the car door for her, small gestures that Martha appreciated.

Johnny Cash stepped into a "Ring of Fire" when George started the car.

"I grew up with Johnny Cash, he was one of Gram's favorites, are you a fan?"

"Definitely, his singing provides the perfect background when I'm in restoration mode."

"His songs make great traveling music too, he kept Charley and me company when we drove back to Baltimore from Pensacola." Persistent, freezing rain didn't help the heavy Friday night traffic. Martha let George focus on driving, and she listened to the music and enjoyed the comfortable silence.

The Blue Hydrangea was tucked into a quiet corner along Thames Street. Martha had been there in warmer weather, and had dined al fresco on a patio overlooking the harbor, but tonight indigo drapes blocked the chill, and candles glowed on every table. Once seated, Martha took a few minutes to peruse the menu, the special butternut squash soup with sage butter caught her eye.

"How's the baking going, were you able to finish all the cakes?" George asked after placing their order.

"I finished the cakes for Thanksgiving weekend, and I can wait until later in December to bake for the Christmas weddings." The server brought their wine and Martha took a sip.

"Mmmm, delicious. I'll fly to Maine tomorrow, help with the café's Thanksgiving orders, then fly back to decorate the wedding cakes and have them ready to pick up on Friday and Saturday."

"Sounds like an exhausting schedule. Where will you celebrate Thanksgiving?" Martha heard the disappointment in his voice—surely he hadn't hoped to spend Thanksgiving with her. That day belonged to families.

"I'll be in the bakery decorating cakes, but Sarah promised me plenty of pumpkin pie to eat." She laughed and rested her cheek on one hand, then got lost for a moment in his warm brown eyes. Embarrassed by her schoolgirl trance, she straightened and said, "How about you, are you going back to Cape Cod for the holiday?"

"No, much to my mother's dismay. I've got a project with a tight deadline, and I decided to stay in Baltimore to work on it. My friends Nick and Mandy invited me to have dinner with them, as did Delia when she discovered I would be here. Does she know you'll be in town?"

"Not yet, and I'm hoping she doesn't find out, because she won't stop pestering me until I agree to have dinner with her family. But the truth is, I'm not feeling much like a family holiday celebration. I'll be happier working; it consumes my mind. Besides, if I don't, I'll never finish four wedding cakes by Saturday." The server delivered their soups and conversation paused for a moment.

"I'll be around all weekend, call me when you need a break. You can't work nonstop, you have to eat, and it helps to step back and get a fresh perspective. We can go for a walk or a run, or grab a pizza. When you're ready for a longer break, there's something I'd like to show you."

"What is it?" Martha's spoon paused midway to her mouth. His vague comment intrigued her. Had he made a discovery about something they saw on their day together?

"Better to see it, let me know when you've got a couple of hours free."

"Sounds mysterious, but that's okay, while I'm baking, I can think of all the possibilities. Tell me about your usual family Thanksgiving, you mentioned your mom's disappointed, do you have a big gathering?" Martha resumed eating her soup while she listened.

"My sister Valerie always comes with her husband and three kids. She lives in Maine and teaches elementary school like my mom. Some years my aunt and uncle come, and sometimes my cousins and their kids come. It gets a little wild with seven boys under the age of eight. My mother finds a few extra people who have nowhere to be for Thanksgiving and invites them as well."

"It sounds crazy and wonderful. My Thanksgivings were always quiet, except for one year in culinary school when a November snowstorm prevented me from going home. I spent it with Delia's family, which bore a close resemblance to yours. So many aunts, uncles and cousins arrived, I couldn't keep track of who was who." Martha chuckled at the memory of that holiday and continued.

"I finally understood why Delia's incapable of silence, she grew up in a house where everybody talked at once. They yelled and teased nonstop, but somehow the threads of conversation wove together, and I didn't have time to feel homesick for Gram." When she mentioned Gram, a sudden wave of grief washed over her. All the sweet memories of holidays in Hope Island Harbor warred with the empty ones when she stayed in Baltimore, and Tony worked. Sorrow for the time lost throbbed like an open wound and threatened her composure. Martha excused herself and left the table.

"I'm sorry, I needed a minute," she touched George's shoulder when she returned. "Did you always know you wanted to be an architect?" Concern flashed in George's eyes, but he followed the change in conversation.

"Pretty much. My dad's a gifted carpenter. He's passionate about preserving and restoring old homes, as well as protecting the shoreline on the Cape from developers. If he had his way, no new houses would ever be built. I worked with him when I was in high school, and before, from the time he thought I could help and stay out of trouble. I learned to see the beauty and hidden possibilities in the old wood from him. Like magic, he'd breathe new life into a house you'd swear was beyond saving." Martha immersed herself in George's story and the harsh edge of her grief softened.

"You admire your dad, is he why you decided to restore old factories and mills?" The server brought their seared scallop entrees and George waited to answer.

"Indirectly, when I went to school, I wanted to design green homes. I could see the beauty in the old homes, but I preferred to create energy-efficient new ones. Despite my dad's wishes, we still have to build houses.

"My senior year in college, I had an internship at a prominent Rhode Island firm. They were building a mini-mansion in Watch Hill and they wanted it as environmentally friendly as possible." George paused, took a sip of wine, and a deep breath. Martha waited, he seemed torn about sharing more. Did he worry about her response, as she had his, when she told him about her broken promise to Gram?

"Elaine had an internship at a cooperating interior design firm and we worked on the same house. We started dating, and after graduation she accepted an offer with a firm in Connecticut. When Winthrop and Delaney offered me a job in their New Haven office, she encouraged me to accept.

"I thought I could influence the customers' choice of designs and materials for the better, but my dad told me I'd sold my soul to the devil, and a few years later, I agreed with him. After Elaine died, I kept working there out of habit, until my friend Nick called and offered me this job." It surprised Martha to learn George had given up on his career dreams. And it sounded as if the job had caused a rift with his dad that still troubled him.

"You must have jumped at the chance to restore old buildings again."

"Yes, after Nick wooed me with free tickets to a Ravens football game."

Martha laughed. "But you love it, I can tell. You're excited even though you're working on Thanksgiving weekend."

"I do. The aged brick and precise lines of the old mills fascinate me." While they finished dinner, Martha pictured the company's signature living walls, studded with plants, that he described in detail.

George stopped and shook his head. "Sorry, I get carried away when I talk about this project."

"You don't need to apologize, I enjoy listening to your ideas and descriptions. I feel the same way when I'm designing a cake." After they shared an exquisite chocolate mousse for dessert, Martha vowed she couldn't eat another bite.

The freezing drizzle had subsided when they left the restaurant, but a raw wind blew across the harbor and Martha tucked her chin inside the folds of her scarf. George took her hand and Martha felt its warmth radiate through her body. He continued to hold it on the drive home.

"I enjoyed tonight Martha, and I'm really glad you decided to run the marathon."

"Me too." Reference to the marathon brought back a mental picture with a tag of jealousy attached. George hadn't mentioned Lucy again, but Martha wondered how much she mattered to him.

"I had a lovely time tonight, but there's something I have to ask you."

"What is it?" Although his gentle tone encouraged her, Martha chewed on her lip, trying to find a tactful way to ask George about the "other woman."

"Some friends joined you at the marathon, I know about Nick and Mandy now, but I can't help wondering about Lucy." Martha feared George would think her question petty or intrusive, but he didn't hesitate.

"Lucy's a childhood friend of Mandy's. She's a nurse and recently moved back to Baltimore. Mandy and Nick arranged a blind date last summer. We've become friends, but I know that's all we'll ever be, and she feels the same way. You can meet her on Thanksgiving, if you change your mind about joining us." Martha had been holding her breath, but she exhaled with relief at George's explanation. She didn't think he would see someone else too, but his answer reassured her. She didn't want to wander down a path of make-believe romance again, and the more time she spent with George, the more she wanted to be with him.

George parked in front of Martha's apartment and faced her. "Remember, if you need a break let me know, and we can get together, even for coffee or a walk."

"We'll see." Spending time with George sounded tempting, but she'd need every minute to finish the cakes.

He walked her to her door, and a second away from inviting him in, reality interceded—she had an early morning flight. When she attempted to put her key in the lock, George looped his arms around her, and spun her to him. He drew her close, resting his forehead against hers. Martha slid her arms around him, nestled her head in his chest, and basked in his closeness.

"I wish I didn't have to wait a week to see you again." His breath fluttered over her ear.

"I feel the same way," she tipped her head up, but kept her arms in place.

"What time is your flight tomorrow?"

"Seven, there aren't many choices going to Portland. Besides, I need as much time as possible in Hope Island Harbor to help with holiday orders. I think everyone in town ordered their Thanksgiving pies from the Sunrise Café."

"I guess that means you're not inviting me in for coffee." His hands rested on her shoulders. "I'll call you during the week." Before she could answer, he lowered his head and kissed her with a mix of longing and regret. Martha responded, and the passion emanating from George fueled her own, until breathless, she pulled back and looked at him.

I want to see this face every morning. Martha questioned again if she wanted to return to Maine. But Sarah's words danced staccato across her mind. "Could you do it? Sell everything? You gave up your dreams once, do you want to do it again?"

Chapter 33

Martha flopped into the window seat like an empty duffle bag. She tipped her head back and closed her eyes, weary after a sleepless night. When George brought her home, she knew he wanted to stay, but as much as she yearned to invite him in, she couldn't. If she allowed him to get that close, she would never be able to leave.

She knew one place where she could heal from this pain and grief. One place where she'd be sung to sleep by the wash of waves, one place where she'd wake to light filtered through the fog and the sound of gulls' raucous cries. She had to be in Hope Island Harbor.

As much as Martha longed to fall asleep snuggled against George, and feel his comforting arms around her, she needed to walk this path by herself. Gram was gone and nothing could change that, but she had to make peace with her delayed return to Hope Island Harbor. She had to find Gram's forgiveness. She had to forgive herself, and she had to do it all alone. It was the only way she would emerge whole on the other side.

Martha needed solitary time to think. She rented a car in Portland and images of George and Gram spiraled through her brain as she drove back to Hope Island Harbor. Every time she thought of seeing George again, her spirits soared.

Although she still felt the searing pain of Gram's death, being with George plucked her from the mire of grief and allowed her to view it from a distance, gain perspective, instead of wallowing in it. Gram's letter weighed on her mind and she wanted to tell George about it, but Gram's message changed her life in ways she couldn't fathom herself. How could she share it with him?

She missed Charley's calming purr beside her as she drove. His presence helped her focus when he listened quietly or commented with his perceptive meows. Since she'd be in Maine for only a few days, Charley stayed behind at her apartment, but the silence of the empty passenger seat unsettled her.

The next days went by in a blur of pie crust and exhaustion. She had spoken on the phone to Jeanette, who'd told her that when the town learned that Martha would be keeping the bakery open, Thanksgiving orders multiplied. People trusted her to be every bit as good a baker as her grandmother.

Originally, Martha remembered, Gram had made three varieties, apple, pumpkin and squash. Over the years she'd added more choices by request, including apple crumb and pumpkin chiffon with a gingersnap crust.

"I can picture her the day someone from away came in to order a cheesecake for Thanksgiving." Jeanette chuckled at the memory. "Jessie told her she could order any of the pies offered, but cheesecake would have to wait until after Thanksgiving. After the customer left, she fluffed her way into the kitchen like a bird disturbed from his nest muttering, 'Imagine wanting cheesecake for Thanksgiving, whoever heard of such a thing. Pie is for Thanksgiving.'" Martha laughed, but tears streamed down her cheeks and she ended the call before sobs overcame her.

Jeanette knew the best system to have all the pies baked fresh for Thanksgiving, so Martha left the schedule in her hands. The ovens would run all night to make it possible for customers to pick them up Thanksgiving morning. Martha wouldn't be there for the baking marathon, but she made sure that every piecrust was ready for its filling before she flew to Baltimore on Tuesday night.

On Wednesday morning, Martha woke in her Baltimore apartment with Charley curled against her back. She dragged herself from exhausted sleep and shuffled to the kitchen to make coffee. While it brewed, she took a quick shower, dressed, and fed Charley. Although every step felt like slogging through wet cement, she arrived at Sweet Selections by six.

"Welcome back, how was Maine?" Sarah looked up from filling the display case and smiled.

"Crazy busy, I've never rolled so many pie crusts in my life."

"Here"—Sarah held out a steaming mug of coffee in one hand and a cinnamon roll in the other—"you look exhausted." Martha took a bite of the roll, Sarah's tasted as good as Gram's and they had become Martha's comfort food.

"Thanks, the weather in Portland delayed my flight, and I didn't get in until late last night." Martha took a sip of her coffee and leaned against the counter.

"Let me know if I can help, I've got a little time before the breakfast rush."

"Just keep the coffee coming," Martha brushed crumbs from her hands and moved towards the kitchen. "I feel muzzy headed, and it's going to be a long day."

Martha removed the layers for the first two cakes from the walk-in freezer, and lined them on the counter. Then she made lemon curd for the lemon almond pound cake and ginger cream cheese frosting for the parsnip chai cakes. While she worked, her mind vacillated between dreams for the Sunrise Café and her desire to spend time with George. The balance kept shifting, increasing her indecision. By the time she finished the fillings, the cakes had thawed, and were ready to frost and decorate. She pushed thoughts of Gram and George to the recesses of her mind and focused on the cakes before her. One required the stacked layers be carved and then, after frosting, decorated with intricate lace patterns to replicate the bride's wedding gown.

Sarah closed the bakery at six, an hour later than usual, to accommodate Thanksgiving orders. "Can I bring you something to eat, Martha? You haven't stopped working all day."

"I'm too tired to be hungry. Besides, Angie brought me another cinnamon roll and more coffee before she left." Martha stretched her arms over her head and added, "I'm hoping to be done in another hour or so, I'll get dinner when I go home."

She picked up her cell phone and saw two messages from George. He asked how she was doing and if she needed a break. She'd been so engrossed in assembling the cakes, she hadn't even noticed the texts. As much as she wanted to answer, she'd wait until she finished, then enjoy their conversation.

Martha didn't leave the bakery until after nine, and arrived home stiff and tired from hours bent over the counter. But she had assembled two cakes. She would finish tomorrow, and the cakes would be delivered Friday morning.

She walked directly to the bathroom, peeling her clothes from her tired body as she went, and stepped into a hot shower. When she finished, Martha intended to call George; however, she wrapped herself in a terry robe and fell across the bed, instantly asleep.

The next morning the phone startled her awake and she jumped from the bed when she saw George's name.

"Oh, George," she moaned, "I'm so sorry I didn't call you last night. I fell asleep before I could call you, eat dinner, or feed Charley. No wonder he's meowing as we speak."

"I figured you must have worn yourself out, but I wanted to say Happy Thanksgiving, see if I could persuade you to come to dinner with me at Nick and Mandy's. It won't be a big production, and you can leave whenever you want."

"I'd love to George, but I can't. I have to decorate two cakes for Friday, and get started on the two for Saturday. I don't think I'll finish much before nine." Martha envisioned a relaxing dinner; it would be fun to get acquainted with George's close friends. She wanted to say, "Yes I'll come," but she'd never have the orders ready on time if she did.

"You've got to eat sometime."

"I'm pretty much running on coffee and adrenaline right now, but Sarah promised to leave a pumpkin pie for me to eat when I need some nourishment."

"When do you think you'll come up for air?" Martha heard disappointment in his voice, and already regretted her answer.

"Probably not until I deliver the cakes on Saturday, at which point I'll go home and sleep until Sunday."

"Okay, I give up, but how about if I take you to brunch on Sunday, and then show you my secret project?"

"That sounds perfect, and George, thank you for understanding. Enjoy Thanksgiving with your friends." The invitation lifted her spirits. She had two grueling days ahead, but then she would see George again.

"Thanks, don't work too hard. See you Sunday, Martha." George's caring tone touched her heart. Tony wouldn't have understood or respected her wishes. He'd have complained about the time she spent at work that interfered with his plans.

Martha fought the urge to call George and tell him she'd changed her mind. She relegated the phone call to the back of her mind and hurried to feed Charley and get to the bakery. She'd overslept, which put her behind schedule.

By noon, she'd finished the two cakes for delivery Friday morning, then she tackled Saturday's. They both entailed elaborate designs. One couple had met on a mountain climbing trip in the Rockies, and wanted their cake to reflect that meeting. Martha had drawn the snow-capped mountain scene she would replicate on the cake, complete with hikers on the trail meeting at the top. The second couple planned to open a flower shop together, and wanted their cake decorated with handmade, botanically correct lilies, the bride's favorite flower.

Immersed in her designs, Martha ignored the coffee she had poured earlier. At four o'clock she put down her pastry bag and stretched. She would take a quick break and start on the lilies, her last project of the day.

Her knife hovered over the pumpkin pie Sarah had left for her, when she heard a knock at the front door. Apprehension froze her in place. She had turned off the lights in the sales area, and didn't want to reveal her presence by opening the door. She waited, heart pounding, hoping the person would give up and move on. However, the knock came again, louder this time.

She debated if she should call the police. Then the handle on the back door rattled and she grabbed her cell phone. Before she could hit 911, she heard someone calling her name.

"Martha, you in there?" Her breath whooshed out in relief when she recognized George's voice and unlocked the door.

"You scared me half to death. I wasn't expecting anyone here today."

"I'm sorry, I sent you a text, but I guess you didn't receive it. I brought you a mini Thanksgiving dinner." He held out a foil-covered plate. "I wasn't sure what you liked, but I figured you wouldn't take time to eat, so I brought a little of everything." Martha drew George into the kitchen and relocked the door. She inhaled the aromas of roast turkey with wild mushroom gravy and sage stuffing, along with nutmeg scented butternut squash and garlic mashed potatoes.

"Oh, it smells wonderful." She took the plate and her heart swelled, he'd taken time from his celebration, concerned about her. "I lowered the volume on my cell phone, so it didn't distract me. I guess I should have checked it now and then, but I got so involved with decorating, I lost track of time. Thank you for bringing me dinner, and please, thank Mandy." Martha ate standing at the counter. "I didn't realize how hungry I was."

"Why don't you sit down and relax for a few minutes?" George pulled a chair over to the counter.

"I need to get back to work, these lilies require total concentration, and I want to finish them before I go home."

"Okay, I'll leave you to it, but finish eating before you go back to work. You can't keep going without any food." He pulled her close for a quick hug and a kiss that left her breathless despite its brevity. "I'll see you Sunday." George left as abruptly as he had arrived.

Midway through the third lily, Martha realized she'd been smiling since George left.

Chapter 34

On Sunday morning, her phone rang at nine o'clock. She saw George's name, and a familiar burst of joy scooted through her.

"Good morning, Martha." His rich baritone and the elation in his voice caused her heart to tap dance in her chest. "I hope I'm not calling too early."

"No, Charley and I are having coffee together, well, I'm having coffee and he's having his first nap of the day."

"Were you able to get everything done and delivered?"

"I did, on time, in one piece, and I came home and crashed. Now I'm ready for brunch." George had been on her mind even when she worked, and thoughts of today had revived her sagging energy more than once.

"How 'bout if I pick you up at ten, I thought we'd go to Sobo Café, they have a fantastic brunch and it isn't far from you. We could walk if you like."

"I'd love to walk. I need to stretch after standing scrunched in one spot decorating for the past few days."

Martha finished her coffee and met George at the door. The sparkling, crystal air made her think of autumn in New England, and Martha looked forward to returning to Maine. But when she tucked her hand into George's elbow as they strolled the short distance to the restaurant, the prospect of more time with him thrilled her. After breakfast, when they walked back, Martha asked him about the mystery he had promised to show her.

"We can be there in about twenty minutes, do you have time now?"

"Absolutely, let's go." He'd piqued her curiosity, and she felt like a child, impatient for her surprise. She imagined a completed mill restoration and looked forward to seeing his work.

They reached Martha's apartment and George opened the car door for her. The crisp day reminded Martha of sitting on drafty bleachers, cheering for her high school football team on Thanksgiving Day, as the freezing air numbed her feet. When she returned to her grandmother's house, the warmth of the woodstove, and the aroma of roasting turkey, had thawed her to a blissful stupor as she set the table. They drove north on Charles Street and she related her thoughts to George.

"Did you ever play football?" She could see him as a wide receiver, with his running speed and large hands.

"No, I was too skinny at that age. I ran track and played soccer; both required more speed than size." Martha glanced over at George and scrutinized his broad shoulders. She thought of the marathon, and the well-defined muscles she'd seen in his arms and legs. They indicated a body conditioned by more than running and designing restored mills, a body familiar with physical work. His hands captured her attention. Sturdy and square, with long fingers, she got lost in imagining how those hands would feel touching her body.

"Martha?" George said loudly, and she knew he had probably said it more than once. "Something on your mind?"

"Oh, I was thinking about the designs for the Christmas wedding cakes." A heated blush spread over her cheeks and she couldn't look at him. "Are you going to give me a hint about where we're going?" His quizzical look implied her change of subject hadn't fooled him, and he didn't believe her answer about wedding cake designs.

"North on Charles Street," he said with a smirk.

"Smart aleck, I can see that." She cuffed him lightly on the shoulder. "Okay, if I guess correctly, will you tell me?"

"I don't think you will, but you're welcome to try."

"I think our destination is related to your work and the recent project you've been so excited about." She was pleased that George wanted to share

215

his work, he must value her opinion. "You consider this your best design yet, and you want to show me the finished product before the world sees it." Eagerness lit her voice, and George glanced at her as he stopped for a red light.

"No, and yes." His twinkling eyes teased her.

"Which means?"

"No, it isn't a mill, yes I want you to see it, and I've enjoyed the work more than anything else I've done in Baltimore, or ever." Martha mulled this over for the time it took to reach the Johns Hopkins campus, a familiar route.

"This is the way to Delia's house," she said. "Are you taking me to Delia's for some reason?"

"No, and yes," he repeated, and Martha laughed.

"You're exasperating, you know."

"Don't you like surprises?"

"I do, so I won't say anymore." Traffic was light, and soon they turned down a street Martha knew well. At that point she couldn't stop herself.

"I knew it, we're going to Delia's. Why are we going to Delia's?"

"We're not," George pulled into the driveway of the house next door.

"You want to show me a house?" Martha frowned in confusion.

When George opened her car door, Martha studied the yellow frame house, its porch open in greeting, and the glistening windows reflecting a friendly smile. She could see why he would enjoy working on it, the house possessed a steady warmth, like Gram's home, and she felt drawn to it. But his desire to show her a house and not a mill, perplexed her.

"It looks happy," she said thoughtfully.

"I think so too, although it appeared a little more forlorn when I bought it. I tried to guide it back to its original charm with the help of paint and a well-directed sander. Come on, I want your opinion on some things." As they ascended the porch steps, Martha visualized children jumping in piles of dried leaves on the lawn. She heard their gleeful shouts, and the imagined smell of woodsmoke wafting on the November air percolated in her mind.

George unlocked the door, took her hand and drew her inside. She stopped and surveyed the sunlit hallway; light glinted off the polished wood bannister and sent rainbows of color shimmering up the stairs.

216

"Wow! Did you do all this?"

"The basic bones are the same, but I stripped and refinished floors and woodwork."

"What did it look like when you bought it?"

"Brown paint everywhere," he showed her a few "before" pictures on his phone. "It masked hardwood floors and this magnificent mahogany bannister, the paint hid all the best features." Martha continued to gaze around the hall in appreciation, thinking how many hours of labor it represented.

"Come on, I'll show you the rest," George led the way upstairs. He guided her through the bedrooms, all cozy and inviting. "Most of the rooms needed a facelift of sanded floors and fresh paint, except the bathroom, which required total remodeling." He described the pink and gray color scheme he had replaced, which made the claw foot tub, pedestal sink, and pale turquoise walls even more appealing. It looked like Cape Cod Bay on a sunny day.

Downstairs, he had joined the kitchen and the sunporch, creating one large, bright room with ample space for a family to gather. Polished white beadboard cabinets accented the pale blue walls, and a round, antique oak table circled by four oak chairs sat in the center. Beneath the sunny windows, a row of shelves held flourishing pots with tarragon and chives. It reminded Martha of Annie's house on the Cape, and it couldn't have pleased her more if she'd designed it herself.

"You moved Cape Cod to Baltimore."

"Or Maine to Baltimore?"

"Yes, I think a bit of Maine got carried along too. How did you do all this and keep up with your work? I mean this isn't part of your job, is it?"

"No, although I think it has more of my sweat and tears than my work does. My job consumes my mind during the day, and sometimes into the evening, but eventually my brain needs a break. Most of the renovations here were straightforward and physical, guide the sander, brush on the polyurethane, replace a wall or two." George made it all sound easy, but Martha guessed the amount of labor required had worn him out more than once.

217

"I get into a rhythm, and my brain is free to wander, sometimes on work designs, sometimes on the next step for the house, sometimes on nothing at all. Even when my mind roams, I have the finished vision guiding me from my subconscious. By the time I call it quits, I'm mentally rested and my body's tired, but relaxed."

"I feel the same way when I'm decorating a cake. The work is painstaking and demanding, but satisfying when I'm finished." George would understand if she needed hours to perfect a design, and she found that reassuring. Tony used to say, "It's just a cake, Martha." She rotated, taking in the detailed molding and quartz counters.

"What do you think?" He sounded hesitant, as if her approval mattered to him.

"I think if you ever decide to sell it, the new owners will be lucky, but I can see you here, the house suits you."

"When I first viewed it last spring, its character and need for attention intrigued me. As I worked to restore it, I saw myself raising a family here, and I pictured you in the house with me. I think it suits you too."

Martha stared at him without saying a word. The visions of the two of them married and raising children, Delia next door, the kids growing up together, rolled through her head. Running beside them were images of big "For Sale" signs on both Gram's house and the Sunrise Café. Did he want her to discard her dreams like Tony had? She shook her head to erase the pictures in her mind.

"Why would you picture me here when you hardly know me?" Dismay edged her voice. Vestiges of Tony's controlling behavior loomed in her mind. They whirled together with Gram's death, her attraction to George, and decisions about the bakery, creating a tsunami of emotion that sucked the breath from her lungs. She needed space. "I can't talk about this now. I have to go home." She left the house without another word.

"Martha, wait," George followed her down the steps. "I didn't mean to upset you, I'm sorry." She kept walking towards Delia's house.

"Never mind, I'll ask Delia to take me home." George caught up with her.

"Delia's not here, come back. I'll take you home and try to explain better this time. I know you're angry."

Martha stopped, but didn't take his offered hand. She studied Delia's house, no children ran about and Delia hadn't come outside to greet them, two clear indications that her friend wasn't home. She sighed and returned to George's car.

"I'm sorry, Martha," he repeated and opened her door. "I never should have shown you the house thinking you'd want to live here. That was my dream, not yours."

"How could you dream that? Until the marathon you'd only spent one day with me." Martha again felt the pressure of someone else's dreams and sank further into her seat.

"I hate apartment living, and when I moved to Baltimore I looked at houses. When I first saw this house, I knew I'd found the right one. It had good bones, and although neglected, it had everything I wanted. I hoped to see it come to life under my hands. I invested my heart in it." George started the car and backed out of the driveway, Martha waited, sensing he had more to say.

"The day I met you, I could see the shadow of pain in your eyes, though you didn't reveal the cause. But I also saw a sparkle of joy, a spirit of fun and adventure, and I wanted that part of you to come alive with me, because I fell in love with you that first day, Martha." George glanced at her. "I know it's not what you want to hear, but I can't help how I feel."

"How could you love me after one day?" She'd been swept away by imaginary love before. Without giving him a chance to respond, she continued. "I broke a promise to my grandmother, gave up my dreams to follow Tony to Baltimore. I thought we shared a dream we'd pursue together, but he cared about his own dreams, mine got in his way. I can't forfeit my dream for someone else's again." Martha looked out the window, her own words reinforced her decision to return to Maine.

"I didn't mean to push my dreams on you," George said, "but the day I met you I knew I wanted to see you again. Then I messed everything up by not telling you about Elaine. I couldn't get you out of my mind, and I was afraid I'd never find you."

Martha looked over at George but didn't speak. George had stayed in her mind too, although she'd tried to shut him out.

"I kept my dream of finding you alive by envisioning you in this house. I knew when I saw you at the marathon, I hadn't imagined my feelings the day we met. I wanted to see you again, and after dinner that night, I got the distinct impression you wanted to see me too." He stole a quick questioning look at Martha.

"I did," Martha whispered. "But my life has changed since the marathon. I feel as if I'm free falling and I don't know how to stick the landing, or where I should plant my feet, in Baltimore or in Maine."

George clasped Martha's hand. "When you came back, after your grandmother's funeral, you said being here made you question going back to Maine. I hoped you meant being with me, but I didn't expect you to suddenly decide to stay because I showed you the house. I knew you'd go back to Hope Island Harbor, even if you hadn't figured it out yet. I wanted you to know how much I hope to stay a part of your life. I love you, Martha."

"How can you love me? You don't know me." Martha drew her hand away, his touch added to her confusion.

"I know all I need to know." He kept his eyes on the road. "I know you love ice cream, and flowers, and life. And you're willing to take time to enjoy them. I know I'm happier and more at peace when I'm with you than I have ever been with anyone else. I know you're an amazing pastry chef, but I also know you've been carrying guilt with you for the past eight years, because you didn't go back and help Gram.

"If your dream is to live in Hope Island Harbor for the rest of your life, and make your grandmother's bakery famous, then do it. But make sure the decision is based on your dream and not your guilt over letting Gram down, because that's not what she would have wanted."

George parked in front of Martha's apartment and she opened the car door. "How can you presume to think you know what I'll do, or what I want and why?" She closed the car door and ran to her apartment without a backward glance. Once inside, she let the tears fall, then she remembered that George knew exactly how much she hurt, and the burden of guilt she carried.

Martha closed her eyes and leaned against the door. She took a long, calming breath, and the chaos in her brain quieted. In her heart, she knew George and Tony were different, and George would never treat her the way Tony had. But the impact of her marriage and divorce still lurked deep in the recesses of her mind, and when it surfaced, a march of doubt beat in her head.

Now she imagined George sitting beside her, hands resting on the steering wheel, and remembered her grandfather. His knotted, weathered hands were those of a workman, callused, strong, and tanned from the sun. Tiny tufts of hair sprouted from the back of his knuckles, and she could see their strength when he hammered a nail, or fit a fieldstone in the perfect spot of a wall, the tendons standing out as his strong fingers grasped the heavy weight. Those same hands became gentle when he lifted Martha to his shoulders or swung her behind him for a piggyback ride.

Martha loved her grandfather, and when she pictured him, she saw his hand holding her much smaller one. She saw the same strength coiled in the stillness of George's hands, felt their tenderness when they brushed tears from her cheek. Strength ran through his arms and into his shoulders, permeated the muscles of his legs and rested in his heart and his head, but his heart also held kindness and compassion.

He cared deeply for her, and she had shoved him away with hurtful words. Why did she do that? She came face to face with reality, her dreams traveled two different roads, each leading to its own rewards. Did either choice close the door on the other path? She felt lured in two directions by the desires of her heart and her dreams for success. Did she have to relinquish one dream to allow the other to come true?

Chapter 35

Delia had left Baltimore the day after Thanksgiving to visit her family, which George knew when he took Martha to see the house. He hadn't wanted Delia to run over to tell Martha how great it would be if she were living next door. Now he speculated on whether he'd made a mistake. Would it have eased the tension between them if Delia's bubbling presence had been part of the afternoon?

He should never have shown Martha the house so soon, or at all, he thought in frustration. He should have waited until they'd spent more time together, he could have told her about the house and let things evolve naturally. But he got carried away by his own passion, and his dream.

Monday morning when he saw Deirdre board the school bus, he walked to Delia's and knocked on her door. Maybe she'd have some advice on how to restore Martha's trust. She asked for space, so he hadn't called her, though he'd come close several times.

"Hi George. You look awful, are you coming down with something?" Delia held the door open. "Come in, I'm feeding the baby."

"I blew it again with Martha." He paced the kitchen and dragged his hands through his hair. "I'll never learn."

"What do you mean? She's crazy about you." Delia poured a cup of coffee and handed it to George.

"Not anymore. I showed her the house and told her my vision for it."

"Why did you buy it, anyway? I've often wondered why a single man would want a family house." Delia spooned oatmeal into Maura's waiting mouth. George explained that he had bought the house because he wanted a project and it needed him. But as he restored it, he pictured Martha there with him. Delia's mouth dropped open.

"And you told her this?"

George nodded regretfully.

"You do know about Tony, don't you?"

"Yes, she told me that she gave up her dream of working in the bakery with her grandmother to follow him to Baltimore. I guess now she thinks I'm asking her to give up her dream, like Tony did."

"It was more than that." Delia gave Maura her sippy cup and focused her attention on George. "Tony fed her a line about how they were going to do everything together, build their dreams together, open a restaurant together. Then it was like somebody flipped a switch when they arrived in Baltimore. He didn't experience instant success, as he expected, and he took out his frustration on Martha. When she found her niche as a pastry chef, he belittled her, told her she had no talent, would never make it without him, and for reasons I will never understand, she believed him."

"What?" Fury took over when he imagined Tony treating Martha so callously, but he lowered his voice when he saw Maura's lip tremble. He hadn't meant to shout. "How on Earth could Martha believe that? She seems, I don't know, in love with life. She's incredibly talented, I saw pictures from the Charm City Chocolate Challenge that were published—she won second place!"

"I know, but she hadn't made a name for herself back then, and she was convinced Tony knew everything. As she drew more notice from the Baltimore food critics, Tony resented the attention she received. The sad thing is, Tony's an amazing chef, but he wanted instant fame, and that didn't happen. Martha worked hard, but the more celebrated she became for her unusual wedding cakes, the angrier he got, and the more he disparaged her. She felt like a failure."

"And now after her grandmother's death, she feels so guilty she has to go back to Maine—if only to make peace with herself." After learning more about Tony, he understood Martha's reaction to the yellow house.

223

"Give her some time, I know she cares about you, but she's afraid of disappointing Gram, even though she's gone. She wants to keep the promise she made, but she also needs to find herself after trying to become the person Tony wanted."

"You're right, and I don't think she wants to see me right now," he rubbed his hands over his face, resignation in his voice. "I'll give her some time to figure things out."

❈ ❈ ❈

After Thanksgiving, Martha returned to Hope Island Harbor to begin the Christmas baking. She sat at Gram's kitchen table drinking coffee and watching sunlight peeking over Hope Island. The day was in a rush to wake up, but she wasn't. Jeanette had told her to sleep in this morning, and Martha readily agreed. Since she'd be in Maine for several weeks, she and Charley had driven back from Baltimore the day before, and an accident on the Jersey turnpike suspended traffic for hours. She arrived in Hope Island Harbor at two in the morning. Despite her fatigue, the turmoil in her mind destroyed her sleep, and she woke when the first shard of daylight pierced her curtains. She hoped a jolt of caffeine would clear the haze in her brain.

Martha sat stroking Charley's soft, purring fur, when she heard a faint knock at the kitchen door. She would have thought she had imagined it, except for the bulky shape, swathed in scarves against the cold, standing on her back porch. *Who can be here at this early hour?* She rose, more curious than concerned, placed Charley on the chair she'd vacated, and in the same fluid motion tightened the knot of the tie on her blue fleece robe. She opened the door.

"Can I help you?" The woman unwound her scarf and Martha drew a sharp breath and put her hand to her mouth as she looked into a pair of turquoise eyes, the exact shade of her own, peering out from the face of her grandmother. The face she had seen in countless pictures, the younger version of the face she'd seen every day growing up, the face of the sad woman holding Martha when she was a baby. Her hair had gone gray and hung in a long braid down her back.

"Martha?" she hesitated. "You look just like your father." Martha remained frozen, one hand on the doorknob, the other covering her open mouth. She couldn't put words together as her mind raced from her grandmother's letter to the picture of the woman holding her as a baby; it flew through the years of growing up and landed in a heap back here with this woman she knew must be her mother. She closed her mouth and opened it again, but no words came out.

"May I come in?" The woman didn't move. Martha regained enough composure to nod.

"Please, sit down, would you like some coffee?" Martha closed the door.

"Yes, thank you."

Grateful for something to occupy her body, Martha's mind tried to make sense out of the situation. *My mother is alive? Here?* Was it really her, or was her imagination playing tricks, was she overtired from the drive the day before, and having an awake dream? But when she poured the hot coffee into a mug, it spilled, burning her. *This isn't a dream.* She ran cold water over her reddening hand.

"I'm sorry," the woman said. "I shouldn't have come without calling, but I didn't think you'd agree to see me." She sounded both apologetic and defensive. "Maybe I shouldn't have come at all, but I wanted to see you. I wanted to come to the funeral, but the Monhegan ferry was fogged in and I couldn't get here. I'm sorry about your grandmother."

"You mean your mother?" Martha snapped as she placed the mug of coffee in front of her guest. The woman made it sound like Gram had been related to Martha, but not her.

"Yes, my mother, I saw the obituary in the paper." She grasped the mug in her hands. "Thank you for the coffee." Martha thought of her grandmother dying without seeing her only child, who lived close by, and found her voice. The questions tumbled out like apples tipped from a basket.

"Where have you been? Why didn't you visit her when she was sick? Why did you leave me? Why didn't you come back? Didn't you love me? I thought you were dead, who allows her child to think she is dead when she isn't?" Martha clamped her jaws shut to stop the tirade and stood glaring down at her mother.

The woman drew in a deep shuddering breath. "I don't know how to answer those questions, except for one, yes, I loved you from the moment I knew I was pregnant, and all the other answers hinge on that. I left and didn't come back because I loved you. I knew your grandmother and grandfather would do what I was incapable of doing, caring for you and watching over you as you grew. I thought it would be easier for you if you thought I was dead than if you knew I was alive, but not here with you."

"Easier for me or easier for you?" She found it impossible to equate love with desertion. If you loved someone you stayed and made it work, like her grandparents had.

The woman Martha couldn't think of her as her mother sighed again.

"I loved your father to distraction, I didn't feel whole without him— not a healthy way to love. We were never apart until you were born." Martha took a sip of coffee, she heard the pain in her mother's voice, but it didn't diminish her anger.

"You looked so like him, he fell totally in love with you, and you with him." At the mention of her father's reaction, she looked at her mother and saw a smile hovering at the memory. "When you were an infant, he could soothe your nighttime cries in a way I never could, and as you got older, he could make you giggle with abandon. You were content with me, but your daddy took your joy to another level that I never could."

Martha felt a stabbing pain of loss for the father she never knew, and tears coursed down her cheeks. Her mother continued, her voice flat and her eyes lost in the distance, as if seeing through Martha.

"Your father didn't want to leave, but he got an assignment to cover the war in the Middle East, and he thought he had to go. When I heard the news of his death, I screamed and wailed, and I frightened you. Every time your grandmother tried to hand you to me, you clung to her instead. But then I wasn't reaching for you either, I couldn't, I just couldn't." She hung her head.

"Didn't you want me anymore?" Martha whispered. Growing up, she had never felt unwanted, but she did now, and she shriveled inside.

"I should have taken comfort in having you, a part of him, but the pain was overwhelming, and nothing helped, I felt like I'd died with your father. Your grandmother thought I needed time, and she was right, I did need time, more than either one of us ever imagined." Her mother stared at her, but it seemed as if her mind had gone far away. Martha stood and retrieved the coffee pot, although both mugs were full.

"I wanted to die, but your father always managed to be there with me. I drove my car towards a steep cliff, and I heard him say, 'Let me drive Maggie,' and found myself back on solid ground. I ran to the middle of the Golden Gate Bridge prepared to jump, but he took my hand and said, 'Let's go back to the car,' and I walked safely off the bridge. I finally gave up. He wouldn't let me harm myself. But the one thing I couldn't do was come back here." Did Martha matter so little that her mother preferred death to being with her?

"Why not?" Martha's hands clenched and unclenched in her lap.

"I felt empty, I had nothing to give you." Her mother took a steadying sip of coffee before she continued. "I traveled around the country to some of the places we'd been, hoping to find him, hoping to heal. Eventually I returned to Maine. I wanted to be near you, even though I wasn't ready to see you."

What about me, what if I wanted to see you? Martha silently shouted, but her throat wouldn't work. She paced the kitchen, too agitated to sit. "I went to Monhegan Island and rented a small cottage. I planned to stay for the summer, but one day led to another, then I started to paint again.

"Tourists bought my paintings, and I sent money to your grandmother. I wanted to help with your expenses, especially when you went off to culinary school. When you got married, I stopped sending money. I'd developed arthritis in my hands, so I couldn't paint as much, prices had gone up on the island, and I needed most of what I made. I followed your progress, but I thought it had been too long to contact you." Martha had stressed about money for school, but she remembered Gram telling her not to worry. If her mother cared enough to help put her through school, why didn't she care enough to visit?

"Why come now?" Martha stared at her mother and saw the torment in her eyes, and she tried to feel pity, but her own rage and anguish prevailed. Everything she believed about her life had been based on a lie.

"I couldn't face your grandmother's disappointment, I let her down. I wish I hadn't waited. I should have come back sooner, no matter how confusing it would've been for you, but I thought you deserved a whole mother, and I didn't feel whole." She met Martha's eyes. "I'm sorry Martha, I know I can't make up for the lost years."

Martha stared blindly out the window. Resentment choked her. After all the years of feeling different, of missing what she'd never had, of carrying an empty place inside her despite all that Gram and Grandpa did, her mother was alive? She remembered the pictures of her parents together, their love shining from their eyes, the love she wanted to find someday. She looked at her mother, and all the hurt and loss spewed out of her.

"Now you come?" She paced as the words fueled her motion. "When it's too late to matter, to her or to me? When I'm grown? When I still feel the unbearable pain from losing Gram, you decide to come now? What do you want from me?" She stopped and faced her mother.

"You're right," her mother's head bowed, "I shouldn't have come." She raised her eyes to Martha. "I came because I wanted to tell you I always loved you. I didn't expect you to love me, but I hoped you could forgive me."

Martha stared at her in silence. After a moment, her mother rose and left, and the door clicked shut behind her. Martha sank back onto her chair and wept into her hands. She had begun to function normally, and now everything was turned upside down again. Charley hopped into her lap, licked her chin, then curled into a purring ball. Her hand rested on his back.

The telephone startled her from her thoughts, and she stood, dumping Charley on the floor to his meowed complaints.

"Good morning, Martha." Martha was grateful to hear Jeanette's lively voice, it anchored her to reality. "I wanted to make sure you're okay after your long drive. Did I wake you?"

228

"Goodness no, Charley and I have been up for a while, I'm trying to collect my thoughts."

"You sound a little strange, you sure you're all right? Are you coming down with a cold?"

"I'm fine, guess I'm tired from the drive," Martha tried to keep her voice steady as she answered, "I'll be there soon, thanks for checking in." She disconnected before Jeanette could ask any more questions, and took a deep breath. She would think about this later, right now she needed to get to the bakery. Martha cleared the coffee mugs and saw a crumpled business card on the table, "Paintings to Order by Maggie, Monhegan Island."

Winter

Chapter 36

Martha planned to return to Baltimore the week before Christmas to complete her last cake orders. She'd stay in Hope Island Harbor until then, although the holiday festivities and decorations intensified her grief. She remembered Christmases with Gram. They had strung popcorn and cranberries to decorate the tree, then rewarded themselves with hot chocolate, and a generous sample of Gram's famous Christmas cookies.

Martha worked through the morning in a daze. A lump formed in her throat as she rolled the delicate dough for lemon butter crisps paper thin, the way Gram had shown her. She cut an assortment of bells, stars, and Christmas trees and sprinkled them with colored sugar, but she would be glad when it was time to go back to Baltimore, where memories of Gram didn't hover in the air.

Jeanette kept casting worried looks in her direction, but she didn't say anything. Martha hoped she would assume fatigue from the drive made her quiet. By noon, she couldn't wait any longer and decided to go to Mr. Berg's office. She had more questions to ask.

"I'm going home early," Martha said, when Jeanette returned to the kitchen from the café area. "Will you be all right for the rest of the day? I guess the drive wore me out more than I realized."

"Don't worry, we'll be fine. Go home and get some rest."

Martha walked the short distance to her lawyer's office, hoping to find him free.

"Hi Martha, nice to see you again," the receptionist greeted her.

"Any chance I can have a minute with Mr. Berg? I'm afraid I don't have an appointment."

"You're in luck. He had a cancellation. I'll tell him you're here." Martha paced as she waited and turned when she heard the office door open. Henry Berg came forward. Martha thought of him as tidy, and she had never seen him without a bow tie.

"Martha, how are you? What can I do for you?"

"I'm sorry to barge in like this, but there's something I have to ask you." He ushered her into his office and closed the door.

Martha remained standing, clasping and unclasping her hands. When the lawyer sat down, she blurted her question.

"Did you know my mother is alive?" He looked startled. Had he lied to her, too?

"No, or rather I didn't know one way or the other and your grandmother didn't either. She told me the whole story was in her letter, although I didn't read it." His answer troubled Martha. Why had Gram trusted him with information about her mother and not her?

"This morning when I was having coffee, a woman knocked on my door. As soon as I saw her, I knew who she was. She looked like a younger version of Gram, and she had the same face as the woman in the picture holding me when I was a baby." Martha repeated her mother's story. "She's been living on Monhegan Island. I have to know if you and Gram knew all this, and kept it from me all these years." If they'd lied about her mother's death, maybe they'd hidden other information. Plus, she'd never been given the chance to search for her mother, Gram had made the decision for her.

"As long as the money kept coming, we knew your mother was alive, but to my knowledge, your grandmother didn't know where she was. If she'd known she lived on Monhegan Island, I'm sure she would have gone to see her. When the money stopped, I think your grandmother worried that she'd committed suicide. I honestly don't know."

234

"I don't know what to do." Martha paced the room. The turmoil in her mind made her dizzy. If Mr. Berg stopped the spinning, maybe she could see the next step.

"Do you want her in your life?"

"I don't know. Gram was the only mother I knew, I have trouble thinking of this woman in the same way, she wasn't here. Giving birth to me doesn't make her my mother. I'm angry and hurt—she didn't want me, she deserted me." Her stomach clenched with the last words.

"My advice is to take some time. She's your last living relative, don't be too quick to cast her aside. Maybe you can't think of her as your mother, but perhaps there's room in your life for her friendship." Mr. Berg stood beside her and gently placed his hand on her arm. "My guess is, she's hurting and regrets her decisions. I think she left you *because* she loved you, and wanted the best for you, which she thought your grandparents would provide. Whatever you decide, remember, anger is a heavy burden, and forgiveness is light."

"You sound like Gram." Martha closed her eyes and heard his words in Gram's voice, but anger clung to her heart. "Thanks for seeing me, it helps to know you didn't know more than you told me." She didn't want to uncover any more secrets.

Martha walked home through the dwindling light of a gray, winter afternoon. She smelled snow in the air; she would start a fire in the wood-stove, then curl up beside it to think.

✖ ✖ ✖

Martha and Charley returned to Baltimore. Part of her regretted missing all the Christmas festivities in Hope Island Harbor, because Jeanette would be disappointed, but when she left Maine, the weight of childhood Christmas memories stayed behind. As she drove, she reviewed her plans for the holiday wedding cakes. They were the last orders placed before Gram died, and she owed it to Sarah, the customers, and to herself to fulfill them as promised.

After a long day of decorating cakes for the weekend before Christmas, hunger rumbled in her stomach. She hadn't eaten all day in her flurry to finish the orders and transport them to the reception sites. Exhaustion consumed her, but when she drove back to her apartment, the lights of the Christmas Village in the Inner Harbor caught her eye. A replica of German Christmas markets, there would be carols playing, handmade gifts, and tasty German holiday treats. She parked at her apartment, and without bothering to change out of her bakery garb, she walked the few blocks to the Harbor. The exercise would help stretch the muscles stiffened by hours bent over her work table.

Despite her fatigue, Martha roamed through the Christmas Village, reveling in the festive atmosphere. She inhaled the loud smells of bratwurst, sweet pastries, and fresh pretzels that floated in the air, and allowed them to drown out the world and soak her in deliciousness. She pushed thoughts of wedding cakes aside and focused on shopping. What could she give Jeanette and Sarah for Christmas? Martha munched on a soft pretzel and strolled amongst the stalls before she stopped at a booth with exquisite handblown glass ornaments. The miniature bells would be perfect for Sarah, because she lived in an apartment and had a tiny tree. Jeanette told her she always had a huge hand-cut tree, so Martha bought her one stunning crystal ball blown around a sparkling gold manger scene.

She discovered a cashmere scarf and mittens, soft as milkweed floss, in the muted colors of the eastern sunset sky, reflecting the vibrant hues painted in the West. *Gram will love this.* Then she remembered, and tears trickled down her cheeks. She longed to feel Gram's arms around her again, wrapping her in love and safety. She fingered the downy scarf, and although she didn't understand why, Martha thought of her mother and imagined her arms holding her. Her mother's words echoed in her mind, "I've always loved you." *I'm not alone, I have someone in my family who loves me.*

Martha continued winding along the path through the tents, sipping hot cider and nibbling on a gingerbread tree. She picked out handmade toys for each of Delia's children. In the last tent, she saw an array of gloves and mittens. Her mother's appearance and the internal disruption it caused had taken over her mind the past few weeks, leaving room for little else. But when she saw a pair of alpaca lined work gloves, images of George pushed in and she pictured him surveying a mill site in the midst of winter, his hands toasty warm inside these gloves. Before she could change her mind, she found her credit card and paid for them. As she turned to leave, she thought she saw George, but he was too far away to be sure, and besides, he was walking in the opposite direction.

Chapter 37

George muddled over his options for Christmas. Should he go home? Should he accept the invitation from Nick and Mandy when Lucy would be there? Or should he go to Delia's, and hope Martha would be there too? He realized he couldn't disappoint his mother and dad again. His sister and her children would be there, and he hoped the time with his family would soothe the sharp edge of missing Martha.

Consumed by work and the yellow house, he hadn't had time for Christmas shopping. He'd start in the Christmas Village in Baltimore's Inner Harbor. He hoped the carols and twinkling lights would spark a holiday mood. George meandered in and out of the tent covered stalls, and stopped before a display of snow globes. The whimsical glass balls contained a variety of winter scenes, snowmen, Christmas trees, and even a sleigh ride, but then he saw an unusual one that looked like spring. When shaken, instead of snow, cherry blossoms fluttered down from the trees and landed on a carpet of tulips and daffodils. Martha would love it.

George continued to wander, and selected handmade toys for Delia's children. In the last tent, he stood before a table festooned with scarves the shades of an artist's palette, and made from the softest material he had ever touched. His eyes lingered on one that captured Cape Cod Bay in the summer, turquoise and blue blended into each other seamlessly, and Martha's eyes swam before him. He saw it draped around her like the bay she described encircling Hope Island Harbor.

As he reached into his pocket for his wallet, he thought he could smell Martha, a spicy, sweet bakery scent floated above the light floral fragrance that was hers alone. Silly thought, she was tucked away in Maine, wasn't she? In the distance he saw a woman who looked like her leaving the Village. She slipped into the shadows and disappeared into the night before George could call her name, but he knew Martha had been here, right at this table, moments before.

The day before Christmas Eve, Martha worked late. She couldn't concentrate and labored to bring life to her designs. The past few weeks, her thoughts had flitted between Baltimore and Hope Island Harbor along with her body. Her decision swung back and forth a thousand times. Which place would become her permanent home, and which would slide gently—or not—into her past?

She thought of George more than she wanted to admit, but he had not called since he had shown her the yellow house. She lost count of the times she had brought up his number, but then stopped before her finger pressed, "Call." What would she say? "I'm sorry I got angry, I'm trying to decide whether or not I want to live with you in the yellow house."

Besides, her primary decision lay elsewhere. First, she had to determine where she wanted to live and which business she wanted to build. Her star had begun to rise in Baltimore, did she want to hang on for the ride? Or did she want to nestle in the coast of Maine, plant her feet in the soil Gram had held so dear, and grow something from that crumbling, but still strong foundation? She refused to base her decision on a man, and yet, no amount of success could fill the hollow place inside her heart, a place the exact size and shape of George.

Martha faced Christmas alone, dividing her time between Baltimore and Hope Island Harbor, pulled in two directions like a piece of taffy, stretched so thin, she felt like a thread of sanity held her together, and she might snap at any moment. Hard kernels of anger rolled around and around

239

in her gullet as she tried to make sense of her life. All the years her mother was alive and she didn't know it, all the years when Martha could have been with Gram wasted, as she steeped in her own pride.

Annie was right, Gram had loved her unconditionally, she would have welcomed Martha no matter what, and she let Gram's love slip away, squandered time until it was too late. She thought of her mother. She came to see Martha begging forgiveness and professing her love, love that had taken her away from Martha all those years ago.

Why hadn't she come back sooner? For the same reason Martha had not come back to see Gram—she felt like a failure. It was too late for Gram; the best she could do was grow the Sunrise Café and Bakery into something even more wonderful and open Laughing Gull Chocolates, realizing Gram's dreams along with her own.

But it wasn't too late to share her life with the one person alive in the world who had loved her since the day she was born. She needed Gram's forgiveness, and her mother needed hers. Martha felt lighter as she decorated the Christmas wedding cakes. Joy ran through her, it started in her heart, raced up to her brain, trickled down through her arms into her fingertips, and shone through the finished designs.

What began as an uninspired effort, came to life, sparkling with the couples' love for each other, and reflecting the love Martha felt for Gram that now spilled over to her mother. She hoped it wasn't too late for George's love. Somehow, she would figure that out.

When she left for the night, well after ten o'clock, there was a balmy breeze blowing, not the Christmas temperatures she remembered from New England. The weather forecast predicted a cold front for tomorrow, and with it some light snow. Baltimore would have a white Christmas after all.

Once in her car, Martha closed the door and slumped over the wheel. She had been working since five in the morning, and she would have to work on Christmas Eve, but she refused to be in the bakery on Christmas Day.

Chapter 38

George intended to leave the next morning for the long drive back to Cape Cod, but he had a delivery to make first. After the older children left for school, he crossed the adjoining yard. Delia opened the back door before he could knock; she held Maura in one arm.

"George, I'm so glad you stopped by, are you going to join us for Christmas?"

"I'd love to Delia, but I'm driving to the Cape. I didn't go home for Thanksgiving, and my mother is sending waves of guilt through my phone and email. Before I'm totally swamped, I want to get back, besides, my sister and her kids will be there."

"I'm glad you'll be with family." She set Maura on the floor, amidst a circle of toys.

"Me too, but thanks for the invitation." He paused. "Will you be seeing Martha?" He hadn't heard from her since Thanksgiving weekend, and he hadn't called, for fear of pushing her further away.

"I'm not sure, I know she's up to her ears in wedding cakes. I'll call her tonight and invite her, but I don't know if she'll come."

"Well, if you see her, would you give her this for me?" He held out a gaily wrapped set of packages, a flat one on the bottom, topped by a smaller square one, and tied together with a brilliant, red bow. "And these are for the children," he extended a large shopping bag of festive gifts.

"How sweet of you George, but you didn't have to give them anything."

"I wanted to. When I see them playing in the yard, I think of my sister's children."

"Thank you, Merry Christmas, and drive safely." Delia reached up and gave him a hug.

❈ ❈ ❈

Martha's phone rang as she arrived at her apartment. "Hi Delia, good timing, I just got home." She slipped out of her jacket and hung it on the wooden coat rack. "How are you? Crazy busy getting ready for Christmas as usual?"

"Of course, but I love it. That's why I'm calling. You're officially invited to join us, even though you know you don't need an invitation."

"I don't know, Delia, I don't think I can face a house full of people. Who's going to be there?" Martha sat on the couch beside Charley and lifted him onto her lap. It would be like Delia to invite George, and she didn't feel ready to see him yet, especially not on Christmas when grief would be her hidden companion.

"If you're asking about George, he isn't coming. I invited him, but he's going to spend Christmas on Cape Cod with his family. So you can relax, even though I don't think you should have stopped seeing him."

"I'll think about it." Delia frequently anticipated Martha's thoughts, and she couldn't decide if she was relieved or disappointed that George wouldn't be there for Christmas.

"You shouldn't be alone. You might like the idea now, but on Christmas morning it'll be too painful. You can't bring Gram back by steeping yourself in misery, like one of her cups of tea." Martha closed her eyes, listened to her friend, and made her decision.

"The kids want to see you, and you'll have fun. It's not going to be a big gathering, just us, and the Townsends will be here for dinner."

"All right, Delia, I'll come."

On Christmas night, Martha put on her coat and hugged Delia. "Thank you, it was a wonderful day, and you were right, I'd have been miserable alone. I loved seeing the kids open their gifts and the Townsends are a hoot! I never would have guessed by their dour expressions."

"I know." Delia giggled, "They look like American Gothic come to life. Are you sure you don't want to spend the night?" The day had been hectic and fun, and thoughts of Gram had flickered in the shadows, but right now, Martha wanted to go back to her quiet apartment and be alone.

"I'd love to, but I'll be up at dawn to finish a cake for an afternoon delivery. Then I'm going to stuff as much as I can in my car and get an early start for Hope Island Harbor Friday morning."

"No chance I can persuade you to stay in Baltimore? George obviously is interested."

"Please don't make it harder, Delia," Martha thought of the lovely gifts George had given her. "You know I've grappled for weeks with this choice. I'm not sure I understand why, but once I acknowledged my need to be in Hope Island Harbor, all the stress of the last two months disappeared. I feel Gram there, my mother lives close by, and for now, I belong there." Martha didn't know what else to say so Delia would accept her decision.

"Okay, I won't say another word, except I want you to be happy. Here, I packed some leftovers for you to take home." She held out a large plastic container.

"I can't eat another bite Delia, or I'll burst." Although often annoyed by Delia's mothering, tonight she found comfort in it.

"You have to eat, and I know you won't take time to cook tomorrow while you decorate and pack, take it." Delia shoved the package into Martha's hands, gave her a final hug, then pushed her out the door. Delia's eyes glistened and Martha knew she wouldn't want to break down in front of her. Martha hurried to her car and swiped her hand across her own eyes.

The day after Christmas, Martha delivered the last wedding cake, grateful the reception was nearby in Fells Point. She came home and gathered her belongings together. When she found George's gifts, she coiled the scarf around her neck, rubbing her cheek against its softness, and shook the snow globe, watching the petals flutter to the ground. She wondered if she would see him again. Had he given up on her? Part of her ached to call him, but she had to solve the emotional puzzle of her life, and her mother's sudden appearance added another baffling piece. She wanted to wish him a happy New Year and hear about his Christmas, but it would be too hard to talk to him, and an email or text might generate a call. She rummaged in a closet for stationery, then sat down and wrote.

"Dear George…"

She thanked him for her gifts and told him about seeing her mother. She shared the resulting turmoil and her decision to stay in Hope Island Harbor. She implied she would like to see him again, once she sorted her life, but not yet. When she finished the pen hovered over the paper. Her heart wanted to write, *Love, Martha,* but her head took control and she ended, *Happy New Year! Take care, Martha.* She would mail it in the morning, maybe.

After she completed the letter, she packed all her remaining possessions into her Honda Civic. She flattened the back seat and used every square inch of space, except she saved room for Charley in his shotgun spot, and herself.

The next morning, she locked the apartment door for the last time. When Martha plunked herself in the driver's seat, Charley stood with his paws resting on the window, as if he too sensed the end of this chapter in his life, and the beginning of a new one. Martha made one final swing past Sweet Selections to say goodbye to Sarah, and to stock up on coffee and treats for the road.

"I'll be right back, Charley, I have to leave the key with Sarah so she can return it to her friend." Martha found Sarah in the kitchen spreading frosting on fresh cinnamon rolls. The bakery smell of sweet vanilla and spice seeped into her, energizing her for the drive ahead, but also tugging at her, urging her to stay.

"I'm on my way, Sarah," she said before she could change her mind, "I brought the key, thanks for returning it to Miriam."

"I hate to see you go, Martha. Sweet Selections won't be the same, and neither will I." Sarah came from behind the work table. "I'll miss you more than I can tell you."

"I'll miss you too, and your support."

"You have my support wherever you are, and there's always space for you here, if you ever decide to return to Baltimore."

"Thanks, but for now, I have to go back to Hope Island Harbor, and see what's waiting for me. I hope you'll come visit, especially when I open my chocolate shop."

"I'll be there, let me know when." Martha embraced Sarah briefly, unwilling to give in to the tears that threatened, then walked out to join Charley.

Martha drove back to Hope Island Harbor, excited by the plans she had for the Sunrise Café. The turmoil in her brain had vanished; she had made the right decision. She arrived home on a swirl of snow-laden air, and the ground would soon be white.

� ✳ ✳

George sat in crawling traffic on the Jersey Turnpike. He had hoped to hear from Martha before Christmas, but her silence continued. Delia said she was busy with holiday orders. Had she gone back to Maine when she finished? He hoped she would still be in Baltimore, and he could persuade her to spend New Year's Eve with him. Nick and Mandy were hosting a party and they included Martha in their invitation. If she preferred a quiet evening, or wanted to spend New Year's Day together, that would be fine with him.

He had planned to be on the road by six Saturday morning, but when a coastal storm dumped a foot of snow on the Cape, his parents persuaded him to wait another day. Now he wished he hadn't agreed. Traffic grew worse the farther south he drove, and the eight-hour drive stretched to ten hours, and then twelve.

After midnight, he finally rolled into the driveway of the yellow house. He dragged his suitcase and a bag of presents onto the porch, thinking of a hot shower and his bed. A colorful box leaned against the door. He flipped on the hall light; the mail lay scattered on the floor beneath the metal slot. A hand-addressed, square envelope caught his eye. The return address, Hope Island Harbor, caused him to forget about the hours on the road. He ignored the rest of the mail and carried Martha's letter and the package, tagged, "Merry Christmas George, from Martha," to his room. George opened the gift and slipped the warm gloves over his hands. His heart lurched. Martha thought of him. His shower could wait, he flopped on the bed and ran his finger beneath the flap on the envelope. He heard her voice, gentle but determined as he read.

Dear George,

I hope you had a wonderful Christmas and enjoyed the time with your family. I spent the day at Delia's and I'm glad I did. Christmas is much more fun when there are children around. Delia's four were thrilled with the gifts you gave them, and I love mine too.

I wore the beautiful scarf all day, the colors remind me of the bay around Hope Island Harbor, and the snow globe is exquisite. I've never seen one that snows flower petals, thank you for such thoughtful gifts. I left one for you with Delia.

I'm leaving for Maine tomorrow morning. Gram's lawyer gave me a letter she wrote, and when I read it, I discovered my mother didn't die when I was a baby as I thought. In fact, she came to see me when I came back from Baltimore after Thanksgiving. The struggle to process this information has consumed my mind as I rushed back and forth through December.

You were right about following my own dream, not Gram's, but for now my dream is in Hope Island Harbor. When I find a location for a chocolate shop, maybe the final pieces of the puzzle will fall into place. I hope you understand, and that you'll come for the opening of the chocolate shop.

Happy New Year! Take care,
Martha

George read between the lines of Martha's letter. She wasn't coming back to Baltimore, and although she wanted him to come to Hope Island Harbor someday, she didn't want to be with him now. He wouldn't celebrate the New Year with Martha. He dragged himself to the shower, then collapsed into bed thinking of her and aching with longing to hold her in his arms. He wanted to get back in his car and drive all the way to Maine, but that isn't what she wanted. Exhaustion overcame his restless thoughts and he sank into a troubled sleep, and dreamed of seeing Martha in the distance, but never reaching her.

� ✗ ✗

New Year's Eve arrived, and though he didn't have a date, George promised Nick and Mandy he would attend their party. He stood in a corner brooding. He knew he should participate in the festivities, but he didn't feel in a party mood. Still, Mandy had worked hard and cooked like crazy, so he would make an effort to enjoy the evening. He prepared himself to mingle when Lucy walked over.

"Hey stranger," she hugged him.

"Hey Lucy, Happy New Year." He leaned down and kissed her cheek.

"You don't look happy, want to tell me what's bothering you?"

"What makes you think something's bothering me?" He frowned at her.

"For starters, you're standing over here under your own personal rain cloud. Besides you were gloomy when I saw you before Christmas. You told me your job's going well, but you seem lost, does it have anything to do with the woman at the marathon? Tell me what's going on, maybe it'll help to have a different perspective." George didn't confide in anyone, except Nick, and even that didn't happen often, but a female viewpoint might help.

"You're right," he took a sip of beer. He told her more about Martha, and how he lost her and found her again at the marathon. How he came alive with her, but he had made poor decisions that led her to her believe he wanted to control her, which he didn't. He wanted her to be happy, he wanted to banish the sadness she carried deep inside her.

"I got a letter from her when I got back after Christmas. She said she needs to go to Maine and figure things out, without me." He had good intentions but flawed methods and now she didn't want to see him.

"Did she say she never wants to see you again?"

"No, she said she's opening a chocolate shop and she hopes I'll come to the opening. I guess she'll let me know when it is."

"That's a good thing, George," she rested her hand on his arm. "From what you told me, she had a tough year. She's confused and hurting right now, and doesn't want to commit to a relationship. Be patient, I'll bet she'll want you there when she figures out what comes next. Give her time to heal." Lucy had offered the same advice as Delia, and she didn't even know Martha.

"I hope you're right, but all I want to do is catch the next plane to Portland."

"Have faith, George." She took his hand, "Come on, let's go sample some of Mandy's famous guacamole."

❈ ❈ ❈

On New Year's Day, Martha called Jeanette. "Want to come for supper? I have clam chowder in the freezer, and I want to talk to you about something."

"Is anything wrong? You okay?"

"I'm fine, but with my frantic holiday schedule, we haven't had time to unwind and talk."

When Jeanette arrived, Martha had rekindled the embers in the woodstove, making the kitchen cozy and warm. She opened the bottle of wine Jeanette handed her, and set it on the kitchen table along with glasses and a tray of sliced apples and cheese.

"I feel like Jessie should be joining us," Jeanette sat down. "We always visited in the kitchen by the woodstove."

"I know, Gram kept busy cooking, even when she was home, and she'd entertain her guests while she worked." They sat in companionable silence and Martha thought about her mother. She couldn't devise a subtle way to include her in the conversation, so she forged ahead.

"I won't be at the bakery tomorrow because I'm going to see my mother."

Jeanette's jaw dropped. "What? I thought your mother was dead."

"I did too, but it turns out she's alive." Martha told Jeanette about Gram's letter and her mother's visit. She explained her distracted behavior the day she found out. "I've been trying to absorb this news, come to terms with it, and it hasn't been easy. At first, I was so angry I didn't want anything to do with her."

"What changed?"

"When I thought about why I didn't come home, because I felt like a failure, I understood she didn't come back for the same reason, she felt like a failure too. Besides, she's the only family I have."

"Where is she?"

"Monhegan Island."

Chapter 39

Martha stepped off the ferry and looked around. Most tourists left by Columbus Day, and this morning she was the sole passenger. She stood on the dock in the empty quiet, a crewman pushing a loaded dolly up the wharf the one sign of life, and wondered if she'd made the right decision. Martha stuck her hand in her jacket pocket and withdrew the crumpled paper her mother had left on her kitchen table. The back of the business card had a scribbled phone number and an address on the island.

She took her cell phone from her pocket and checked for service, then hesitated. Her uncertainty tossed out every negative outcome she could imagine. Suppose her mother said she didn't want to see her after all, or didn't answer because she didn't recognize the number? Suppose they had nothing to talk about? Suppose her mother wasn't even here? She hadn't called since she didn't plan to stay overnight.

Martha walked to the small general store at the end of the dock, and could see by the flyers it also served as the post office, ticket booth, and real estate office. She opened the heavy door. A small Franklin stove burned in the corner, its heat not reaching the door.

The woman behind the counter looked up, glasses perched on the end of her nose, and a long blond braid bisecting her down jacket. "Happy New Year! How can I help you?"

Martha showed her the card and asked her how she could find the address, and how she might get there.

"I'm leaving soon. I can take you myself, if you don't mind waiting a few minutes and riding in the delivery truck."

Martha stood on the small front porch of a gray shingled cottage. *My mother's house,* how strange that thought felt tumbling in her mind, over and over, each time wearing away a few more rough edges, until it stilled in a corner of acceptance.

She lifted a jittery hand and imagined the anxiety her mother must have felt when she stood on Martha's front porch. She took a deep breath and knocked. Her mother opened the door with a tentative smile, but when she recognized Martha, her eyes widened and joy lit her face.

"Martha, you came. I can't believe you're here, but I'm so glad you are. I've been praying I'd see you again." She stopped abruptly, "I'm babbling, come in where it's warm." She stepped back, opening the door wider for Martha to enter. "Would you like some tea? I just made a fresh pot."

Martha took another calming breath, her mother looked as nervous as she felt herself. "Yes, that would be lovely, the wind is relentless. I wasn't sure the ferry would run."

"It takes a lot to stop Hank, he's the best pilot I know." They walked into the tiny kitchen, designed for summer days when you wanted to be outside, and stopped for a quick cup of coffee on your way to another island adventure. A small wooden table with two chairs faced the windows and the expanse of ocean far below.

"This room sees the most spectacular sunrises," her mother gazed over the water. "It drags me out of a cozy bed to sit and watch the show."

"And paint?" Martha moved to stand in front of the easel sitting in the far corner of the room. She studied the beginnings of a sunrise, but not one from her mother's window, across the vast Atlantic, she saw the intimate view from Gram's porch, with Hope Island in the distance.

"Sometimes."

"The color is magnificent—do you paint from a photograph?"

251

"Yes, in my head." Martha's mother poured tea from a chubby white china pot, then placed a plate of homemade oatmeal bread, warm from the oven, beside it. She cut a thick slice for Martha, and offered butter and a jar of blackberry jam to accompany it.

"Did you make the jam too?"

"No, my friend Rosie made it, we swap bread for jam. She says her bread is always like a brick, and I don't want my hands torn up with blackberry thorns. Besides, she knows all the secret places for wild blackberries, including the edge of her backyard."

Martha sipped her tea and gathered her courage, but her mother broke the silence.

"Why did you come? What made you change your mind?" Martha pondered for a moment how best to explain the emotional river flowing through her, transforming her feelings as she rode the current.

"Christmas," Martha said. "I was exploring the Christmas Village in Baltimore, looking for gifts, and I automatically searched for something special for Gram. When I remembered she wasn't going to spend this or any other Christmas with me, I wanted to crumble into a heap." Martha faltered, but her mother remained quiet.

"I thought of all the Christmases I could have come back to Maine but didn't, because I felt like such a failure in my marriage, the marriage Gram wanted me to postpone. When it ended in divorce, I wanted to accomplish something to make her proud before I came back." Martha took a sip of her tea, seeking comfort in the ordinary ritual. "I had qualified for the Charm City Chocolate Challenge held in October and I signed up to run the Baltimore marathon the week before. I planned to return after completing them, but by then it was too late. I let Gram down, but I know she never stopped loving me. I wanted to hear her words of forgiveness, but I waited too long to ask." Martha's throat caught, and she stopped, her head down.

"I felt the pain of Gram's loss in every cell of my body, then I realized that's what you felt when my father died, but worse, because you lost your partner in life." She looked up and saw her mother brush the tears from her cheeks. "I understood why you thought you couldn't come back, because you'd failed me. You asked for my forgiveness, and I want you to know that you have it. I hope we can get to know each other, become friends, and not wait until it's too late." Her mother moved towards Martha and clutched her in her arms. Martha buried her head on her mother's shoulder and sobbed, as her mother wept. When she regained some control, Martha lifted her head, and her mother gave her a watery smile.

"Can you stay for a few days?" Her voice wavered, "It's not much, but I have an extra room."

"I expected to be here for the day, so I didn't bring any extra clothes." Martha wished she'd called earlier; she could have made plans for a longer visit.

Her mother stood and swept her hand over Martha's head. "You could borrow some of mine—" Martha heard the uncertainty in her voice, but she also felt the tenderness in her mother's touch and the last shreds of tension from this morning disappeared.

"Okay," she clasped her mother's hand. She would send Jeanette a text later and tell her about the change in plans.

"I could use a walk, is your coat warm enough?" Her mother reached for her own jacket, hanging on a peg by the door.

"I may have lived in Baltimore for a few years, but I remember Maine winters, and I'd love a walk."

When Martha boarded the ferry two days later, her mother held her in a tight embrace. "Come back to Monhegan whenever you can."

"I will, and promise you'll come to Hope Island Harbor soon," her mother's scarf muffled Martha's words.

A month later, Martha stood on the dock waiting for the Monhegan Ferry to arrive. A series of winter storms had curtailed its scheduled trips, and her insides felt a bit like the sea, the gale had passed, but the remnants of restless waves continued. She looked forward to seeing her mother again, but fragments of hurt and anger surfaced at unpredictable moments.

Her mother stepped off the ferry with a large bundle under her arm, after giving her a quick hug, Martha offered to carry it, but her mother declined, with an enigmatic smile.

Back at Gram's house, Martha made tea and put fresh ginger scones on a plate.

"Would you like to go see the changes at the bakery? There are a few things to complete before the grand re-opening, but we're serving breakfast again."

"I would love to, I haven't been there for so many years." Martha trampled the threatening blip of resentment; she didn't want to start their visit on a painful note. They finished their tea and her mother retrieved the package she had stowed on the chair, under her coat.

"This is for you." She handed the parcel to Martha.

Martha slipped off the string and folded back the brown paper wrapping, then gasped. "It's incredible." She couldn't take her eyes from the painting; it depicted the Sunrise Café in such detail the smell of cinnamon rolls wafted in her mind. "Thank you, I'll hang it in the bakery."

"I hoped you would." Her mother's eyes glistened.

"Did you have this photograph in your head, too?"

"Since the day I left." Martha hugged her mother close and healed a little more.

"Let's go to the bakery, I have the perfect spot for this."

Chapter 40

Martha left the house, her schedule for the day already rolling in her head. Every time she entered the Sunrise Café, the new welcoming space confirmed her instincts to expand. She had purchased the vacant former post office attached to the bakery and opened the wall between them, creating a cozy but roomier dining area, complete with a gas fireplace for frosty winter mornings. Gram would have approved.

She flipped the switch on the fireplace, relishing the sudden burst of heat, then proceeded to the kitchen to tackle her mental list. Ever since the grand re-opening brought reporters from local newspapers, as well as a featured spot in *Down East* magazine, business had soared. The long hours didn't bother Martha. As she gathered ingredients for the daily special, gingerbread muffins, her mind roamed to her plans to open a chocolate shop across the street. When the owner of the barbershop decided to retire and move to Florida, she had purchased the building and placed a sign on the lawn, "Coming soon—Laughing Gull Chocolates."

The bell on the bakery door jangled, and Martha smiled as she looked up from filling the display case with warm muffins. Tony walked through the door, and her smile vanished. She stood in stunned silence.

"Hey, Babe," Tony acted as if he had seen her yesterday and they were still married.

"I'm not your babe," her body stiffened. Tony held up his hands, like stop signs.

"I know, I'm sorry, force of habit."

"What are you doing here? How did you know where to find me?"

"News travels, plus I bumped into Delia. I know you're surprised to see me, but I came to apologize." He moved closer, "And to say I think we should try again."

"What?" How could he possibly think she would try again, after the way their marriage had ended? Flashes of Tony's anger, and his cruel words blinked like neon signs in her mind, sending the familiar wrenching signals of distress through her body. The last thing she wanted was to try again.

"Listen! Will you please listen?" He lowered his voice on the second request.

"Not here Tony, lunch customers will be coming in soon, I can't talk now." She needed time to gather her thoughts. Tony's unexpected appearance had scattered them like leaves in the wind.

"Will you meet me for dinner?"

"I don't think that's a good idea."

"Please, I only want to talk. I've changed since the divorce. Let me buy you dinner." For a moment, Martha saw the charming handsome man she had married, why had he shown up now?

"All right, but just dinner, and then you have to leave."

"Okay then," Tony turned and winked as he opened the door. "See you at the Scallop Shell, say six?" Martha nodded mutely. Jeanette came from the kitchen carrying a tray of warm pesto buns.

"Martha, you all right? You look like you've seen a ghost."

"I did, sort of, can you cover for me? I need some air. I'll be back before the lunch crowd."

"Of course."

Martha threw her apron on the counter and marched from the café. She strode along the shore road, head down. The cold rain that fell through the night had moved on and a brisk wind had swept away the clouds, leaving a glacier blue sky. She hadn't grabbed a jacket and the winter breeze blew through her thin T-shirt, but she didn't notice. Her feet crunched on the gravel, and she took in huge gulping breaths, confounded by Tony's unexpected appearance. She faced the bay, and memories of the last day with Tony flooded her mind. Martha allowed the wind-tossed rhythm of the waves to consume her until her breathing slowed, and her hands unclenched.

Calmer, she walked back to the bakery. Martha bet Tony had more reasons for being here than he implied, and she wanted to know what they were, but she would deal with him later. Right now, she needed to help Jeanette serve lunch.

At the end of the day, Martha removed her apron and ran a comb through her hair. She resisted the urge to go home and change, she didn't want Tony to think she cared about impressing him, and went straight to the Scallop Shell. Perched on a point overlooking the harbor, Martha remembered the seafood shack it had once been. She and Gram used to come here for a treat and Martha could never decide between the lobster and the rock crab, both fresh from cold Maine waters. Sometimes they each ordered one and shared.

The aromas of freshly baked bread and clam chowder greeted Martha when she opened the door. She missed the salty charm of the old Scallop Shell, but Tony would prefer the present casual elegance created by the maple captains' chairs, dark blue tablecloths, and huge fieldstone fireplace.

Martha observed Tony sitting in the dining room at a table by the window. *Already nursing a drink.* A finger of apprehension shivered up her spine at the prospect of dinner with Tony after he had a few drinks. She looked around at the clam rakes and hods hung on the inside walls, and comforting memories of the old shack returned. After taking a moment to compose herself, she walked over to the hostess who looked up from her station at the dining room door.

"Hey Martha, you here to pick up the dessert order for tomorrow?" Martha derived additional business by providing desserts for the restaurant every day.

"Hey Joyce, Jeanette already took the order on the phone. I'm meeting someone, but I see he's already here so I'm all set." Joyce followed Martha's gaze. Tony grinned at Martha.

"Wow! Where've you been keeping him?" she looked back at Martha. "Everything okay? You don't seem too happy."

"Long story, but I'll be fine." *As soon as I figure out why he's here.*

Tony rose when she approached, "Thanks for coming, Martha."

"I don't see the point."

"I know, but please hear me out. Our divorce was a real wake-up call, and I've changed."

"It doesn't matter, Tony." Martha wished she hadn't come; she should leave now. Judging by the glass in front of Tony, nothing had changed.

"I think it does, and you might agree if you'll listen—" The waitress came over mid-sentence and Tony pointed to his drink.

"Another one like this." Martha ordered a glass of white wine, hoping it would calm her nerves. When the waitress left, Tony picked up his glass.

"I know what you're thinking, nothing has changed and I'm still drinking. But, take a sip." He held the glass out towards Martha. She took it, but didn't taste the contents. The bubbles from the seltzer tickled her nose, but she couldn't detect the scent of alcohol as she expected.

"I'm in AA, I got a sponsor, and I've stopped drinking. I've been faithful to the weekly meetings."

"You don't have to tell me all this." The lack of alcohol surprised her but didn't solve all the other problems.

"I do, because I want to assure you I've changed. My sponsor recommended I go for anger management counseling. I didn't really think I needed it, but in time, I agreed with him. I should never have hit you."

"No kidding." Martha spoke louder than she intended and lowered her voice. "It took an anger management class for you to realize that? It's done, Tony. It happened, it's over." The waitress returned with their drinks and asked if they were ready to order dinner. The knots in Martha's stomach left little room for food, but she ordered a bowl of clam chowder. The creamy broth, brimming with chopped clams, provided a soothing reminder of her grandmother.

258

"I wish I could turn back the clock. I got started down the wrong road, and every mistake I made led to another, each worse than the one before. I regret striking you the most. I never wanted to hurt you Martha, you have to believe that." The remorse in Tony's voice tugged at Martha and she felt the tension in her body ease. "Remember how much fun we had in school, the plans we made, the nights we spent together?" Tony switched to his seductive voice.

Although vaguely aware of sounds around her, the gentle bump of silverware against a plate, the tinkle of glassware as dishes were cleared, subdued voices from nearby tables, they didn't register in her mind. Martha heard the sound of the surf when she and Tony had walked on Narragansett Beach.

She remembered feeling Tony's hands on her arms, sliding up and down, turning her to mush with a kiss that seemed to go on forever. She felt her pounding heart and the excitement of being close to him. Had he changed as much as he claimed? She was so smitten back then she thought she would break in two if they separated.

A waitress dropped a plate across the room, and the sharp sound of breaking china acted like a slap, flinging her into the present moment.

"I can't do it Tony, I can't go back there."

"I don't want you to go back, Martha. I want you to go forward, with me. I'm not suggesting we move in together, I'm asking if you'll see me and give me a chance. Despite what you might believe, I still love you, I never stopped loving you." He reached across the table to take her hand, but she moved it to her lap.

"Do you have a day off?" Tony didn't give up easily. He never had, Martha thought.

"Mondays tend to be the slowest day, we stay open, but I try to steal a little time away." She had no desire to get back together with Tony, but he deserved a chance to make amends.

"Well, how about next Monday? No pressure, let's go somewhere fun or take a walk, whatever you want. Think of it as getting to know a new friend. I've changed Martha, I really have."

Martha reluctantly agreed, but when she walked home, she wondered what other reasons Tony had for coming, beyond an apology. She pulled her cell phone from her pocket and called Delia.

As soon as Delia answered, Martha said, "Tony's here, he came into the bakery today."

"What? I'm sorry Martha, I'm afraid that's my fault. I saw him by chance when Jimmy and I had dinner in Baltimore. He asked about you, but I didn't expect him to go to Maine. You told him to take a hike, right?"

"No, I had dinner with him and agreed to see him Monday, when I finish work."

"Why?" Delia's disapproval didn't surprise Martha.

"I know it sounds crazy, but if he really came to apologize for everything, I want to give him the chance to do it. I have a feeling he has other reasons for being here, and for my own peace of mind I want to find out what they are. Otherwise I'll always wonder, this way I can put Tony behind me and move on."

❊ ❊ ❊

Martha arrived at the bakery at seven Monday morning, the day she reserved for paperwork. The bakery business also required paying bills, ordering supplies, and scheduling help. She preferred the hands-on portion of the business, which is why she treated herself to a few hours off on Monday, once she finished the tedious chores. The sooner she finished, the longer she had to relax, although time to herself often meant studying real estate ads, and imagining the perfect spot for a bed and breakfast.

Today she had trouble concentrating, her mind insisted on straying back to her dinner with Tony, and then ahead to lunch today. She'd agreed to pack a picnic and meet him for a walk and a late lunch at two. But she wanted to call him and cancel, she could claim too much work, since she had accomplished next to nothing in the five hours she had been sitting at her desk.

She decided on a solitary walk, in the hopes of clearing her head before meeting Tony. He insisted that he had changed, but even if that were true, Martha had changed also. No longer a shy, retiring, country girl who hung on his every word, grateful for his attention, she had established herself as a top pastry chef and chocolatier, first in Baltimore and now in Maine.

If Tony had truly turned his life around, she felt happy for him. She had forgiven him for hitting her, but that didn't mean she wanted to start again. She didn't love Tony, she loved George.

Where did that come from? She loved George? She hadn't allowed herself to admit or even consider loving him. When he showed her the house, she had felt cornered and lashed out at him in anger. But since she returned to Maine, she harbored a huge empty space in her heart, and Tony could never fill it.

She tucked that revelation aside for later, but she would call Tony and tell him she'd meet him after lunch, for a short walk, she had too much to do. Then she put her head down and went to work. She finished the last of her paperwork while nibbling on a spinach salad, then grabbed her water bottle and headed for the point.

They had agreed to meet on the shore road, where the wave's constant flow would ease her nerves. She stood on the hill above the spot where Tony waited, hands in his jacket pockets, and speculated again on what he wanted.

The sight of him brought back memories of walks on the beach when they were in culinary school. Those walks often led to evenings of more passion than she wanted to remember. For another brief moment, Martha wondered if Tony had changed. Could they make a life together? *Not a chance.* She took a deep breath, shut the door on the vexing memories, and jogged down the hill to where he stood.

"I knew you'd come, we still have the same attraction between us. Admit it, you feel it too." He grinned at Martha.

"I'll admit nothing except we're different people, hopefully we've both grown up and moved on. I'm happy for you if you've conquered your demons. I know I've conquered a few of my own, but I don't want to begin again." It had taken her too long to heal.

"Do you forgive me, Martha? I hope you will, then we can start over with a clean slate." He sounded sure of himself, as if her forgiveness negated his behavior and their divorce.

"I do forgive you, what's past is past, but I don't want to start over, not now, not ever." She didn't tell him it took longer to forgive herself for allowing him to rule her life. She could have stood her ground and come back to Hope Island Harbor the summer after graduation. She could have had more time with Gram. The realization haunted her.

He grabbed for her hands, but she shoved them in her pockets and walked a few steps down to the remains of a stone pavilion. Her grandmother's generation had picnicked there, but too many winter nor'easters and a few fall hurricanes had reduced it to a pile of rubble.

Martha closed her eyes and heard the sounds of children, and saw her grandmother rowing across to Hope Island. Then she opened them and regarded the glistening bay.

"I love this view."

"Me too." Tony detested life beyond the city limits, but when Martha glanced at him, he studied her. She shook her head and would have brushed by him, but he grabbed her and drew her into a firm embrace then claimed her mouth. In spite of herself she felt a stirring deep inside her, but it was her body's traitorous response to loneliness, not her heart's response to Tony. She placed her hands on his chest and shoved him away.

"Stop it, Tony."

"Come on, Martha, you know the spark is still there." He tried to embrace her again.

"There are no sparks," Martha pushed past him. Tony caught up with her and kept talking as if she hadn't spoken.

"When you sell the bakery, we'll have enough money to buy that restaurant, like we dreamed, but now we both have the name to back our investment. You'll be the pastry chef and I'll be the executive chef, and we'll put it on the map, Martha. It'll be the most popular new restaurant in Baltimore. What do you say?"

Bingo! She should have guessed the real reason for Tony's visit. Some things would never change. Tony might have his anger under control, but Tony's world would always revolve around Tony, and her sole purpose would be to fund the spinning of that world as he wanted it.

"You don't get it, do you? I'm already living my dream by putting Gram's bakery on the map and opening a chocolate shop. I'm staying here, Tony, Hope Island Harbor is home for me."

Martha returned to the bakery alone and left Tony in the past, where he belonged. She didn't need him to feel whole.

Spring

Chapter 41

Martha flipped the calendar page. She couldn't believe it had been one year since she signed the divorce papers. It felt like a lifetime, and in a way it was. She had transformed her world, rebuilt her life and begun to heal. In Pensacola, she perfected her passion for chocolate, and added owning a bed and breakfast to her dreams. She came back to Baltimore hoping to claim a spot in the pastry and chocolate world, and unexpectedly found—then lost—new love. Sorrow from her grandmother's death continued to ache inside her.

George had honored her request for time alone to follow her dream, and she had kept herself busy expanding the bakery and café and preparing for the opening of Laughing Gull Chocolates.

Martha sat on the porch swing, staring across the bay to Hope Island, and thinking of her grandmother. She had refused to move from the place she loved to follow the man she loved. She would have let him go because she couldn't leave, her soul would die if she moved away. She hadn't expected Grandpa to stay in Hope Island Harbor, but he had. He hadn't wanted to be anywhere except with her grandmother.

She thought of her mother, her grandmother had said, "Her heart died with your father." Two women who loved deeply, but differently. Which path did she want to follow? Her success in Hope Island Harbor surpassed her expectations. The Sunrise Café had gained widespread recognition, people came from up and down the Maine coast seeking her pastries and wedding cakes.

She scheduled the grand opening of Laughing Gull Chocolates for May twelfth, Gram's birthday. Darcy had helped her with the design, and would arrive in time to assist with the opening. Martha loved every minute of the long days spent creating and filling the cases with exquisite handmade chocolates.

Despite all this, her heart didn't dance in her chest, but stretched towards Baltimore. When Gram died, George's tenderness and compassion had provided a soft landing for her bruised soul, smoothing the jagged edges that wounded her—both had been missing with Tony. Every night when she crawled into bed, she thought about George and imagined spending the rest of her life with him. But his life belonged in Baltimore. His designs had become the gold standard for mill restoration, and were featured in national architectural magazines. How could he leave?

What was she supposed to do? She had followed Tony when she should have come home to Hope Island Harbor. Now as she realized her dream in Hope Island Harbor, one half of her heart remained with George, in Baltimore.

She couldn't live in the yellow house he had restored; she couldn't leave Hope Island Harbor again. Not because of Gram and her promise to return, but because she had found home here. The salt air and changing tides, and the people whose roots grew as deep as the rocks that lined the shore, nourished her soul. One half of her heart had reclaimed peace here, the other half yearned to get in the car and drive south. Her heart was ripped in two. How could she bring the pieces together, or choose which half would be happy?

Martha collapsed into bed that night with George on her mind. The snow globe he had given her for Christmas sat on her nightstand. She shook it and smiled as the petals fluttered down. She fell into a troubled sleep and woke to the sound of the wind, like a freight train circling her house, and a clap of thunder that rattled the windows.

She heard a bang and flew out of her room and down the stairs, her feet skimming the treads. She didn't need a light; she had the footprint of the house ingrained in her mind. At the bottom of the stairs she turned left and raced through the living room, down the hallway and into the kitchen.

The wide-open back door banged in the punishing wind. *I know I locked it.* And then she heard the creak of heavy footsteps in the pantry, but she was alone in the house, wasn't she? The pantry door opened, and a man emerged, "You!" she shouted in alarm.

Then she retraced her steps to the bedroom, locking each of the four doors behind her, but as she tried to turn the key in the remaining one, he came through it. "What are you doing here? How did you get in?" She yelled as panic gripped her throat. He smiled.

Martha woke with her heart pounding and the sheet clenched in her hands. She had the same dream three times that week. Once, the man had been Tony and twice it was Jake, but never George. Dreams of George came later, when she lulled herself back to sleep.

Sometimes she dreamed she was dancing in his arms as he sang to her in his rich baritone, his breath tickling her ear, and sending delightful shivers through her body. She woke with Charley nestled next to her head, loudly purring and his whiskers tickling her.

Sometimes she dreamed their bodies were entwined with nothing between them to prevent his muscular body from sliding against hers. She woke from those dreams smiling and tingling with anticipation, until she realized the bed was empty except for Charley, and then the ache in her heart returned.

The restlessness that had plagued George all day followed him home from work. He tried to convince himself an unresolved design problem was causing his current agitation, but it didn't work. The empty evening loomed before him and he failed to find an appealing project to fill it. He changed into shorts and a T-shirt and headed out the door. A run would clear his mind and the solution for the mill might surface. It had been a year since he met Martha, the balmy air reminded him of that April day, and he left the mill behind. He visualized every detail from his immediate attraction until he made the mistake that cast him into limbo. He'd fallen in love with her and lost her before the day ended.

He jogged up and down the streets of his neighborhood, where children played in the yards and lights in the windows blinked on one by one. Would his children ever play in the yard of the yellow house? Would he always live there alone? George could picture Martha there with him, but he regretted showing her the house. He'd pressed his dreams on her, and she thought her dreams didn't matter to him. The past year revolved in his mind as he ran; he'd spent half of it hoping to find Martha and the other half waiting for her to decide if she wanted him in her life. Her chocolate shop opened in two weeks, but he didn't know if he could wait that long.

Her Christmas gift and letter had thrilled him, they said she still thought of him. But they said other things too, messages he heard though they weren't written on the page. "I'm not prepared yet to meet or even talk on the phone. I'm trying to find my way back to me. I hope you'll wait until I'm ready before you come to Hope Island Harbor."

He'd waited impatiently the past months, adding more furniture to his house, to fill the space in the rooms and in his life. All the extra bedrooms had unused beds. He readied the gardens for planting, reclaiming old beds and adding new ones, but he didn't feel like gardening right now. His job continued to challenge him and keep his mind occupied during the day, but at night, Martha haunted him. On the weekends he watched football with Nick, until the season ended, then they switched to baseball.

When he asked Delia about Martha, she relayed the progress on the chocolate shop, and reminded him, "Just a little longer." In other words, Martha didn't want to see him yet. When would she be ready? He longed to talk to her, hold her, and counted the days to May twelfth.

A voice in his head kept saying, "Go see her, go see her now." He wanted to know she was okay. He needed to know whether he had to let her go, and get on with his life, or figure out how they could be together. He didn't want to make the same mistake again, but he yearned to see her. His patience evaporated. He couldn't wait two more weeks.

When he came back from his run, he found a late-night flight to Portland, he'd rent a car there and drive to Hope Island Harbor in the morning. Once he booked it, a sense of calm replaced his unease. He'd see her, and stay for the weekend, and when he returned for the chocolate shop opening, he hoped she would want him to stay longer. George raced to make the flight. His heart swung like a pendulum between fear and elation. He couldn't wait to see her, but what if she said good-bye?

Chapter 42

The sun snaked fingers of gold across the lavender sky, marking a new day as Martha jogged along the shore road. The breeze ruffled the sea grass, and a red winged blackbird called a cheerful *chick-ta-ree* as her sneakers crunched on the unpaved road. She absorbed the rhythm of the waves and the squawk of a raucous gull flying overhead, *home*. She would stay, like her grandmother, she needed roots. Her mind launched plans for a bed and breakfast then circled back to the details for opening Laughing Gull Chocolates, two weeks away. Her dreams were coming true, except for one.

She took thoughts of George and stuffed them in the closet of her mind where they lived during the day, reappearing at night in her dreams. When she woke in the morning, she missed him all over again. Martha filled her lungs with the early morning air she loved, and focused on her appointment with the real estate agent this afternoon.

Considering her success at the café, and the well-publicized opening of the Laughing Gull, she hoped the bank would approve a loan for her to buy the old Ames Farm homestead. She would renovate it room by room until it became the bed and breakfast she pictured in her mind. She hadn't told anyone, she wanted to be sure of the loan before she got Jeanette's hopes up, along with her own.

"Martha, did you hear?" Jeanette spoke excitedly before Martha could shut the bakery door. "Someone bought the old Ames Farm, including the surrounding fifty acres. Rumor has it he plans to turn it into a bed and breakfast, and he's going to raise his own organic herbs and vegetables. I saw him leaving Hollis' Real Estate office, and he's so handsome!" Jeanette clutched her hands in front of her heart and pretended to swoon. "I think he's your type, you should go introduce yourself."

Jeanette's words tumbled out so fast Martha had trouble keeping up, but the information landed like a sucker punch to her gut. She had an appointment today to look at the farm, the perfect spot for a bed and breakfast. The house required improvements and she couldn't afford the renovations all at once, but she eventually could turn it into a thriving business. A pang of loss gripped her; did she have to erase this dream? Jeanette continued, but Martha's shock muted her voice.

"If I were ten years younger, I'd be interested." Martha didn't share Jeanette's enthusiasm, she shook her head and mumbled, "It can't be sold, it can't."

"You all right?" Jeanette finally noticed Martha's reaction.

"I have to go, Jeanette." Without further explanation, Martha escaped from the kitchen. Distracted by her anger at Pam, the real estate agent, she collided with the man entering the bakery. His hands reached out and steadied her, then about to apologize, she lifted her eyes to find a familiar face smiling at her.

"George? What are you doing here?" His unannounced arrival prompted a rush of happiness, she'd missed him even more than she admitted to herself.

"I thought I'd check out the neighborhood, I heard there's an amazing chocolate shop opening soon." Then Jeanette's words raced through her mind. "Someone bought the Ames Farm, he's so handsome, I think he's your type," and she ignored George's attempt at humor and the words she hadn't said, "I've missed you, I've thought of you every day."

"You? You're the one who bought the Ames Farm?"

"I looked at it. I didn't buy it, but you don't look happy."

Martha heard George's confusion, but still responded with annoyance. "Why would I be? I had an appointment with the realtor to see it this afternoon. Once the chocolate shop is up and running, I hoped to buy it and open a bed and breakfast. I needed a little more time to get my finances together." Disappointment fanned her frustration, she'd been so close to realizing the last piece of her dream and finding redemption for her broken promise.

"What makes you think I bought it?"

"Jeanette, the bakery manager, said someone bought the Ames Farm and planned to open a bed and breakfast and grow his own vegetables. She said she saw a handsome man leaving Pam Hollis's office. I figured that must be you."

"I'm sorry for the misunderstanding Martha, I drove into town and saw the For Sale sign. I remembered you talked about wanting to own a bed and breakfast someday, and it looked like the perfect spot. I did go to the realtor's office, and she showed it to me." He shook his head, obviously mystified by Martha's assumption. "I must have mentioned it would make a great bed and breakfast, with plenty of room for a vegetable garden. The small-town rumor mill took over from there. I didn't buy it, I didn't even make an offer.

"Pam told me there was another interested buyer, but I had no idea she meant you. I wanted to surprise you, see if we could work on it together, I thought if I did the renovations, you could run it."

"Under your direction, I assume?" Martha folded her arms across her chest. "Because that's the only way you think I can be successful?" Tony's words played in her head, *You need me, you'll never make it without me.* She thought George was different. Had she been wrong?

"No, that's not what I meant!" They both noticed the café had quieted, and all eyes were on them. George spoke first.

"Look, this isn't the place to discuss it. I'll let you get back to work. We can talk later."

"So, you can persuade me to do things your way?" Tony said they'd be a team, then he took over and shoved her dreams aside, and worst of all, she'd let him, but not this time. She hurried past George and out the door.

George looked over at Jeanette who stood behind the counter. "I blew it, didn't I?"

"Maybe not, give her some time."

George ordered a coffee to go and went outside. He wanted to follow Martha, but chose to take Jeanette's suggestion and give Martha some time. He took out his cell phone and called the agent.

"Hi Pam, George Henderson here. Listen, I don't think I'll get back again today for another look at the house."

"Are you sure? It's a phenomenal property, and the house is solid."

"I know, but I need to give it more thought." He should have spoken to Martha before he went to see Pam. Once again, he'd followed the wrong impulse.

"Would you like to see other properties in the area, something smaller?"

"Not right now thanks, but I'll let you know."

George drove back to the inn where he was staying and changed into running gear. He jogged along the quiet roads that wove in and out around Pemaquid Point, and he could see why Martha loved it here. Today held a raw beauty as waves crashed on the rocks, and the salt spray flew against the sun, but last night in the moonlight, the sea had been a whisper, and the breeze a caress. It reminded him of Martha, stubborn and strong, determined to follow her dreams, but fueled by a tender heart. She belonged here, and he would not ask her to leave.

Peace enveloped him as he ran, and he knew he would talk with her again. If she wanted to buy the Ames Farm, he'd support her. He hoped she would allow him to do the renovations, but she would be the boss. He would do whatever she desired, he could live anywhere, but her roots were planted here. He finished his run, showered, and drove back to Hope Island Harbor. He should wait until dinner, but that was too far away. He'd try to spirit Martha away for a quick lunch.

Martha fumed her way to the shore road. She stopped beside the rocks, letting the waves and the sea breeze calm her frustration. What was the matter with her? She had been missing George, dreaming of him every night, dreaming of the bed and breakfast during the day, and here he was, offering her both. She had told him about her bed and breakfast dream, and he had found the perfect spot. The old farmhouse would come to life under his hands, and the renovations would be flawless. He didn't suggest this because he thought her incapable, but the opposite. He could envision her dream and he wanted to be part of it.

Martha sighed and retraced her steps to the bakery, she would meet George tonight and apologize, but right now she needed to get back to work, she had a wedding cake to finish. She took her cell phone from her jacket pocket.

"Pam, it's Martha. Something's come up and I need to cancel my appointment this afternoon." She wanted to explain her outburst to George. When would she stop responding like a runaway train?

"Are you sure? There's been some serious interest in the farm, I don't think it will stay on the market long."

"I'll call and make another appointment soon." She would wait to tour the Ames Farm until she and George could work out a plan together.

"Seems to be a lot of second thoughts today."

"What do you mean?"

"Oh nothing, let me know when you want to reschedule."

Martha entered the bakery and went directly to the kitchen. Normally she stopped to chat with customers in the café, but she had too much on her mind. She wanted to call George, but feared he would hang up on her after her rude response. She was engrossed in the final touches of the three-tiered cake she frosted, when Jeanette flew through the door.

"Where do you find them?" She startled Martha from her frosting flower reverie.

"Where do I find what?" Martha continued to shape rose petals when she spoke.

"Not what, who. Where do you find these handsome, drop dead gorgeous men? This is the third one who's come here looking for you."

"What are you talking about?" Martha set the finished rosebud aside and started on another.

276

"First it was the gorgeous leading man with long eyelashes and curly hair." Jeanette ticked off Martha's visitors on her fingers.

"That would be Tony, my ex-husband."

"This morning a rugged man arrived with a smile that would knock any woman's heart off kilter."

"You mean George," a wistful smile crossed Martha's face and her hands paused, "but I'm not expecting another man. Of course, I didn't expect them either, they just showed up, I can't think of anyone else, unless Annie and Dan have arrived to surprise me. Dan's arresting enough to turn your mind to mush."

"Well, if he looks like a tall, blond Viking with piercing blue eyes, then it must be him." Martha's hands froze above the cake, then a shiver ran down her back, and the delicate flower she was holding fell from her hand.

"Jake," she whispered. She thought of her recent dreams, had she conjured Jake with them?

"You don't look pleased, what's going on? Do you want me to tell him you're not here? Or call the police?"

"Neither. I'll see him." Martha dropped the ruined flower, brushed her hands on her apron, and fired by anger, slammed through the swinging door without noticing the late morning rush or acknowledging the locals who greeted her. She stopped a foot from Jake.

"You wanted to see me?" she skipped the social niceties.

"Hi Martha, it's good to see you again." Jake smirked, and his eyes roved over her. "Did you get your sandals back?"

"What are you doing here?" A creepy unease slithered down her spine, had he been plotting to find her again since last summer?

"I wanted to see you. I thought you'd like to finish that sail we started, it ended rather abruptly. You're surrounded by a beautiful bay Martha, and I'd enjoy taking you for a sail. In fact, I like your town, I think I'll stay for a while." Martha refused to be coerced, and she didn't budge.

"You need to leave," she said, her voice hard and flat.

"What, you mean you won't let me sample your delicious treats?" Jakes eyes remained riveted on Martha's face.

"You're free to buy what you want, then enjoy your sail back to wherever you came from." As Martha spoke, she nodded toward the bakery door and saw George come in smiling. She met his eyes and tried to telegraph her distress. When he approached her, his face grim, she knew he heard her silent message, and the brief touch of his hand on her back spread a wake of relief in its place.

"Hey Martha, sorry I'm running late." He kissed her on the cheek then looked up at Jake and offered his hand.

"George Henderson, Martha and I are partners." Although his words were friendly, the tone was not, nor were his steely eyes. Martha had told him about Jake, and he must suspect Jake had followed her here. Martha watched as George glowered, and though Jake shook George's hand he couldn't hide a wince.

"Jake Whitfield. Martha and I are old friends." He ended the contact first.

George stepped closer to Martha, his arm around her back. "I'm sorry we can't take time to visit, we have an appointment with a realtor. Be sure to try a cinnamon roll on your way out." Before Jake could answer, Martha saw Ray Solomon amble over. He didn't say much, but Martha recognized his support because he stopped in every day, even after a long morning setting lobster traps.

"Hi Martha, cinnamon rolls are as good as ever. Everything okay?"

"Fine thanks, Ray, Jake is just leaving. Perhaps you could show him the easiest route to navigate our harbor when he sails out."

"My pleasure." Martha saw a hint of a smile. Ray was eager to add some local reinforcement. He nodded towards Jake. "Want a coffee to go?"

Anger flashed in Jake's eyes and he stalked out without responding. Martha released her breath in a whoosh when Jake left.

"Why did you say we're partners?" She remained in the curve of George's arm.

"I wanted him to know I had your back, that's the first thing that came to my mind."

"Thank you, I'm glad you were here, and I'm sorry about this morning," she saw George's surprise. He had probably been prepared for her usual huffy declaration of independence.

278

"You're welcome, and no apologies necessary. I didn't know you were interested in the Ames Farm, but regardless, I should have talked to you before I looked at it. I told Pam I wouldn't be returning to see it again." George moved his arm then clasped her hand in both of his. "I'll leave and stay out of your life if that's what you want, but I hope it isn't. Can we go grab some lunch and talk?"

"I'd like that, but can we make it dinner? I have to finish a cake for delivery this afternoon." Martha smiled and squeezed his hand, "Call me later." She slipped back into the kitchen.

❊ ❊ ❊

Jitterbugs danced in her stomach when Martha arrived at the Scallop Shell. She couldn't believe George was here, but uncertainty niggled at her brain, what would she do if he asked her to live in Baltimore? She couldn't leave Hope Island Harbor. She returned from her worry mongering when Joyce greeted her.

"Hi Joyce, I'm meeting someone, but I'm running late so he's probably already here."

"You look much happier than the last time you said those words, though I'm not surprised, I know I'd be happy if he were waiting for me." She nodded towards the dining room and winked. "Corner table by the windows."

"Thanks Joyce." Martha felt her cheeks turn pink. George rose when he saw her and Martha quickened her steps.

"Sorry I'm late, I had to deliver a wedding cake and it took a little longer than I planned. Have you been waiting long?"

"A few minutes, and I've been enjoying the view." He gave her a kiss on the cheek, and she floated on a giddy cloud into the chair he held for her. "Would you like a glass of wine?" George asked when their server came over.

"That sounds lovely." The air around her shimmered with doubts, unanswered questions, and desire. A similar mixture of uncertainty and longing resided in George's eyes. She held his gaze but didn't know how to begin, and when she did, they spoke at the same time.

"George—"

"Martha—" Her tension evaporated as they laughed. "You first," George said. Martha twisted her glass. She had never been uncomfortable with George, and their conversations had been honest, even when they hurt. She took a deep breath.

"What made you come now?"

"I've missed you, I thought about you every day. It took all my will-power not to come sooner, but I wanted to give you time to grieve and figure out your life. Delia kept me up to date on your progress with the café, and told me the date for the opening of the Laughing Gull." He curled his hand around hers. "I planned to come that weekend, but a voice in my head kept saying, 'Go now,' as if someone shoved me out the door. I had to be here, I couldn't wait even one more day."

Martha reviewed the encounter with Jake, and she knew who had urged George to come. *Thank you, Gram.*

"How did you know about the Ames Farm?"

"I didn't. I followed an impulse to look at it."

Martha thought for a moment before she responded. She wanted George to understand her desire for the Ames Farm, because it connected to the reason she needed to stay in Hope Island Harbor.

"When Tony and I divorced, I didn't think I'd ever be whole again. But that affected me like a bump in the road compared to losing Gram. I felt hollow and shattered, but being here in the town that was woven through her, seeing the café flourish, and preparing for the opening of the chocolate shop has helped me heal. I finally understand what Gram kept telling me.

"'Follow your heart Martha.' She didn't mean follow your romantic heart, but follow your heart to find your true north. Do what makes you whole and not what somebody else wants you to do. I love being with you, George, but I can't live in the yellow house."

"I know." The tenderness Martha heard in those two words disarmed her.

"You do?"

280

"I can't say I didn't hope you'd change your mind in time, but when I saw Hope Island Harbor, I couldn't ask you to leave. You're as entwined with this place as your grandmother. I don't care what your dreams are, or where they take you Martha, I want to be with you."

"What about your job in Baltimore? What about the yellow house?" Her heart drummed in disbelief. George would leave Baltimore?

"I do most of my job on the computer anyway, and I can fly to Baltimore when I need to. Besides, there are plenty of old houses in need of restoration in Maine. Perhaps I'll phase out of the mill business. The house is just a house without you in it. I'll put it on the market and find a family who will be happy there. I can work anywhere, but you're here Martha, and that's all that matters." He squeezed her hand, and a wave of joy washed over her. All the dreams that had ripped her heart in two, all the nights of longing she'd buried in the crevices of her mind broke free and spun her in a dizzying circle of amazement, *George loves me.*

"I don't know what to say, I prepared myself for you to pressure me to go back to Baltimore. I can't believe this is real." Doubts simmered beneath her smile. *What if I'm not meant to be in a relationship? What if I'm wrong again? What if I fail again?*

"How long will you be here?" She needed time to absorb George's words.

"I'd planned to stay through the weekend, but I fly out in the morning. I left in a rush, and I have to deal with an issue at the mill. But I'll be back for the opening of the Laughing Gull." She saw promises in his eyes. "I'll return, I'll stay longer," and more—igniting a spark of shivery desire.

Chapter 43

At 4:00 a.m., Martha stood in the kitchen waiting for coffee to brew, too excited to sleep. Laughing Gull Chocolates opened today, the culmination of endless hours of work creating unique flavors and designs. George had texted the night before to say he'd be here before the opening, and happiness settled around her like summer sunshine.

Martha took her coffee outside on the porch, and as she searched the fading darkness, a shooting star sliced the end of night sky and she deemed it the sign of a perfect day ahead. Gold flowed over the water below her, like a giant highlighter, touching a lobster boat as it emerged from the shadows. Buoys marking the lobster pots, invisible when she first came out, appeared magically as the morning spotlight fell on each one.

As a teenager, Martha had hated dragging herself out of bed in the wee hours when she wanted to sleep. But now, she loved the peaceful stillness of dawn. In winter, she went to the bakery in darkness while the town slept, except for fishermen. This time of year, light touched the hilltops much earlier, and woke the birds now singing their morning songs. Spring often brought lingering swaths of cold, dense fog, but the sun would shine today, May twelfth, Gram's birthday.

"I did it, Gram," she whispered, "Laughing Gull Chocolates opens today. Thank you for believing in me."

The kitchen door opened and Darcy joined her, Gram's colorful afghan draped around her shoulders, and her hands clutching a Sunrise Café

282

coffee mug. She had flown in a week ago to help with final details of the opening.

"You couldn't sleep either?" Martha said, smiling.

"No, besides I smelled coffee, and I knew you were awake." They savored the quiet of the sleeping world in companionable silence.

"I'm impatient to go to the shop and make sure everything is ready."

"I felt the same way the morning the Dancing Dolphin opened. Last night we left the shop prepared for today. I doubt anything has changed since then. Let's have breakfast, then we can go check on it."

"Jeanette will have opened the café for the lobstermen." Martha didn't want to wait any longer. "We can grab something there, although I'm too nervous to eat." In spite of her desire to be at the chocolate shop, Martha took time to gather her wavy brown hair into a neat twist on top of her head, and apply mascara, blush, and a bit of coral lip gloss. She didn't bother with make-up when she spent the day baking, but today photographers from *Down East* and *Maine* magazines would be present, excited to feature Laughing Gull Chocolates and its creator.

The Chocolatier, a national trade magazine, had mentioned her in a November article on the Charm City Chocolate Challenge, but lost in grief, she'd paid no attention. They wanted to do a follow-up story about the second-place winner and the opening of the Laughing Gull. During the last few weeks, local newspapers and radio stations had featured stories of the opening too, and Martha hoped all the publicity would net an abundance of customers.

Darcy and Martha arrived at the Sunrise Café as Jeanette took the first batch of cinnamon rolls from the oven and slid in a large pan of wild blueberry cake in its place.

"I knew you wouldn't sleep late, even though the Laughing Gull doesn't open for hours," Jeanette teased.

"I couldn't sleep and neither could Darcy. Do you need any help here?"

"No, Kelly will be here shortly to help me with the baking, and Manny and Dianne will cover the front. Why don't you sit and have some coffee, make sure these cinnamon rolls meet with your approval?" She winked at Darcy and spread a thick layer of vanilla icing over the warm rolls.

Martha poured coffee but refused the offered roll. She watched Darcy, who didn't suffer from opening jitters, reach for a roll, fragrant with butter and cinnamon. Martha fidgeted at the table while Darcy ate, until she couldn't sit still any longer.

"I'm going to go check the chocolate shop, take your time here. I know there isn't much to do, I just need to be there." She carried her mug across the street and took a moment to study the small brick building, painted snow white with blue trim, to match the Sunrise Café and Bakery. "Laughing Gull Chocolates" marched in black script over the cornflower blue door and launched the silhouette of a gull into the sky. Several of her mother's paintings hung on the walls of the chocolate shop, the rocky coast and crashing waves, lighthouses, gulls, and fields of wild lupines. Martha's favorite, the painting of the Sunrise Café, hung in the bakery.

She had dreamed of owning her own chocolate shop as a teenager and she sensed Gram beside her whispering, "It's perfect." The ache of missing Gram lingered, but each new success helped heal the pain of failing her.

She opened the door and breathed deeply; a rich chocolate fragrance greeted her in the dimness. Why the smell of chocolate melted tension from her body she didn't know, but peace swept over her, and replaced her earlier angst. Martha switched on lights in the kitchen, and they glowed over the showcases as she circled the display room and scrutinized the chocolates she had created.

They represented a glimpse into her childhood, and satisfaction welled within her, she'd fulfilled her wish to honor Gram. She surveyed the selection of truffles with flavors inspired by Gram's favorite recipes, warm cinnamon bun and caramel maple cream. If they didn't spark the desire to start the day with chocolate, the Maine sunrise duet of dark chocolate espresso and chocolate cappuccino would.

The summer berry explosion assortment brought memories of helping Gram make pies bursting with local fruit, their juices bubbling over the crust. Wild blueberry, blackberry bramble, and raspberry wave, each had a fruit flavored ganache enrobed in a rich, silky, Swiss chocolate shell. In her mind, she smelled Gram's herb garden, which she'd highlighted in truffles with hints of lavender, peppermint, or rose geranium.

In the remaining cases, strings of marzipan pearls filled dark chocolate scallop shells. Chocolate starfish, gulls, and clams nestled in small fluted paper cups, and the Lighthouse Collection, tucked in small white boxes, held replicas of the Pemaquid Lighthouse, plus three other Maine lighthouses, Cape Neddick, Bass Harbor, and Portland Head Light. "I remember when we visited every one of them, Gram." A river of sadness spilled over her happy memories.

As Darcy predicted, everything looked perfect, including the front window framing a large chocolate Laughing Gull perched on a chocolate lobster pot, with chocolate lobsters trapped inside. Peekytoe crabs crawled amongst rocks, along with starfish, scallops and mussels, and a replica of the Pemaquid Light stood guard over the ocean below, all created in chocolate.

Martha heard a knock on the door. She opened it for Beal and gave her a hug.

"Hi Beal, looks like you're excited for the day to begin too, are you ready to start so soon?"

"No, but I wanted a chance to see the shop before the crowds arrive. I'll start playing at the café around eight and remind people about the opening here at ten. Where do you want me to set up?" Beal would play her guitar and sing to entertain the Laughing Gull customers, and Martha looked forward to hearing the Celtic melodies from Cape Breton Island that Beal loved.

"Near the small tables and chairs in front of the shop. I know your voice will draw attention here, and people can sit and listen while they wait to come inside." Martha hoped there would be a line out the door, and she didn't want customers to become impatient while they waited.

"Where's the rest of the crew, still sleeping?" Martha asked.

"Sarah was making coffee when I left, but Annie and Delia were enjoying the luxury of sleeping in. They'll be here before you open to get their assignments for the day."

"Thanks for collecting them at the airport and letting them take over your house." Beal had suggested the arrangement, and Martha appreciated being free to focus on last minute details.

Beal admired the chocolate displays and then left for the bakery. Martha glanced at her watch; the morning rush would soon crowd the café. She had placed a poster there, on an easel beside the spot where Beal would sing, listing the performance schedule at Laughing Gull Chocolates.

Martha went outside and adjusted the position of a table or chair here and there. A breeze carried the smell of spring and ruffled the edges of the white tablecloths with "Laughing Gull Chocolates" embroidered in blue.

"Looks perfect," George's voice startled her.

"George!" She saw his eyes focused on her and blushed with pleasure. "I'm so happy to see you," she gave him a quick hug, then withdrew when he would have lingered. "I'm sorry I'm a little distracted, I have a few more things to do inside before I turn over the 'Open' sign. Come see what you think." She took his hand and led him into the shop, then waited quietly watching him. She wanted more than a passing, "Looks great," she wanted him to appreciate the hours of work and the importance of her dream. He walked from case to case studying the chocolates in amazement.

"It's unbelievable Martha, you're an artist and a flavor magician. I predict empty cases by the end of the day. Any chance I can take you to dinner tonight to celebrate your success?" Martha followed him outside. His reaction thrilled her, not because she needed his approval, but because her success didn't threaten him, it delighted him.

"First let's wait and see if you're right. I can't believe I'm really opening a chocolate shop. Delia and a couple other friends who offered their help will be here soon for instructions, and I can't think beyond this moment."

"It'll be awesome! I'll let you get back to work and see you at the end of the day." George disappeared across the street to the café, and a minute later Martha's mother approached. "It's perfect." Shivers prickled Martha's skin, she heard Gram's voice, but felt her mother's arm pull her into a sideways hug. Martha rested her head on her mother's shoulder.

"I'm glad you're here." Martha and her mother had met a few more times after her mother gave her the painting. They dealt with the guilt and anger that surrounded their first meeting and grew closer over multiple cups of tea.

"I wouldn't have missed it," her mother squeezed Martha's shoulders, "and I know it's going to be an over-the-moon day. What can I do to help?"

"You may regret the offer. I think it's going to be a busy day." Martha ushered her mother inside and introduced her to her friends when they arrived.

"It all looks so tempting," Annie said, "I want to try every single truffle."

"I couldn't have done it without Darcy."

"We're a good team," Darcy said, "but you would have been fine on your own." Martha gave them directions and they each donned a blue apron embroidered in black with Laughing Gull Chocolates. She took a deep breath and flipped the sign to "Open." Strains of "One for the Morning Glory" floated around her, as Beal began her set beside the line that had already formed outside the chocolate shop.

The long narrow space didn't offer much extra room inside, enough for a single line to snake past all the display cases and end at the cash register. Customers waited patiently, seated at the small tables, or standing in line to enter the Laughing Gull, while Beal's melodic voice carried them away. Time passed unnoticed and Martha wove through the waiting sea of people, offering samples to melt on their tongues, sweet as a lover's kiss. They closed their eyes and sighed, "Mmmm," when they tasted buttered rum, and Irish coffee truffles, and Martha heard no complaints if they had to wait an hour before they could purchase their own treats.

After a parade of endless customers, media interviews, and photos, Martha turned over the "Closed" sign at six o'clock and declared the day a success. Though exhausted, she invited her helpers to dinner and texted the same invitation to George, "Dinner at the Scallop Shell, my treat."

❆ ❆ ❆

The chocolate shop remained busy after the opening, and since Sarah and Darcy stayed for a few days to help with the steady flow of customers, Martha had a valid reason for not spending time alone with George. She had dinner with Sarah and Darcy every night and always invited George to join them, but she knew he would prefer to be alone with her. The more she saw George and longed to be with him, and the closer they became, the louder the voice of doubt shouted in her head. *It will be your fault when this relationship fails.* It warred with the message from her heart. *He's the one, your true love.*

Sarah and Darcy planned to fly home the next morning, but George did too, and when he called and asked if she would have dinner alone with him, she agreed. They sat at "their" table, at the Scallop Shell, and Martha felt the tension rippling around him. She opened her mouth to ask what was wrong, but he spoke first.

"Martha, everything you dreamed about for Hope Island Harbor has come true, but something's bothering you. Have you decided there's no room in your dreams for me? Because if you have, I wish you'd tell me."

"What? No! I know we haven't had a chance to be alone, but—" She stopped, she could have made time to be alone with George, her friends would have understood. George deserved an honest explanation for her hesitancy, not flimsy excuses.

She gathered her courage to continue. Martha traced George's face with her eyes, she loved him and didn't doubt his love or desire to be with her, but that demon in her head persisted.

"But I'm afraid. It's why I've avoided being alone with you." Encouraged by the understanding she saw in his eyes, she continued. "I failed at my first marriage, I'm afraid there's something wrong with me, that I'm not meant to be with anyone. I'm afraid I'll fail at this relationship too." George clasped Martha's hand in his, stroking the back with his thumb. The familiar tingling at his touch traveled through her body, nudging her fears aside.

"You're not the only one who's afraid, I failed the first time also. It doesn't mean there's anything wrong with either of us, it means we'll work harder to avoid making the same mistakes again. We aren't the same people we were then. I love you Martha, and whatever we need to do, whatever challenges we face, we'll figure it out together."

A few nights later, Martha sat on the porch swing and thought about the last year. She had rediscovered lost pieces of herself, and now she delved inside and found strength. The chorus of "What ifs," and "Maybes" no longer played in her mind. She had healed.

She could pursue success alone, but she wanted to experience it with George. She trusted him. *George loves me because I'm me.* Capable without, but wanting with, they would share tears and laughter, bodies and souls, and dream their dreams together.

She took out her cell phone and called George.

"Hey, I wanted to say good night, and—"

"I'm glad you called—and what?"

"I want to open a bed and breakfast, and I know I'd be okay alone, but I want us to buy the Ames Farm together. Will you look at it with me?"

"That's what I hoped to hear. I'll get back as soon as I can."

Chapter 44

hree more hours. Martha hadn't seen George in two weeks and anticipation rattled her nerves. She shopped at Harkin's store on the way home, tossed her parcels on the bed, and started dinner. Preparations finished, she fidgeted through the house, smoothing a wrinkle from the couch, adjusting the flowers on the table, and checking the salmon in the refrigerator. After opening the oven door five times, she abandoned the chocolate soufflé, now a chocolate pancake. Strawberries drizzled with chocolate ganache would suffice for dessert. She didn't think George would care about the menu.

Martha removed the lacy underwear from the bags and lined them on her bed. Unable to decide in the store, she bought a bra and matching panties in both pink and black. Beside them laid the barely there dress in aquamarine silk, the exact color of her eyes. It skimmed her body, following her curves, and a wisp of aquamarine lace circled the plunging neckline.

After intense contemplation, she chose the black. When she stepped from the shower, she changed her mind and reached for the pink. The doorbell rang. *George! Early!* In a panic, she threw the dress over her head, and it shimmied down her body. She stepped into matching strappy heels, scooped up the underwear, and threw it in a drawer.

Martha opened the front door, and a trace of apprehension darted through her.

George's smile held a hint of mischief. Did he know what was under her dress, or rather what wasn't? They stood for a moment drinking each other in. Martha felt her body about to spontaneously combust under George's seductive eyes.

She experienced an instant of panic, but he traced her cheek with one finger, sliding it like the whisper of a butterfly wing down her neck to the hollow of her throat. He stepped toward her without taking his eyes from her face, and leaning down, placed delicate kisses in the same path he had traced with his finger.

Her knees melted as sparks erupted from the places where his lips grazed her skin. He moved forward and she backed through the door until they both stood in the front hall. George closed the door. Martha heard the latch click, then the lock, and she swallowed against her paralyzed throat.

Dinner waited in the kitchen, she had intended to put the salmon in the oven and toss the salad after he arrived. She swallowed again.

"Are you hungry? Dinner's almost ready."

"Starving," George scooped Martha into his arms and headed towards the stairs.

"What are you doing?" But she wriggled closer, dinner could wait.

"Having dessert first." He proceeded up the stairs. Martha liked that idea, no one had ever claimed her as dessert before. She twined her arms around his neck and nestled her head in the hollow there, enjoying the unique smell that sent her heart racing and her insides trembling, a blend of fresh air, woodsy soap and George. She breathed in, and when he paused at the top of the stairs, she pointed towards her room.

George used his foot to close the door—Charley would not be joining them. He set her on her feet, enclosed her in his arms, and kissed her with months of pent-up longing, it sent electricity from her lips all the way down to her toes, making critical stops along the way. He found the zipper in the back of her dress and slowly slid it down, his eyes locked on hers. She shivered and he rested his hands on her shoulders.

"You okay?" He would go no further if she stopped him, but Martha didn't want him to stop.

"Yes." Her dress slid soundlessly to the floor.

Martha woke to the smell of coffee. She stretched and savored delicious memories of the previous night. Before she could follow the coffee aroma to the kitchen, George entered carrying a tray with coffee, scrambled eggs, fresh fruit, and homemade muffins. He had even added a vase with a single late blooming daffodil.

Martha sighed, "Breakfast in bed, what a treat, it smells yummy. I like a man who knows his way around the kitchen."

"I'm a master of scrambled eggs and fresh fruit, but I confess I raided your freezer for the muffins." He set the tray on the bed then leaned over to kiss her. She raised her hand to caress his cheek and would have drawn him down beside her, but Charley chose that moment to hop on the bed and the tray tilted sideways. Martha grabbed the tray and George hoisted Charley into his arms. He nuzzled his head then deposited him in the hall, shutting the door behind him.

"Sorry Charley, your breakfast is in the kitchen." He turned back to Martha, who sat holding the tray and giggling. George removed the tray from her hands.

"How do you feel about reheated scrambled eggs?"

"My favorite," and she slid beneath the sheet.

On Monday morning, Martha and George had a ten o'clock appointment with Pam Hollis at the Ames Farm. They drove along the narrow, winding driveway until the house emerged from the trees, a solid, gray shingled presence, wise with the generations who had lived here. Despite the drooping shutters and salt sprayed glass, it appeared sturdy beneath the surface wear.

Martha stared at the house. Dormer windows reminded her of eyes looking out over the sea, and although trees and shrubs blocked much of the view, she caught glimpses of the bay far below.

292

"I remember coming here as a child. Gladys Ames and Gram were friends; she and her husband Bennett grew most of the fruits and vegetables for Gram's pies." Martha got out of the car, and her memories paraded through her mind in colorful detail. "This time of year, he brought rhubarb and the sweetest strawberries I've ever tasted, then peaches and raspberries in the summer. Bushel baskets of apples, pumpkins, and squash arrived in autumn. When they died, none of their seven children wanted to manage the farm, so the house has been vacant for several years."

"This farm means more to you than a good location for a bed and breakfast, doesn't it? It represents another link to your grandmother."

"I hadn't thought about it until now, but you're right, seeing it brings back so many memories, all good." In those days, the farm had been vibrant and alive, and it saddened Martha to see it neglected. If she transformed it to a thriving bed and breakfast, the house would have a purpose again, and the thought delighted her and gave new meaning to her dream—and it would have pleased Gram. George opened the barn door and Martha poked her head inside. Though empty, it held the lingering smell of horses and hay.

Pam arrived and greeted them, then unlocked the door that led into the kitchen. The old cast iron cookstove still scented the air with burned wood, a boarded-over fireplace occupied one wall, and a huge, square oak table filled the center of the room.

"Since you've had the tour George, you can show the house to Martha, if you have any questions, let me know." Pam retrieved her phone and walked outside.

Martha rubbed her hand over the worn table and her mind traveled back in time, as she half-listened to George's enthusiastic voice.

"We can make the necessary changes for a bed and breakfast and keep the farmhouse charm. For example, if we restore the fireplace and remove the woodstove, there'll be room for a commercial refrigerator and range."

"Maybe—" She wanted to keep the woodstove; Mrs. Ames had baked delectable treats there. She would ask George to devise a different solution.

"We can replace the oak table with a smaller one, to allow for more counter space or even an island."

Martha shook her head. "This table has been here since I was a child, and probably before then. Mrs. Ames used to roll pie crust here, and I sat and ate warm molasses cookies there while I listened to Gram and Mrs. Ames exchange recipes and gossip. I can't discard it."

"How about if we move it to the sunporch?"

"We definitely need more work space." Martha tapped a finger on her pursed lips. She hadn't realized change would be so hard, it felt like discarding her memories. "I'll think about it. Let's go upstairs, I've never been beyond the first floor."

Martha laced her fingers with George's and they wandered from room to spacious room. Built for a large family, the house had six bedrooms. Martha envisioned them painted in seaside colors—blue, turquoise, and sand, and bathrooms stocked with fluffy white towels and robes. The aroma of the lavender goats' milk soap from a nearby farm wafted through her imagination. The grimy windows cast spotty shadows, but once washed, they would welcome the spring light. After sharing ideas for the second floor, they returned downstairs.

George and Martha strolled around the yard; the lush gardens Martha remembered had grown into a tangle of weeds. Fog obscured the sun today, and the spring dampness that chilled the house soaked through their jackets. They walked to the bluff overlooking the distant gray blur of the bay. George captured Martha in his arms.

"What do you think?" He drew her closer. "Is it what you want? Are we what you want? Do you still have doubts?" George didn't want her to be someone else or give up her dreams. He wanted to share her dreams, and she wanted to share his.

"It's what I want," she looped her arms around his neck. "We're what I want. I have no doubts George, I love you."

Epilogue

O n a flawless June day, while the breeze skipped over the grass and played hide and seek with the birch trees, Martha waited beneath the lattice arbor on the back lawn of Ames Farm. A cherry-red Blaze rose climbed overhead and butterflies of excitement fluttered in her stomach.

She wore Gram's simple princess style wedding gown in ivory peau de soie.

Martha thought about the changes she and George had made since they bought the old farm last June. They had renovated the house and tamed the gardens. Beside the road, pink beach roses, *Rosa ragosa,* smothered the old gray fieldstone with their heady fragrance, and lupines marched inside the front wall, a riot of precession in shades of purple and blue. The backyard cottage gardens had yet to reach their summer height of flamboyant chaos that she remembered from her childhood, but fuchsia peonies, purple irises, and pink roses dotted the beds, with the promise of more to come.

Martha wished she had time to check on the food once more; it would take her mind off her nerves, though she knew Annie, who arrived a few days before to help, had everything under control. She pictured the wedding buffet, Gram's clam chowder, succulent lobster drizzled with melted butter, mussels steamed in garlic and white wine, and roasted asparagus. It would be served in the sunroom that George had transformed into a dining area, where Ames Farm guests could enjoy breakfast while morning light graced the rooftops of Hope Island.

The wedding cake, made from layers of almond pound cake sandwiched with lemon curd and frosted with her secret buttercream recipe, stood apart on a special table. A string of white chocolate pearls filled with raspberry ganache encircled each of the three tiers, and wild roses cascaded from a cluster on the top, in a widening band to the bottom.

"Everything's ready," Martha felt Annie's arm slip around her. "You okay? Nervous?"

"No, just excited, and thrilled this day has finally come. Well, a little nervous, but I know Gram's here with me. I think she'd approve of George."

"I know she would." Annie gave her one more hug and Martha watched her walk to her seat beside Dan. Sarah and her husband Zach, and Jeanette and Darcy, filled the rest of the row. Behind them, Delia and Jimmy bookended their four children. A surge of gratitude for her friends enveloped her, they'd seen her through a year of sadness and traveled to celebrate the highlight of a year of joy. Martha grinned when she remembered the secret Annie had shared with her last night. Annie's wish would come true in late autumn, and Martha couldn't wait to welcome Annie and Dan's daughter into the world.

George's family sat across the aisle. Since Nick was George's best man, Mandy, their children, and Lucy joined George's family. Martha smiled, happy that Lucy could make it with her work schedule. They had become friends the past year. Longtime residents of Hope Island Harbor who had known Martha since her childhood occupied the remaining chairs. White satin bows and clusters of New Dawn roses from Gram's garden, embellished the aisle chair in each row.

When Beal played the first familiar notes of Pachelbel's *Canon in D* on her violin, Martha took a deep breath and stepped from the arbor. Her mother—her sole attendant—preceded Martha down the aisle. She knew everyone stood and watched, but Martha's gaze fastened on George, the one who made her heart dance. He waited at the bluff where two rocks converged, and the wild roses divided to reveal a clear view of the bay, a distant ribbon of blue.

While Delia and Annie read from the Bible, and Beal sang "The Wedding Song," she held fast to George's hand, calmed by its strength. She heard the minister speak about the importance of love, kindness, and for-giveness, and saw his words reflected in George's eyes. Her voice faltered on the vows she had written, but George's smile steadied her. Then George re-peated his vows and Martha heard his love in every word. When the minister pronounced them husband and wife, she floated into George's outstretched arms, and he kissed her breathless.

After they cut the cake, George and Martha stepped onto the wooden dance floor. While Beal's voice drifted around them, George took Martha in his arms and his mellow baritone rumbled in her ear, but this time, it wasn't a dream.

Gram's Hermits

10 Tablespoons oil (such as canola)

1/4 cup molasses

2 Tablespoons unsweetened applesauce

1 Tablespoon water

1 egg

1 cup packed brown sugar

3 cups sifted flour

1 teaspoon baking soda

1 teaspoon ground cinnamon

1 teaspoon ground ginger

1/2 teaspoon salt

1/2 teaspoon ground cloves

1 cup raisins

Whisk together first six ingredients-oil through brown sugar.

Sift together dry ingredients and stir into first mixture.

Stir in raisins.

Chill dough for easier handling.

Preheat oven to 350 degrees F.

Divide dough into thirds and form into strips, about 8 inches long, 3/4 inch high, and 2 inches wide, on greased cookie sheets. (Use 2 sheets to allow enough room between strips.)

Moisten top of strips with water and sprinkle with coarse sugar.

Bake 15-18 minutes, don't over bake, cookies will be soft.

Let cool slightly on cookie sheet, then slide onto rack to finish cooling.

When cool, cut strips down the middle, lengthwise, then crosswise, on an angle, in strips about 1 inch wide.

Store in airtight container. Makes about 4 dozen.

About the Author

*D*ebbie Kaiman Tillinghast is the author of *The Ferry Home,* a memoir about her childhood on Prudence Island, Rhode Island. Her writing has appeared in *Country* magazine, and her poetry featured in five anthologies published by the Association of Rhode Island Authors. *A Dream Worth Keeping* is her first novel. Visit her at www.debbiekaimantillinghast.com

Made in USA - North Chelmsford, MA
1206569_9781952521607
12.04.2020 1740